"Aral the jack, formerly th[...]
is the best kind of hero: dama[...]
yet needing only the right cau[...]
—Alex Bledsoe, auth[...]

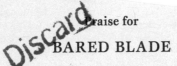

Praise for

BARED BLADE

"The second Fallen Blade fantasy stars an interesting hero with an irreverent, self-deprecating attitude . . . Fans will appreciate the magnificent McCullough mythos." —*Genre Go Round Reviews*

"Full of action, fun characters, and an interesting plot."
—*Whatchamacallit Reviews*

BROKEN BLADE

"Creative world-building really helps the reader to immerse themselves . . . A strong beginning to a new fantasy-mystery hybrid series." —*Fantasy Book Critic*

"*Broken Blade* explores a different side of dark fantasy than the typical European/medieval fare . . . I could definitely spend hundreds of pages wandering around in the wilds of McCullough's newest creation." —*Flames Rising*

"*Broken Blade* is a compelling read that was hard to put down . . . Mr. McCullough has the ability to make even his dastardly characters sympathetic." —*Fresh Fiction*

"Filled with multifaceted characters, layered plots, and the type of quixotic scenarios that only the imagination of Kelly McCullough could possibly create. The author, once again, crosses genres . . . Stories by Kelly McCullough are one of a kind—just like him. I found Aral's world to be compelling and highly addictive. Brilliant!" —*Huntress Book Reviews*

continued . . .

"McCullough's atmospheric little tale of betrayal and skullduggery is brisk, confident, intelligently conceived, and suspenseful . . . With as promising a start as this, McCullough's new series is looking like one sharp blade indeed."   —SF Reviews.net

"*Broken Blade* is perfect for a fan of political/hierarchal conspiracy in a fantasy series . . . It's also filled with some heart-pounding action . . . The story is positively bursting with excitement."   —*Whatchamacallit Reviews*

"The world McCullough sets up was certainly the highlight of the book for me. I enjoy fantasy-world politics and dark humor, both of which are in abundance here."   —*Night Owl Reviews*

More Praise for Kelly McCullough

SPELLCRASH

"Simple and elegant . . . McCullough is the true demigod of Web magic. Brilliant!"   —*Huntress Book Reviews*

"The book is filled with action and suspense. The world-building is awesome, the plot intense, and there is plenty of pathos and humor."   —*Three Crow Press*

"Entertaining and rapid-fire."   —*San Francisco Book Review*

MYTHOS

"A smooth, flowing tale that entices the imagination."
                    —*Huntress Book Reviews*

CODESPELL

"A hint of cyberpunk, a dollop of Greek mythology, and a sprinkle of techno-magic bake up into an airy genre mashup. Lots of fast-paced action and romantic angst up the ante as Ravirn faces down his formidable foes."   —*Publishers Weekly*

"One long adrenaline rush." —*SFRevu*

"Imaginative, fascinating, with a lot of adventure thrown in . . . Mr. McCullough has followed his first two books with a worthy sequel. *CodeSpell* will keep the reader on edge."

—*Fresh Fiction*

CYBERMANCY

"McCullough has true world-building skills, a great sense of Greek mythology, and the eye of a thriller writer. The blend of technology and magic is absolutely amazing." —*Blogcritics.org*

"McCullough has the most remarkable writing talent I have ever read." —*Huntress Book Reviews*

WEBMAGE

"The most enjoyable science fantasy book I've read in the last four years . . . Its blending of magic and coding is inspired . . . *WebMage* has all the qualities I look for in a book—a wonderfully subdued sense of humor, nonstop action, and romantic relief. It's a wonderful debut novel."

—Christopher Stasheff, author of *Saint Vidicon to the Rescue*

"Inventive, irreverent, and fast-paced, strong on both action and humor." —*The Green Man Review*

"[An] original and outstanding debut . . . McCullough handles his plot with unfailing invention, orchestrating a mixture of humor, philosophy, and programming insights that give new meaning to terms as commonplace as 'spell-checker' and [as] esoteric as 'programming in hex.'" —*Publishers Weekly* (starred review)

"This fast-paced, action-packed yarn is a lot of fun . . . weaving myth, magic, IT jargon . . . into a bang-up story." —*Booklist*

BLADE REFORGED

Kelly McCullough

ACE BOOKS, NEW YORK

THE BERKLEY PUBLISHING GROUP
Published by the Penguin Group
Penguin Group (USA) Inc.
375 Hudson Street, New York, New York 10014, USA

USA | Canada | UK | Ireland | Australia | New Zealand | India | South Africa | China

Penguin Books Ltd., Registered Offices: 80 Strand, London WC2R 0RL, England
For more information about the Penguin Group, visit penguin.com.

BLADE REFORGED

An Ace Book / published by arrangement with the author

Ace Books are published by The Berkley Publishing Group.
ACE and the "A" design are trademarks of Penguin Group (USA) Inc.

For information, address: The Berkley Publishing Group,
a division of Penguin Group (USA) Inc.,
375 Hudson Street, New York, New York 10014.

ISBN: 978-0-425-26232-0

PUBLISHING HISTORY
Ace mass-market edition / July 2013

PRINTED IN THE UNITED STATES OF AMERICA

10 9 8 7 6 5 4 3 2 1

Cover art by John Jude Palencar; dragon © iStockphoto/Thinkstock.
Cover design by Judith Lagerman.
Interior text design by Laura K. Corless.
Maps by Matthew A. Kuchta.

For Laura, without whom I would be lost.

And in loving memory of
Michael Matheny,
one of my oldest writing friends and coconspirators.

Acknowledgments

Extra-special thanks are owed to Laura McCullough; Jack Byrne; Anne Sowards; my mapmaker, Matt Kuchta; Neil Gaiman for the loan of the dogs; and cover artist John Jude Palencar and cover designer Judith Lagerman, who have produced wonders for me.

Many thanks also to the Wyrdsmiths: Lyda, Doug, Naomi, Bill, Eleanor, Sean, and Adam. My Web guru, Ben. Beta readers: Steph, Dave, Sari, Karl, Angie, Sean, Matt, Mandy, April, Becky, Mike, Jason, Todd, Jonna, and Benjamin. My family: Carol, Paul and Jane, Lockwood and Darlene, Judy, Kat, Jean, and all the rest. My extended support structure: Bill and Nancy, Sara, James, Tom, Ann, Mike, Sandy, Marlann, and so many more. Lorraine, because she's fabulous. Also, a hearty woof for Cabal and Lola.

Penguin folks: Kat Sherbo, Anne Sowards's wonderful assistant; production editor Michelle Kasper; assistant production editor Jamie Snider; interior text designer Laura Corless; publicist Brad Brownson; and my copy editor Mary Pell.

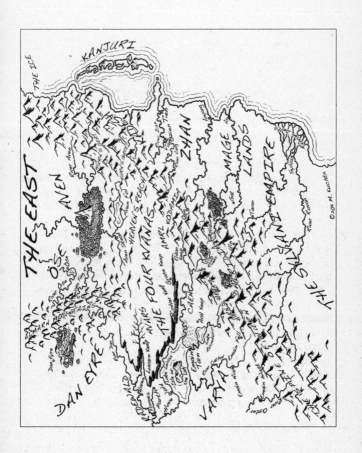

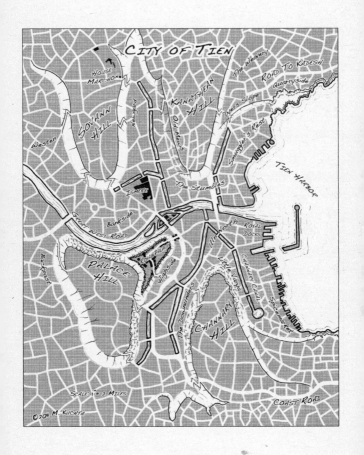

1

———✦———

The present *is* the past. Every today is built atop the
mounded corpses of a thousand yesterdays. Mine was
no exception. Broken furniture and filth surrounded me in
what had once been the tavern known as the Gryphon's
Head. A place that had once been my home was now a shattered ruin, empty save for myself, my partner, and trouble.
The past calling the present to account, as it always does.

Trouble wears a thousand faces and comes in a million
shapes. In my case, trouble had herself a new dress. It looked
damn good on her, too, and no surprise there. My trouble
had a name: the baroness Maylien Dan Marchon Tal Pridu,
and she always looked good. Tall and lithe, with long brown
hair and a lovely set of curves that she'd sheathed in green
velvet. My sometime lover, sometime client, and the un-
acknowledged heir to the throne of Zhan was a beautiful
woman . . . and trouble. Lots and lots of trouble.

"Have a seat." I gestured to the open chair across from
me with the half-empty bottle I'd found in the wreckage,
and whiskey slopped out over the cracked lip. "Let me pour
you a drink."

"I don't think either of those would be such a good idea, Aral," said Maylien. "In fact, I was rather hoping I could convince you to leave with me so we could have this conversation someplace else. Someplace safe."

"But I like it here." I swung the bottle around to take in the whole of the dark and empty bar, with its boarded-up windows, tumbled and broken furniture, and thick layers of dust over everything. "It's one of the few places I've ever felt at home." I was slurring my words. Not a good sign, but I didn't care. "Or at least, I used to, before whatever the hell happened here happened. Speaking of which, I'm guessing you showing up here right now, means you know something about that."

Maylien sighed and directed her attention to the dim shadow I cast across the table in front of me. "Triss, is there any chance of you talking some sense into Aral? Or do I need to play this out here?"

The shadow shifted, transforming itself from a darkened mirror of my own form into the silhouette of a small winged dragon.

It, or rather, he, flicked his wings angrily. "If I could talk sense into Aral, would he be sitting here drinking and waiting for the fucking Elite to show up and nail his hide to the wall and mine with it? No, of course not. But why would he listen to me? I'm just his familiar. It's not like I'm right nine times out of every ten that we disagree. Or, wait . . . no, it's exactly like that." Triss shook his head. "He's hopeless."

"There you may have a point." Maylien pushed her dueling blade to one side and sat down on the dusty chair across from me, doing untold damage to that fancy dress. "What do you want, Aral?"

That was a good question. What did I want? Once upon a time, I could have answered that question with ease: I wanted to be the instrument of Justice. That was back in the old days, when they had called me Aral Kingslayer and I was among the most feared assassins in the world, one of the fabled Blades of Namara, the goddess of justice. But that was before the other gods murdered her and ordered her followers put to the sword.

For a long time after that, what I most wanted was to turn back time to the days when Namara yet lived, to restore the temple, and to return my friends and fellows to life. To undestroy my world. Some days I still wanted that more than anything. But life wasn't as simple as I'd once thought it was. Or, maybe, I wasn't as simple. These days I couldn't even mourn the me I'd once been without second-guessing everything.

Fuck it. I took another drink, careful to avoid the jagged edge. The whiskey tasted of smoke and honey as it burned its way down my throat. Damn but it was good. Even so, I sighed and set the bottle down, because I didn't really want to drink myself unconscious either. Not the way I would have a year or two ago.

I snorted, then looked Maylien square in the eyes. "I honestly have no fucking idea what I want, but why don't you start by telling me what happened here."

The Gryphon's Head was a sleazy tavern in the depths of one of Tien's worst slums, or it had been anyway. Now it was a boarded-up ruin. For years after the fall of the temple I'd lived in a rented room over the stables. I worked out of the taproom then, paying my bar bill by playing the shadow jack—a freelancer on the wrong side of the law. But that me, Aral the jack, was gone, too. Not as dead as the King-slayer maybe, but definitely sleeping.

"Well?" I prompted, when Maylien didn't answer me right away.

"My uncle happened here," she said finally, her voice bitter.

Maylien's uncle was Thauvik Tal Pridu, current king of Zhan and successor to the one I'd slain for my goddess all those years ago. Not one of my biggest admirers. Despite shedding no tears over the assassination of his half brother, Thauvik had set the largest price on my head of any of my enemies. He seemed to feel that letting me live after I'd removed his predecessor from the throne might set a bad example. His involvement told me all that I needed to know about the destruction of the Gryphon's Head.

"What you mean," I said, "but are entirely too polite to say, is that *I* happened here. The king would never have even known this place existed if I hadn't made it my home."

"My *uncle* did this, not you—" Maylien began hotly.

But I cut her off. "He did it because of me, because he wanted to punish those who'd once given me shelter, whether they knew who I was or not."

She shook her head. "He did it because he's a monster, Aral. Just like my father and my sister. In case you hadn't noticed, the poisoned apple doesn't often fall far from the Pridu family tree."

The shadow of a dragon suddenly rose up between us, flapping his wings angrily. "How about we actually *do* something about the problem instead of sitting here and playing *guiltier than thou* until the king's men show up to cart us all off to the headsman? I know that's less dark and brooding and 'oh the world is an awful place' than either of you like to do things, but I've had about all I can take of that shit for the moment."

Maylien's answering grin was pained but genuine. "You sounded just like Heyin there."

I didn't smile, but I had to admit that Triss might have a point. Heyin, too. The chief of Maylien's baronial guard and her oldest friend, Heyin didn't like me much at all. That didn't make him one bit less wise. Quite the contrary. He disliked me because he felt I made a wholly inappropriate bedmate for his baroness. He was absolutely right. Maylien had more than enough strikes against her in the eyes of her fellow nobles without adding a broken-down ex-assassin to the list.

First off, she was a mage, which meant she had certain advantages that undermined the entire central structure of the Zhani hierarchy—the formal duel of precedence by which anyone of noble blood could challenge any relative for their titles. Secondly, her brand of magery was particularly scandalous. She'd once been a member of the Rovers, a traveling order dedicated to keeping the roads free of brigandage. She'd spent most of her formative years as a homeless wanderer rubbing elbows with the sorts of people most Zhani nobles wouldn't deign to spit on.

Just then, a harsh squawk sounded from the kitchen—where both Maylien and I had entered. It was followed a moment later by the advent of a miniature gryphon by the name of Bontrang. The little tabby-patterned gryphinx was Maylien's familiar and he flew straight to his mistress. Landing on the thick pad sewn into the shoulder of her dress, he mrped worriedly in her ear.

She nodded and rose from her seat. "The guard is on its way, Aral. We have to leave. Or, I do, at least. I can't draw the shadows around me like a cloak the way you can." She looked pointedly at Triss. "Will you come with me? I can tell you more of what I know about what happened here if you give me the time."

"Is Jerik dead?" I asked. The owner of the Gryphon's Head was . . . well, not exactly a friend, but I owed him.

"Not the last I heard."

"Will you help me find him?"

She nodded. "I know where he's being held."

"I'll come."

Jerik looked terrible, sallow and pale with loose skin on his cheeks and neck where he'd lost weight, and red blotches all across the old scar tissue where his left eye and much of his scalp had been ripped away by a gryphon. The fact that he was upside down, or rather, that I was and he wasn't, didn't help things. No one looks good that way.

There's just no getting him out of there, I mindspoke to Triss.

Not from here, no. We'll have to try another route, but why don't we talk about it later, someplace a bit less hazardous?

Point.

I bent double and caught hold of the rope looped around my right ankle, hand-over-handing my way up the few yards that put me in the shadow of the overhang. I'd set a pair of spikes into the gaps between blocks there. Anyone watching from a distance would have seen little more than the merging of one shadow into another, larger one. That's if they saw anything at all in the dim light of the waning moon.

The greatest advantage the Blades of Namara possessed was our partnership with the Shades, elemental creatures of darkness, bonded both to our souls and our shadows. Semi-corporeal shapechangers, they were capable of expanding into a cloud of darkness to hide their human companions. In a world where spells cast their own light for those with the eyes to see it, a Shade's penumbra was the closest thing there was to true invisibility. Triss had shifted away from my eyes so that I could see Jerik for myself, but other than that I was entirely contained and concealed within an enveloping cloud of darkness.

Once I had a grip on the line connecting my spikes, I reached down and slipped my ankle free. Then, bracing myself between two of the corbels that supported the overhang, I started working the spikes free. Whether I ended up coming back this way or not, I didn't want to leave any traces for the guards to find.

Below me the surf snarled and slithered through the miles of jagged coral surrounding the little island where the prison stood. The angry noise more than covered the quiet grating of steel on stone as I pried my anchors loose. The next bit was going to be tricky, so I reached through the link that connected me with Triss and gave him a gentle nudge. In response, he let go of consciousness, sinking down into a sort of dream state as he released control of his physical self to me.

My world expanded to include the darkened cloud around me when I added Triss's inhuman senses to my own. Light and shadow took on something like taste where they directly impinged on the diffuse blob of shadow that was Triss's substance. The effect was intense and visceral, with bright spots registering as a spice too hot for the tongue, and the deepest bits of darkness reminding me of the richer notes in a good whiskey. For dealing with greater distances Triss possessed something I thought of as unvision.

His field of view encompassed a complete globe, looking outward in every direction, but it was dimmer than human sight and darker. He had no real ability to distinguish color and only a limited sense of shape. Light intensity and textures dominated. Was something flat and reflective, or nubbly and absorptive? Those were the questions that Triss's unvision answered best. Once I'd grounded myself firmly in Triss's alien worldview, I reached out and found the edges of my larger self, pulling inward until what had been a broad, spherical, cloud of shadow contracted to little more than a second skin a few inches thick.

That freed up enough shadow-stuff that I was able to form thin claws on my finger and toe tips. Drawing nima from the well of my soul, I poured that life energy through the familiar link that bound us, hardening shadow claws into something truly corporeal. Moving quickly, because it was no trivial drain on my soul, I reached out and up, inserting points of congealed darkness into the narrow gap between stones in the overhanging wall. Like some wall-crawling lizard, I made my way past the bulge that underlay the crenellations and up onto the battlements of the prison fortress known as Darkwater Island.

Jerik's cell stood high in the easternmost corner of the prison, facing the open ocean, and continually hammered by wind and wave. A giant magelight topped the tower that rose up from where I slipped onto the wall. It warned ships away from the jagged reef lying inches below the surface for miles in every direction. I paused briefly in the lee of the tower to release Triss again.

He returned to full shroud form, leaving only the thinnest slit for me to see through. While he was doing that, I mapped out my route back to the supply ship that had brought me here. It was docked at a narrow pier extending out from the landward side of the reefs about a half mile from the prison proper. At the head of the pier a small building stood on stone pilings anchored deep in the coral—the same construction used on the prison.

On a calm day, a lucky man might be able to make his heavy-booted way from the base of the prison wall to the pier by walking carefully along ridges in the submerged coral. More likely, he would slip and fall into one of the many deeper channels that ran through the reef. Between the currents, the razor edges of the coral, and the colony of demon's-head-eels the Crown had encouraged to infest the reefs, it wasn't the best place to go for a swim. The only reliable way to get from the dock to the prison was riding in one of the long narrow baskets that traveled back and forth along an enchanted cable between the two points. Or, in my case, *underneath* the basket.

I had to avoid several guards walking the rounds as I made my way back to the cable-head, a trivial task given their general lack of interest in their surroundings and my shroud. It was sloppy, but not surprising considering the isolation and reputation of Darkwater Island. No one escaped from the island, and very few were released. Mostly it was a place the Crown sent prisoners to die slowly. And to suffer.

The latter came home rather forcefully when one of the doors that led down from the battlements into the prison depths opened and spat out one of Thauvik's torturers. Through the narrow gap in my shadow covering I watched him come toward me. The stylized, laughing devil face-paint made him look utterly inhuman, matching appearance to soul by my lights.

The Ashvik whom I had slain had mandated the masklike paint when he first created the royal office of agony. The official reason was to increase the fear the masters of pain instilled in their victims. If it also served the purpose of effectively masking the identity of Ashvik's pet monsters from those who might be moved to retribution, well, that was just fine, too.

I hopped up into the darker shadow between two merlons and crouched down as the torturer passed, briefly closing my eyes to avoid reflections. Triss hissed angrily but silently into my mind as he went by, and I found myself in hot agreement with the sentiment. There is never any excuse for torture.

This man might not be one of those who had tortured my fellow Blades after the fall of the temple. That distinction belonged to the office of Heaven's Hand. But he was of the same monstrous breed as those who served as the disciplinary arm of the Son of Heaven, chief priest of the eleven kingdoms, and the man I hated more than any other that lived.

The torturer continued another dozen yards past my hiding place and then slipped into the limited shelter offered by a bend in the wall to light a small pipe—most likely some blend of tobacco and opium. He settled into a gap like the one I currently occupied to have his smoke. I might have simply moved on then if he hadn't rubbed red-stained fingers together and chuckled happily in the manner of a man enjoying a recent memory. It was a small noise, barely audible above the wind, and his makeup hid any smile that might have gone with it. But it was that one step too far.

I crossed the intervening distance without really noticing I was doing it. Before the torturer had time to even register the sudden darkness that had cut him off from the safety of the prison walls, I formed my fingers into a spear and drove the tip deep into his throat. He let out a brief gagging cough as he spat out his pipe, but that was all. It's hard to scream with a crushed larynx. Harder still when you're falling a hundred feet onto jagged coral at the same time. One twisting punch in the chest and he was gone.

Fire and sun, Aral! Triss yelped into my mind. *What was that?*

Justice. I turned and continued toward the cable-head, easily slipping past a guard.

I could feel my familiar's startlement echoing down the link that connected us. *I can't say that I disagree, but Namara preferred to aim at the masters that held the reins of that sort, the ones the law couldn't touch.*

I'm not Namara.

No. . .

And if you think the law was ever going to touch one of Thauvik's personal abominations, then you've learned nothing of humanity in your years among us. I was absolutely spitting mad, and not entirely sure how I'd gotten there.

Calm down, I didn't say that. You're right enough about the chance of any normal sort of justice finding the likes of that one, and I'm not at all sorry to see him die. It's just that I'm . . . surprised to see you act on that sort of impulse.

. . . So am I, actually. It needed to be done, so I did it. Something that had been lying beneath the surface of my thoughts for a couple of months suddenly broke through into the light then. *Namara's gone, Triss. She's not coming back. I've known that for years, but I think I've been avoiding thinking about what that* meant.

I had been groping toward what it meant to be a Blade without a goddess for more than a year now, ever since Maylien first hired me and forced me to confront what I'd become in the absence of the goddess. I think I finally had a big piece of it.

I can't just let the world go to hell because I don't have someone telling me how to fix things, Triss. Kings and generals and high priests didn't stop going bad when Namara died. They just stopped having to worry about paying for it.

Are you taking this where I think you are?

Maybe. People like that torturer shouldn't be certain that they can make a life of hurting others without ever having to worry about paying for their crimes.

And you're going to fix that?

Hold on.

I paused and let another guard go by. At night, or in any environment with heavy shadows, the shroud form of the Shade all but guaranteed his companion Blade would remain unseen. Even in bright light, most people simply ignored the blind spot it created unless it stopped directly between them and something they were looking at.

Master Kaman had told us it was because the human

mind wasn't properly equipped to cope with the magic of elemental shadow, especially expressed in the diffuse-boundaried form of a shroud. I didn't know if that was what was really going on, or if it was some gift of the goddess that had continued beyond her death, or something else entirely. What I did know was that even with intense training, my own eyes had tended to slip right past shrouded friends without registering them, day or night, unless I was actively looking for the telltales.

I started moving again, considering Triss's question as I went. *Am I going to fix it?* I shrugged. *Maybe? Sometimes? When I can? I'm a homeless drunk and I don't know that I'll ever be able to see the world in the same black and white way I did when I was a young Blade, but sometimes the right thing to do is pretty clear. Not acting when I know what I should do is a kind of cowardice. I don't think I can bear to indulge my fears anymore. Take the torturer back there. I knew that if I didn't act to stop him, he was going to finish his pipe and go back downstairs to hurt and kill people. Could I really afford not to act in that circumstance?*

While I applaud the sentiment, sent Triss, *I do wonder where it's coming from. Faran was right when she called you sentimental for a Blade and said you didn't like killing people who weren't directly in your way. That was only a few months ago. What happened?*

When we rescued the lost apprentices at the abbey we killed a couple hundred of the Son of Heaven's people. A lot of them weren't in the way.

And?

It very nearly broke me, but it didn't quite. I survived and I made the people who put me in a position where I had to kill like that suffer. I spared a moment then to worry about how my apprentice was healing—Faran had been badly injured in the abbey assault—but there was nothing I could do about it but hope the healers could mend what I could not. *I feel stronger now than I have in years, Triss—since before the fall of the temple, really. I think all that death*

*was a fire that burned away some of the sentiment. I think
it burned away a* lot *of the old me, actually.*

I'm not sure I like the sound of that. Triss's mindvoice
sounded worried.

*I'm not sure I like it much either, or whether what's left
of me is going to be someone I can live with, but I don't see
that I have a whole lot of choice in the matter.*

I knew that I sounded hard and cold, and to some extent
that's the way I felt. At the same time, I didn't think I was
going to forget the crunch of the torturer's throat under my
fingers or the sight of him falling away to his death anytime soon. That was good. I had just killed a man, and it's
not something I ever wanted to do lightly, no matter how
much someone deserved it.

I guess what I'm saying is this, I continued. *I'm an assassin. I kill people. It's what I do, and I'm very, very good at
it. Talent, training, calling, they all point in the same direction. The world is an ugly place and it needs people who
can do what the goddess made me to do. Her death doesn't
change that. By pretending it did, I've been betraying her
memory, and, perhaps more importantly, I've been betraying what I am.*

By then, we'd reached the cable-head and I needed to
focus on getting aboard a basket to work our way out of the
prison. So, as he so often did, Triss got the last word.

*I think that you may have finally found your way back
to what you once were. It's what I've wanted for years, and
yet, now that it's come, I'm not sure that I have been wishing
the right thing for you.*

2

The Marchon baronial great house stood atop the Sovann Hill in the northwest corner of Tien proper. It bordered the royal park, occupying some of the most expensive real estate in the city. If I lived a thousand years, I would never grow comfortable with the sort of wealth and power expressed by the building and its grounds, beautiful though they were. I had been raised to *kill* people who owned places like this, not have tea with them. Namara's priests brought us into the temple at the age of four and trained us in the arts of death for the purpose of bringing justice to the corrupt nobles and crooked priests who were too powerful to receive it in the courts of the eleven kingdoms or at the hands of their fellows. Royal monsters, too, like Maylien's sister and father, both of whom had died by my hand, the latter in front of this very house.

Aral? Triss spoke into my mind, and I realized it was the second time he had done so in as many minutes.

I blinked and mentally stepped back into the moment, refocusing my attention from the Marchon estate of the past to the one of the present. I stood on the third floor balcony that opened off the baronial sitting rooms. Below me, a few lonely flowers bloomed here and there, testament to the mild winters of Tien and the dedication of the gardeners.

Sorry, old friend, I sent. *I was far away.*

And long ago, he added. *I could see you wandering the streets of the past, and didn't want to interrupt, but I think Maylien will be joining us shortly, and we have things to talk about before that happens.*

I grinned. *Not while it's happening?*

Our ability to speak mind-to-mind was a relatively recent development and, as far as we knew, unique in the history of Shade/human pairings, though I too often took it for granted. The living shadows had provided my order with familiars and companions since our very inception, and when I remembered to think about our special relationship I rather enjoyed being the first of my kind to share such a deep bond with his partner.

I felt Triss's answering smile. *Not if you don't want Maylien to spend the evening giving you hard looks because you're distracted. I would have thought that when Faran caught us speaking mind-to-mind, that would have been enough for you to want to be more cautious about when and where we do so.*

Before I could respond, the balcony doors opened and a pair of servants brought out a tablecloth and tea service. I noted that they only set two places, which meant that Maylien had won her argument with Heyin about this first conversation since my return from Darkwater Island. There were two pots as well as two cups, plus assorted plates and all the other paraphernalia that the nobility dragged into the simple act of having a cup of tea. Because I really didn't much like the stuff, my pot was both cooler and much milder than the rich smoky green that Maylien and most of her fellow Zhani preferred.

She commented on it as she came out and took a seat at the table, placing Bontrang on a perch beside her. "Really, Aral, are you sure you wouldn't prefer tea, instead of that lukewarm water you favor?"

I dropped into the chair across from her. "I don't actually favor it. It's just that it's better for me than the whiskey I'd prefer, and the less I can taste it, the better. I'd prefer plain water or fruit juice, but the latter's out of season, and drinking city water without tea in it's a sure recipe for spending the next three days in the privy." Though, to be honest, I agreed with those who thought it was the act of heating the water rather than adding in the tea that prevented disease.

Maylien shook her head, but poured for me anyway, an action that would have given her footmen palpitations if she hadn't already sent them back into the house—her past as a Rover showing again. "At least, stir it properly, so I can pretend I'm not serving you slop."

I sighed, but picked up the little brush and mixed the powdered tea at the bottom with my lukewarm water, giving it just the faintest yellow green tinge. The action made my teeth itch because it always reminded me of making a hot cup of efik. Efik! The taste, the smell, the way it smoothed the harshest mood without the jangling of the nerves that accompanied strong tea, everything about it was superior. Mostly these days I didn't crave it anymore, except when I had tea, or wanted a drink and couldn't have one, or the muscles in my back knotted up over a mission, or . . . well, leave it there. I couldn't have it, not if I wanted to end my days as something other than a sleepwalker slicing his arms so he could rub powdered efik into the wounds for a faster effect.

I had just taken my first sip of tea when Maylien leaned forward and touched her fingers to my cheek. "I think I liked your old face better, though this one's more handsome. I understand why you had to make the change after you were exposed to the world in that business with the Durkoth, but I wish you hadn't erased all the old lines when you did it. They gave you character."

"An assassin doesn't want character," I replied. "Character makes people remember you. That's a good way to get caught and killed. Once the wanted posters with my old face went up, it became a potentially terminal liability."

"I didn't think you liked that word 'assassin' either, and I'm sure I don't. I still think of you as the 'last Blade of fallen Namara.'"

That was what Maylien had called me in the letter where she asked me to help her kill her corrupt sister so she could assume the baronial seat.

"I don't like it," I replied. "Not really, but it's more honest than the other. I'm no Blade anymore, and, truth be told, what was any Blade other than an assassin in Justice's name?"

She dropped her hand away from my face and leaned back in her chair. "You've changed since the last time I saw you, and far more than your face."

"I have that, and I think I'm not the only one." It'd been over a year since the last time I'd seen Maylien, and she hadn't looked half so comfortable with the trappings of her high state then. "But talking about what once was and is no more is not why I asked to see you today."

Maylien nodded and her expression lost its wistfulness as she put on the face of a peer of the realm. It was . . . instructive, and for me, more than a touch off-putting. Maylien the Rover, whose bed I'd shared more than once, vanished underneath the surface of the Baroness Marchon, my natural prey.

She picked up her tea and took a careful sip. "You have the floor. Tell me about Darkwater."

"I was wrong and you were right. It's impossible. Staging an assassination is nothing like breaking someone out of prison. Getting into Darkwater was actually much simpler than most of my old assignments for the goddess. I was able to get in close enough that I could have easily killed Jerik without ever being in any real danger of getting caught. But there's simply no way I can get him out, especially not as weak and sick as he looks."

Maylien nodded. "I told you as much."

"You did. The prisoners are too closely watched. I wouldn't have ten minutes from the time I cracked the wall and broke his chains to the alarm being sounded, and that assumes I kill the guard that's in charge of the eyespy watching the cell and the one that's stationed outside his door beforehand. Then I'd have to get him down to the water and out across the reef to a waiting boat."

"Which wouldn't set off nine and ninety alarms why?"

"Exactly," I said. Besides, he'd never make it in the state he was in, and I ached for the beatings he'd taken in my name.

"We could probably come up with a way of concealing the boat," said Triss, shifting out of my shadow and into dragon shape to insert himself in the conversation. "Tie it to a landmark in the coral and leave it sunk till we get there, or something, but there'd be no way of hiding it that wouldn't involve significant time to undo."

"I'd be willing to support you with money and men," said Maylien. "I still have ties to the underworld from the years I spent hiding from my sister. But I don't see that they'd help enough to make this work."

I shook my head. "They wouldn't, and I could put together my own team if I thought it would do any good. I may have changed my face since my jack days, but I know who to talk to if I need hard things done shadowside. But there's really no way to get Jerik out of there short of a major assault on the prison, and the chances are pretty good the main result of that would be getting him and a bunch of the others killed. All of the important prisoners have death wards inscribed on their manacles. Any guard can snuff out any of their lives with very little effort. More important guards, like the fellow watching the eyespys, can murder whole cell blocks with the touch of a ward. No, there's only one sure way to get Jerik out."

Maylien canted her head to one side. "That's one more way than I can see."

"It'll need your full cooperation."

She straightened her shoulders, and inclined her head ever so slightly. "I owe you my life and my honor, not to mention my coronet, and I pay my debts. If it's in my power to give, you shall have what you need from me."

"Don't agree to this blind, Maylien. It speaks well of you that you feel that way, but you're a baroness now. You have obligations that outweigh anything you owe me."

For the first time since she'd found me in the boarded-up remnants of the Gryphon, Maylien looked something other than confident, but only for a moment. "I don't think you'd ask anything of me that would compromise what I owe my people, Aral."

"I guess that depends on how you see things."

"Do get on with it," she said, more than a little exasperated.

"All right. I'm going to kill your uncle and, if you agree, I'm going to help put you on the throne of Zhan in his place. Then, you will release Jerik as well as most of the other prisoners. You will also shut down the office of agony and all the other abominations your uncle has slowly been reviving from the reign of the last king of Zhan I had to assassinate."

"You're going to what?" demanded Maylien.

Have you thought this one through, Aral? Triss asked into my mind.

"I'm going to assassinate your uncle Thauvik. If we do this right, you will be the one to assume the throne when he dies. That's going to take more than a little risk on your part, and, if we fail, your head is going to get nailed up over traitor's gate right next to mine."

Maylien set her tea down and growled at me. "You are the single most difficult man I've ever known. You do know that, right? Because, as I recall, the last time we had a conversation about putting me on the throne, I came within about two inches of begging you to help make me queen so that I could put a stop to the horrors Thauvik's been committing in my family's name. Then, you told me that you simply couldn't do it. What's changed?"

"As you noted earlier, *I* have."

Triss spoke into my mind. *That's how I remember things going, too, and I agreed with you then. A little warning* before *you jump off a big cliff like this one would be appreciated next time.*

Sorry, Triss. I didn't want to have to explain myself twice.

To Maylien I said, "I turned you down before because if I'd killed Thauvik then, I would have been doing it for you, and, as much as I care about you, love you even, that's not the right reason."

"Then what is?" She was hiding it well, but I'd hurt her there.

I was sorry for that, and I felt I owed her the full explanation. "When I met you, I was at my low point, broken, bleeding inside, drunk, a wreck. I'd lost my goddess and, with her, my purpose. I was pretty much waiting to die. When you came along, you gave me something to believe in for a while, a purpose outside myself. I'd forgotten what that felt like. It was exactly what I needed and you probably saved my life by doing it."

Where are you going, Aral?

Just follow along and you'll see.

"I'll be forever grateful to you for that, but it would have been so easy to substitute your needs and orders for the ones I lost when my goddess died. When we met, I was a tool without an owner. If I'd killed Thauvik for you, I'd have remained that, a tool for another's hand, and honestly, I wanted that. I wanted to give myself up, to become nothing more than an expression of someone else's will once again. I wanted it more than I want a drink or a cup of efik on my worst nights. I wanted to give up on being me so bad it was scorching my soul."

I got up and began to pace. "But the life of a tool isn't really living at all. I'm not entirely sure how I figured that out. Maybe it was all those years as a jack. I got to see some awful people and some pretty good ones, and I learned that the difference between the two isn't in who they are, it's in what they do and why. Only you can be responsible for what you become. Whatever the reason, I could see something then that I hadn't as a Blade; even if I did become a tool again, the responsibility for what that tool did would still be mine. At some point we all have to take ownership of ourselves."

"I never wanted to reduce you to an instrument of my will, Aral," said Maylien, her voice low and throaty.

I shrugged. "What we want and what we do aren't always the same things. I don't blame you for it, and I don't think you had any idea that was what you were asking for, but that doesn't change what it would have done to me."

"Why is it different now?"

"Because I'm going to kill Thauvik no matter what you decide. I hope that you will agree to work with me to take advantage of the opportunity, but if you don't, it's not going to change my decision one whit. I'm not doing it for you, but I might be doing it *with* you."

"What about me?" Triss asked angrily. "When exactly were you going to bring me into your decision? What if *I* don't want to kill Thauvik? Would *that* change your mind?"

I looked at the shadow of a dragon and I couldn't help but smile. "I'm sorry, Triss. You're normally the one pushing me to do the right thing. It never occurred to me that, knowing what we know about his rule, you might not want to kill Thauvik. Are you against it?"

He flicked his wings rather sheepishly. "No. He's very nearly as bad as his half brother was. It's just . . ."

"Just what?" I asked, keeping my tone as deadpan as I could manage. "Thauvik is a murderer and a torturer, and the only way he'll ever see justice is if we deliver it. It's that simple."

"Well, yes, but . . . Wait a second," he said, suspiciously, "are you pulling my tail? Because that sounds a lot more like something I'd say than something you normally would."

"Maybe a little bit," I replied. "But only in the way I'm talking about things, not the sentiment behind them. It's rare that the path to justice is so easy to see, but Thauvik deserves to die if any man does." It wasn't all that long ago that we'd managed to prevent him starting a war between his neighbors. "We're among the very few who could manage it. Knowing that, do we have the right to turn away from our responsibility to justice?"

"When did all this occur to you?" Triss sounded more than a little dazed, and I can't say that I blamed him.

From the outside it must look like I'd become an entirely different person, changing who I was as completely as I'd changed my face, and all rather suddenly. Some days it felt like that from the inside, too.

"I'm not sure, Triss. I think it happened in the instant that jackal torturer laughed on the wall of the prison, though it took a while to sink in. It's been years since I felt as sure about anything as I was about the fact that what he was doing was evil, and that if I didn't stop him right there and then, I'd be complicit in whatever evil he did going forward. I might not have thought about it at the moment, but if what the torturer was doing was evil enough to kill him for it, how much more evil were the actions of the king who ordered him to it? If I had to stop the one, don't I have to stop the other? Once you've asked that question, the answer isn't something you can turn away from."

Triss nodded. "I think you're right, but I'm still surprised. You sound so decisive, and that's not something I've been used to hearing from you these last few years."

"It's not something I'm used to feeling. Back in the old days, before the fall of the temple, I was certain all the time. Some days I think that's what I've missed most in the years since Namara died, that sense of knowing what was right. There's a pleasure to that, that I can't even begin to see anywhere else, though I didn't even know it was there till I'd lost it. In the shadow-jack years, I wasn't certain of anything."

"You seemed pretty sure about wanting to get drunk," he said, but without the heat that comment would once have held.

"No, not even that." I glanced over at Maylien who was doing an excellent job of pretending she wasn't listening to every word we were saying. "For all that I couldn't stop myself drinking, I never once felt like it was a good idea or

what I ought to be doing. Hell, that uncertainty is half of
why I wanted to drink so much, and more than half of why
I still want a drink more days than I don't, even today."

"Wait a second," said Triss. "I thought you just said you
were sure about what you had to do. Now you're saying
uncertainty makes you want to drink."

"I'm certain about Thauvik, and that's good, better than
having a drink by far." I laughed a bitter laugh. "But that's
the only thing I'm really sure about. For the rest, I'm still
wandering in a fog. I know what we need to do tomorrow
and probably the next day, and the next, at least until
Thauvik's dead and Jerik's free. After that? I hope I can find
something else to be sure about, but I'm far from sure that
I will. It's enough to drive a man half-mad and maybe more
than half."

I turned away then and walked to the rail of the balcony.
Behind me, I could feel Triss sliding along the shadow trail
that connected us. A moment later I felt a tight pressure
across my back and shoulders as he wrapped his wings
around me. He didn't say anything, just held me tight for
three long beats, then dropped down to hide himself in
my shadow. Maylien's chair scuffed on the tiles of the balcony.

"I'm very sure about something," she said, coming closer
as she spoke.

"What's that?" I didn't turn around.

"That the man I asked to help me with my sister was a
damned good one, whatever he might have believed about
himself at the time. That's not the end of it, though, because
the man he's become in the year and a half since is an even
better one. I'll help you with my uncle, and I'll take the
throne if we can put me there. I'll do it because it's the right
thing to do and I've a duty to the people of this kingdom
every bit as important as my duty to the people of my
barony."

"I'm glad to hear it, we'll start tomorrow."

She came into view on my right then, leaning one hip

against the balcony and smiling at me. "I'm sure about something else, you know."

"What's that?"

"I like you decisive."

"Do you, now?"

"I do." The corner of her mouth quirked up, and I was reminded once again that she was a beautiful woman and of what had been between us in the past.

"That's good, because I think I feel another decision coming on."

"What's that?"

"This!" I leaned over and scooped her up into my arms.

Her smile broadened into a grin as I carried her toward the doors. "Good decision."

I kissed her then as Triss opened the door for us, while Bontrang followed along purring happily.

Captain Kaelin Fei, Tien's perfect model of a corrupt cop, and my . . . friend? Ally? Once and future nemesis? Whatever you called her, the captain was a power in Tien and, by extension, all of Zhan. We'd saved each other's lives at least a couple of times in the middle of the mess with the Durkoth, and because of that she was one of the few who recognized the new me as well as the old one. When I pulled back the curtain on her private booth at the Spinnerfish, she gave me a very hard look.

"What's this about, Aral?"

As I slid into a seat across from her, I let the curtain fall behind me, magically cutting off anything we might say from potential listeners. The private booths at the Spinnerfish were *really* private. They were also one of the very few places in Tien where people could meet with their enemies as safely as their friends. The owner, Erk Endfast, a onetime black jack, maintained the tavern's neutral status by the simple expedient of killing anyone who violated the peace of the house. Since it behooved the powers of the city to have someplace like the Spinnerfish exist, he almost never had to ghost anyone beyond the actual transgressor. If all that wasn't enough to recommend the establishment, there was always the fish—some of the best in Tien.

I smiled at Fei. "Why does this have to be about anything other than old friends getting together for a quiet romantic dinner?"

Fei snorted. "We could start with the fact that you've never once in the years I've known you asked me out for a social dinner. Or that I don't particularly like boys, nor really girls all that much, though I've been known to change my mind on the latter. Add in that you completely vanished from the city late last summer, and that this is the first I've heard of you since. Finally, heap on top of that the fact that it's the middle of the night, which is the best time for you to vanish once this is over, and yeah, I get suspicious. Not that I wouldn't be suspicious if you'd asked to meet me at noon in the middle of the square on Sanjin Island. I can't help it, suspicion's an old cop habit. So, again, *what do you want*?"

"Some of Erk's excellent fish as a starter," I said, mostly because I wanted to rile Fei up a bit before I got down to business, put her off balance.

"It's on the way. I ordered for both of us when I got here and told Manny Three Fingers to start it when you came in the door."

"But you didn't even ask me what I wanted." Not that anything Manny cooked ever came out less than excellent, but there was the principle of the thing.

"I told him to give us two of whatever was best tonight, and that if he tried to fob me off with something they had too much of they'd have to start calling him Two Fingers instead. I also told him to slather enough salamanda sauce on yours to burn the top of your head off."

"I can imagine his response."

"I bet you can. He told me that if I wanted one of his fingers that bad he'd give it to me right now." Fei made a rude gesture. "Then he assured me that the sawfin was incredible tonight and he'd save me two good steaks. Now, can we finally get down to why you're here? Or do I have to pretend that you've got me all flustered to get you to cough up whatever crazy thing it is you're planning to spring on me?"

"Fine. Be that way."

Fei crossed her arms and raised her eyebrows at me, but didn't say a word.

"I'm going to kill Thauvik."

"Good. It's about fucking time someone did it. Who are you planning on replacing him with? The Marchon girl? I like her, though her bastard status will count against her, especially with the example of Thauvik so fresh in everyone's mind. They're calling him the bastard king more and more of late, and that's going to make it a tougher sell to put another illegitimate ass on the royal seat cushion. Not to mention the fact she's a mage, though I don't think that'll matter as much just now."

I blinked several times. That was not the reaction I'd been expecting. Fei was a corrupt cop, but not for the usual reasons. She didn't break the law to enrich herself, though it surely did that. She did it because it was the best way to do what she thought of as her real job, which was keeping the peace and protecting the citizens of Tien.

In Fei's city, you could sell all the opium or caras dust you wanted to, but if you tried to cut it with something lethal, she would see that your body was found, or the important bits of it anyway. Likewise with gang fights. The Cobble-Runners were welcome to kill all the Bonebreakers they wanted, and vice versa, but if either side involved civilians, she would fall on them like a burning building full of red-hot iron.

"I'm . . . surprised," I said after a moment. "I thought you would be worried about the chaos that a change in the Crown inevitably brings."

"That's because you haven't spent the last six months in Tien. Thauvik may not be as bad as his late unlamented brother yet, but there's no doubt he's headed that way fast.

I'd rather have a few buckets of blood spilled in the streets in the process of toppling him from his throne tomorrow than the great vats of the stuff I expect to see if the madman stays on his fancy chair for another year. So, is it the Marchon girl?"

"I hope so, yes. We have a paper signed by her father before his death that legitimizes her and her sister."

Fei nodded. "If it's real, that *would* change things. Hell, it'd put her place in the succession *ahead* of her uncle's, at least technically. But you can't bring it out after he's dead. No one will buy it for a second then, no matter how authentic it actually is. And if you put it out there beforehand, Thauvik's going to have her killed."

"He'll try to, but I'm not going to let that happen. We're going to deliver the declaration that legitimized her directly into the hands of the chancellor at the Winter-Round court."

"That's insane . . . how can I help?"

I told you we wouldn't have to lean on her, Triss thought smugly.

3

A faint scratch sounded from my chamber door, loud enough to draw attention but not to disturb. I was getting tired of that and of the deference it implied.

"Enter," I said.

An older woman opened the door and peered into the dimness. "Lord?" She was carrying a slim gray bundle.

"I'm over here, and no lord."

"Close enough for a seamstress like me." She crossed to where I sat and set the bundle on the desk. "I'm finished with the first set, my lord."

"Thank you." I didn't bother to correct her again. It hadn't taken the last five times I'd tried and it wasn't going to take now. "I appreciate it."

She bowed and left without another word. As I turned my eyes to the things she had brought me, Triss shifted into dragon form on the wall above the desk.

"Don't hover, Triss." I still hadn't touched the bundle.

"I'm not. I just want to see this. It's been so very long."

I swallowed hard. Now that the moment had come, I found myself strangely reluctant. If it hadn't been for Triss's obvious excitement, I think I would have stuffed the bundle in the bottom of a drawer and tried to forget I'd ever thought this might be a good idea.

"Go on," said Triss.

With a sigh I put my hand on the top item in the pile. Raw silk met my fingers, whisper soft, but rough and specially finished, so that it drank light instead of reflecting it the way the shimmering fabrics the nobility favored did. I wondered briefly what the seamstress thought I had wanted of something so drab. I flipped over a fold, revealing the nature of the garment, a loose pair of pants. A shirt and vest of the same design lay beneath, each with many small pockets sewn into the interior. On the bottom was a yoke and cowl with its outer seams sewn double to give it more shape. I ran my fingers along one sleeve, admiring the watermarking that broke up any hint of a straight line. It reminded me of a fine marble or threaded sandstone.

"Aren't you going to put it on?" demanded Triss. "You have to see that it fits properly."

"I'm quite confident in Maylien's seamstress." But he was practically dancing on the wall, so I finally nodded and stripped off my robe.

Where Zhani pants would have buttoned or closed with a simple drawstring, these had an elaborate double tie to cinch the waist tight. My fingers tied the traditional knots without any input from my mind. Then they went right on from there to pull on the shirt and long vest—tying and adjusting as needed—and finished up by slipping the cowl over my head. The wide belt and low boots had been delivered the day before and I put those on over all, leaving only my worn harness and trick bag to complete the outfit.

When I was done, I turned to the mirror and found myself facing a Blade of Namara.

Seven years had passed since I last wore the formal clothes of my order. Seven long brutal years. The pain of it should have left lines etched into my face, *had* left lines, but those were gone along with the features they had once marked, erased like my order and my goddess. The assassin in the mirror was a stranger. Oddly, that made it easier. I think that it might have broken me to find Aral Kingslayer looking back at me out of the glass. The man in the mirror now was a different Blade, forged from the same steel perhaps, but someone else. Maybe it was even someone who could bear the weight of the events that had broken the old Aral. I had to hope that it was so.

I turned my eyes to the shadow that hung in the darkness behind my shoulder. "Well, what do you think?"

Shadow wings wrapped around my chest from behind and a dark and scaly cheek pressed against my own. "I think you look absolutely magnificent."

I reached back and scratched the soft spot behind his ear, happy for him being happy for me, even if I couldn't be happy for myself. As always, the different messages of scale and shadow sent by fingers and eyes provided a strange contrast, reminding me of the way Triss's dual nature rode the line between is and is-not.

He sighed contentedly under the attention. "It wants only your swords showing to make it perfect."

Stung, I stopped scratching. I didn't make the mistake of thinking even for an instant that he meant flipping the lovely new set of Tienese dueling blades Maylien had given me a few days before so that they showed over my shoulders. They were of the best mortal steel, and any smith in the city would have been proud to have forged them, but they would never—could never—touch the divinely created swords my goddess had given me on the day she made me a full Blade.

After a moment, I answered him. "No, Triss. I gave them back to Namara, and she can keep them."

"Laid them in her tomb, you mean."

"If you prefer it. Yes. Would you make me a grave robber?"

"I hardly think that—"

But I cut him off. "Triss, don't." I shook off the wings that wrapped me round and turned to face my familiar. "Just, don't."

"It's not theft to take back what is your own."

"They were never mine. They always belonged to Namara, and I only ever carried them in her name and service. In the normal course of things she would have reclaimed them on my death, drawing them back into her soul and using their essence to shape a new set for the Blade who took up the cause in my stead. When she died, that possibility vanished, a door forever closed. But my service ended that day, too, and with it, any claim I had on those swords. They belong to the goddess, I have returned them to her, and there the story ends."

I could see that he didn't fully accept my argument, but sense or mercy prevented him from pushing it any further. I changed back into my regular street clothes, and put the assassin's grays in the carved rosewood trunk at the foot of my bed, though I was more than half tempted to throw them into the room's small fireplace. I was having a hard time reconciling how simultaneously right and wrong having them felt, and the seamstress had promised me another set in silk, as well as a heavier woolen version with a matching poncho to be delivered in the next few days.

It made my teeth itch, and I couldn't help but long for a steaming pot of efik to soothe my nerves. I'd been able to keep a pretty good grip on my drinking the last few weeks, but the more time I spent sober the more the older craving had grown stronger. I shuddered briefly and forced myself to once again picture the sleepwalkers that used to haunt the alleys of Emain Tarn in Varya, the open slashes on their arms packed with ground efik and covered in flies as they slowly grinned their way into the grave. I was going to beat this.

"I hate wearing this." I tugged at the loose jade green sleeve that covered my left arm.

"Then don't come," replied Maylien. "You said yourself that you don't think we're going to be in any danger this morning."

Heyin nodded. "The king won't dare make a move

against Maylien at a meeting of the Council of Jade, no matter how much he wants to. That's why we decided to wait to deliver the declaration of Maylien's legitimacy to the chancellor until today at the Winter-Round court. It's afterward, when we're on our way back to Marchon House and in the days that follow that we'll be in the most danger. That's why I suggested you wait for us outside the great gate and shadow us back here."

I shrugged. They were both right, and I really did hate wearing the green and gold uniform of Maylien's baronial guard. Pretending to be part of the very sort of hierarchy my goddess had so often sent me to decapitate always made me twitchy. I'd done it on missions in the past, but somehow this felt very different. I didn't mind killing Thauvik. Removing corrupt rulers was the work I had been born for. But putting Maylien in his place ventured into territory that my goddess had always avoided—the politics of succession. The role of the Blade was to act as a threat, never a promise. We didn't choose sides.

"I know," I said after a moment. "I even mostly agree with you. But what if we're wrong and he's even crazier than he seems? I want to be in the chamber when Maylien delivers her papers."

Now Heyin shrugged. "If you insist, I won't oppose you. Gods know, I've no one better to guard her back."

The sky was still dark as our small troupe left the gate of Marchon House. Heyin walked in front with a pair of his lieutenants. Maylien would come immediately behind on an open-work ivory chair set in a palanquin with the silk curtains in the green and gold Marchon colors pulled aside— the baronial seat on its way to sit before the throne.

"I wish I could walk," she said to me as they were affixing the narrow chair to the palanquin. "It's a terrible way to travel, but the tradition's a thousand years old, and so's the damned chair. Whatever Marchon it was originally made for must have been three feet tall and knife-edge skinny."

"Do you ever wish you could just step away from all this and go back to the Rovers?"

"Every damned day. When I first set out to take the baro-nial seat from my sister, there were things I hated to lose about that life and things that I didn't mind giving up. How could I not miss walking under a clear blue autumn sky with an open road and nowhere to be? These days I even miss the icy winter rains of Radewald and slogging through ankle deep mud in hopes of finding an inn. I hate this role and I hate the choices it forces on me."

She looked longingly back at the house where Bontrang had been placed in a cage to prevent him following her to the palace. Her magery was deeply troubling and bordering on criminal as far as her fellow nobles and the law of Zhan were concerned. That had made her challenge of her sister and assumption of the baronial seat almost impossible, and it continued to make her an outcast among the peerage. It was also going to make putting her on the throne that much harder, though I had to assume Fei knew what she was talk-ing about when she said it was less of a problem than her bastard status.

But then the palanquin was ready for her and she had to climb up into her narrow ivory chair. I fell in at the back of the procession with a couple of her guards. Within a few minutes of hitting the main thoroughfare leading from the Sovann Hill down toward the river and the palace, we encountered the coterie of the Earl of Anaryun, and had to pause to let his people move out in front.

We stopped again when the Duke of Jenua claimed pre-cedence in front of the earl. Later, as we left the Sovann behind, a couple of baronets fell in behind us. Then, as we approached the Sanjin Island bridge, the Duchess of Kijang coming down the river from her estates west of the city bumped everyone back a place. She ranked fourth in the peerage, behind only the Duke of Anyang, the Duchess of Tien, and the king himself.

The streets directly in front of the palace gates were an absolute madhouse, with every high noble of the realm and their entourages jockeying for proper position in the march of the peers. Most of the baronets and clan lords and lesser lights weren't high enough in the peerage to be granted entry to the meeting of the Council of Jade, but they had to attend the Winter-Round court that followed or risk formal censure by the Crown.

For that matter, Maylien's participation would normally have been limited to a gallery seat for the Council of Jade, because of the relatively minor position of the Barony of Marchon. Only her uncle's formal recognition of her and her sister as *official* bastards of his late brother allowed her to claim a place at the council table, informally ranking her with the earls and dukes and counts. That was also the only thing that made it possible for me to attend—each of the jade councilors was allowed an unarmed personal attendant whose job was to kneel behind their master's chair and await commands.

The Council of Jade met at the high table in the largest of the palace's formal chambers—built purpose specific for the twice annual event. The king sat on his throne at the head of a long table that jutted out into the center of the room on a raised platform. The lesser peers placed their chairs of office around the councilors on three sides, sitting on the lower level of the floor. I set Maylien's chair on the left side of the table, very near the foot, then joined the other attendants, going to one knee at the edge of the dais holding the council table.

The first twenty minutes or so of the convocation was eaten up with a brief welcoming speech by the king and other court formalities that left me quietly thinking that if I ghosted Thauvik now at least he'd shut up. That was followed by the official presentation of credentials by the participants, starting on the king's right with the Duchess of Tien who also served as chancellor of the realm, and then alternating back and forth across the table in descending order of precedence. Mostly it was a matter of each noble rising and stating their antecedents, which the chancellor dutifully attested to the king, who acknowledged them with a nod.

Occasionally however, a seat had changed hands either

through the normal course of succession or by right of challenge in the previous few days and the new holder had to petition for the formal recognition of the Crown. In both instances, the newly made noble had to bring their documents up the table to be formally examined by the Duchess of Tien. In the case of traditional succession, they presented wills and certificates of legitimacy. With challenges, they brought documentation of blood relationship to the challenged and witnesses' statements as to the conduct and outcome of the duel. It took nearly an hour for the presentation of credentials to reach Maylien, who sat third from the end, a position determined by order of precedence.

"The Baroness Marchon," said the Duchess of Tien, in a loud formal voice.

I slid Maylien's chair back as she rose to speak. "Thank you, Chancellor. Your Majesty, Chancellor, peers of the realm. I am the Baroness Maylien Dan Marchon *Dan* Pridu, and I ask permission to approach the throne to present my credentials and formally claim the titles of Duchess Pridu and Crown Princess."

The Duchess of Tien, who had seemed practically asleep in her chair, abruptly sat up straight, "Pardon? What did you just say, Baroness? *Dan* Pridu?"

Though she was so old that no one expected it ever to become an issue, the Duchess of Tien was also the current Crown Princess and formal heir to the throne, though not the Duchess Pridu, due to her lack of sufficient royal blood. That title was currently unclaimed. The king didn't move, but his eyes, never warm to start with, went suddenly icy. The "Dan," which replaced the "Tal" Maylien had used until now, indicated a legitimate claim to the Pridu name that Thauvik Tal Pridu himself didn't own. The surrounding sea of lesser nobles, which had been very quietly chattering away, slowly quieted as they realized that something unusual was happening at the high table.

"I asked permission to approach the throne so that I may present my credentials," said Maylien. "While examining the cellars in Marchon House, I recently came across a document which I am forced by law and custom to present to this body and the Crown. It seems that shortly before his death, my father, the late Ashvik the Sixth, formally adopted my sister and I as his heirs, legitimizing us. While I would never dream of claiming precedence over my uncle, who has been a wise and just ruler, I cannot in good conscience refuse the duty to the throne and succession placed on me by my late father with this document."

Maylien bowed formally to the head of the table. "For the second time, I am the Baroness Maylien Dan Marchon *Dan* Pridu. May I approach the throne?"

The duchess jerked at that and the king now sat up straight as well, while the whole vast room went utterly quiet, with many holding their breath. The throne was the only noble seat not directly subject to the Right of Challenge under general circumstances. But there *were* exceptions, most notably if the Crown refused to cede certain acknowledgements to the top dozen or so members of the royal family in direct line of succession for the throne. If Maylien's papers of adoption were adjudged to be real, she would fall into that select group, and refusing her permission to approach the throne three times would allow her to issue challenge.

Maylien straightened the dueling blade that hung at her left hip. "For the third time—"

The king flicked his eyes at the Duchess of Tien and inclined his head the barest fraction of an inch.

She rose from her chair and bowed to Maylien. "Provisional on the acceptance of your claim, you may approach the throne and present me with the documents, *Baroness* Marchon."

As Maylien slow-marched around the foot of the table and up the dais to hand her papers to the chancellor, I slid back off the dais and paralleled her on the floor below. I had to force myself to break training and let my feet make noise as I walked. Perfect silence would actually have drawn more attention to me in the greater silence of that long walk. When we reached the Duchess of Tien's seat, Maylien stuck a hand out to the side without looking and I passed her the silk-wrapped scroll—it would have been beneath her formal dignity to carry it herself or to acknowledge my existence. She slipped off the silk sheath and handed the document to the duchess.

The duchess took it without seeming to look at Maylien, much less pay any attention to me. She continued to ignore Maylien as she unrolled the scroll and gave it an initial glance. The proclamation of adoption and legitimization was short and simple—quickly read. Within moments the duchess had moved on to checking the seals and chops. After another minute or two, she looked up at Maylien and her expression was now deeply troubled.

"Baroness Marchon, would you please step to my left"—the king's side, a very telling choice—"and make room for the Lord Justicer and the Warden of the Blood to join me." Respectively the chief legal authority of the realm and the woman charged with validating all issues of family relations with regards to succession.

As Maylien passed to the duchess's left, I did the same on the floor below.

Aral, another Shade's been here! Triss's words came as a mental shout of alarm. *The shadow trail is very fresh, no more than two or three hours old and it leads toward the throne.*

I forced myself not to show any visible reaction to Triss's news, but immediately began scanning the area around the throne for deeper pools of shadow. Another Shade almost certainly meant another Blade.

Do you recognize the spoor? Best would have been my sometime apprentice Faran, come to keep an eye out for her teacher, but I didn't hold out much hope for that. Neither for her, nor for Siri or Jax or any of the tiny handful of other survivors who still retained some loyalty to the memory of Namara.

Not quite. It tastes almost familiar, an older master perhaps, but not one I know well. There's something else there, too, something . . . ancient and wrong.

How so?

I don't know. It's not a knowing *thing. It's tasting and feeling and shadows of something I can't quite touch.*

I didn't like the sound of any of that, but I couldn't do anything about it without more information. If it wasn't Siri or Faran or one of Jax's people, it almost had to be one of Kelos's renegades—the Blades who had gone over to the Son of Heaven after the destruction of the temple. Traitors to everything we had once held sacred, they called themselves the Shadow of Heaven. My eyes flicked across the king on his throne for perhaps the dozenth time as I tried to spot someplace where a shadow-cloaked assassin might hide. Something about the position of Thauvik's head drew my attention back to him with a sudden snap. He was looking up and somewhat back, as though he were trying to see something positioned above and behind his chair, but couldn't afford to be seen to turn his head and actually look.

The velvet curtain that created an alcove for the throne hung from four large marble pillars that approached but didn't reach the ceiling. I tried to see if I could make anything out in the shadows that clung to the gaps above. The king—who had leaned forward a bit, as though idly glancing at the documents his councilors were so carefully reviewing—slid his left hand even further forward. Then he made a tiny cutting gesture with one finger.

I moved without thinking, lunging to grab the back of Maylien's belt and yank her off the dais. As I pulled her down flat behind the Duchess of Tien, alarmed gasps broke out from the lesser nobility behind us, as well as the dukes and earls seated across the table. The duchess herself half turned in her chair, and I was looking right into her eyes when the tiny poisoned dart meant for Maylien struck her in the neck.

She let out a gasp and stood straight up, knocking her chair and the Lord Justicer off the dais. Then she fell face-first onto Maylien and me. The room exploded into cacophony. Several hundred people leaped to their feet, variously yelling, running for the exits, or reaching for dueling weapons as the notion took them.

If I hadn't been lying practically at the king's feet, I would never have heard him shouting over the uproar. "Kill them! Kill them all!" There was a wild, half-mad quality to his tone that set fingers of ice clawing at my spine, and I knew in that instant that something was deeply wrong with Thauvik.

Behind him, the door reserved for the king burst open and a pair of the Crown Elite came rushing through. They had weapons in their hand and spells uncoiling like curls of glimmering fire at their fingertips. On either side of the Elite, the giant stone dogs who familiared them slid silently up through the marble tiles of the floor, rising from the cold ground beneath, where they had been lying concealed. Elemental creatures of earth, the stone dogs could swim through dirt and rock as easily as any fish through water. They left no marks on the tiles when they emerged.

Grabbing Maylien, I cried out with my mind, *Triss, shroud!* Darkness swallowed us as he spun himself into a cloud of blackness.

I expected the king to make his exit then, drawn away by his most loyal guards. But he waved them off, remaining on his throne to watch the carnage. The last thing I saw before night blocked my sight was the king's half-mad grin when one of the Elite blasted the Warden of the Blood aside with a spell that nearly tore the woman's head off.

Dragging Maylien with me, I rolled wildly away from the dais. I aimed for a gap in the first rank of ivory chairs where a wild-eyed clan chief had cleared herself some fighting room. We smashed into her shins and sent her staggering toward the dais, and she stabbed downward in response, snapping her sword on the stones. She swore and turned, obviously trying to spot what had hit her, but we had already moved beyond easy reach. Without the forced awareness of contact, she would have a hard time spotting us now.

Even one of the Elite—who were trained for such work— would have had difficulties picking us out amid the swirling chaos of angry lords, jumbled furniture, and fallen bodies. Still, I spared a moment to thank the memory of my goddess for whatever magic made it so hard for people to spy a shroud even in relatively good light. And another to hope that the Elite who had come in past the king hadn't spotted me before we went dark. There was lots of visual turbulence to draw hostile attention away from a shadow that wasn't supposed to be there, but it would be better if they weren't actively looking.

Maylien hissed, "What the hell's going on, Aral?" for perhaps the fifth time as I staggered to my feet and pulled her with me.

I finally had the attention to respond. "Enemy Blade," I said. Then I scooped her onto my shoulder. "You need to stay inside the shroud if you don't want to go the way of the duchess, so hug me tight."

I dashed toward the nearest wall—where I could hopefully find a servant's door—zigging and zagging as I ran.

4

Down! Triss shouted into my mind, and I dove for the floor.

A chain of green fire lashed across the wall in front of me, shattering thirty feet of teak paneling and sending out a shower of burning splinters. A narrow gap was revealed a couple of yards to my left—that servant's passage I'd been hoping for. Steep stairs spiraled away into darkness in both directions.

"Aral, stop, we have to go back," Maylien gasped—I'd landed on her pretty hard. She pushed herself off my shoulder.

I rose onto hands and knees, covering her with my body and the shadow that surrounded me. "Like hell we do." The green chain fell somewhere off to my left, destroying chairs and drawing screams. I hoped that meant that the lash that had nearly cut us in half was a lucky shot then, not aimed.

"We've got to get my adoption papers," said Maylien. "This whole disaster will be pointless if we don't." And damn me if she wasn't right.

"Bad idea," said Triss. "There are more Elite coming

through the king's door right now, and an army of Crown Guard can't be far behind. To say nothing of the rogue Blade back there."

Triss, my eyes. He uncovered them as I glanced back over my shoulder toward the high table.

A few yards behind me a stone dog tore at the corpse of a fallen baronet. Beyond, I could see a half dozen Elite fanning out from around the throne. They were blasting away with magic, though nowhere near as indiscriminately as the king's order had called for. In fact, the vast majority of their spells were falling on inanimate targets.

One of the mage soldiers started to step over a fallen clan leader. The apparent corpse suddenly whipped his sword up and across the Elite's lower belly, spilling her guts. Before he could do more, a spear of black fire punched a fist-sized hole in his skull and he fell again, this time truly dead instead of shamming.

A glance in the other direction showed the main doors clogged with panicking and heavily armed nobles. More than a few bleeding bodies showed where they had slain one another in their haste to escape. Mercifully, the Elite seemed to be avoiding the crowd with their magical attacks. But there was no way to tell how long that might last, or how much worse things could get. I had to get Maylien clear.

I pointed her toward the servant's stairs and started nudging her along. "I'll go back for the papers, but not till you're through that door. They won't do anyone any good if you're too dead to use them, and without Triss to cover you, you wouldn't make it ten feet. I've a much better chance of managing this alone."

She looked mighty unhappy, but crawled with me toward the broken door anyway. It was a long distance to go on hands and knees, but with the green chain smashing this way and that, it seemed the better choice. As soon as Maylien had spiraled up the stairs and out of sight, I slipped back down to the door, crouching in the shadows there while I surveyed the hall and planned my approach. Much had changed in just the few minutes since my last look around.

Though the king remained on his throne, most of the madness had faded from his expression. He was leaning back and to his left, and looking more bemused than any-thing. The numbers of the Elite had climbed to a dozen or so now, the nearest of whom was attending to the one who'd had her guts opened, while two or three stuck close by the king. Others were taking command of the numerous Crown Guards who had started to arrive on the scene as well. Either at the king's orders, or on their own recognizance, the Elite had stopped flinging spells around.

The jam of screaming and fighting chaos around the main doors was still going strong, though some of those at the back had started moving away from the conflict as they realized that the immediate danger had passed. Some had sheathed their weapons, but more had not, and all were eyeing the Crown Guard and the Elite with more than a little hostility. Barring active combat breaking out between those two groups, this was probably my best chance to collect Maylien's document. The calmer things got, the harder it would become to approach the throne unseen, and with the room as well lit as it was, the thing was going to be damned hard no matter what. I assumed full control of Triss and started forward.

As I shadow-danced my way through the king's guards, I briefly entertained the idea of simply killing Thauvik now. Though I was supposed to be unarmed and had been care-fully searched by the Crown Guard before being allowed to follow Maylien into the council room, I had managed to secrete one or two things about my person that would allow me to do the job without actually having to get close enough to touch him. But until Maylien's claims to the Crown had been officially acknowledged or refuted, killing the king would only make Maylien's road to the throne more dif-ficult.

I was perhaps fifteen feet away when I finally noticed that the document in question was no longer on the table in front of the duchess's place. *Dammit.* I glanced at the floor where her body had fallen since either she or the Warden of the Blood might have dragged the thing with them when they fell, but it wasn't there either. At least, not that I could see. As I edged closer still, one of the Crown Guard rolled the body of the warden over, exposing the space beneath her and reducing the possible number of hiding places by one.

I froze as one of the stone dogs emerged from the floor a scant yard in front of me, and held my breath when it sniffed once or twice and looked in my general direction. I got a far closer look at the lion-like face of the great brute than I cared for as it sniffed harder, working its heavy jowls and nostrils. But then its master called and it turned away from me. I slipped forward another three feet, having to move a good ten left and right to manage it. Finally, I was kneeling right over the crumpled body of the Duchess of Tien.

The cone of the dart had already fallen to the floor, dropping away when the crystallized poison that made up the point and shaft melted. In the scramble that followed, the brittle ceramic cone had been crushed, leaving only a tiny, barely identifiable wound in the duchess's neck as evidence she'd been struck—more proof that it was a Blade dart. Maylien's proclamation of legitimacy was nowhere to be seen. I took a risk by giving the corpse a shove to tip it aside, but it didn't pay off. Then the stone dog was coming back my way and I had to move, sliding to my left until I was practically in the shadow of the throne.

As I tried to decide where to look next, I heard Thauvik speaking very quietly. "But I don't want to." And then, after that, an angry hiss of, "Fine, let's go then."

The king rose and called out, "Vyan, come out from under that table and attend me."

After a long beat, a querulous voice sounded from beneath the table, "Your Majesty?"

"Are you going to make me repeat myself?" the king asked, his voice low and dangerous.

The Lord Justicer practically shot out into the light, bowing deeply as he stood up. "Of course not, Your Majesty."

"Good. I would hate to lose another member of my high

council today." The king turned and walked to the door behind his throne. At the threshold he paused and said over his shoulder, "Don't make the mistake of thinking I didn't notice your craven dive under the table when you should have been thinking of my safety, Vyan. Or that it will be easily forgiven."

The Lord Justicer swallowed heavily. "Of course not, Your Majesty." Then he started after the king.

"Tell me, Vyan, what became of that paper my niece tried to foist off on us?"

"I'm not sure, Your Majesty. I thought the Duchess of Tien had it in her hand when she . . . fell." He stepped through the door behind the king.

For lack of a better plan, I followed them. I had just reached the threshold, when my borrowed Shade senses gave a harsh jangle and I tasted the sharp smoky notes of an extremely fresh shadow trail on the floor. Though I had been practicing regularly with Faran much of the spring, I would never have a tenth the palate for such things that Triss did. All I could really read from the trail was that it had been laid down within the last few minutes. Ahead of me lay a small and very dimly lit presence chamber. The king and the Lord Justicer had stopped in the middle of the room, and I slowed and slipped to the left side as soon as I entered.

I could taste that the Blade who preceded me had done the same, so I froze. Rather than take a single step farther, I leaned back against the wall and forced myself to breathe shallowly and slowly. As always at moments like this, I found myself missing the efik, which would have made the effort of controlling my heart rate and breathing *so* much easier. Using Triss's senses I did a slow scan of the room. But if my rogue Blade was in there with me, I simply couldn't see them. Which was probably the express purpose of whoever had hooded all the magelights in the room.

Triss, wake up, I mentally whispered—no noise was involved but I couldn't help but extend the effort at silence to everything I did.

What is it?

I'm following the king and I've hit that shadow trail you mentioned earlier. But I'm no good with the nuances. How close behind them am I?

Don't move!

I'm not. That close?

That close, though I still don't recognize the spoor. I never thought I'd say this, but I wish this room were brighter. There's just too many places one of us could hide in here.

Before he could go on, the Lord Justicer said something that drew my attention back to their ongoing conversation, and I mentally shushed him. I didn't dare get Triss to uncover my eyes, but he did let what information was coming through his senses flow through the link that bound us, giving me a Shade's-eye view of the situation.

"No, Your Majesty, I really don't know what happened to the Marchon girl's papers," the Justicer was saying. "I heard you order the Elite to find them. If they couldn't, I can only assume that she grabbed them when she fled. The chancellor had them last I saw, and she practically fell on top of your niece. What *I* want to know is how the girl got out of the hall without getting caught."

"We have some ideas about that, don't we?"

Thauvik turned half away from the Lord Justicer and nodded to a rather darker patch of thin air in a way that suggested his choice of "we" wasn't the royal one. It was always strange watching people through Triss's unsight. He couldn't see things in the conventional sense, so, instead I had to interpret the textured interplay of light and shadow through the focus of years of training. Faces and expressions were all but impossible to read, and I had to rely on broader cues of movement and posture to give me emotional context.

For example, the way that the Lord Justicer sagged slightly whenever the king's focus shifted away from him suggested both terror at being in the royal eye, and an underlying exhaustion that prevented him from fully hiding his relief whenever he passed out of the king's direct focus. The shift back the other way was a much subtler thing. He was far too skilled a courtier to jerk tight when the king looked at him directly, but with each passing second of royal regard his body tightened and grew more erect.

"You got a good look at the document, Vyan. Tell me about it. I would have preferred to have it in hand, but since you couldn't manage the simple task of hanging on to it when my niece made her move against us, I'm stuck with your word for how the thing looked. Do you think it was real, or just a ploy to get her close enough to issue her illegal challenge?"

Fire and sun but what is he talking about? Triss demanded. *There was no challenge and Maylien didn't make a move to harm him.*

I think we are seeing the official version being formulated, I replied.

"Of course not, Your Majesty," said the Lord Justicer. "How could it be real? Everyone knows that you are your brother's rightful heir. It had to be a forgery."

Thauvik nodded. "True, but was it a well-made one? Do you think it might be used to convince discontented peers to support a pretender?"

Tiny diamonds of reflected light had appeared on the Lord Justicer's brow—beads of sweat not at all in keeping with the chilly temperatures of the presence chamber. Vyan knew he was dancing on the edge of the abyss with every question and every answer, and this was the most dangerous yet.

"It would never convince anyone who gave it a proper examination, Your Majesty, I'm sure. But who can say what a traitor already looking for an excuse might choose to see in such a forgery."

"Who indeed?" The king gave the Justicer a suspicious look. "I need you to draft a proclamation declaring my niece outlaw and decrying her rebellion against the throne. Be sure to include the complicity of the Duchess of Tien, and as many of the slain as you think reasonable." He canted his head to one side. "I think the Warden of the Blood ought to be a martyr, slain while defending me from my niece's assassination attempt, don't you? Oh, and have the formal Winter-Round court postponed indefinitely."

"Of course, Your Majesty. It will be just as you say. Would you like me to start now? I can have one of the Elite bring me a list of the fallen."

The king didn't say anything for a couple of minutes, then he suddenly looked up at the Justicer and glared. "Are you still here?"

"No, Your Majesty. I was just leaving." He practically bolted for the door leading deeper into the palace.

Once he was gone, the king reached up and started absently rubbing at his cheeks. "That didn't go well at all at all," said the king in a half singsong, "it didn't go well at all." He brushed distastefully at a blood spatter on his sleeve. "This will have to be burned, and I need a bath." Then he followed the Justicer out, still rubbing away. "Yes, a long hot soak, that would be just the thing . . ."

Bring me up to date, said Triss. *Thauvik seems to be following his late brother round the bend, and I need to know if I missed anything important while I was in dreamland.* I did so as quickly as I could, and when I mentioned overhearing what sounded like the king taking orders from our hidden Blade, Triss hissed mentally. *I don't like the idea of Thauvik bowing the knee to one of Kelos's traitors. That implies a connection with the Son of Heaven that's very worrisome.*

I hadn't thought it through that far yet, but you're right. Still, we haven't time to do anything about it now. We need to catch up to Maylien and make sure she gets clear of the city before we can worry about anything else.

I went back through the dining room, since I wanted to take one last look for the missing adoption papers. But I had no more luck than the first time. The guards had started to sort out the bodies, laying them along the back wall, starting with the Duchess of Tien and the Warden of the Blood. As I looked at the row of corpses, my eyes fell on the clan chief who'd had half his head blasted away by the Elite.

The ruin the wound had made of the man's face reminded

me of Jerik and the huge scar where the gryphon had tried to bite his head off. A sharp pang of guilt hit me, and I wondered how much my old friend was suffering right now, and whether this mess was advancing the cause of getting him out or I was just adding to the world's pain to no point. But there was no way to know that until I finished what I'd started or died in the attempt, so I pushed it aside and went on to the next step.

With all the chaos created by the slaughter at the Council of Jade and the subsequent rats heading for the exits effect, getting from there out into the grounds was a trivial task. I didn't bother to follow Maylien up the stairs. She was more than competent to escape the council building on her own. By the time I reached the gates that led out of the palace complex, the Elite had taken control. They were frantically checking everyone who left, which told me they hadn't grabbed Maylien yet.

I had a lot of faith in both her and Heyin's abilities, so I slipped out of the gate and started toward the Sovann Hill, scanning faces as I went. I found one of Heyin's sergeants waiting for me at the head of the Sanjin Island bridge. Her name was Lineya and she'd ditched her jade and gold uniform for a peasant dress.

"They're out?" I asked as I slipped up beside her.

She didn't turn. "They are, lord, and heading for Marchon house on a couple of stolen horses. Heyin wanted the baroness to leave the city immediately, but she refused to go without warning her people at the house and collecting Bontrang."

I was sure that latter was the more important of the two. If it were somehow possible to separate us, I wouldn't have let anyone else go after Triss for me either. "How long ago was that?"

"You won't catch them at the house if that's what you mean," said Lineya. "She said that if you could come in the next few hours, you should meet her at the place where the two of you landed on the glorious day that you flew together. Otherwise, she said that you would have to seek her at Exile

House." Then, without looking at me or saying another word, Lineya headed off into the crowd.

"Crazy woman," I said, though not without affection.

Lineya? asked Triss.

No, Maylien, calling that desperate sail-jump we took off the Channery Hill cliff a "glorious flight." It was neither glorious nor flying. It was hardly even a sail-jump—more like falling and getting it wrong.

Point . . . crazy woman?

I saw where he was going there, but this was a more mundane sort of craziness than the hereditary insanity that had taken her father and now seemed to be at work in her uncle.

Not that way, Triss. The only one whose safety Maylien ignores is her own. In that way, she's practically the polar opposite of Ashvik and Thauvik.

I didn't include Maylien's sister in the list. Sumey had fallen to the curse of the restless dead. Somewhere in the years she spent in exile—far from the safety of the court and the baronial guard—she had become one of the risen. How or where she'd encountered the risen that had infected her with its particular variety of the curse of the restless dead was something Sumey hadn't shared before her death. Neither that nor how she'd managed to learn how to prolong her human seeming far beyond what was normal among her kind. While she had been subject to bloody hungers that somewhat mimicked the madness of her older relations, they came from a wholly different source. It was a fact Maylien would do well to remind herself of whenever she had one of her periodic panic attacks about going the way of the rest of her family.

Come on, I sent, *we need to meet Maylien.* I would have to get rid of the borrowed uniform on the way.

The Downunders was one of the shabbiest neighborhoods in a city rife with slums. Lying on the south side of the city, it had started out as a series of temporary markets and shelters for the drovers and teamsters who brought in the goods that didn't travel well by ship. That was half a millennia ago. The city bounds had long since swallowed those temporary buildings whole, but it had never quite gotten around to tearing them down and starting over. Instead, people had tacked brick sheds onto canvas tents, and then later covered over the tarps with rough plank roofs, and replaced canvas flaps with poorly fitted doors—all without ever knocking down the original tent posts.

The area where I was supposed to meet Maylien had a touch more polish and architectural stability, but that was only because the Elite colonel who was trying to burn us out of the sky on our way down had started a dozen buildings on fire in the process. The residents had replaced them in much the same way that buildings were always replaced in the Downunders: by scavenging in the wreckage and adding the permanent on top of the temporary, but at least the canvas was new and the mortar between the charred old bricks was fresh.

The burning leather shop where we'd landed had been replaced by a lopsided teahouse. I found Maylien sitting at a tiny table on the porch outside despite the chill. She was wearing stained leather and wool in the browns and greens the Rovers tended to favor. She had her calves resting on the chair across from her, though her well-worn boots hung over the edge so as not to get mud on the seat. An oversized pack lay on the planks beneath her knees with Bontrang perched atop it. She had a steaming cup of tea in her right hand and her left resting on the hilt of a utilitarian sword. All in all, she looked more right and happy than I had seen her at any time since she took her sister's coronet.

When she saw me approaching, she nodded and smiled, dropping her feet off the chair. "I wasn't sure if you'd make it, but I ordered you a cup of tepid slop anyway. Now that you've arrived I'm sure they'll eventually deliver it."

"I didn't get the paper." There was no point in holding the worst news back from Maylien.

She sighed. "I'm not surprised, really."

"I followed your uncle and the Lord Justicer to see whether they'd recovered them."

"And?"

I quickly described what I'd witnessed. "If either of them had it, they pretended not to, though I can't see why they'd have done so."

Maylien snorted. "At court lying is like breathing. The one only stops when the other does. But I don't see any gain in it for either of them here."

The owner of the teahouse arrived then and rather unceremoniously dropped a chipped pottery cup on the table in front of me. The water was hot and the brown bits on the bottom suggested that he'd dumped a few ancient and twisted tea leaves into it. That or rat droppings. It was hard to tell the difference from the flavor, but I didn't like tea anyway, so it was kind of a wash.

While the two of us were dealing with the tea, Maylien tipped Bontrang off her pack and undid some straps that bound what I had taken to be a fold in the canvas but was instead a separate piece. Bontrang squawked and flew up to Maylien's shoulder as she passed what turned out to be a second, smaller pack to me. I undid the flap and glanced in at a tangle of wool and silk and leather straps all tumbled together—my gear, including the Blade's garb that her seamstress had made for me.

"I didn't have time to pack it properly," she said, "but I thought you'd want it. This, too." She picked up an oblong bundle that had been hidden under the pack until now. "Your swords and the longer knives," she said very quietly.

"Thank you."

"I knew you'd need them." The door banged shut as the owner vanished into the depths of the tea shop, and Maylien let out a long breath. "If we don't have the paper and they don't have it, where do you think it went?"

I shrugged, there were too many options. "It could easily have been destroyed with the way the Elite were throwing around magic there at the beginning, though I'd have expected to see some remnants if that were the case. Or it might have gotten buried in the wreckage of the chairs. One of the nobles could have grabbed it, or that rogue Blade if the document stayed on the table when the duchess fell. It was within easy reach of the king's seat and the shadow trail was all over there."

"Devin?" Maylien asked the question with a deceptive sort of calm.

I winced. Not all that long ago she had spent some time with Devin, my onetime best friend who had since turned into an enemy and traitor to our goddess. He'd chained her up and threatened her familiar's life as a way to keep her from using her magic to escape. That was back when Devin had been working to put Maylien's sister on Thauvik's throne—rather ironic considering present events. I suspected that Maylien hated him even more than I did.

I shook my head. "No, even I'd have recognized *that* shadow trail, and Triss didn't know who this was. One of the lesser masters of the previous generation, probably. Someone who either never had the opportunity to distinguish themselves, or simply didn't have the talent."

"I'm not sure whether I'm glad about that or disappointed," said Maylien.

"Devin's not all that great a Blade either, so it's probably even."

"You misunderstand me. I'm disappointed that I won't get the chance to kill him myself, but glad that you won't have to." Now she laughed. "Don't give me that look. I've seen the two of you talking, and I've heard you talk about him. I know how hard it would be for you to have to kill him, and since I care about you, I'm glad you won't have to make that choice."

I didn't want to talk about Devin, so I asked, "What will you do now that the document ploy has fallen apart?"

Maylien took a deep breath. "The slaughter at the Council of Jade will have turned many against my uncle, and it can't go unanswered. I will go to war against the Crown. What other choice do I have?"

5

Life is identity. When you kill someone, you rob what remains of the body of any true relationship with the person that once inhabited it. That was never clearer than when you saw someone's head on a stake. No matter how perfectly preserved the features, the *person* was simply gone.

The Duchess of Tien's head went up first, a lump of dead flesh impaled on a stake and nailed over the traitor's gate. I watched from the edge of the square as it was followed by more than two dozen more heads, including two earls, five counts, eight barons, and a dozen mixed clan chiefs and other lesser nobles. The other thirty or so casualties of what was being called the Jade massacre were being hailed as martyrs for the Crown and given a mass state funeral paid for by the king's personal house purse. At least, that was the word on the street.

The rumors said that Thauvik was claiming that funding the memorials out of his own pocket was the least he could do to honor the fallen patriots who had given their lives to save his own. They were also saying that more arrests and executions were expected at any moment, which sounded to me like a not so subtle signal to any nobles who might want to dispute the official version of events.

The Lord Justicer himself supervised the display of the heads, an operation that took well over an hour. The thick oak beam where they nailed up the stakes didn't have the room for even a dozen traitors, so while one crew was putting up heads and branding their cheeks with the inverted crown of the traitor, another was mounting two more beams. A huge crowd gathered in the square during the process, and not the typical bunch of local knockabouts and urban poor for whom the displaying of traitors provided a cheap morning's entertainment.

Oh, they were there as well, and pleased as always to see their overlords suffering some of the same rough justice that usually fell most heavily on those who could least afford it. But there were as many or more in the crowd that had calluses built with dueling swords, or the more utilitarian weapons of personal guards, as there were those whose rough hands came from the tools of laborers. That spoke volumes about the way the ruling class felt about the deaths of the previous day.

What said even more was that not a single one of the many nobles and their guards wore the crests and colors that their respective stations would normally have required. Cowls and hoods were much in evidence as well, far more than the slight chill would reasonably have justified. The nobility did not want to be seen to be in attendance. That suited me just fine, as it made my own cowl and loose poncho that much less visible.

Once the last head was nailed in place, the Lord Justicer mounted the scaffolding the soldiers had used for the work and, with a face the color of yesterday's rice, unrolled a huge scroll. This was the proclamation of outlawry for the dead, and its first reading here at the traitor's gate was the main reason for the noble presence.

The Lord Justicer took a deep breath and began, "Let it be known that on this, the second day of Winter-Round, His

Royal Majesty, Thauvik the Fourth, has decreed that the following individuals have been adjudged guilty of high treason against the Crown of Zhan, and are forfeit of their lives and titles: Jiahui Dan Tien, once Duchess of Tien and Countess of . . ."

The reading of the names and titles took a long time and the crowd grew steadily quieter and angrier as each of the dead was announced. More and more hands fell to rest on sword hilts, and the Lord Justicer kept looking steadily paler and paler as the names and titles rolled out into the silence.

Odds on whether the crowd put his head up with all the others when he's finished speaking? Triss asked.

At the moment I'd call it an even bet. The nobility don't like to see their own cut down at the best of times and in ones and twos. The sheer number of the fallen here puts this on the edge of the knife.

I wonder if that's Thauvik's plan? Concentrate the angriest of his peers in one place and provoke them into the open slaying of one of the great officers of the realm? That would certainly give him an excuse to execute the lot.

I don't think he can afford that kind of bloodshed so soon after yesterday, not with so many of his nobles more than half ready to start an open rebellion. Besides, if he wanted to do that, he'd have the alleys packed with Crown Guard instead of city watch. If Thauvik's trying to provoke them into tearing his Lord Justicer apart, it's more likely because he wants to get rid of the last reputable witness to the legitimacy of Maylien's papers of adoption.

Now, there's a thought. I could see Thauvik thinking that was a grand idea.

I nodded and then another idea occurred to me. *From his point of view it might also serve as a way to allow his lords to vent some of their anger on a proxy for the throne in a way that costs him nothing he values.*

As the potential for violence grew, more and more of the common folk wisely slipped from the square. By the time the last name was read out, there were very few left in that square who didn't possess noble blood or carry arms for those who did, and I began to think that Thauvik really had chosen to throw the Lord Justicer to the wolves.

". . . Clan Lord of Reshi," said the Lord Justicer, concluding the roll of the condemned.

Total silence fell in the square while the crowd waited to see what further names or penalties might be read out. This was the moment when it could all go bad and I slid deeper into the doorway where I'd taken station, ready to shroud up or break the door's lock and duck inside as necessary.

The Lord Justicer paused and took a deep breath before continuing. "It is customary in times of open rebellion, such as this, for the Crown to name those outlaws who remain at large and to levy penalties on the families and estates of those who have been adjudged traitors to the realm, and today is no exception. The Crown declares the Baroness Maylien Dan Marchon *Tal* Pridu an enemy of the realm and all her lands and titles forfeit along with her life. A reward in the sum of ten thousand gold riels is levied for the delivery of her head to the palace gates at any time of day or night."

I was surprised by that, actually. It was only one-fifth the sum that Thauvik had put on my head, and all I'd done was put him on his throne. The crowd remained silent.

"Further," said the Lord Justicer, "anyone, noble or commoner, who delivers the head of the sorcerer-baroness to the Crown will receive the Barony of Marchon and all its entailed titles and fiefdoms, for themselves and their heirs, unto the end of the kingdom."

That created an angry buzz in the crowd, and no surprise. Some were no doubt unhappy at the thought of one of their peers picking up such a choice title. But I suspected that it was the inclusion of commoners in the potential rewardees that really rankled. It had been at least a hundred years since the last time any commoner had been raised to the nobility outside of special recognition for valor on the battlefield. In the entire half-millennia-long history of the Pridu dynasty, a grant of rank that lifted a commoner into the peerage couldn't have happened more than a handful of times.

Further, I couldn't think of a single historical instance of such falling on anyone not already in service to the Crown.

This unprecedented reward created the possibility of someone cutting purses in the alleys of the stumbles one day and sitting down to dinner with the great families of the realm the next. And while *I* might not see all that much of a difference between your gutter criminal and any high noble, I was pretty sure that wasn't how the peers of the realm viewed things.

Before the buzz could grow into a roar, the Lord Justicer held up both hands. "Citizens of Zhan, allow me to finish before you make any decisions. The Baroness Marchon is the only name on my list." That brought a bit of quiet, though it didn't erase the angry glares. "Further, the king believes that the sorcerer-baroness used magic most foul to charm and compel the participation of many of those displayed here." He gestured over his shoulder at the nailed-up heads and was answered with a sort of low growl from the crowd.

He continued nonetheless. "While it is possible that some among the nobility joined the sorceress's plot of their own free will, the Crown feels that there is no way to know that for certain. Therefore, though the only possible punishment for rising in arms against His Most Royal Majesty is a traitor's death, the Crown will not be levying any further penalties against the houses and heirs of the traitors here displayed. Nor will it take any actions in regard to the normal course of succession to the titles of the condemned."

A moment later a familiar voice whispered, "Clever" in my ear, and I did my best not to jump half out of my skin. "That might do it."

"Hello, Scheroc. How are you?" I asked while I looked around for Captain Fei—the little air spirit's bond-mate.

I missed seeing her the first time my eyes flicked across the place where she was standing, mostly because she was out of uniform. I might have missed her a second time, too, if not for the matching scars on her cheeks. One pale stripe was twenty years old, the other only eight months and probably a goodly part of why she'd agreed to help us get rid of Thauvik. Fei had chosen to hold up a piece of wall just to the left of a small alley that lay maybe twenty or so yards around the back of the square from me. I'd checked the spot out myself, but passed on by because of all the yellow and black uniforms hanging out in the depths—the city watch swarming among the trash-strewn depths every bit as ominously as the huge wasps they resembled. But, of course, the "Stingers" would leave Fei alone.

Not only were her officers officially a part of the same organization, but they mostly scared the liver out of their fellows. The Silent Branch, or the "Mufflers," as they were more commonly known, had the equivalent of a letter of marque from the powers of the city. Their job was to see that things stayed quiet in Tien. If that meant that the occasional regular officer of the watch ended up facedown in an alley for making too much noise, well, there were plenty of new recruits ready to sign on to replace 'em.

Once I made eye contact with Fei, she headed my way. The Lord Justicer had finished speaking and now the noble section of the crowd was beginning to follow the commoners out of the square.

"What do you think?" Fei asked me as she got close enough to speak quietly.

"Too many ears around here. Let's walk."

"Good plan. I'll meet you at the intersection where the Last Walk runs into Sailmaker's Street." She jerked her chin toward the road that led from the traitor's gate to the Smoke-yard, where the Crown held those sentenced to the block or the stake.

When I cocked an eyebrow at that she said, "There's Stingers in every alley here and I'd rather not have too many of them see me with someone who looks like you do right now."

I nodded sullenly as though I'd just been told to move along and started walking fast toward Render's Way, while Fei sauntered up the Last Walk. I needed to cover eight blocks for her five. When I finally caught up to her, she'd pulled up the hood of her street clothes, making it much harder to spot those scars.

I fell in beside her and tugged at the lip of my own cowl. "We make a fine pair at the moment, you and I. Someone's going to mistake us for a couple of our betters."

"You, maybe. But there's not a noble alive that would be caught dead in this rag." She shrugged the shoulders of her patched and worn wool cloak, and I had to agree. "Speaking of which, are you wearing what I think you're wearing?"

"I am."

"Don't you think that's a little risky?"

"Not really. The world believes that my kind died out almost a decade ago. Besides, we were always more legend than reality for most—a few hundred half-mythical shadows hiding amongst the untold millions who people the eleven kingdoms. In the old days the goddess twisted the tongues of those who would have described us in more than the sketchiest of detail, just as she blurred the memories of any artist who tried to draw one of us."

"So, you're a ghost?" Fei sounded more than a little skeptical.

"In more ways than you can really imagine, yes."

We're not quite dead yet, Triss whispered into my mind. *Not completely anyway.*

Fei shrugged. "Good thing I'm not frightened by ghosts then. So, now that the ears are fewer, what did you think of Lord Vyan's little speech back there?"

"Smart. Very, very smart," I answered. "Show them the naked blade in the form of that line of noble heads, place the blame squarely on Maylien, then offer up the candy of no further reprisals. I'm actually surprised that Thauvik was able to restrain his tendency to spill blood long enough to make it happen."

"Oh, I'm sure the king reserves the right to add more heads to the wall as the whim takes him. I'll be downright shocked if the first of those doesn't go up within the week. The king has mostly avoided indulging his more violent impulses among the peers, but I know for a fact there's at least a double dozen more noble heads he'd love to see off the shoulders that currently support them."

"How do you know that?"

Fei smiled. "The wind blows many tales to ears that are ready to hear them."

Scheroc, then—the qamasiin sure came in handy for its bond-mate. "Has the wind blown you any whispers about a link between Thauvik and the Son of Heaven?"

"No. Should it have?"

"Possibly. I wasn't the only shadow behind a chair at the Council of Jade."

"Another Blade?" she asked, and I nodded. "And, that would imply a connection with the Son of Heaven how? Wasn't your friend Devin planning to replace Thauvik with Maylien's older sister?"

"He's not my friend, though he was once, and . . . it's complicated."

"So, buy me a drink and tell me about it. I've a few complicated things of my own that I need to share with you."

"Spinnerfish?" I asked.

Fei shook her head. "No, Erk would keep anyone from actually listening in or interfering with us, but his doors are open to everyone. At times like these that means spies holding down a lot of the chairs out front. There's no way we could get in and out without someone marking who I was, that I was out of uniform, and getting a very good description of who I was there with. I presume after all the trouble you went through to erase your old face, you'd rather not have this one showing up in anyone's official reports."

"All right. Where then?"

"I'm not sure. We could buy a flask and keep walking. That's got its plusses by way of making it very hard to listen in, but the longer we stay out in the open, the better the chance of someone spotting me and sniffing along behind, playing the hound."

"That or trying to eavesdrop mage-style," I said.

"Wouldn't do them much good. I've got a really nasty little drum-ringer in my pocket. Anyone tries to cock a magic ear our way is going to hear bells loud enough to half deafen 'em."

"Mine's a subtler version, it garbles as much as it drowns out. I've an oil-smear to foil eyespys as well, and a compass bender to prevent findings and mappings." There was a reason my Blade's vest had so many little inner pockets. "I presume you're carrying similar toys, but the mere fact that we're both loaded with blinds and countercharms is going to tell any mage-nosed hound things I'd rather they didn't know. How about you?"

Fei shrugged. "I don't think it's any secret I prefer muffler business stay as quiet as I try to keep the city, but the fewer people who know how much magic I carry the better. Do you have a thought?"

I nodded. "I think so. I know a very quiet spot, if you don't mind putting off our chat till nightfall."

"I have things that need doing, so that works for me."

"I'll have to check in with the . . . proprietor—to make sure it's all right. Meet me on Sanjin Island's north bridge an hour after sunset. If things are good, we can walk from there. If not, we'll have to come up with another plan. Hire a sampan maybe."

"Oh yeah, that'd be great fun, out on the river playing tag with the customs boats."

"Hopefully it won't come to that."

"You really know how to reassure a girl," said Fei. "See you then."

As Fei turned and walked away Triss sent, *Harad?*

There's nowhere quieter than a library.

Do you think he'll go for it?

Only one way to find out.

The Ismere Library was a private facility associated with the club of the same name. Both were founded several hundred years earlier by a Kadeshi-born merchant who had wanted to put a sheen of legitimacy on a family name whose fortune had its roots as much in smuggling and banditry as legitimate trade. The effort had taken several generations, but the fact that yesterday's Council of Jade survivor's list had included the name Nasima Dan Ismere, Countess of Zien said all that needed to be said about its success.

Harad, another Kadeshi who had headed south looking for a better life, was the master librarian of the Ismere, and one of my few real friends. He was also one of the most powerful sorcerers I'd ever met, a teacher at the Temple of Namara well before my birth, and personally older than the Pridu dynasty. As usual, I entered via a long jump from roof to roof and a drop from there onto a third floor balcony.

When I landed, the wards flared so faintly I wouldn't have even noticed them if Harad hadn't shown them to me the day he set them up to fry any Blade who wasn't me. He'd since changed them to allow Faran to come and go as well, but she was the only other exception. I found Harad himself wandering in a row of shelves on the second floor, setting the day's misplacements to rights. I waited for him to finish the row before clearing my throat to draw his attention—not that I made the mistake of believing he didn't know exactly where I was.

"Hello, Aral. It has been some months, and I expected to see you sooner. Did your trip to the south not go well?"

"Better than I feared, worse than I hoped."

"The very story of life. Young Triss?"

My familiar shaped himself into a dragon's shadow on the floor between us and bobbed his long neck in a bow. "Most honored Master Harad. It is good to see you."

The librarian smiled at Triss's use of the greeting normally reserved for a senior Blade. "I share the pleasure, *Resshath* Triss." He glanced at me. "Where is your apprentice Faran? I trust that she is well."

"Not as well as I'd like. She took a serious injury in our business to the south, a blow to the head that very nearly cost her an eye. She's staying with friends while she recovers."

"I'm sorry to hear that." Harad shook his head sadly. "I quite like the child. What do the healers say?"

"That they hope she will regain her sight and that the headaches will fade, but that they are not at all certain."

"I don't like the sound of that." He frowned for several

long seconds before finally nodding and saying, "I think that *would* be best. Bring her to me. I do not generally involve myself in business beyond the bounds of my library these days, and it has been a good two centuries since I last seriously practiced the healing arts, but I think I must make an exception here. Yes, bring her to me." He made a scooting motion.

"She's in Dalridia," I said.

"Then fetch her back. I have resources not available to the general run of healers, I may be able to do things for her that they could not."

"I appreciate the offer and the sentiment, Harad. And, I promise that if I live through the next few weeks that I will go and get her for you, but there's nothing I can do about it right this moment."

Harad peered skeptically down his long nose at me.

"It's true," said Triss. "If we leave the city now, many lives that might otherwise have been saved may be lost."

"I take it then that you are involved in the forthcoming civil war?" he asked, not at all happily. "On the Marchon girl's side as you were against her sister?" I nodded. "I suppose that does take precedence then, but I absolutely will not accept the idea that you dying should interfere with me doing what I can for Faran. That's just sloppy thinking on your part, Aral, and shows no consideration from properly arranging your affairs to deal with the high risks of your profession. I want your promise that you will send a message to Faran telling her that she must come visit me."

"In the middle of that forthcoming civil war you mentioned?" I asked, though my voice sounded weak even to me.

"If necessary, yes. Don't tell me that she couldn't slip in to see me without either side ever catching sight of her. I know her better than that."

Triss hissed sharply and interjected, "Then you ought to know her well enough to know that the only way to keep her out of that war, injury or no, is to prevent her from hearing of Aral's involvement before it's wrapped up."

"You may have a point there. All right. Then you must

promise to arrange to have a message sent after the war in the event of your death."

"How about if I just tell you where she is, and you take care of that part yourself?" I said with some exasperation.

"Hmm, yes, that would work. We'll do that. Where is she?"

So I gave him detailed instructions as to how to contact Jax and Faran. He didn't bother to write them down, but somehow I wasn't worried that he'd forget.

"Now," he said, when I'd finished, "you never got around to telling me why you came in. Are you here for a book, or just conversation?"

"I'm actually here to ask a favor. I need a quiet place to talk to Captain Fei."

"Well, there's no place quieter than my library. Go and fetch her."

So I set out to do just that, taking the chimney road upriver a brief way from the top of the Ismere to the roof of a once-grand tenement overlooking Sanjin Island Road. I was perhaps a quarter hour ahead of the time Fei was supposed to meet me, so I slipped into the shadow of the building's little water tank, where I had good view of the north bridge, and settled down to wait.

Do you think Harad can really help Faran? asked Triss.

I don't know, I hope so. He is a very powerful sorcerer and . . . I trailed off then as I spied Fei coming through the square on the island below. Her face was hidden and she'd changed her clothes, but I recognized the walk. . . . *Now that's odd.*

What is? asked Triss, whose ability to distinguish things over distances was somewhat limited.

There's half a dozen young jackals trailing along in Fei's wake.

Do you think they're going to try a bit of grab and stab? His mental voice came through somewhere between worried and amused.

I shared the sentiment. *Wouldn't they regret that!*

Fei was a jindu master as well as a vicious street fighter.

Any petty criminal who thought she'd make an easy mark was in for a brief and brutal education in the consequences of choosing the wrong game. However, that didn't feel like what was going on.

I don't think that's the play, I sent. *They're not sticking close enough together for a simple mobbing, but they're not really placed for anything more complex either. I'm not even sure they'd register as following her if we were down at street level. There's a lot of churn up and down the street like they're on someone else's turf and trying to keep from getting blindsided or looking scared.*

Professional hounds then? Playing at looking like a gutterside gang that's out to build a rep by turf skating?

I nodded. *That's what I'd say if it was anyone but Fei they were following.*

But? asked Triss.

But it suggests a major player on the shadowside making a move on Fei, and short of them expecting that she's not going to be a factor in the near future that'd be seriously stupid.

Which means someone thinks she's on her way out.

Or they're planning on giving her a shove, yeah. Hang on. I pulled a slip of paper out of one of my pockets and scrawled "You're being followed—I'll take care of it—Ismere—side door—knock." *Now, shroud me up and let's go down and politely explain what a bad idea that is.* Once I was hidden in shadow, I quickly climbed down the side of the building and headed for Fei and her followers.

6

There is a joy to doing something difficult really well, a joy that no other experience can touch, not alcohol, not drugs, not sex. Nothing comes close. I had forgotten the sheer pleasure of being good at something in the years since the fall of the temple, drowned it in booze and buried it with so many of my friends.

In the midst of all my other losses I hadn't even realized it was gone. Not till now, the very moment it returned. Having it come back to me all in an instant, totally unexpected and unlooked for, felt like taking a knife to the heart, a knife forged from purest happiness. I can't really express it any other way. There I was, slipping along the edge of the street, preparing to hand off my little note to Captain Fei, and suddenly I remembered what it felt like to do what I had been born to do, and to *know* that it was what I had been born to do. Not just remembered it, but fell suddenly and completely back into it.

This! This was why I existed, to become a part of the night, to do the work of a Blade. Even with my goddess slain and my compatriots mostly gone into the grave or over to the forces that had destroyed us, this was why I was. Without thought or will, tears suddenly wet my cheeks.

Are you all right? Triss sent, his voice caught halfway between worried and hopeful.

No. I'm not. I'm good! For the first time in seven years, I'm good.

Triss didn't say anything in response to that, but I could feel his love and his support flowing silently through the link that bound us as his worry subsided. I could also feel his curiosity and hope.

It's complicated. I'll tell you more about it later, I sent.

I can wait.

My experiences at the abbey had burned away big pieces of my soul. At the time, it had nearly destroyed me, and I had thought I might never recover. I *still* thought that. But, if my almost destruction was the price I paid for the gift that had just been given back to me, I would count the injuries I had taken to my soul a fair trade and more than fair. It had been a very long time since I was last whole, and I was no longer certain that such a thing was even possible for me.

Perhaps I had become something like a jar in the shape of Aral, a jar that held some of the pieces of the man I had once been, but not all. Never all. If that was my new truth—and I had begun to suspect that it was—then what I had to hope for was to find and hold on to the best pieces, and this joy-in-action was one of those.

As I slid along the street, moving toward Fei and the hounds that hunted her, I found myself aware of my surroundings and the night as I had not been since my goddess died. No detail that might affect what I was doing, no matter how small, seemed beneath my notice.

That bit of pavement had more grit on it than the one just to its left and would make more noise if I stepped there. So, place the foot just there. . . . The illumination from the bridgehead magelight fell like so. By angling my torso back and to the left I could use the natural slant of the light to help conceal the darkness that I wore as a second skin within the greater darkness of the night. Twist and . . . Fei's left hand, hanging just above the hilt of her dagger, was perfectly placed for me to slip the note unseen between her fingers. I barely had to think, my body picked up the cues from my senses and acted as needed to make things happen without my conscious direction.

Recognition, intention, action. I *was* the flow of one into the other. I *needed* this, and I had forgotten it even existed.

Fei didn't see me coming, of course. She jerked slightly when she realized that she had something in her hand, but covered it well. I was already past her by then, seeing her reaction through Triss's unvision, as she slipped farther and farther behind. While she paused under the magelight to glance seemingly casually at her hand, I moved on, heading toward the trailing hunters.

My original intent—formed as I had climbed down the building to the street—was to create a distraction that would draw the attention of the little group's foremost members. Then I could slip around to grab one of the stragglers and ask a few questions. Instead, as I approached the front pair, I reached under the back of my poncho and put my hands on the hilts of the swords hanging on either side of my spine. Before I had time to think, the blades were free of their sheaths and dropping down and around to clear them fully.

It wasn't until I swung double beheading strokes as I passed between them that my thinking mind fully caught up to my acting mind. From above, I had seen Fei's hunters as a collective entity, a group creature following her with the intent of seeing what she was up to and possibly waylaying her. From the street, I could see the way the individuals held their bodies and how they moved, recognize some of them, even though I couldn't make out faces through the dark curtain of my shroud.

The man leading the pack on the left was Dian, a black jack in training and lieutenant to the woman second from the back. Rehira was her name and she was one of Tien's better hired killers, perhaps the best of the ones who had no magic of their own. The man just in front of her didn't move like the others. Not a hunter, but some other kind of shadow-sider. There was something familiar about him, but I couldn't name him right away. The first pair hadn't finished falling when I ran the third through. That's when I finally recognized the fourth as Ru-jin Eight Dogs, a minor nail-puller—sort of a freelance version of Thauvik's officers of agony. I snapped his right knee with a kick as I passed to keep him from legging it.

Rehira was every bit as good as her reputation. She had a pair of short axes in her hands by the time I got to her. She even managed to turn in the right direction when I slid to one side to come at her from another angle. She died facing me, slowing me down enough that between her and dealing with number five, the tail guard had time to turn and run. I picked up one of Rehira's axes and aimed at his fleeing back, but at the last moment I changed my mind and threw it into a door frame instead. Then, I returned to Eight Dogs, keeping my shroud in place.

"I'm going to ask you this once, and only once. Who hired you and Rehira?"

He was sweating and shaking, holding his knee and clearly terrified. "Rehira hired me. I don't know who hired her. She always kept her cards facedown and never brought you farther into the play than she had to. She said it was a big noble and if this went well we'd be living in the fat, but that's all I've got. Please don't kill me."

"I won't. Not today. But I'd suggest you find a new line of work between now and the next time I see you, because this is a onetime opportunity to build a new and potentially much longer life."

He said something else, but I was already jogging silently away and I didn't bother to listen. Fei would be waiting.

You let two of them live. Triss sounded more confused than concerned.

The runner wasn't a threat anymore.

What if he tells people that he was attacked by a Blade?

I snorted. *I doubt he's got any idea that's what happened.*

*Even if he figures it out, who's going to believe he went up
against a Blade and lived? I suspect he'll say they ran into
bad magic and leave it there.*

*All right, but what about Eight Dogs? He's a torturer,
not all that different from the one back at Darkwater Island.
Why treat him differently?* From his increasingly puzzled
mental tone I could tell that this was one of those times
where Triss was genuinely baffled by my behavior and won-
dering if he'd missed something about the way humans
thought.

*Eight Dogs answered the question. He's also not going
to be hurting anyone else anytime soon. Not until that knee
heals a bit. Who knows, maybe he'll take my advice and
find a new line of work once he can walk again.*

Do you really believe that?

*I'd like to. People change. I've changed. Maybe he
will, too.*

What if he doesn't? asked Triss.

Then, the next time I see him, I'll kill him.

Oh well, that makes sense then. Good.

We caught up to Fei about a half block short of the
Ismere, but I didn't yet drop my shroud. I was still taking
too much pleasure in concealment. I waited silently while
Fei knocked on the side door. Harad opened it at once. I
slipped in right on Fei's heels, stepping to one side as Harad
latched the door behind us.

As he was doing that, Fei turned and looked right at me.
"Would you please stop that? It's seriously creepy."

Triss collapsed back down into my shadow and I canted
my head to one side. "How did you know I was there?"

"You might be invisible, but I imagine that you still stir
the air when you move," said Harad.

"Scheroc," I said.

"Just so," agreed Harad. "I was, of course, alerted by the
wards as soon as you arrived on the doorstep with our good
captain. Go along now, I've brewed a pot of tea for the two
of you and left it in the third floor reading room that you

favor, Aral." Then he turned and headed back for his apartments.

As soon as he was out of earshot, Fei glared at me. "How does he know about Scheroc? You didn't tell him I was a mage, did you?"

"Of course not." I started toward the back stairs and the reading room. "That's your secret, I wouldn't give it away. Not for free anyway, and no I haven't. Harad's a librarian. He knows lots of things."

Fei sighed rather resignedly and fell in behind me. "He's not just any librarian. He's a serious mage. According to my sources he's been the head librarian here for more than a century."

I smiled. "Really, you don't say. . . ."

"You knew that?"

"I'm an assassin. I hide in the dark. I listen. I know lots of things."

Fei laughed. "But not as many as a librarian?"

"No. Not this one, anyway."

Fei fell silent and nothing more was said for a few minutes while we finished climbing the steep and narrow back stairs. The main set out front was eight feet wide and sheathed in marble, rising in a beautiful double spiral. I led the way to the reading room and ushered Fei in ahead of me. There were little seed cakes and spring rolls as well as the tea.

Fei poured for both of us, then leaned back and put her calves on the corner of the table as she began to sip hers. "Oh, before we start, I presume the librarian is listening to every word we say?"

"I expect so, but he's very good at keeping secrets. He's known I'm a Blade since before I killed Ashvik, and I've never heard any hint that he's even whispered it to another soul. I trust him."

"Good enough for me, under the circumstances. So, tell me about this other Blade hiding in the shadows at the council meeting, and about Devin and Sumey, and why it all means the Son of Heaven might be involved. When you're done, I've got some stuff to share with you as well. Or, would you rather start with this"—she dropped my note on the table—"and whatever happened back there on the bridge?"

I put my own calves up on one of the other chairs and sipped my tea. It was a delicate jasmine flavored concoction and just as awful as every other cup of tea I'd ever tasted. The spring rolls on the other hand . . .

"This." I picked up the note and used a simple cantrip to burn it to ash. "It's more immediate and we can always come back to the Son of Heaven."

"Fair enough." She took a seed cake. "These are fabulous, by the way. Do you think he'd share his recipe?"

"I wouldn't bet on it. Secrets."

"Pity." Fei stretched and sighed. "Is it just me, or do you feel really at ease and secure for the first time in ages?" She paused and suddenly looked less so. "Spell?"

"Possibly, though I think it's just the Ismere. Harad once told me that in its entire history there's not a single record of the Crown or anyone else violating the integrity of the library."

A voice spoke out of the air, "I said that no one has ever *successfully* violated the integrity of the library. Many have tried over the years. One reigning queen even."

"What happened to them all?" asked Fei.

But her only answer was the silence of the library and perhaps the faintest echo of a quiet little laugh.

"That's almost as creepy as you sneaking around in the shadows," said Fei. Then, "Do you think he'd be willing to help out with our little problem with Thauvik?"

I thought about it for a moment. "No. I don't think that he likes to take action beyond the bounds of the library. If there is a civil war and it directly threatens the Ismere, he might intervene, but I don't see it happening short of that or beyond the immediate threat to the library."

"Too bad. But, you were about to tell me about that little band of marauders you ghosted on my back trail."

I nodded. "I presume Scheroc gave you the basics?"

"Yes, though he's a bit hazy on things like who it was you ghosted and how many of them there were to start with. He *was* quite firm about you letting two of them live. He's always happy to deal with numbers low enough that he can count them successfully, and he doesn't really do well above three. I love him dearly, but he's a much more limited sort of elemental than your Triss."

At the sound of his name, Triss shifted from my shape to his own, though he remained on the wall behind me where the reading light painted him, and said, "Don't count him so lightly."

Fei shook her head and smiled. "I don't, but I do know his limitations . . . like counting."

I grinned. "There were six. Rehira, four of her people and a 'puller, name of Eight Dogs."

"That's not news I like to hear," said Fei. "Rehira's not cheap, and she's not stupid. She wouldn't take a job on me without major backing and some sort of surety there'd be no reprisal from the Mufflers once I was gone. Who hired her, and who'd you let live?"

"Some heavyweight noble paid the undertaker's bill, at least according to Eight Dogs. He's one of the survivors. The other was muscle and I didn't get her name."

Fei's eyes went far away and she held up a hand to stop me from saying anything more for a few moments. Finally, she nodded. "The Count of Uron's youngest cousin, probably. The lean and hungry one. That'll be the result of the Lord Justicer's speech this morning."

"I think I missed a step in there."

"Under normal circumstances, the Count of Uron would succeed his aunt as Duke of Tien, since she had no children of her own. This cousin, the baronet of something or other, has had his eye on the ducal seat for years. He even went so far as to try to issue challenge to the old duchess on one occasion. She's surprisingly spry for seventy years old, or she was anyway. She sliced his larynx without bleeding him out—a very neat piece of sword work—then told him he'd better not come within a hundred miles of the city ever again. Now, with the duchess gone and Thauvik saying that all successions will happen in the normal fashion, he's going to want another crack at it."

"And, if he succeeds, he'll be the Duke of Tien and the ultimate head of the city watch. Your boss."

"My successor's boss, more likely, if he can manage it. He doesn't like me any more than the old duchess . . . or any woman for that matter. At least not out of the bed or the kitchen."

"One of *those*."

"Yes. You'd think their mothers would strangle them in the crib and save us all the trouble of having to fix the problem once they've grown up. Well, at least you'll have given him something to think about by ghosting his chosen assassin."

"I wonder why he picked Rehira," I said.

"Probably thought it would be funnier. That, and either way, there'd be one less competent woman in the world to make him wet his bed. You know, I'm glad you let those two live for now. It'll make sure the news gets back to him. I hope you don't mind that I'm going to have to track them down and kill them both in a few weeks."

I shrugged. "Not my lookout. I refrained from killing them. I didn't promise no one else was going to hold them to account."

"Okay, that's settled. Now, tell me about this Blade at the council and why that means church involvement."

Where to start . . . ? "What do you know about the fall of the temple and the destruction of my order?" I said, after a beat or two.

"Not much, to be honest. Not beyond the official story anyway. You know it well enough, I'm sure. The current Son of Heaven felt there was evidence that Namara was a false goddess. So, as chief priest of the eleven kingdoms, he went to petition the gods in the person of the Emperor of Heaven to do something about her. Then, when the gods agreed and decided to execute Namara, the Son of Heaven sent his forces to destroy her temple and put her followers to the sword. But that's all I've heard. I guess it never really interested me."

"That's just rot . . . I . . . oooh, fire and sun!" Triss was all but snarling with rage.

"Triss," I said, "hush. Fei's right. That's the official story, as you well know."

"I do, but every time I hear it, it makes me so angry I want to tear a hole in the world and toss the Son of Heaven's entire corrupt operation into it."

Fei looked curious. "Could you really do that?"

"Not the entire church," said Triss. "Not all at once anyway, and probably not the buildings, but I could certainly make a good start on sending the priests and soldiers off to fall forever through the everdark."

Fei looked a question at me and I nodded. "I saw him do it once. It's not a clean death."

"Remind me not to piss off the Shade."

"That's always a good choice. Here's how the fall of the temple looks from our side of things. We're quietly working away at doing the bidding of our goddess. We make sure that justice applies equally to all and generally see to it that the worst excesses of the powerful don't go unchecked. Suddenly, an army shows up on the temple doorstep and starts killing everyone in sight. The priests and Blades are crying out to our goddess to protect us, but nothing happens because while the human army of the Son of Heaven is murdering my people, the other gods are murdering my goddess."

I got up and started to pace. I simply wasn't capable of sitting still while I talked about these events. "But that's not the whole story. I wasn't at the temple when the attack happened or I'd be dead now. So, I didn't find out any of what comes next until last year, when I helped Maylien against her sister and Devin." I'd learned more since then, but not anything I was willing to share with Fei. "It seems that at the fall of the temple the Son had his people offer a deal to all the Blades they managed to capture. If they were willing to transfer their allegiance from Namara to him, he'd let them live, even have some autonomy."

Fei whistled. "Him personally, not Shan?" I nodded. "How many took the deal?"

"I have no idea," I replied.

"Because that's the kind of news that would have an awful lot of people looking over their shoulders. Blades serving the Son of Heaven, and freelancing when they're not. . . . If there are more than a half dozen of them, that would completely change the blood trade. Pricing of assassinations, options on the sorts of targets no one is willing to try right now, cost of bodyguards . . . everything!" Her eyes went far away. "I wonder if it's already happening. . . ."

I raised an eyebrow.

"The great khan's heir fell off his horse and broke his neck about two weeks ago while hunting on the Avarsi plains," said Fei, then nodded when she saw my expression. "And no, you're not the only one who finds that *very* hard to believe. But he was riding with friends and his full bodyguard. They all agree no one was anywhere near him when his horse stumbled and threw him, and none of the mages saw any hint of spell-light. They searched but couldn't find a slink's hole or anything else that would have tripped the horse either." She looked speculatively at Triss. "Could you do that? Make a hole into this everdark thing for a horse to stumble on and then make it go away later without showing magic?"

"Not without dropping Aral's shroud, but I wouldn't need to do it that way," said Triss. "If Aral were willing to get in close and have only partial cover for a time, I could just grab the horse's leg. Much easier to do, and not half so dangerous."

"I don't suppose the khan's heir had recently said anything nasty about the Son of Heaven?" I asked.

"Funny you should mention that. It happened about two days after the heir claimed the entire theoarchy of Heaven's Reach was built on land stolen from the people of the Kvanas. He also said he'd make the Son pay tribute for it when he took the throne. The Son is calling the heir's death the judgment of the gods on an impious man."

"That's . . ." I couldn't find any words strong enough to express how sick that made me feel.

I quite literally wanted to vomit. If one of my former colleagues had been a part of that, it was perversion of everything the goddess had created us to be. Somewhere in my head I'd known things like this must be going on. It was the only reasonable conclusion to be drawn from what I'd learned from Devin, and later, from Kelos. Somehow I'd been able to put it aside in a dark corner of my mind with so many of the other things that hurt me, like my current worries about Jerik's torment.

But I couldn't avoid it any longer. After what felt like ages of trying to say something and failing, I put my face in my hands and squeezed. Triss didn't say anything either, wrapping shadowy wings around my shoulders and resting his chin on my head instead.

After a couple of minutes, Fei coughed quietly. "Are you just going to sit there moping, or are you going to kill the bastards that make you feel that way?" A pause. "I'm good either way, but I suspect you won't be."

It wasn't the most gentle and loving nudge I'd ever received, but it got the point across. "Right." I pressed the heels of my hands against my cheeks one last time, then opened my hands and raised my eyes to meet Fei's.

"There," she said. "That's much better. If I hadn't been expecting that death stare, you might have even made me jump a bit. So, if these rogue Blades of yours are working for the Son now, and they're helping Thauvik out, why was your, ah . . . onetime colleague Devin trying to put Maylien's sister on the throne last year?"

I shrugged. "That's a great question, and I have no idea what the answer might be. Could be that things have changed since then in the Son's thinking. Could be Devin was freelancing at the time. Could be the Blade at the council is freelancing now. Hard to say without more evidence. The key thing is that Thauvik has a Blade up his sleeve."

"Yeah, that's going to make things a lot tougher for the leaders of the coming rebellion. Speaking of which, I have a number of messages that I've been asked to pass along to the Baroness Marchon should I get the chance. There are a lot of nobles who think it's way past time Thauvik took a long rest in a pretty wooden box, and not only the lesser lights."

"Nothing in writing, I presume."

Fei rolled her eyes. "You jest, right? I'm supposed to deliver them in person, of course. I was going to ask that you have her meet me somewhere in the city so that we could talk. After tonight though, I'm thinking it might not be a bad idea for me to make it very clear I'm still among the living and deeply pissed. Then I should probably vanish for a little bit. That will get a few hearts beating faster. I presume Maylien's gone into hiding in the wilds again. Can you take me to her?"

"When do you want to leave?"

Before Fei could answer, a faint rap came at the door of the reading room and Harad poked his head in. "Aral, Captain Fei, I think the two of you might want to see this." Then he turned away.

We followed him through the shelves to another reading room, this one on the corner of the building where the alley met the street in front of the library. Harad put his finger to his lips as he dimmed the reading light almost to nothing. Then he opened the door onto a front-facing balcony and stepped out. Once we had joined him at the railing, he pointed off to the right where a pair of Crown Guards were leading a half dozen city watchmen along the front of the library.

As they were about to come even with us, a dozen men and women in the scaled armor favored by the clans who occupied Zhan's Chenjou Peninsula slipped out of the alley mouth. Most were armed with long-bladed spears of the sort most often referred to as woldos—essentially a short staff with a sword on the end. These had their blades darkened with oris juice for night work. Their leader had a noble's dueling blade hung from her sash of mourning, and had blackened the steel monkey-face of her helm, another sign of official mourning. More of the clan's warriors cut off the street behind the guards.

Fei looked like she wanted to intervene, "Are they going to—" but Harad raised a hand sharply, cutting her off.

"Wait. Watch."

7

———

I have seen too many deaths. They no longer move me, and I am less human for it. When you see a death or, worse, cause one, you lose something. Innocence certainly, but so much more. A tiny part of yourself falls away with each new corpse.

We are, all of us, a part of each and every person we meet and it is that part that dies in the instant of another's death. Some, it drives mad. Some, it makes into monsters, incapable of seeing themselves in others, cutting them off completely from any understanding of others' humanity. People become things for them. Most, it wounds too deeply ever to heal, though the scars don't show most of the time. A few, and I count myself in this number, learn how to put that part of ourselves in a sort of box, to cut off our own humanity for a little while.

It only works for a time, and never without a cost. Whenever you do it, whenever you put your humanity into that box, even for a little while, you run the risk that you won't be able to find the key. And then, how different are you from the monsters?

Fei tensed beside me, but I put a hand on her shoulder, shaking my head. Now was the time for boxes. Even if Fei could have gotten down to the street in time to intervene, there was nothing she could do against such odds without giving away her mage status. At which point, the very Crown Guards she would have just rescued, along with some of her fellow city watch, would become her sworn enemies. There was no way she could win here.

Fei deflated, perhaps realizing that. "I . . . damn."

Harad spoke quietly, "Their previous clan chief had his head nailed up over the traitor's gate this morning. They are angry, but not without honor." He looked over Fei's shoulders at me. "Or justice. You will see."

The clan chief stepped forward, and formally bowed to the soldiers and guards. "My father died in the palace yesterday, murdered by the Bastard King. His body was burned to ashes, and his head is to follow once it rots. I am not allowed so much as a lock of his hair to place in the family tomb. This cannot be forgiven or forgotten, and I have vowed to place a score of heads in his empty coffin to appease his angry ghost."

"You'll have to take them," the taller of the two Crown Guards said defiantly. "That won't be so easy, even twenty against eight."

"Against two," replied the clan chief. She looked past the Crown Guards to the watch. "My quarrel is with the king, not the city. If you wish to claim the king's side, you may choose to do so. If not, you are free to go, taking your weapons and my blessings with you."

They didn't hesitate for so much as an instant, putting their weapons up and backing away from the doomed Crown Guards. After that, it was over quickly and quietly, with the heads going into a pair of sacks and the bodies into the river. This clan had obviously seen a lot of night raiding.

"That's the second time tonight," Harad said once we had returned inside. "Same spot, same ambush, same results."

"Which means that the first group of guards didn't report the ambush," said Fei.

"Would you?" I asked. Then it really hit me, and I whistled low and appreciatively. "If she lives to be fifty, that woman stands a good chance of becoming chief of chiefs for the Chenjou Peninsula."

Triss poked a dragon-shaped head out of the top of my otherwise human-seeming shadow. It was quite a disconcerting effect. "I think I missed something, there," he said.

"Assume for a moment that she collects that score of heads in pairs," I said, "and that every time she does it, another half dozen city watch walk away without a scratch."

"Yes . . ."

I smiled. It was kind of nice seeing something Triss didn't for once. "Those six Stingers have now more or less officially separated themselves from the side of the king, whether they realize it yet or not. At some point they're going to figure out that if the king is victorious in the coming civil war, there will always be a chance that he'll find out what happened down there. We can't have been the only witnesses, and the clan chief was pitching her voice to carry."

"That she was," said Fei, who had clearly already seen where I was going.

I continued. "If the king does find out about what happened here tonight, each and every one of those Stingers is going to wind up tortured to death. They all have to know it. Where do you think that puts them for how they hope the war turns out? Along with any friends they can convince? If our clan chief out there can talk any of her fellows into taking their revenge in a similar manner, it'll drive one hell of a wedge between the two biggest armed forces in Tien."

My shadow shifted fully into dragon form, his mouth agape. "Oh. My."

" 'My quarrel is with the king, not the city,' " I quoted. "That's fucking brilliant, and I'm sure she didn't come up with it by accident. Harad, do you happen to know her name? I suspect that Maylien will want to have a word with her sometime in the near future."

"Her name's Prixia Dan Xaia, and she's the new clan chief of Xankou," replied Harad.

"Given the pronunciation, that's got to be somewhere near the base of the peninsula on the north side, right up by Kadesh," said Fei. "That'd explain how sharp her warriors are. Lots of raiding back and forth across the borders, and none of it sanctioned by either throne. You're as likely to get hung by your own side as the other if you get caught. Very dangerous game."

Fei cocked her head to one side as if listening, then nodded. "And that's my exit line. Scheroc tells me that I have something that needs attending. Aral, how about I meet you at Westgate an hour before sunset tomorrow and we go find your baroness? I'm sure I'll have more messages by then, and there are things I can do for her in the city without compromising my position. We'll have lots to talk about."

I nodded.

Harad gestured toward the stairs. "I'll see you out, Captain Fei. Aral, come find me if you need anything more. Otherwise, good night."

Again, I nodded.

Are you all right? Triss asked as I started back toward the other reading room, and the balcony by which we normally made our exit.

I don't know. The fight in the street out front brought it home in a way that I couldn't ignore.

Brought what home?

By acting to put Maylien on the throne, I've just started a war. That wasn't my intent, of course, but I'm not entirely sure that matters. A lot of people are going to die because of me, a lot of people who haven't done anything wrong.

Maybe, replied Triss, *though we're a long way from armies facing each other in the field yet. But a smart man once said to me that "Thauvik is a murderer and a torturer, and the only way he'll ever see justice is if we deliver it." He also pointed out that if we had that power and chose not to use it, we would be complicit in Thauvik's evils going forward.*

A smart man? Really? Because I sure don't feel very smart right now.

I think so, yes, and an honorable one. Triss shifted around in front of me and spread his wings, bringing me to a halt. *There is almost certainly going to be a war, and you can be said to have started it. I can't deny that. But you've seen what Thauvik is like, what he can do. Last year we stopped him from starting a war between the Durkoth and Kodamia. How long before he found a way to start another one? Look at what happened at the Council of Jade. This is not a sane man. He has to be removed from the throne.*

You make it sound so simple, Triss.

It's not. It's terribly, terribly hard, and there's going to be a price, a damned big one. But I don't think you made the wrong choice. Everyone we've talked to agrees that Thauvik's been following in his brother's footsteps. You remember where those footsteps lead, don't you? They lead straight to rivers of blood.

Can we be so sure of that? I asked. *And, if we can't, what right have we to start a war over what Thauvik* might *do?*

Triss winced. *Perhaps we can't know it, though I don't doubt it for a moment. I don't have a good answer for your other question either. I don't think there is a good answer. Let me ask you a counter question. Knowing what we know about Thauvik, about the way he is oppressing and murdering his people, could you really live with yourself if we'd walked away without trying?*

No, it's just . . . dammit! I slammed the heel of my hand into the wall in a killing strike. The thick wooden paneling shivered with the impact, but neither it nor my hand broke. *This isn't how it was supposed to go.*

I know. Better by far if we could have done it quickly and neatly. But things don't always go the way they should, and we cannot allow ourselves to be prevented from acting at all because of things that might happen. Sometimes you don't get to choose the right answer, just the least wrong one and then you have to do what you can to make it better.

Any idea how we go about that?

Win the war, or better yet, find a way to kill Thauvik without fighting it in the first place. That's what we're best at, isn't it?

I'm an assassin. There are very few people in the world who are better at killing than I am, at least on an individual basis. I'm proud of that, but it means exactly shit in the business of groups of people killing other groups of people. It probably shouldn't have come as such a surprise, but I'd never really thought about it before I started trying to make sense of Heyin and Maylien discussing tactics and lamenting their lack of a good field general with the strategic skills necessary for commanding larger bodies of soldiers.

It wasn't quite gibberish. I had been trained in the strategy and tactics of dealing with small groups of soldiers in the shape of royal and clerical bodyguards. But the techniques a lone assassin needs to employ against groups defending a single target were radically different from those employed when even a score of soldiers faces another similar body on a battlefield. Realizing that I wasn't going to be a whole hell of a lot of help with the actual war part of the war, and admitting it to Maylien, was downright humbling.

It was also what had me clinging to the wall beside a third-floor window on a small keep in the fief of Xankou. I quietly tapped on the shutter for the second time. In response, a faint scraping sound came from the other side, followed by a gentle pitter-pattering like rain in the distance.

I was still trying to figure out what might have caused that latter when a woman's voice called out, low and soft, "The shutters are open."

I pushed lightly on the farther one, and it silently pivoted inward. "May I come in, Clan Chief Xaia?"

"I should probably say no, but you seem too polite for an assassin, and too articulate for one of the restless dead.

While I could be wrong about either case, I'm curious. Come ahead, but no further than the window ledge, if you wish to prevent the conversation from escalating to words of steel."

I was rather charmed by her attitude and pushed the other shutter aside, though I didn't yet step down onto the window ledge. "What, no worries about the creatures of wild magic?"

"Somehow, I don't think the hunting host would speak Zhani with the accents of Tien. They are not known for favoring cities."

I hadn't realized I had that pronounced an accent—I probably ought to work on it. "Fair enough," I said, "though I must note I'm not from Tien originally."

"No, somewhere in the barbarian west if I'm any judge, but it seemed rude to comment."

I leaned down so that I could peer in through the top right corner of the window. My hostess might sound very charming indeed, but that didn't make me want to offer myself as a big dark silhouette at her window. Not before I'd made sure she wasn't being charming while she got her crossbow lined up anyway.

The room was a large, quarter-round tower room with the door occupying the sliced off point of the wedge. It was also much darker than it was outside—only Triss's borrowed senses allowed me to see anything. A big, canopied bed stood close to the door, and my hostess, the clan chief Prixia Dan Xaia, was about halfway between it and me, a dueling blade held loosely in her right hand. She was alone. I dropped my shroud and released Triss—no point in showing what I was if I didn't have to.

I sure hope you know what you're doing, Triss said into my mind as I stepped down onto the window ledge. There was a faint aroma of jasmine in the room.

Me, too.

"May I sit, Clan Chief?" I said aloud.

"Please do."

As my foot touched the floor, it made a very quiet crunching sound. "You scattered rice when I knocked?" I asked. That would explain the pitter-patter noise—dry and scattered the rice would make moving silently in the room all but impossible.

"Yes, I thought it prudent."

Which meant she kept a bowl by the bed just in case. "But you hadn't bothered before I arrived?"

"Oh, no, there was enough under the window and in front of the door to wake me if anyone tried to enter, but I try not to leave a big mess for the maid if I don't have to."

"Prudent and considerate, I approve."

"So did my mother. Could we skip to the part where you tell me why you're here? Because if you don't do it soon, one of the guards is going to notice the open window and then there are going to be all sorts of interruptions and bother."

"All right, my name is Aral and I'm here to see if you'd be interested in joining the army of the Baroness Marchon."

"Don't you mean the rightful queen?"

"Well, she's that, too, but I—"

"Then make sure you say it every chance you get. This sort of battle is won in the minds of the people as much as it is on the field of war. If you would make the baroness a queen, Blade, then proclaim her so every time you speak."

"Blade? Who said anything about Blades?" This encounter was not going at all the way I'd planned.

"I did, Kingslayer, and there's no need to pretend to look surprised, I can't see your face at all in this light."

"But what if I really am surprised?"

"Then you are being foolish. Xankou has been attacked by Kadeshi marauders at least twice a year for my entire life. They come in the night and they kill with stealth. Sometimes they attempt the castle. They are some of the best night raiders in the world, and not one of them has ever gotten within a stone's throw of the keep before, much less all the way to my window. Though Thauvik the bastard made every effort to keep it quiet, it has long been rumored among those with ties to the army that there were Blades involved in the conflicts that happened around the time the baroness took the Marchon coronet from her sister. The rumors are at least partially substantiated by the deaths of so many Elite at the time."

I blinked at that. I suppose that I should have realized that would get around, though the rumors had never filtered down to the level of the Gryphon's Head.

Prixia continued. "Later, when it was revealed that the Kingslayer had been hiding out in the Stumbles for a number of years, those of us who knew of the earlier rumors put two and two together and determined exactly who must have helped Marchon to achieve her seat. So, when a man knocks at my window in the middle of the night after passing silently through my guards, and introduces himself as an emissary from the rightful queen, the conclusion is obvious. It would have been so, even had you not given me your name."

She's smart, said Triss.

Which is exactly what we're looking for. That and savvy.

"So," she asked, "why are you here?"

"Zhan's rightful queen needs a general."

Prixia froze for a moment, the first sign of uncertainty I'd seen in her, but only for a moment. "I imagine she does. What does that have to do with me?"

"I think you might be that general."

"Really, why?"

"I first saw you operating in Tien the night after your father's head was nailed up over the traitor's gate. The way you handled the watch and the Crown Guard was quite brilliant, alienating the one from the other with mercy and a knowledge of how that mercy would play with Thauvik. Afterward, I asked around. According to my contacts in various places, you are considered one of the borderers' most promising young military commanders. Long thinking and quick in a fight, both."

"There is a small chest about five feet to the right of the window." She gestured with her sword. "Why don't you close the shutters and take a seat there. This will be a longer and more interesting conversation than I originally thought, and I don't want to have to argue with my guards about you for a quarter of an hour in the middle of it."

The room went utterly dark once I closed the shutters, but I'd memorized the positions of all the furniture and had long training in moving in the dark. It was easy to find the chest, though every step crunched on the way there. Assuming she'd practiced with the rice and a blindfold—and, given her general competence, I had no reasons to think otherwise—Prixia knew exactly where I was. It was a clever technique, though I could think of at least three ways to subvert it, including one that used the very sound of the rice as a tool of deception to make a listener believe I was where I was not. The lid of the chest creaked distinctly when I sat down, and I awarded her another point for cleverness.

"Now," she said, "tell me more. Like what Her Majesty thinks about this."

"She's not completely convinced, but thinks that I've had worse ideas and that she would like to meet you and talk with you. For that matter, *I'm* not completely convinced, but everything I've learned so far leads me to want to learn more."

"As flattered as I am, I have to ask the obvious question."

"Why not a more experienced commander?" I supplied.

"No, why not a more socially acceptable one? I'm a Chenjou clan chief, which puts me a half step above a roadside brigand in the eyes of most of Zhan's proper nobles. Why not the Duke of Jenua? He's got the military reputation and the blood. Giving him command of the queen's armies would immediately increase her legitimacy in the eyes of the peers."

"Start with the fact that he hasn't offered," I replied. "He's still technically on Thauvik's side, though he might well jump, given the right opportunity. Thauvik's a good general himself and unlikely to let Jenua have a real command, for more or less the same reason Maylien can't."

"Which is?" And the way she said it told me she knew the answer.

"That the second he's got command of an army he's as much of a threat to the throne as Maylien is. His blood might not be as royal as either Thauvik's or his niece's, but his birth doesn't have the cloud of bastardy hanging over it, and he's well respected by the peers. If Maylien stumbles, or Thauvik's rule becomes even a little bit shakier, Jenua would have an excellent chance of taking the throne for himself."

"Maylien's no bastard anymore, or at least that's what I hear from those who support her claim." Prixia's voice was deceptively sweet.

"Then I presume you've also heard that the paper that proves her legitimacy has gone missing?"

"I might have."

"I thought so," I said. "Look, I'm not going to play coy with you. Maylien's claim is a shaky one. The bloodline is good, and even if the paper never turns up, there are many who will be willing to accept that the reason for the massacre at the Council of Jade was that her adoption papers were genuine. But she's also a mage. Nothing anyone says or does can change that, and it means there are many among the peers who will never accept her as a legitimate claimant to any title in the realm. You know as well as I do that there are a good dozen generals of strong reputation that she might be able to call on to join her in her fight against Thauvik, but . . ."

"But she can't be sure to control any of them if they suddenly decide they want to have a go at the throne themselves."

"Or second-guess any of her decisions, really. She, as Thauvik has painted her, is the sorcerer-baroness, and that means that she's going to have real trouble controlling anyone with real clout."

"Whereas a barbarian from the borders would rise or fall based entirely on whether Maylien rises or falls. Yes?" I heard a faint crunch as Prixia shifted in the dark, the first such noise she'd made. "That's got the sound of something that could really bite me in the ass if she falls."

"If you join her and she loses, your head's going up next to your father's and the clan seat will fall to whichever of your relatives is most willing to stab your reputation in the back."

"That sure makes it sound like a great opportunity," Prixia said dryly.

She's got a point, said Triss. *Are you sure you know what you're doing?*

Hush, Triss.

"If she rises, on the other hand, she's going to be riding a tiger. The peers will attempt to undermine her. The army, which put then-chief marshal Thauvik on the throne after the death of his brother, will be furious that one of their own has fallen to a mage, of all things. The peasants will be nervous about the idea of another member of the Pridu dynasty taking the throne, especially a mage. *And* they'll be convinced she's going to go as mad as the rest of her family."

"You're not selling this very well," said Prixia. "I thought you should know that."

"Every single bit of that's true, and more besides, but I heard another thing when I was asking around about you. Two things actually."

"What things?"

"First, that you're ambitious. This is the one and only chance you are ever going to get in your entire life to do something like this. If Maylien wins with you as her general, you are very likely going to be the next chief marshal of Zhan. If you walk away from her now, the best you will ever achieve is to become the local chief of chiefs, little more than a glorified warlord."

"There's that." Prixia's voice came calm and steady, but I could hear the husk underneath. "What's the second thing you heard about me?"

"That you are honorable. Thauvik had your father killed, more or less by accident. Then he declared him a traitor and burned the body to hide the fact. He dishonored your father, your family, and your clan. If you don't fight to unthrone him, what does that make you?" Before she could respond, I continued. "But even more than that, if you are honorable, and you believe that Maylien belongs on the throne, and is your liege and queen, how can you refuse her?"

"What makes you so sure that I believe she is the rightful heir?"

"Would you be listening to all this if you didn't?" I asked.

"Probably not. All right, you've made your point, and you know you've got me. But there must be a couple dozen lesser lords and minor chiefs with a reputation as good or better than mine. Why pick me?"

"Like so many things, it's mostly luck. If I hadn't seen you in the street that night, Maylien would likely never even have known you existed. It might not have even occurred to her to try a relative nobody as a commander. But I did see you, and I pushed to find out more about you, and now here I am."

"Lucky, lucky me."

8

———◆———

"**I**f Thauvik has a Blade, why haven't they tried to kill me yet?" Maylien took a long pull from the leather water bottle, then gave a sip to Bontrang before hanging it off the back of her camp chair again. "Or any of my more prominent allies or lieutenants for that matter?"

It was a good question. "I don't know," I replied. "It doesn't make any sense to me."

I rubbed the bridge of my nose between thumb and forefinger. Six weeks had passed since the Jade Council massacre, as it was now being called, and despite more than one slipup on my part, no other Blade had yet made an attempt on Maylien's life. Nor even come sniffing around, as far as I could tell. Six weeks filled with minor skirmishes—more in the way of street fights and roadside ambushes than battles, though the effectiveness of those had been going up since Prixia had started organizing the campaign. I got up from my place at the little table and began to pace back and forth in the limited space.

My footsteps echoed hollowly in the back gallery where Maylien had set up her temporary offices, and raised the smell of damp stone and old ashes. The series of abandoned sewers we'd moved into had once housed an illegal tavern called the Nonesuch. It had been destroyed by fire and the collapse of a couple of galleries during a running battle I'd had with the Elite and a group of Durkoth the previous summer.

Later, Faran and I had dug a new entrance and a couple of rabbit runs to set the place up as a fallback. At some point, some other enterprising soul would almost certainly crack into it from one of the rebuilt buildings above, and then it would lose its utility. In the meantime it made an excellent base of operations for Maylien while she was in Tien—hidden, relatively secure, and big enough to house both her and her guard with their own separate rooms.

We'd returned to the city a few days before because Maylien needed to meet with several wavering peers in hopes of talking them over to her side, something no proxy could do for her half so well. It was another step in the slow buildup of the alliances we would need to carry the battle to Thauvik, a process that had been greatly hampered by the king's bizarrely passive and gentle behavior since the massacre. The blood-mad impulses that had become an ever more prominent part of his reign over the past few years were nowhere in evidence at the moment.

"I hate this," I said. "I don't understand what's going on with the king, or the Blade he's got up his sleeve, or the freaking court politics you're having to play out, or even the way the war is going. I'm no good at the things you need, Maylien."

"You're doing a fine job as the head of my bodyguard," she replied. "No one's assassinated me yet."

"No one's tried," I replied, flatly. "That's got nothing to do with me. Heyin is more than competent to keep your back covered and your escape routes open."

"But he can't stop a Blade." She put her hand out and caught my arm as I passed by her chair.

I shrugged it off. "I can't either," I said, finally admitting to Maylien what it had taken me most of the last six weeks to admit to myself. "Not with the resources you've got. Give me a major strong point like the fortress at Kao-li, the guards to defend it properly, *and* your promise not to move from the royal apartments, and I could *probably* keep you safe from a Blade. But the second you left, you'd be vulnerable again."

"Thauvik holds Kao-li," said Maylien. "Even if he didn't, I couldn't afford to stay in one place like that, not with the army and half the peers still siding with Thauvik. I've got to keep moving and working to shift the opinion of the more important nobles. You know that."

"I do. It's my whole point, actually. I can't protect you from a Blade. Not by following you around and trying to catch the assassin at the point of attack, anyway. Triss and I have been discussing it, and there's just no way."

"What do you think of that, Triss?" Maylien shifted her gaze to my shadow.

In turn, my shadow flowed up the curve of the nearest wall and into dragon form. "I don't think either of us ever realized just how badly the mere existence of a hostile Blade/Shade pair changes things for one of our targets. Not until we started trying to figure out how we could stop one. I mean, we *knew* it, that's part of our training. But knowing in the abstract and knowing in your gut are very different things."

"Look at what happened to Ashvik," I said. "He had some of the best bodyguards in the world in the person of the Elite and their stone dogs. He had a multilayered defense that included using the restless dead to hunt the sewer beneath the palace. He had it all, enough to kill the first three Blades that tried even."

"But in the end," Triss continued, "Aral and I were able to get through and kill him in his bedroom. No one is completely safe."

I nodded, and once again felt the sick feeling that had been building in my stomach for over a week. "Triss is leaving out the worst of it."

"No one is safe isn't the worst of it?" said Maylien.

"Well, it is, but maybe not in the way that immediately comes to mind. I wouldn't have believed it was possible then, but the destruction of the temple was actually even more horrible than I had imagined at the time. In destroying our goddess while allowing some of us to escape, the Son of Heaven and his god removed the only outside check on our actions. While Namara lived, no one but the unjust ever had to fear a Blade. Now, the only thing preventing any of us from slipping out into the night and killing whoever we want, is conscience. Fine for me, maybe. At least for now."

"But not for Devin," said Maylien.

"No, not for Devin. Nor probably for any of the other Blades the Son took into his service. The sort of people who are willing to give their allegiance to the very priest who's just murdered their friends and family are not people you want running around with the power of a Blade, and nothing to hold them back but conscience."

"So, what do you propose to do about it?" asked Maylien.

"Why does it have to be me?" I whispered. But I wasn't really asking Maylien, nor even myself. It wasn't even a question. It was a lament to the goddess who had failed to save herself and her followers.

"Who else is there?" Maylien countered.

"No one," I replied.

"Then it falls to you, or it fails," she replied, and I couldn't help but remember that this woman wanted nothing more than to be a wandering vagabond, but was well on her way to becoming a queen. It shamed me.

"I know," I said. "I've known for at least a week, but I haven't wanted to face it. They're my friends, Maylien, my family even. Or they were once, and I love them still. Even Devin." I paused then because that wasn't quite true. "At least, I love the idea of what they were, though I hate the idea of what they've become. It's hard."

"Again, I ask: what are you going to do about it?" There was no pity in her tone, just as there had been none for her sister two years previously.

"I don't know. What I do know is that I'm useless in the role I'm playing for you right now. I think that duty calls for me to do what I can to put you on the throne first, since I got you into this mess." She raised a skeptical eyebrow at that, but didn't respond otherwise. "Besides, there's a Blade involved here, and any effort to right the wrongs of my fellows begins by finding out about the connection with Thauvik. I need to get into the palace to find out what's going on, and to kill Thauvik if I get the chance."

"So, you'll be leaving me?"

"Yes, for now, though I'll contact you as I can."

"When will you go?"

"Now that the decision's made I can't see any reason to stay longer than it takes to bring Heyin up to speed on what few ideas I have for slowing down a Blade. This evening? Certainly no later than tomorrow night."

"You might want to hang around a little while longer," a voice called from the entrance to the next gallery.

Captain Fei ducked through the low arch and came up the sewer's dry spillway, with Heyin following close behind. The barrel-vaulted gallery Maylien had adopted as her apartment fed into the main line—where her guards had set up their headquarters—at about a thirty-degree angle. It was much lower ceilinged than the larger sewer it had once fed. A normal-sized person could only stand upright in the center of what used to be the channel.

"I take it you have news?" said Maylien.

"She does indeed," said Heyin.

"So, what is it?" Triss was still hanging on the wall behind Maylien and I could feel a sort of satisfaction coming from him—probably because he didn't have to hide here and with these people. The necessity of always concealing his existence wore at him.

"A little bird tells me one of the king's high officers is thinking about switching sides."

"Who?" demanded Maylien.

"Lord Justicer Vyan."

"That's excellent news," said Maylien. "If he's sincere.

I've never trusted the man, and the events at and after the Council of Jade haven't improved my feelings. Do you think he knows about the king's Blade?" She inclined her head my way with the question.

"I don't know," I replied. "It didn't seem like it during the conversation in the presence chamber, but things will have changed since then. With the chancellor and the Warden of the Blood both as yet unreplaced and Thauvik himself falling into this passive funk, Vyan's more or less running the place in consultation with the Royal Monetist."

"Tell me more," Maylien directed Fei.

"My source says that he's growing more and more worried about Thauvik and the state of the kingdom. I think the main reason he hasn't already tried to sell the king out is that he fears the king. That and he doesn't know who he can trust as a go-between."

"What makes you so sure of your information?" asked Heyin. "He could be loyal to Thauvik."

"I don't think so. He's holding one of the high cards in the play for the throne, and has been since the day of the massacre, one no true loyalist would conceal from the king."

"He's got the adoption papers," I said. "*That's* what he was hiding from Thauvik when I listened in."

"Put a golden badge of merit on the man's cap," said Fei. "He does indeed. He's not sleeping much either, and he's talking to himself rather a lot."

"I don't suppose you want to tell us how you got the information this time, either," said Heyin.

Fei shook her head. "I protect my sources."

I didn't say anything either, though it was obvious to me that Scheroc was listening to the Lord Justicer gibber to himself. Fei hadn't chosen to share her secret with Maylien's people and I had no reason to betray her.

"It doesn't matter," said Maylien. "You haven't steered us wrong yet. Can you contact the Lord Justicer for us? Or do we need to take care of that?"

"My source inside the palace is one-way at the moment.

I don't dare expose them to the kind of scrutiny sending messages in would generate, and Vyan hasn't been getting out into the city much of late."

Maylien turned back to me. "Aral, you'll handle that."

I nodded. "I wanted to go have a look around the palace anyway. Do you want me to talk with the Lord Justicer directly, or would you prefer I deliver a note?"

"A note." She grinned. "It'll be like old times."

I smiled back at her. When we'd first met, it was because she wanted me to break into the Marchon estate and deliver a letter. Of course, the person I'd actually been delivering the letter to was me, though I hadn't known it at the time. And the only reason I had to bring it to Marchon House was so that I would be forced to see events that took place there.

"I'll write it up in a moment," said Maylien. "Leave it someplace Vyan can't miss it, and if you scare him a bit, that's all to the good. If fear of my uncle is the main thing keeping him from switching sides, letting him know that he's not safe from me either will give him something to think about. Do it tonight."

I'd slipped into and out of the palace complex dozens of times over the years. With a perimeter more than a mile around, it was virtually impossible to secure against any talented mage, much less a Blade. I climbed in over the wall that looked out across the Highside streets toward the sea. There, the additional height of the bluff on which the compound sat added about thirty feet to the climb. A bit more work, but worth the effort to avoid repeating the path from my most recent visits to the palace.

It also had the advantage of somewhat reduced guard vigilance. Highside was a well-lit neighborhood, heavily populated by the city's more wealthy sort of Crown loyalist. The patrols on its streets, both public and private, meant that any thieves or assassins would have to run quite a gauntlet to even get to the palace. It wasn't as vulnerable on that front as the back slope, but it was still easier to crack than the riverside, where the Crown Guard focused their attention most heavily.

Getting into the palace proper presented a slightly greater challenge, but it was still a great sprawling building, with hundreds of windows, and only moderately difficult for someone like me to penetrate. I'd never had any call to sneak into the apartments set aside for the Lord Justicer before, as they were at the far end of the palace from the tower that housed the royal family. Since the Lord Justicer was second only to the chancellor among the great officers of the kingdom under Thauvik, who acted as his own chief marshal, I expected to encounter some real challenges once I got close.

Imagine my surprise then as I kept finding tiny, but perfectly placed holes in the security arrangements as I went along. Here, a patrol didn't come quickly enough on the heels of the one that preceded it. There, a corner that should have had an extra magelight to expose a narrow hiding place high on the wall between two intersecting arches remained dark. Around the corner, a ward of alarm was of an older design that allowed it to be effectively nullified by a charm of blinding and the presence of a Shade. It was subtle, and I don't think anyone but a Blade could have exploited all of the holes that I found. But for any Blade, the web of guards and wards around the Lord Justicer was little more than a cleverly crafted illusion.

It made my bones itch. I kept looking for the teeth in the trap, but I couldn't find any hint of them. By the time I was one floor below my target and slipping into the shaft of the dumbwaiter that fed the Lord Justicer's private dining room, I wanted nothing more than to turn right the fuck around and head for anyplace that wasn't so easy to get into. I had just closed the little door behind me and started up the narrow stone chimney when I tasted a patch of something very faintly through Triss's senses. It was an odd sort of almost-trace like a Shade's ghost might leave, but too faint for me to make anything of it. It was perhaps a yard above the door.

Triss? I sent as I released him from the sleeplike state that allowed me to assume full control of his shadowy substance. *Triss, wake up.*

What is it?

What do you make of this? I placed my palm against the front wall where the patch of shadow flavors lay.

Hmmm. I could feel his mind going far away as he struggled to identify the trace. *It's like a Shade's been here some time ago, but* not . . . *and the taste* . . . *echoes? Yes, it echoes strangely. It's very muddled and indistinct, and* . . . *Wait, I think I might have it! How did the door open? I mean, how did it feel?* He shifted around to the dumbwaiter's entrance.

I don't know, it was very loose and easy, like it had been oiled recently. . . . .

Did it hang open, or swing closed by itself?

Hung open. Here, I'll show you. I pushed the door loose of its catch, and swung it wide. Swiping a fingertip along the hinge revealed oil recently applied. I brought it to my nose, but it had almost no scent, so I touched it to the tip of my tongue. A familiar and deeply bitter taste greeted me. *Thalis nut oil.*

I quickly rubbed a corner of my shirt on my tongue to strip away as much of it as I could. Even with the tiny amount involved and wiping it away as soon as I recognized it, a rather unpleasant tingly numbness spread outward from the point of contact. The combination of that lack of scent and the fact that it could double as a poison made the oil of the thalis an old favorite with my order despite its great cost. Not conclusive evidence of the passage of a Blade here, but certainly suggestive.

Let me think, Triss sent as he examined the patch of shadow residue. *There are cobwebs here, old ones freshly broken by your hand. Where is the window in the room beyond?* I felt the shadow that had been covering me flow away out through the little door, and then return to reshroud me, closing the door behind him on the way. *Yes, that makes sense.*

What does? I asked.

I think the trace here is doubled, or quadrupled, really, since each of them both came and went.

I missed a step there, Triss.

I believe that two different Shades passed through here a few hours apart, going both up and down. It happened several days ago, maybe as long as a week. It's more than dark enough to hold a trace that long. Later, probably some hours later, someone tried to burn it away by leaving the door open. It didn't work completely because bounced sun doesn't chew as deep and the cobwebs partially protected this patch. Even so, with your reduced ability to use my senses, you would never have noticed it if they weren't familiar traces.

Traces? I asked. *Two of them, and familiar? Why do I think I'm going to hate where this is going?*

Because you're no fool, replied Triss, *no matter what I say when I'm angry with you. The only reason you registered the residue here is because you've tasted these shadow trails before, both of them, and spent time setting them in your mind.*

Oh, but I didn't like where this was going. *That limits things, rather a lot. I presume one belongs to the Blade from the Jade Council massacre.*

It does.

Faran I hope I'd recognize, even as faint as the trace is here. Though I wasn't absolutely sure of that. *It's not her?*

No, nor any of Jax's people, nor Master Kelos.

That only left one choice. *Devin.*

Yes.

Dammit! Dammit! Dammit! And he's been here at least a week?

Maybe. The trace is faint and it's been sun scrubbed. It could be as recent as a couple of days old.

But there's nothing saying the first thing he did when he got in was climb Vyan's dumbwaiter. He might have been here much longer. Fuck! I shouldn't have waited so long to break free of Maylien. If I'd come back here sooner . . .

You might have found evidence of Devin's presence, or you might have found nothing at all. If not for Fei's news this afternoon, you wouldn't be climbing around in Vyan's dumbwaiter, you'd have been looking around the royal apartments. We don't know what Devin's here for, so there's no way to be sure that would have led us to discover his presence any faster than we already have. Don't guess at things that might be, work with what you know. Observe. Assess. Act decisively.

You sounded more than half like Master Kelos there, I replied. *That was always one of his favorite lessons.*

It was a good one. You humans are too prone to acting before you think. It's kind of endearing . . . when it's not driving us crazy, that is. I felt his smile.

Then, in the interest of preserving your sanity, I should bring you up to date. I proceeded to quickly outline the things that had happened while he was asleep, with a special emphasis on the security arrangements, or lack thereof, for the Lord Justicer.

Interesting. I wish that we knew who set that up. It would tell us a lot about why there's a Blade-shaped hole in things. Does the king want a way to eliminate his Lord Justicer that doesn't point back to him? Do Devin or our unknown Blade want a way to get at Vyan? Or, all of the king's high officers, if it extends that far? Does Vyan himself want a Blade ally to be able to visit him easily? Without more information, there's no way to know what the answers are.

What now? I asked. *I'd originally hoped to approach the king's suites after we finished up here and maybe take a run at our unknown Blade if I got the chance. But with two involved the risk goes way up. I'm in much better shape than I was the last time I fought Devin, even if I'm not yet the Kingslayer again. I'm pretty sure I could take him or all but a few of the best of the lost Blades in a straight fight now, but there's no guarantee I wouldn't have to face both of them at once. That's a far chancier proposition.*

Especially with the potential for interference by the Elite and the Crown Guard. We deliver Maylien's letter first, I

*think. We said that we would, and this route has gone
unused for some days. I'd say the odds are with us there.
After? Well, let's talk about that once we finish here. Do
you need me to let you take over again?*

*Let's see how things look in Vyan's rooms first. If
arrangements are as lax up there as they've been along the
way, I shouldn't need that fine a control.*

I quickly hand-over-handed my way up the dumbwaiter
rope, which was both recently replaced and of a heavier
gauge than it really needed to be—more than adequate to
support my weight. The door at the top—the Lord Justicer's
apartments topped the tower—opened silently on freshly
oiled hinges after I'd listened long enough to assure myself
of the emptiness of the room. The dining room—big enough
to hold a dozen guests and their servants—was dark and
silent, as was the receiving room beyond. A dim light shone
under the door of the withdrawing room, however, and faint
noises from within suggested some servant or guard
remained alert there.

After dropping my shroud and taking on dragon shape,
Triss poked his nose underneath. *Two of them, playing cards
at a table in front of the door to the Lord Justicer's bedroom. Vyan's personal livery, not Crown Guards.*

No surprise. The Lord Justicer was an earl in his own
right, in addition to holding Crown Office. *How do you
suppose Devin got past them?*

Hang on a beat. The deep darkness of the receiving room
gave Triss the freedom to expand far beyond his normal
area, and he quickly flowed outward, brushing across every
available surface. *Secret panel,* he said after a couple of
minutes.

Where?

Here.

I felt a gentle tug through the line of shadow that connected us, and the last panel on an elaborate enameled
screen went briefly darker than the others around it. It was
hanging on the wall that separated us from the withdrawing
room.

I crossed to the indicated spot and examined the panel. *How did you find it? And how do I open it?*

There's more thalis on the slides at top and bottom as well as on the catch. Whoever applied it was sloppy and got a bit on the floor in front of the panel or I'd never have found the seams. The catch is behind the shiny sort of round bit there. He indicated a stylized tortoise.

Maybe press the head? I did, then twisted when that wasn't enough. I was rewarded with a sharp pop as the right side of the panel suddenly sank about an inch into the wall behind it. Then I was able to slide it behind the next panel over, exposing a narrow space about the depth of a coffin, with stone walls on three sides. A crude ladder had been built into the wall opposite the outer one. I slipped sideways into the gap—there wasn't enough room for anything else.

That's when I heard the door to the withdrawing room creak open.

"Is someone in here?" a voice called quietly.

9

————◆————

As silently as I could, I slid the hidden panel into place behind me, though I didn't yet close it. I didn't want to run the risk of it popping again.

"You're imagining things," a second voice spoke out on the other side of the panel.

"I am not," replied the first. "Something snapped in here, and it's not the first time. I want to check it out."

Kill them? asked Triss.

I'd prefer not to. Let's see if I can . . . yes.

The panel latched by means of a pair of spring-loaded metal rods at the top and bottom. Rather than simply pushing the panel in place by means of the handle, I grabbed hold of the rods and held them while I leaned against the door, then slowly eased them into place. There was still a faint pop when the latch clicked shut, but this time I felt it more than heard it.

A moment later, quiet footsteps echoed through the panel as the guard drew close. The panel creaked, but only briefly, and then the footsteps moved away.

A few minutes later, a voice said, "I told you it was nothing."

"Maybe, but I still don't like it."

"Do you want to wake his lordship up and explain to him that you've been hearing things?"

"No, he doesn't wake friendly."

"Then you'll stop stomping about and get back to the game. Don't think I didn't notice that you didn't get all alert until right when you started losing."

The door to the withdrawing room creaked shut again, and I found myself silently thanking whoever had failed to oil it.

The shadow trail is stronger in here, and it's definitely Devin and the unknown. Triss drew my attention to the traces as he spoke into my mind—I didn't have anywhere near as fine a control over his senses when he remained awake like this. *But it's still weaker than it ought to be, given the level of darkness and no good way to sun scrub in here without giving the secret passage away.*

Maybe they used a magelight? I said, proposing one of my own pet ideas.

We'd had a number of discussions about how to get rid of shadow trails since Triss had shared their existence with me. Back when the temple remained a going concern, he'd been forbidden from telling me about them. Though all Shades could taste them, the trails had been an official secret of the order, only ever revealed to its human members when they joined the shadow council that ruled the temple.

I don't know, replied Triss. *You and I never managed to make a bright enough magelight.*

I still think that's because it's got more to do with the type of light than its intensity.

Maybe. He sounded dubious, as he had every time I'd tried that argument, but then he sighed. *I don't know how you would make a magelight with a light all that different from what we can do. Not safely, but I don't have a better guess.*

I didn't know how you'd do it either, but then I was never terribly good with spellcraft. What I really wanted to do was talk it over with Siri. She was far and away the best mage of my generation among the Blades, but no one knew where she was, or if she was even still alive. When I was with Jax in Dalridia, she had told me there were rumors Siri had gone south to the Sylvani Empire after the fall of the temple. They said she'd vowed to live out her life among the Others and renounce all contact with humanity forever, but Jax hadn't put much stock in it.

Never mind, I sent as I started to climb. *The how's not really important, and talking about it is burning time. We don't want to run into Devin or the unknown, and the longer this takes the greater the chances one of them will pick up our shadow trail.*

At the top of the ladder a narrow pass-through allowed us to slip into a gap between the plaster ceiling and the stone cap of the tower above. From there, it was clear that the little space I'd just climbed out of was concealed by a fireplace and chimney using an overwide and hollow false façade. The shadow trail ran along a roof beam and down into another narrow ladderway—this one masked by the shaft of a garderobe. At the base, another sliding panel opened into the Lord Justicer's dressing closet, the door of which was well oiled with thalis.

From there, six short steps took me to his bedside where I slipped Maylien's letter under the sheets a few inches from his face. My initial impulse had been to lay it on his pillow. But I didn't want it easily visible should another Blade follow my path into his bedroom this side of morning.

I wonder where he's keeping Maylien's papers. I glanced around the room.

Fei said she didn't know. Whether that's because Scheroc never saw Vyan accessing them, or because Scheroc is terrible about physical details, is an open question. Do you want to look?

I was tempted, but I shook my head. *No, it would take*

*time we don't have and there's no guarantee the document
is even in this room. Besides, there are too many places we
couldn't check without making noise or otherwise running
the risk of waking Vyan.*

So, what now? Triss asked as I started back toward the
secret panel.

*I want to look around the rest of the palace a bit. With
two other Blades running around, chances are good that
our passing will be detected. I'd like to get in as much recon-
naissance as we can now,* before *they become aware of our
visit and change anything.*

*They had to have twigged to our shadow trail at the
Council of Jade. Do you really think they won't already
have taken measures?*

*That was six weeks ago and we haven't made any incur-
sions since. They might have let their guard down a bit.* I
slid the panel closed behind us.

*Do you think this passage is why they put the Lord Jus-
ticer in these rooms?* Triss asked as I started up the hidden
ladder.

*Perhaps. It wouldn't surprise me at all to learn that all
of the important suites have hidden access of some kind or
another. There've been a lot of ambitious and powerful high
officers of the realm over the years the Pridu have ruled,
yet they still hold the throne.*

Once we'd worked our way back out of the Lord Justicer's
apartments, I checked the initial legs of the routes leading
into the apartments of several of the king's other high officers. All of them looked to have been set up to allow Blade
access, though I didn't detect any further traces of Devin or
the unknown. Admittedly, several of those suites of rooms
were vacant after the Jade Council massacre, but that didn't
seem to have had much effect on the security arrangements.
It took several hours to manage the task, and morning was
fast approaching as we finished up.

Time to go? asked Triss.

I hesitated for a long time. Leaving was the sensible

choice, but I felt like we hadn't really accomplished anything. Oh, we'd delivered Maylien's letter right enough, but
that was her goal, not mine. I'd originally wanted to come
to the palace to find out more about our unknown Blade,
and I hadn't really learned anything at all. That rankled. So
did knowing that Devin was here, but nothing about what
he might be up to. And, this really might be my only chance
to catch them unprepared.

*I should say yes, but I still want to see if we can't find
out a little something about what Devin and the unknown
are up to. Let's see how close we can get to the royal tower.*

Bad idea.

I know.

Half an hour later I was hanging from the underside of
a balcony I hadn't visited since the night I killed the last
king of Tien. *Now, this is spooky,* I sent to Triss.

I agree. Can we leave yet?

It had been very nearly as easy to get to the royal tower
as it had been to get into Vyan's chambers. When I'd killed
Ashvik, it had taken me weeks to get so far. All of the old
security was still in place, at least on the surface. Some of
it had even been upgraded, or made to look like it had. But
just as they had with the arrangements around the Lord
Justicer's apartments, someone had carved a Blade-shaped
hole in Thauvik's protections.

Hang on, one last thing. I poked my head up over the
edge of the balcony to check out the ward there.

Where once that would have been possible only for a few
seconds every six hours or so, I felt no risk in doing it now.
Several static guard posts had been converted to active
patrols, a measure that, done right, could have made what I
wanted to do all but impossible. Instead, it created regular
large gaps in the coverage of the balcony.

Really? I said into the quiet of my mind where only Triss
could hear me. *Really?*

It would appear so.

The elaborate ward that I had worked so hard to defeat
all those years ago had been replaced by something both

much fancier and less effective. Better if you wanted to keep out thieves with no magic, but all but useless to prevent a Blade's approach.

I can't believe Thauvik would choose to make himself so vulnerable to one of us, I sent.

I don't know, replied Triss. *If he believes he controls a Blade or Blades and doesn't want his Elite to know of their comings and goings, wouldn't he have to carve out a route for them to visit unobserved?*

Why would he want to hide anything from the Elite? They are completely loyal to the Crown. Thauvik is all but a god to them.

True, but they hate us as they hate few others. Five rulers of Tien have fallen to the servants of Namara over the last four hundred years. Every one of them represents a failing of the Elite. We have cost them more in blood and prestige than any other circumstance short of war. I can't imagine they would take it at all well if Thauvik told them to play nice with any of us.

Maybe . . . I grimaced—it didn't feel right. *But I'm not convinced.*

What other answer is there? That Thauvik has surrendered control of his personal security to a rogue Blade that answers to the Son of Heaven? You might just as well claim he's surrendered control of his kingdom. It's much the same thing, and just as ridiculous. The sun will be up in less than an hour. Can we go? Or do you really feel the need to stick your hand deeper into the slink's nest?

I thought about it. If arrangements within the tower continued as they had a decade ago, the Elite were as thick as bees on a comb from here on in. And, I wouldn't be able to use my old route, not without leaving a giant sign saying that Aral Kingslayer was here for any who could read the writing. On the other hand, the rest of the guards and wards had been arranged to allow easy and swift passage for any Blade. Why should that change as we got closer to Thauvik?

Just as far as the council room, I sent. *I promise.*

Triss sighed in my mind, but didn't otherwise challenge my choice.

I quickly cast a pair of lesser blinds, one for silence and one for a light foot. Each created a tiny flash of spell-light. I'd never have risked such a trick if security had remained as tight as it once was. Then, up over the lip of the balcony, and across to the door where I paused to listen for ten long heart-beats before slipping a shadow tendril into the shiny new lock someone had installed. Feel out the tumblers, and feed nima to the shadow so I could solidify it without losing too much of my shroud. That created another bit of spell-light. Twist my shadow key . . . and step through into darkness.

There, we're in the council room, Triss said into my mind. *Can we get out now?*

Ten beats more, Triss. Twenty at the most. I crossed to the far door, pulling a cornerbright from my trick bag as I went.

I listened briefly at the door, then lay my length on the floor, sliding the slender instrument just far enough under-neath to put the tip out the other side so that I could see what was happening beyond. The cornerbright, essentially two tiny silver mirrors connected by a tarnished strip of the same metal and a very weak sort of spell that let one mirror show what the other reflected, provided a low-risk way to see around corners. Though it did shine faintly with spell-light, the magic was minor and chances were good that no one with magesight would notice it unless they happened to look at exactly the right place at the right time. The silver mirrors were actually a bigger risk, but sometimes you had to take a chance.

What the cornerbright showed now was an empty and dimly lit hallway. I angled it so that I could see the wards on the doors—every door and window in this part of the castle had some sort of spell of protection on it. In the case of the hall doors, the wards had been designed to screech an alert for the patrolling Elite if the door opened without a countersign. It would also sound if the patrols didn't renew it with a touch of magic every so often. From what I could see, the door wards had changed since my last visit, too.

They would still register being opened, but the intervals at which they had to be renewed by patrols, lest they sound an alarm, had been extended.

The last time I had come this way, I'd carved a pass-through in the base of the door, and another on the one opposite. That had allowed me to slip across the hall without alerting the guards, sneaking into the then-empty suite of one of the murdered princes. I could have done it again now, given more time, but just as it had back then, doing so would leave traces of my passing that couldn't be concealed. I was still tempted. Thauvik had no heirs of his body, so the other suite was unlikely to be—my thoughts crashed to a halt as the suite's door swung suddenly wide. I yanked back my cornerbright and shifted position so I could flip to my feet in an instant if I needed to.

A moment later, I heard the door across the way snick shut ever so quietly. Too quietly, in fact, and without any sound of footsteps. Whoever had come out of the door was trained to stealth.

Triss, take a look.

I'll have to unshroud you.

I know, just do it.

The shadow that surrounded me collapsed into a thin pool between my chest and the floor. A heartbeat later, a dragon crept from beneath me and slipped his nose under the door, only to jump back with a sharp mental hiss.

Fire and sun, Triss yelped into my mind, *Kitsune!*

What? I knew many stories about the nine-tailed foxes. Who in Zhan didn't? But it seemed a strange thing for my familiar to get so worked up about unless . . . *Oh fuck.* The *Kitsune? Nuriko!*

Yes. Now can we go?

I sure as hell hope so.

I was not ready to face that nine-tailed fox, not here surrounded by my enemies, maybe not anywhere. Moving as quietly as I ever had, I pushed myself to my feet and carefully backed toward the balcony exit, never letting my attention leave the hall door.

You're sure? I sent as we slipped onto the balcony.

No other Shade would take the shape of the nine-tailed fox. Not after what happened the last time. And she carried only a single sword, half as long as she was tall.

I slipped over the rail and started down the wall. *But she's supposed to be dead, a hundred and more years dead.*

Apparently, no one told her that.

As I made my way out of the palace, I couldn't help but remember all I had learned about Nuriko Shadowfox, the greatest failure of my order, up until the day the temple fell. Child of one of the seven Kanjurese Rimaru, or sword kings, she had been forced to leave the islands at the age of eight when it became apparent that she possessed the mage gift as well as the familiar gift. The latter, manifested alone, marked out those who would go on to bond with the sentient swords that companioned the nobility of the islands. Though the people of Kanjuri treasured both gifts in isolation, they did not permit their own to become true mages. To be born with both gifts anywhere in the islands was to be born outcast.

Though Nuriko's father was one of the most powerful men in the Kanjurese Isles he had not been able to save his daughter from banishment. It was said to have broken the Rimaru's heart and that he died within a year of sending her out into the world, but the details had grown fuzzy with the passing of time and had acquired the veneer of legend. For the Rimaru had been unwilling to have any child of his high blood fall into obscurity. In hopes of preventing such dishonor, he had sent his daughter to the temple of Namara on Lake Evinduin, there to become a Blade.

In the days when I was taken to serve Namara, no child over the age of five was ever considered for the training, but that was not the rule when Nuriko arrived some three hundred years before me. In fact, it was the advent of Nuriko and what followed that caused that rule to be made along with several others. The child of one of the greatest living masters of the greatsword, Nuriko arrived at the temple with skills no other recruit had ever possessed.

Her first toy was a tiny sword, her first words came from the rituals of training in jurida, the Kanjurese way of the sword. She was the dark star of her generation at the temple, and the greatest assassin in the world on the day she received her sword. Yes, sword. Alone of all the Blades, she was granted a special boon by the goddess, a single blade designed to mimic as much as possible the greatswords of Kanjuri.

For a decade she was the pride of Namara, a demigoddess of death in the name of justice. But then something went wrong. No one knows what or why, but one day Nuriko had come away from the island of the goddess in a cold fury. She had gone straight to the stone orb that held our holy kila, the daggers that symbolize our bond with our goddess, and struck the hilt off of hers with her great dark sword.

Then she had left the temple never to return. For many years no one heard anything more from her. Then, one day, the high lord of Dan Eyre, a just and merciful ruler, was killed while addressing her people, struck down by living shadow. A dagger was left in the heart of the high lord, a dagger inscribed with the emblem of the nine-tailed fox. Nuriko had returned, as a true assassin, killing for money.

Namara condemned her to death the same day. For almost a century Nuriko and the order played a game of knives in the dark that ended time and again with a fallen Blade left with the dagger bearing a nine-tailed fox. Finally, Master Kelos had tracked her down and ended her killing spree, bringing her sword back to lay at the feet of the goddess. It was considered the greatest feat of Kelos the Deathwalker.

Do you think it was all a lie? I sent as we slipped out of the palace. *Do you think Kelos conspired with the Shadowfox to let her live?* It hurt me to even be able to contemplate such a thing about the man who had made me what I was today. But then, as I had so recently learned, much of what I had believed about my former master was a lie. *When did he first betray Namara? Could it have been so long ago?*

It's possible. He carried that severed finger for nearly

eighty years before the fall of the temple, and that was a betrayal of Namara, too.

Point. What the fuck is going on here? Why is the Kitsune involved? And what was Master Kelos thinking to let her live?

I don't know, and we can't be sure that's what happened. He did bring her sword back to the temple, after all. And she is a legendary trickster. He might have believed he killed her. There's no way to know what's true and what's a lie where she is concerned.

You sound almost frightened, Triss. We had reached the outer wall of the palace complex by then, speaking to each other only in brief bursts as we avoided the various guards and wards. *I don't think I've ever heard you sound this worried about anything but me drinking myself to death. Why does the idea of the Kitsune frighten you?*

Thiussus, he whispered into my mind.

What? It was a Shade word, but not one I recognized.

The Kitsune's bond-mate. Have you never wondered why her Shade is almost never named? Thiussus wasn't . . . quite sane. At least, that's what the stories that were told after all the humans had gone to sleep said. The elders said that Nuriko should never have been chosen, that no right-minded Shade would ever have tied their soul to hers.

I slid between two sets of patrolling soldiers and rolled over the parapet to begin climbing down the outer wall. We were almost clear of the palace, but I couldn't shake the feeling that things had gone suddenly and horribly wrong. *I've never heard of a mad Shade before.*

Nor should you have. It's always been a rarity among my kind, and great care was taken to prevent any such from making their way into this world, even before Thiussus and Nuriko. Afterward, the thoroughness of those measures was examined and they were tightened, but none of the elders who knew Thiussus was ever convinced anything would have stopped her.

I don't understand. I know how careful Shades can be, what's so special about Thiussus?

Power. Both of soul and of mind. Thiussus had it all, smart, strong, clever, a natural leader. She was not the sort of Shade that normally expresses any interest in crossing over between the worlds. Triss paused, and I felt an uncertainty coming through our link that felt wholly unlike him.

Triss?

How can I put this so as not to hurt you . . . ? The Shades that choose to leave the everdark and companion your people are not . . . well thought of by our people. It is not a thing done by the mighty among us, not normally. We are, all of us who cross over, outcasts and considered a bit less than normal. Usually, that disregard starts well before we've made our choice. Thiussus could easily have become a . . . I suppose "ruler" is close enough. That such a one chose to pass between the worlds was considered a high honor by the Shades who had chosen to join with your people, and she had the force of mind to push aside almost any possible objections that might have arisen. Knowing that she still lives is . . . troubling. Triss's mental voice fell silent, and I could feel that he wanted time alone.

We had reached the bottom of the wall by then, and I started to lope east toward the road that would take me across the river and back into the northern half of the city where most of my fallbacks lay. I didn't want to return to Maylien right away. Not until I'd had time to think about things a bit more and make certain no one had followed me.

A flicker of light, like a skipping stone briefly reflecting the moon. That was all the warning I got. If I were still the Aral of even a year before, the dagger would have found my heart and ended my life. That it didn't, I owed to Maylien for pulling me out of the gutter, to Faran for pushing me to practice and practice and practice until I was worthy to teach her, to Jax for putting me in the place that burned away the last softness of my soul, and most of all to Triss for never giving up on me. I didn't have time to draw a blade or dodge, and only barely enough to block the blow with the inner side of my forearm. The steel of my own knife in its wrist sheath deflected the blow a scant few inches as I twisted my torso back and sideways.

Instead of sinking into my chest, the blade drew a line of blood and pain across the front of my left shoulder. The follow-up came almost as fast, but I expected that. I was able to crow-hop back and out of the way, drawing my left-hand sword with the flapping motion of my arm.

"Very good." The voice spoke out of shadow. A lacuna of night created an impenetrable blot in the unvision I had borrowed from Triss, a void of nothingness in front and to my right somehow deeper and darker than any shroud ought to be. "I'm impressed, Kingslayer." It was a woman's voice, clear and low, yet secret, like dark water.

I didn't answer. I turned my left side toward the void, lifting that sword to point at its center while I drew my other and brought it into a low guard.

"Steel first, words after?" asked the voice, and this time it held a note of playfulness like a slink with a wounded bird. "I can respect that, though it might mean the words never blossom, and that *would* be a pity. Ah, well—"

Aral! Triss shouted into my mind.

The flicker came again, this time from behind and to my right. I threw myself forward as the dagger sliced through the place the back of my neck would have been. I touched down briefly on the knuckles of my closed hands before vaulting into a sort of handspring to land on my feet again. It hurt, and I cracked a pinky on the stone of the road, but it was that or let my swords go. As I landed, I spun in place, bringing my swords into a crossguard, but the Kitsune hadn't advanced.

She stood just where she had been when she took a swing at the back of my neck, and about nine feet from the false shroud her familiar had created to focus my attention on the wrong place. She was tall like most of the islanders, taller than me, and there was something wrong with her skin. It gleamed gold in the moonlight, like the metal, not the more normal brown gold typical of Kanjuri. The hilt of a great-sword stuck out over her left shoulder, a greatsword whose guard shone blue in the moonlight with the Unblinking Eye of Namara. . . . But I didn't have time to think about what that meant right now.

I don't know where she came from, Triss sent, his mental voice sounding more than half frantic. *It's like she simply appeared there, behind us.*

"Nice trick," I said. "And throwing your voice like a puppeteer, too. Very clever."

"Hardly that, child. Merely another test. You passed, by the way."

"Oh, what do I get?"

Careful, Aral, Triss whispered into my mind. *Careful.*

"Why, I would have thought it would be obvious," she replied. "You get to live, of course. For now."

The false shroud suddenly collapsed into the shadow of a huge nine-tailed fox, throwing its head back in silent laughter.

I opened my mouth to answer her, or tried to anyway. My lips didn't respond. Neither did any of my other muscles.

Triss! I cried with my mind.

A paralytic poison on the dagger. She . . . Triss's mental voice trailed off, or perhaps, I did.

10

———◆———

Every Blade knows their career will end in the coffin. It's the stuff my nightmares are made of, the feel of the winding cloth on your bare skin, the narrow box, the smells of earth and mold and death, the darkness of the tomb, the silence of the grave. It's part of the price you expect to pay for justice.

It's horror to dream about going into the tomb, but even worse to wake up and find yourself buried. Before I opened my eyes, before I even knew I was awake, I understood in my bones that someone had put me in the grave. I felt a scream bubble up from somewhere below conscious thought rising slowly to . . . nothing. I was still paralyzed, though consciousness was slowly returning.

Triss?

Long seconds slid past before his mind voice answered from faint and far away. *I'm here, Aral. It will be all right.*

Where are we? What happened?

I'm . . . not sure. After you fell, Thiussus swooped down on top of me and forced me into stillness while Nuriko

poured something in your wound. They said it was an anti-
dote to the poison she'd just given you, that you had fought
well and deserved to live, and that Kelos would be angry if
she killed you. Then she laughed and Thiussus did some-
thing to my mind. I went away for a while after that, wan-
dering the quiet everdark of a youngling's memory, and
only came back when you called me a moment ago.

I tried to stretch. This time my muscles responded reluc-
tantly, but something more kept me from moving more than
a few fractions of an inch. *Is this really a winding cloth?*

Yes. You're laid out as for burial, and I think we're in a
coffin of some sort. The edges of the lid are sealed with
lead. Hold on a moment . . . there!

I heard a sharp pop, and found it suddenly easier to
breathe, though I hadn't realized until then that it was growing steadily more difficult. *It's a good thing I woke when I*
did. I might have suffocated otherwise.

I don't think so, Triss sent as he started cutting away the
swaths of silk that bound me. *I can't quite remember what's*
happened while I've been away, but I feel that you were
safe. I don't think they could have sent me so far from myself
if you were not, but I don't know how I know that.

I guess I'll take your word for it. As Triss cut my arms
free, I reached up and pushed on the lid of the coffin. It
didn't move. *This is a heavy bastard.*

Wait, I'll help.

Once he finished freeing me, I rolled over in the tight
space and got onto elbows and knees. Then, as Triss levered
at the edges of the coffin lid, I braced my back against it and
pushed with my whole body. With a harsh grinding of stone
on stone, the lid began to move. By tipping it to the side, I
was able to shift it a few inches farther. A dim flickering
light filtered in through the cracks. That, in conjunction with
the stone coffin, really made me wonder where the hell I
was. Four or five more rounds of lifting and tipping, and I
finally had a big enough gap to slip through.

A moment later, I was standing in a small boxlike room

entirely faced with expensive marble. The coffin lay atop a low marble platform, and it was easy to see both why the lid had been so heavy and who it actually belonged to.

"Ashvik!" I put a hand on the chest of the life-sized figure sculpted atop the thick stone lid of the coffin. "She buried me in fucking Ashvik's tomb?" That explained the light, too; the eternal flame was part of the traditional burial of Zhan's kings and peers.

So it would seem, Triss sent. He'd been speaking aloud less and less when he addressed me.

I took a half step back and stumbled when my foot came down on something that crunched softly. *I just stepped on Ashvik himself, didn't I?*

Yes, the crunch was one of the long bones in his right leg.

I turned around and looked down on the fallen-in face of my greatest success. Considering how carefully he ought to have been prepared by the royal embalmer, he had decayed far more than I would have expected. He looked almost as bad as a Kadeshi mummy of similar vintage. For several long beats I stared into the voids where his eyes had once been and thought about this ultimate result of the Blade's mission of justice. I don't know if that was why the Kitsune had placed me in this particular tomb, or if it was a result of a deeply twisted sense of humor and honor. Whatever the reason, it was a reminder of what I was at core, a killer of men. That was all right. Some people needed killing.

The Kitsune, for one, and just as soon as I could manage it. *She had her sword back,* I mindspoke to Triss.

What? But Master Kelos laid it at the feet of the goddess! That's one thing that all the stories agree on, and no counterfeit would have fooled the other masters, much less the goddess herself.

Then she must have gotten it back somehow, because the eye of Namara looked at me over her shoulder. She's a consummate trickster, Triss. Maybe she stole it.

From Namara? How?

*I don't know. I—*It wasn't until that moment that I

realized that Nuriko had defeated me without ever bothering to draw her sword. She'd beaten me with a fucking knife, and not even a particularly long one. That stung.

It doesn't matter, I sent. *Let's just get out of here.* I glanced at the front of the tomb. *Do you think she left the door open?*

After she went to all the trouble of lead sealing the coffin?

Point.

I was tempted to light Ashvik on fire and blow the door of his tomb across the royal necropolis in order to send Nuriko a message. Instead, I chose to return Ashvik to his coffin and pick the lock, closing the door behind me. Leaving silently and without being noticed would send a message, too, a more effective one. It was dark outside, around midnight by the stars. An impression confirmed a bit later by the ringing of the bells of Shan.

It wasn't until I'd made my way down the outer wall of the palace compound that it occurred to me to wonder why neither my shoulder nor my broken knuckle were hurting me. What I found when I slipped into a corner between two buildings and looked at my injuries was deeply unnerving. The finger seemed completely recovered, without so much as a knot in the bone to mark it had ever been broken. The slice on my shoulder was likewise healed, though a thin scar marked the line the knife had drawn, one more among many. But what really disturbed me was a dark brand centering that scar, a nine-tailed fox burned into my flesh as with a heated signet ring. It, too, looked long healed.

How long *was I in that tomb?* I wondered.

I don't know. Triss sounded alarmed, and it wasn't until Triss responded that I realized I'd unintentionally shared my thoughts. *We need to find out. . . .*

"**Three** days, as it turned out," I told Maylien when I shared her bed the following evening.

She'd taken one look at the expression on my face when

I showed up in her hideaway in the old sewers and led me back to her pallet. She shushed my attempts to explain what had happened, and called to her guards that she was *not* to be disturbed as we went. It helped, more than I wanted to admit.

After, Maylien rubbed a finger along the scar on my no-longer-wounded shoulder, stopping at the fox brand. "That's deeply creepy, Aral. I'm so sorry helping me put you in a tomb, especially that one. It's not a good omen."

I shrugged and didn't say anything about it being the price I'd always expected to pay for what I did. I didn't need to. Maylien was going to be a queen, and I was quite sure she understood what that could mean for the people she would be sending into danger.

"It's not so bad," I said. "It didn't feel anything like three days. But even that's not nearly long enough to have healed my injuries so thoroughly." I rolled my pinkie between the fingers and thumb of my other hand. "Especially the broken knuckle." Bones take forever to heal even with magical aid. That this one hadn't was wrong and worrying, especially since neither Triss nor I had any useful memories of what happened—not even dreams.

Maylien pressed the fox one last time, then pulled her hand away and sighed. "This makes me wish I didn't have to ask what I'm about to ask."

I raised an eyebrow at her.

"Lord Justicer Vyan got the note you left and arranged to meet with me."

"And?"

"He's admitted that he has the documents, but he's not willing to turn them over to me until I've proved he can do so safely. He's utterly terrified of my uncle and he doesn't believe I'm going to be able to take the throne. He wants to hang on to the adoption papers until I've proved him wrong. He feels that offers him the most insurance, since he can always pretend to have recovered them later if he needs a way to calm Thauvik in a dangerous moment."

"Then, why is he willing to even talk with you?"

"*Because* he's terrified of my uncle. Vyan's certain that my uncle is going to have him killed the minute he thinks he can do without him."

"Likely enough. What does Vyan want from you?"

"He wants me to kill my uncle . . . or have him killed."

"Oh." I nodded. "I see where this is going."

"I thought you might. Vyan says my uncle is planning a public event to help repair the damage the massacre at the Council of Jade caused to the reputation of the royal house of Pridu. The Lord Justicer has offered to arrange for me or my agents to get close to the king during the event. The instant my uncle is dead, he will declare for me and tell the people that he has authenticated my adoption papers and that he will produce them in a few hours. He thinks that done right, it will put me on the throne without the bloodshed of an actual war."

My shadow slid out from under me and became the dragon. "What about Devin and the Kitsune? Without a plan for dealing with them, this isn't going to end well."

Speaking of which, Triss sent, shifting to mindspeech, *we need to warn Fei about the Kitsune. I don't know if Nuriko can detect Scheroc, but I wouldn't put it past her. She's terribly dangerous even to something as diffuse and hard to hurt as the qamasiin.*

You're right. We'll have to do it as soon as we leave here. Too bad we can't just send a message with one of Maylien's runners.

Too many secrets.

Unaware of our side discussion, Maylien continued. "I asked Vyan about that, though I couldn't name your rogue Blades at the time. He said that he had a plan for dealing with 'Thauvik's invisible friends.'"

"Did he say what that plan was?" I asked.

"He told me parts of it. He's going to arrange the thing so that there's no good place for them to hide close to Thauvik. Then he's going to create a distraction that will take them away from the king for a few critical moments."

"How's he going to manage that?" asked Triss.

"He wouldn't say."

"But you want to do this anyway," I said.

She nodded. "I don't think I can afford to let the opportunity pass. I don't want to fight a civil war if I can avoid it. Everyone who dies in the fight between me and my uncle is one of my rightful subjects. Every scrap of destroyed property, every injury to life or limb, every bit of harm falls on the people it is my duty to protect. The longer I drag this out, the more I hurt my realm and my people."

"And you want me to help."

Maylien nodded. "I do. I don't want to ask you to risk your life for my goals again, but your presence will make all the difference in stopping this civil war before it really gets started. I have to put the good of the kingdom above my personal wants and needs, even where that means people I care about may die. Will you help me?"

"Of course. I got you into this mess, it's my duty to do what I can to get you out."

"No. You keep saying that, but you didn't get me into this mess." She touched my lips with a fingertip when I started to respond. "Wait. I'm not finished. Yes, you did get things rolling in the fight against my uncle, but it's nothing that I wouldn't have been forced to do myself sooner or later. My duty is to this kingdom, and my uncle is a monster of a king. There was no other possible outcome than that the two of us must come into opposition. The only question was when."

"But I—"

"No! No buts. I will not hear another word out of you on the subject. This is my battle, and it was inevitable. You bear no guilt for that, and I will not allow you to take this on your shoulders. Cease. Stop. Halt."

"That sounds an awful lot like a royal command," I said.

"It is."

I grinned because, as silly as it seemed, Maylien's order helped. "All right then. I shall do my best."

"Yes, you will." She leaned in close and gave me a kiss.

"Is that a royal command, too?" I raised a speculative eyebrow.

"Uh-huh." She kissed me again, and for a little while we pushed the cares of the world away.

This just might work, I mindspoke to Triss as I settled the helm with its crowned dragon nasal bar into place—it felt awkward and heavy.

Vyan is a better plotter than I would have expected, agreed Triss.

Behind me, Xaran Tal Xaia, the bastard half brother of Maylien's new general, the clan chief Prixia Dan Xaia, quietly slit another throat. The Crown Guard was housed in groups by its smallest unit, a lance of eight men, including the under-officer who commanded them. Most were placed in the several large barracks halls within the palace. But, due to the extreme tensions after the Jade Council massacre, several hundred of the best guards normally stationed at various smaller Crown properties around the perimeter of the city had been brought into the palace compound. Crack rural units had moved into the vacated spaces, filling out the thinned ranks. Vyan had arranged to poison the tea of one of the many displaced units, a lance tucked away in an isolated tent in a corner of the palace hedge maze.

"Done," Xaran said quietly. "No one will think to check for poison now."

"Good. If this goes wrong, that'll give our Lord Justicer better cover."

As Xaran put on his own helmet, I checked the fit of my vambraces for the third time. I didn't like wearing the armor over my wrist sheaths—it interfered with the action, and I was going to really have to snap my elbow on the draw—but it was part of a Crown Guard's dress gear and we had a special duty this morning. When I finished with my own armor, I inspected each of the seven warriors that Prixia had chosen for the mission, five men and two women. All but Xaran had served in the personal guard of some high noble and had experience in dealing with Crown soldiers.

When we left the tent, I took the sunniest route to the

palace gates. It was still early summer, but the sun was already bright and hard. With Triss hiding deep in my own shadow, our trail wouldn't last twenty minutes. I showed our orders to the duty guards at the gate and they waved us right through. It was a short march from there down to the Sanjin Island bridge where we took over for one of the pair of lances holding the center of the span.

"You're late," growled the corporal I was replacing. "I ought to report you for that."

I bowed deeply and held it. "Apologies. We're in temporary quarters on the far side of the grounds, and I did not realize how long it would take us to get through the crowds this morning. There was a lot more saluting to be done than I had expected."

The corporal sighed. "I suppose it is only a minute or two, and the palace does look like someone kicked over a beehive with a few too many fancy drones. All right, I'll let it slide."

I rose out of my bow. "Thank you."

"It's going to be a hot one," said the corporal. "I don't envy you wearing all the gilt and gewgaws out here in the sun." He tapped the gold enamel paint covering my breastplate with a fingernail. "You're going to roast in those things."

Since his own lance had covered the dawn watch and weren't going to be there for the king's arrival, they were wearing simpler and more practical armor. "That'll be punishment enough for your tardiness." He turned and led his lance away.

"Looks like we're set." Xaran asked me, "What now?"

"Stand still and look pretty." I glanced up at the sun and realized I could already feel my armor heating up. "That, and roast."

I grounded my spear and adjusted my helmet before settling in to wait, making sure the cheek guards and nasal bar concealed most of my face. When Triss and I had discussed the details prior to the actual mission we had decided against bonewrighting my face into a new shape. None of the wanted posters that had been put up after the Council of Jade had anything close to a good likeness of my current face on them. I was mentioned and pictured, but only as a nameless servant wanted for questioning. No one at the Council had really looked at me before the massacre—servant's invisibility—and I'd vanished into shadow the second the fighting started. Add in the concealing nature of my Crown Guard dress helmet and there hadn't seemed much point.

You all right? I sent for perhaps the dozenth time.

I felt acknowledgement through our link, though Triss didn't say anything—conserving his strength here in the brightest part of the day. As we'd approached and then passed noon, the high spring sun had driven him ever deeper into the shelter of my shadow. I'd known it was going to happen, and that he would ultimately be fine, but that didn't prevent me from worrying about him. We normally arranged things to avoid venturing outside in the parts of the day that were painful for him, but Vyan's scheme demanded it this time, specifically because it was such a bad time for Shades and their companions. If I was having troubles, so would Nuriko and Devin.

While my lance of picked volunteers and I waited for our chance at the king and slowly broiled in our armor, a steady stream of royal engineers and artificers flowed back and forth across the bridge. They were erecting a high platform at one end of the island's temporarily closed and cleared market square. The goal was to give people as far away as the riverbanks a good view of Thauvik and his Jade Council at work, while still keeping them too far away for anything like a reasonable bow shot. In addition to the six lances guarding the bridge, other Crown Guard units and officers of the Elite were scattered all up and down the bank and across the nearer rooftops to keep an eye out for any longer-ranged trouble.

The only people allowed across the bridges to Sanjin

Island beside the engineers and artificers were soldiers of the Crown and nobles of the realm. There weren't half so many of the latter as there had been at the original council meeting. The holidays and ceremonies that had drawn the rural and outlying nobles into the city had long since passed, and many of them couldn't be summoned back to Tien on the single day's notice the king had given for this restaging of the Winter-Round meeting. Among the few who did make it was a young clan chief named Prixia Dan Xaia. The one servant her invitation allowed her was a tiny beautiful young woman no one would ever suspect of being a deadly knife fighter.

Prixia had been much in the city of late, settling affairs related to her late father's holdings. At least, that was the official story given out to explain her presence so far from home while she worked with Heyin and Maylien on plans for the civil war we were all hoping to avert. Neither she nor her servant had so much as looked at me or her half brother when they passed by my lance. She and several other nobles who had gone over to Maylien were there to provide us with a small reserve force on the island in case of an emergency. Another group of Prixia's chosen fighters had doffed their uniforms and positioned themselves among the many onlookers gathering on the southern bank of the river—the palace side.

Shortly after the bells of Shan sounded the hour past noon, the gates of the palace opened and the royal cortege began its march down to the island. My lance and I could see the gates from the bridge, though buildings hid the actual procession for perhaps five hundred yards from there until it turned onto Sanjin Bridge Road. The streets between the palace and the island had been carefully cleared of any traffic, though citizens had been allowed to take up places along the verge after being checked for weapons.

The king's cortege soon made the turn, following behind a column of Crown Guards and flanked by a dozen of the Elite. Watching them come straight down the path the lance and I had taken to reach the bridge, I was glad we had such a hot bright day so early in the season despite the heat and the misery it had inflicted on Triss. Even if Devin and the Kitsune had concealed themselves within the group around the king, they wouldn't have any warning of my presence. The sun would long since have burned away every vestige of my shadow trail.

As the king and his company came closer and closer to my position at the center of the bridge, I tried to guess what was going to go wrong with the plan. Something always did. That was practically the first rule of plans. If I was lucky, it would be something minor. But, just as the column of guards started to pass my lance, the sounds of a disturbance came from somewhere at the back of the column. Vyan's promised distraction was arriving right on time. Heads turned and the whole procession slowed at the exact moment the king passed in front of me.

I slammed my right fist into my breastplate right above my heart; the first half of the royal salute. I felt like I had all the time in the world as I snapped my arm forward, using the second part of the salute to flick the knife free of my wrist sheath. The blade dragged against the straps of my vambrace as expected, but only for an instant. Then it slid neatly into my hand as I continued the motion of my salute. Only, instead of extending my fist at shoulder height, I flipped the knife around and stepped forward, driving the blade in between Thauvik's ribs. I stood on his left, and the knife went in perfectly, punching straight into his heart.

That's when things went wrong. Horribly, horribly wrong. I felt it first through the hilt of my knife. I *knew* the blade had gone home properly, and yet it couldn't have. When you stab someone in the heart with a knife or sword, you can feel it beating through the hilt. It's a subtle thing and brief, easily missed the first couple of times, but after a while you become attuned to it and the feeling is unmistakable. But there was no pulse here, no indication that Thauvik was a living breathing person.

I knew something was wrong, but I didn't realize what it was until the king turned and smiled at me. That's when

I knew that the reason Thauvik didn't feel like a living man was that he wasn't. He was one of the restless dead. Risen, probably. Like his niece Sumey, sustained in a human appearing state by frequently bathing in fresh blood, and, quite, quite immune to my mortal steel.

11

———◆———

How do you kill a dead man? It's a ridiculous question, and yet, it was the only one that mattered in that moment. Unfortunately, the answer was that you couldn't. Not with the resources I had to hand. Though my knife had pierced Thauvik's heart, it had no effect on a corpse that walked.

He leaned toward me then, still smiling and very deliberately drew a breath. "You must be the Kingslayer."

Even as he spoke, the Lord Justicer shouted a bit prematurely, "The usurper is dead, long live Queen Maylien!" That was going to cost him.

Thauvik ignored Vyan, continuing to speak to me. "Nuriko warned me that you'd been sniffing around, but I hadn't expected to get the chance to meet you so soon. It's funny, you don't look at all like the posters."

But I wasn't really listening anymore. I was acting. I took a deep breath, filling my lungs even as the king swept his arm in a gesture that took in my whole lance and said loudly and clearly, "Assassin! Seize him. Seize them all, and the Lord Justicer, too."

With a jerk Thauvik pulled himself free of my knife and stepped back, vanishing behind an onrushing curtain of guards. Xaran leaped in front of me, trying to cover me, but I was already in motion and hating myself for what I was about to do. Without turning, I lunged backward. The coping atop the low stone railing of the bridge hit me in the backs of the thighs and I flipped over, dropping backward into the river—abandoning my men. Failing them just as I had thus far failed Jerik.

As I hit the water and started to sink into the dark and icy depths, I felt Triss jolt back into full awareness. My ceremonial armor took me down fast. Triss and I worked frantically to cut away the straps holding it in place while I twisted around to get my feet underneath me before I hit bottom. The water was deep and fast and I touched down in the muck somewhere under the arch of the bridge. That probably saved my life as a chain of fiery green links lashed through the water above, drawing a sizzling line of bubbles behind it.

Other spells struck around me as well, driving bright spikes of orange and purple deep into the river with explosive results as water flashed into steam. I did my best to ignore it all and kept working on the straps. I couldn't hold my breath for too much longer, despite training that included lowering my heart rate and slowing my breathing to aid in concealment and ambush. Triss and I had barely gotten the breastplate and greaves off when I felt a stirring in the silt surrounding my feet and calves.

Up! I sent as I kicked off, and Triss pushed hard, too, helping me break free of the thick sediment only just in time.

Something huge and heavy smashed into the balls of my feet, striking at an oblique angle and sending me tumbling even as it threw me up and away from the river bottom. My right leg went numb almost to the knee and I lost my sense of up and down when the current caught me again.

Stone dog! sent Triss.

You don't say. I wrenched off my helmet, leaving only

my vambraces and the cuisses that guarded my thighs to
drag me down.

He ignored my sarcasm. *Yes, and there are more of them
churning around in the muck down there. If we fall back to
the river's floor, they'll tear you to pieces.*

*If I don't get to the surface and grab another breath soon,
it won't matter one way or the other.*

Triss tugged at my right ear. *Up.*

I turned that way and started to kick—Triss had sliced
my boots away with the greaves, which helped. *You sure?*

That's where the sun is. Then he flowed out and around
me, briefly covering me in a cool second skin that felt like
iced silk, before pushing farther outward to enshroud me in
shadow.

I could feel the weight of my remaining armor tugging
at me, but it wasn't enough to keep me from breaking the
surface and sucking in a huge lungful of air. I couldn't see
with my own eyes because of the shroud, and borrowing
Triss's sense didn't really help at the moment. The bright
afternoon light rendered him very nearly as blind as I was,
at least above the water. As soon as I'd drawn breath I let
my armor pull me under again, but that wasn't fast enough
to keep us both from catching the edge of another lash of
the green chain—a favorite spell of the Elite.

Triss shrieked into my mind as the spell fire burned a
track through his cloud form. Then he collapsed back into
my shadow, unshrouding me. I swam down and away from
the light that I could now see filtering through from above.
Working with the current, I tried to put a weight of water
between me and the Elite. I don't think it would have protected me for very long. But when the next couple of spell-
bursts struck around me there was a great stirring in the
waters of the river as *something* rose up from the bottom
with a terrible roar that I could feel in my bones. A great
cloud of silt came with it and I had only a brief impression
of a huge and scaly horror before the roiling muck once
again blotted out all sight.

Triss? I mindspoke.

But I got no response and my bond-mate's presence felt quiet and far away. Before I could send so much as another word, something that simultaneously felt as big and solid as a runaway cart and as soft and supple as a sheet of silk caught me. It dragged me through the water first this way and then that until I lost all sense of direction. After perhaps a double score of beats of my racing heart I felt the pressure change around me, as though I had left the main course of the river and entered a much narrower channel. The pulse beating in my temples became a slamming trip-hammer and I clenched my jaws and pinched my nose, trying desperately to control the reflex that would have me breathing in the churning water. If my ordeal didn't end soon . . .

But just when I thought I couldn't bear the pressure any longer and that I would have to draw breath no matter the cost, the waters calmed and light returned. Magelight now instead of sunlight. I stroked toward the light and my head broke the surface a moment later.

Breathe! For several long moments that was all I could do, and damn me if the Elite or some other enemy came. But in time the need passed, and I got a chance to look around. I was treading water in a clear pool like a small reservoir, perhaps twenty feet on a side and ten deep. It was housed in a cavern-like room half again the size. Overhead, the stones of the barrel vault were studded with a dozen green and blue magelights arranged in a shape like a Zhani glyph, though of such an ancient mode that I couldn't read it. More lights clustered around the open end of a passage that entered the big room several feet above the level of the water.

A ladder was carved into the tank's wall on that side and I swam to it now. But, when I reached a hand out to grab the nearest rung, the water pushed me back and something like a slow geyser bubbled up in front of me. It rose into a column and then rose again, twisting and broadening itself to become the bearded face of a venerable river dragon peering down at me with a somewhat troubled expression.

Now what am I going to do with you? it asked in a mildly irritated mind voice that seemed strangely familiar.

Triss? I called, hoping the river dragon wouldn't hear.

Coming, give me a few minutes more. Again, he sounded faint and far away.

You needn't summon him to defend you, sent the river dragon. *I won't harm you. Not if I can find any better solution, anyway.*

"Stop frightening the boy, Shanglun. It's not kind." The voice came from somewhere behind the dragon, and echoed the familiar tones. "You can let them out of the tank now."

This time I recognized the voice. "Harad?" I called.

The old librarian stepped out of the mouth of the passage, nodding as Shanglun slipped to one side. "Yes, and I'm quite put out with you. I do not like to reveal my secrets, and Shang is by far the greatest of those."

Not to mention the prettiest, added the dragon. *And the wisest.*

A couple of strokes took me back to the side of the tank, where I tried to pull myself up out of the water and failed. It was only then that I registered the enormous drain of nima flowing away down the line that connected me to my shadow familiar, a sure sign his injuries were worse than he'd admitted.

"I seem to have a problem," I said, as I made another feeble effort at dragging myself out of the water.

"Shang," said Harad.

The water beneath my feet suddenly solidified then rose, lifting me up so that I stood on a level with the dry floor of the room that held the tank. As I stepped from water to stone, I had a brief impression of the reservoir filled entirely with snaking loops of dragon—green and blue and gold, yet clear at the same time. I started to walk toward Harad, but my knees buckled and I went down in a heap instead.

The librarian hurried over and squatted down beside me. "Your ki is very weak and it's getting weaker by the moment." He snapped his fingers and an intense white light appeared just above his palm. It threw my shadow starkly back and away, into the water that held his dragon familiar. "Shang, the Shade needs strengthening."

The dragon's head collapsed into a rough column of water that splashed back into the tank. A moment later the entire contents went as black as ink, making it impossible to see where my shadow lay. I felt the drain on my nima quickly slow and then fade to nothing. After a few minutes, the flow reversed itself and a fierce cold strength began to pour back through my connection to Triss. Without really thinking about it, I rolled back onto my shoulders and palms and then flipped forward onto my feet.

Harad rose from his crouch, and the water cleared, revealing my shadow running back and down, across the floor of the tank. But only briefly. As I watched, the shadow twisted into an elongated and far more serpentine version of Triss than his usual form. With a flick of his wings he rose out of the water and looped himself around me three or four times in a constrictor's hug.

"I! Feel! Better!" he belled.

Harad closed his fist, putting out the light, and Triss dropped back into his normal dragon shape, stretching himself out on the floor between us.

Then, Triss bowed deeply, first to Harad, then to Shanglun. "Thank you. Thank you, both."

"I begin to see why you thought you might be able to do something for Faran where other healers could not," I said.

Harad smiled. The great dragons were known for their near miraculous ability to cure the worst of diseases and injuries. Many of the healing springs of legend had housed a dragon whose mere presence in the waters served as a remedy for the more common sorts of ailments without any conscious effort on the dragon's part. It explained Harad's age as well. True dragons lived as long as they wished. To have one companion a human was rare indeed, so rare that there were no schools of magery involved. Dragons bonded with mages solely on affinity, unlike the vast majority of familiar pairings. No ritual or training of the sort I had undergone to shape me into a proper companion for a Shade could ever hope to bring such a linkage about. Dragons happened. They did so when and if they wanted to, and that was all there was to it.

"Now," said Harad, "let me get you some tea."

"**Thauvik's** one of the restless dead." I took a sip of my boiled leaves and pretended to like it. "I'm guessing that he's risen."

"Because Maylien's sister Sumey was?" asked Harad.

"That and the way he's holding up. Like Sumey he seems almost entirely human, and, also like Sumey, he's in a position to bathe in buckets of human blood if he needs to. That's the only way I know of for one of the restless dead to keep the appearance of life and to hold on to some of their mind, and I'm only sure that it works for the risen."

Harad snorted. "That's because you don't read enough. There are at least a dozen types of restless dead who can keep or put on the appearance of life by feeding on the ki of the living. The blood bath is merely the crudest and most wasteful way to accomplish that."

"Does that mean you don't believe that Thauvik's one of the risen?" Triss asked from the place he'd sprawled on one of Harad's couches.

"No, not at all. It's certainly the most likely explanation, and the steadily increasing blood madness that goes along with it fits the way Thauvik has ruled well enough." Harad's eyes went briefly far away. "I wonder if it wasn't true of Ashvik as well."

"What do you mean?" I asked.

"Long ago, when you told me about the night you killed Ashvik, you mentioned that there was a big red marble tub in his bedroom. It struck me as a bit odd then, though not enough to comment on it. Later, you mentioned a very similar tub in Sumey's torture room. Until this moment it had never occurred to me to connect the two."

"But Thauvik's heart wasn't beating. That was how I realized something was wrong when I tried to kill him. I stabbed Ashvik in the heart, too, and . . ."

I thought back to that night and tried to remember whether I'd felt it beating through my swords. It was a long time ago, and he was the first man I'd ever killed. *Would* I have noticed? Somehow, I didn't think so.

"I guess he could have been," I said, finally. "But how would that happen? Not one, but two kings of Zhan in a row taken by the curse of the risen, and an heir. It's not like the restless dead are just roaming the halls of the palace."

"Actually," said Triss, "they are. Or, were, anyway. When we killed Ashvik we had to fight off the attack of that risen that came up out of the garderobe."

"That was part of Ashvik's security system," I replied. "It's different. The Elite would never have let the ones in the sewers get close to the king."

"It was in the garderobe. How much closer would it need to get?"

"The only reason it was able to come at us was because I pulled the spill pipe out to make an escape route. It wouldn't have fit otherwise."

"I think you're looking at this the wrong way," said Harad.

"What do you mean?" I asked.

"What if the king didn't get the curse from the risen in his sewers?" he asked. "What if he gave it to them?"

I frowned. "I think I missed a step there."

"Look, Thauvik was no ordinary victim of the risen curse. Neither was Sumey. If that tub in Ashvik's bedroom was what I think it was, then Ashvik wasn't either. They all knew enough about the curse to use blood to control its progression, and they all started doing so early enough in the process that they retained their human appearance and much of their mental faculties. That doesn't sound like an accident. That sounds like a plan."

"You think the royal family of Zhan is deliberately

converting themselves into creatures of the undead?" I asked incredulously. "Now, *that's* crazy."

"They also surrounded themselves with risen in more decayed form as watchdogs," said Harad. "Or, at least, Ashvik and Sumey did. We don't know about Thauvik. They were using the curse to their benefit."

"Well," I asked, "if they were converting the whole family, why not Maylien?"

"Because she's a mage," Triss said suddenly. "The curse wouldn't work on Bontrang. You might be able to give Maylien the curse and let her die only to raise her corpse, but you couldn't bring Bontrang back with her. He would die when she did, but he wouldn't rise again. If you make Maylien into one of the risen, there's no way to hide that you've done so."

Harad stroked his beard thoughtfully. "Hmm. Aral, when you and Maylien killed Sumey, you believed that she was trying to take the throne from Thauvik?"

"Not right then, no, but when Maylien found the adoption papers later, it became pretty clear that was her plan. Why do you ask?"

"I'm not sure. It just feels like the right question, and when you get to be my age you come to trust your feelings on such things. If Thauvik gave the curse to Sumey after getting it from Ashvik, wouldn't he have taken more precautions to prevent her blood madness from being directed his way?"

"I don't know. Maybe that's how Devin and Colonel Deem got involved . . . No, that doesn't make sense either. There's something important we're missing here. I just can't believe anyone would voluntarily submit themselves to the restless dead."

Harad looked unhappy but nodded. "Well, probably not to the risen curse anyway. It's simply too destructive over the longer term. But I still don't think that infecting two kings and a baroness who might be queen happens accidentally."

"But what would anyone get out of driving the rulers of Zhan blood mad?" asked Triss.

"I don't know," said Harad. "But, figure that out, and you will likely find the one responsible." He poured me another cup of tea. "The more important question is what will you do about it? I imagine this changes the calculus of the civil war."

"I don't know. There's no way to kill Thauvik quickly with the weapons we have to hand. That means assassination is probably no longer an option."

"If you had your goddess-given swords, you could do it easily enough," Triss said, raising his head hopefully.

I shot him a hard look. "Even if I were willing to reclaim them, it would take two months' travel time to get to the temple, and another two months back. Do you really want to leave Maylien alone and fighting against a risen king and two rogue Blades for four months?"

Triss's wings sagged. "I hadn't thought of that."

"I could probably shorten the time it would take to get you there," said Harad. "But there's no way around the time it would take you to return."

"It doesn't matter," I said. "I'm not going." I paused as a thought occurred to me. "Harad?"

"Yes, Aral."

"Why are you helping me?"

"What do you mean?"

"I've always known you were a powerful mage, but I've only recently started to realize how powerful. You companion one of the great dragons. You could probably be a Magearch if you wanted to be, at one of the university cities like Ar or Uln. Despite that, you're running a private library in Tien. You rarely venture beyond its walls, yet you keep helping me."

"Oh, that." Harad smiled. "I *was* Magearch of Uln, long ago and under a different name. I won't say which. It got old after half a century or so, as most things do. Even the exercise of power. I do not generally exert myself beyond these walls because I don't find the idea particularly interesting."

"Then why do it for me?"

"I would have thought that it was obvious. You are my friend, young Aral, one of the very few I have who still live. You caught my interest the first time you broke in here. First because of what you were, a Blade breaking into a library. Then, and far more importantly, because of your reasons. You simply wanted to read a book to make the world go away for a while. 'A slight volume,' you said, a whimsy. How could I not love you for that? One of the world's great assassins breaking into my library for the simple pleasure of reading a bit of escapist fluff?"

I blushed.

"Since then, you have never once asked me to do anything more for you than find you the occasional book to borrow or read here."

"That's not true," I said. "I asked you to lend me your balcony for a meeting with the Durkoth last year, and that reading room to speak with Fei just a few weeks ago."

Harad gave me a half-pitying look. "And you think those are greater things than my letting you leave the building with one of my charges without being a member or properly checking it out? Truly?"

"I . . . Wait, are you putting me on?"

"Not really, no, though I'm probably enjoying telling you the truth rather more than I might if it didn't so obviously confuse you. I trained some of your teachers, Aral, as I've told you before. I believed that your order was doing important and necessary work and I grieved at the fall of your temple."

I looked down at my feet. I couldn't bear the weight of sympathy in the old man's eyes.

"I have done both great good and great harm in my life," continued Harad. "I have the capacity for both still within me, but I have chosen to turn away from the use of power, to disengage with the world. I no longer have the drive or the certainty necessary. Because of that, I have made rules for myself that I am loath to violate. That doesn't mean that I don't see the need for the world to change. In you, I see someone who would make the change that I no longer find it wise to attempt. And so, perhaps foolishly, it gives me pleasure to help a friend who still believes he can change things."

"And that's why you sent Shanglun to rescue us today?" asked Triss.

"No. I did no such thing. Your battle happened beyond the bounds I have set for myself. What Shang did, he did of his own free choice and with no prompting from me."

"But until now, we've never even seen him before," I said. "Why would he do that?"

"You *have* seen him before, though you may not have known it at the time. About a year ago, in the bay, when you were with the Dyad. He helped you then, rousing Tien Lun, just as he helped you today, and for much the same reasons. Shang has seen *you* many times. Through my eyes. If you look deeply enough into them, you will see him looking back. He is one of the great dragons, and I am his bondmate. I am never without him and he knows that I care about you. Go ahead, look."

I leaned forward and looked into Harad's eyes. For a long time there was nothing. Then, something shifted. In his irises I saw the same twisting coils I had seen in the pool. Blue and green and gold all looped around the black pupil where a dragon's face appeared for an instant, smiled at me, then vanished into the depths. I leaned back in my chair and reached for my tea again only to find the cup empty.

"I can make more," said Harad.

"No, I'll take that as a sign. Today's been a disaster all around, and one that might well have cost me my life without your . . . without Shanglun's intervention. I have to see Maylien. Prixia and the others will tell her what they saw, but I can't be sure they saw enough. She needs to know that her uncle carries the same curse her sister did, and how much harder that's going to make the job."

I rose to my feet and bowed to Harad as I would have to one of my masters at the temple, making sure to look deep into his eyes as I did so. "Thank you, Harad. And thank you,

Shanglun. I owe you both for what you have done for me and for Triss."

You are welcome, Shanglun said into my mind, *though I think you would have saved yourself had I not saved you. The cost would have been greater, but I do not think that you would have failed to pay it.*

Triss slipped off the couch and bowed as well, then fell back into my shadow and my shape as I turned to the door.

12

———◆———

There is a weight to emptiness, a weight I felt pressing on me as soon as I entered the passage to Maylien's sewer hideaway. Long before I reached the far end and opened the hidden hatch I knew I would find the chambers abandoned. Darkness filled the tunnels, and silence, and a sort of loneliness that can only be found where people once were and now are no longer.

My first concern was that they had been discovered, that one of the members of the lance I had led and left behind had been tortured into revealing this location before Maylien and her people had time to scatter. As soon as I conjured up a temporary light, I knew that wasn't the case. The old sewer showed signs of hasty departure, but no evidence of a fight. If any of my lance had been taken alive, they hadn't yet cracked. But it was likely only a matter of time. That was why I had come up from the active sewers below, entering by way of a rabbit run I hadn't revealed to anyone but Maylien.

Knowing that the forces of the Crown might arrive at any moment, I moved quickly, heading straight to Maylien's quarters to see if she had left me a message. It was low on the back wall, scratched crudely into the muck to make it look like graffiti. Three lines.

"Under the willow. We set aside many cares. An island in time."

That was all it said, but that was enough for me. On the night before Maylien challenged her sister, Sumey, we had shared a brief hour of peace and passion under a willow tree on a small island in the Earl of Anaryun's private garden. That was where she wanted me to look for the next message, but it would have to wait till full dark even though the earl was one of Maylien's secret supporters. I destroyed all trace of the message she'd left me, and then headed back into the sewers.

I slipped off my boots and rolled up my pants before stepping into the cool dark water. A carefully planted band of lily pads concealed a shallow path that allowed the earl's gardeners to tend the island without having to use his personal boat. I moved slowly and carefully, but couldn't avoid a bit of splashing.

"Aral?" Maylien's voice came from beneath the low hanging curtain of willow leaves.

"You shouldn't be here." I ducked to enter the hidden bower, using Triss's senses to get a read on what lay within as I did so.

"It's you, all right." Maylien was seated cross-legged on a thin blanket with Bontrang perched on a small basket beside her. "Neither Heyin nor Prixia know about this place, and only one of the three of you would start a conversation with Zhan's future queen by telling her what she should or shouldn't be doing."

The gryphinx cooed at me as I collapsed my shroud and sat down, putting his head forward for a skritch under the beak. The moon was nearly full, providing just enough light for my dark-adjusted eyes to register big details. The oval of Maylien's face, the faint glint of her eyes as she shifted her gaze, the pale outline of the blanket. The spring smells of jasmine and osmanthus sweetened the air.

"You know what happened at the palace?" I said as I indulged Bontrang with more skritches.

"I know what Prixia saw, and I can extrapolate from there to figure out some of the things that didn't make sense to her. My uncle is no more among the living than my sister was, is he?"

"How did you guess?"

"Prixia told me that she saw the knife in your hand, and saw you strike, but that Thauvik didn't fall. She thought maybe he'd twisted aside at the last moment or something. I knew better. I know you. You don't miss. But Prixia has never seen a member of my family take a blade to the heart and keep right on going, whereas I've delivered just such a blow."

"I'm sorry," I said. "I wanted to end this without a war. Now, there's no way. Even if I could get in close again, I can't kill Thauvik quickly. And if I can't kill him quick, the chances are good I won't be able to kill him at all. That's got to be why the Kitsune hasn't been coming after you or your people. He's keeping her close so that she can defend him. Now that Devin's arrived, the balance has changed again, and for the worse. You need to get out of the city and raise an army so you can defeat him in the field and then execute him."

"You killed Sumey. . . ."

"I used Devin's goddess-made blade and I gave it back afterward as I promised."

"But he's here, now," said Maylien. "Couldn't you steal one of them from him?"

I snorted. "Not without killing him first, and I'm not even sure that would work. There was a . . . I don't know, a special kind of magic involved." I thought back to the moment when I had slain Sumey, and the feeling that, if only for an instant, my goddess had been with me again. My throat tightened. "He gave me the sword of his own free will. I don't think it would work if I had to take it from him by force." Justice didn't steal.

"Maybe Triss could throw him into the everdark, like he did that chunk of wall when you rescued me."

Triss slipped out of my shadow and into dragon form, an action more felt than seen. "Possibly, if he didn't move away fast enough, but I doubt it. It takes time and effort to push things into the everdark, and they resist. Smaller things are easier than big things. Soft things are easier than hard things. Things without magic are much easier than magical things. The restless dead carry a powerful curse, and Thauvik's blood baths make it stronger by far. It would take a very long time for me to force him out of our world, if I could manage it at all."

"So much for the easy solutions," said Maylien. "That basically leaves fire, acid, and heavy-duty spellwork, all of which require time and some way to prevent my uncle from getting away."

"War and execution," I said. "Which means you need to get on the road, and I need to figure out what I'm going to do next."

"Not quite yet. Move over, Bontrang." She gave the gryphinx an affectionate shove and he hopped down from the basket with a grumpy *mrp*. She opened it to expose a dim red magelight, shining on several covered dishes and a small bottle. A faint aroma of ginger and garlic wafted out. "I brought us dinner."

I raised an eyebrow, then realized she wouldn't be able to see it. "I'm not sure now is such a great time for a picnic, Maylien." Though it smelled wonderful.

"You're half right," she said low and wicked, and her teeth flashed in a sudden smile. "Because I have something else in mind first, but we *are* going to have a picnic after."

I licked my lips as I tried to figure out what to say to such a mad proposition. "Your uncle's forces are looking for both of us. You know that."

"Yes, and they may well kill one of us before we get the

chance to see each other again. Even if they don't and we win, I will be a queen, and things won't be the same between us. The last time we were here, things were rushed and muddy and we didn't know if we'd ever get the chance to be together again. It was also wonderful. Once more, we don't know if we'll ever have the chance again, but I thought this time we could make up for the rushed and muddy part." She reached into the basket and pulled out the little bottle and I tensed as I fought down a bitter craving for something harder than wine.

"I can't drink with you." Not if I wanted to stop, anyway. "And, you should put out the light." It wasn't bright enough to be seen from more than a few yards away, but even that went against deeply ingrained habits, making me nervous.

"Hush," she said. "It's only cold tea. I know you don't really like the stuff, not even fresh and hot, but it's what I could manage under the circumstances and given . . ." she trailed off, obviously realizing that what she'd been about to say was impolitic.

"Given my drinking problem, it's an excellent idea. Thank you, that was thoughtful."

"You're welcome. I'm glad you didn't take this the wrong way"—she poured the tea into a couple of wine cups and handed one to me—"because I really wanted to drink a toast with you before everything changes." She raised the cup, and recited the verses she'd left for me on the wall. "Under the willow. We set aside many cares. An island in time."

"An island in time," I repeated, and we drank.

Later, when we had recovered our composure and our clothes and I had told her what I needed to, she poured more tea while I unpacked the basket. There were small plates for each of us and I served up the cold noodle salad and other dishes. It was an excellent meal, and the company was of the finest. We were almost finished when Triss flickered into dragon shape. He had disappeared back into my shadow to give us a greater illusion of privacy.

"There's something wrong with the shadows on the garden wall where we came in," said Triss.

"What do you mean?" I asked.

"I've been watching a pale patch among the potsherds—when we came over I broke a bit off this side of one piece to create a fresh surface that I could watch. It just vanished and then reappeared."

Like most serious walls in Tien, the Earl of Anaryun's was topped with iron nails and jagged-edged bits of broken pottery, in this case fine porcelain. The better to show off the earl's wealth and good taste, I guess.

"Devin?" I rose into a crouch, reaching for my sword rig.

"Perhaps. I can't tell from here. Could be the Kitsune, or even a common thatchcutter who just happens to be coming in exactly along our backtrail."

I glanced at Maylien as I settled my swords into place and whispered, "You need to get out of here, and not by the path I came in on. Now. Swim if you have to."

"I borrowed the earl's boat. It's on the far side of the island. I left some of my guard by the house. Should I send them to help you?"

"There's only been a single occlusion so far," said Triss.

I added, "If it's Devin, we can handle it. If it's the Kitsune, I'd rather not get anyone else killed. Wait for the sounds of a fight to cover you before you push off. Go."

She didn't argue, just touched a kiss to my cheek, scooped up Bontrang and slipped out the far side of our little willow tent. That practicality was one of the things I loved about Maylien. As Triss enfolded me in a shroud of darkness I slid out from beneath the willow and walked down to the edge of the water to wait.

Whoever it was would have to come at me through the lake and they'd have to do it slow if they didn't know where the trail was. That or slip off into deep water. Either way, I would have a distinct advantage if I attacked them in the last five feet while they dealt with unknown and slippery footing.

Any chance our shadow trail could be followed across the water? I sent. *It's awfully still. . . .*

No, not accurately. Not this long after we crossed. If

whoever it is, is foolish enough to try, they'll end up in deep water.

Good. I wasn't sure.

Normally the natural movement of the water would quickly erase any remnants of such a trail, but the earl's artificial lake looked more like a mirror than living water at the moment, a fact that registered in Triss's unvision even more sharply than it would have to my eyes. I popped the catches that held the hilts of my swords tight behind my hips and slid the blades free of the sheaths strapped to my back, though I still held them up and back, to either side of my spine.

Minutes dripped past with no more signs of any trailing presence, far longer than I would have expected for someone to take simply to get from wall to water. I practiced stillness, breathing quietly and evenly, schooling my heart to beat in slow time as I had been taught. Patience is one of the assassin's most important skills, and I had spent many frustrating hours as a child mastering the discipline. Flesh, like stone.

Finally, long after it should have come, I saw the water ripple at the far bank. One foot entering the water. A second. Something was moving toward me. Ripple and ripple again. Slow. Quiet. Patient. Then, the faintest of splashes. A long pause. The water returning to stillness. I continued to stand and wait.

"Aral, I know you're there." It was Devin's voice, worried, angry. As he should be. If he was alone, he had to know I had the advantage here. He continued. "I circled the lake and your trail doesn't come out anywhere. I want to talk to you."

It's a trick, Triss mindspoke. *He's trying to get us to give away our position.*

"Aral, dammit, don't make this harder than it has to be."

Breathe in. Breathe out. Be a pillar of rock standing on the shore. Devin would have to come to me on my terms or turn back. Either way, I was winning.

A ripple. Another. A bigger splash as he strayed too far to one side.

"I'm going to kill you some day, Aral. For this, if for no other reason. But not right now. Right now I need you to talk to me."

He was close and getting closer. Another dozen steps and I would be able to reach him with a leap. Two more after that and it would be a lunge. Soon . . .

"Aral . . ." The voice was close now.

Another foot. The water rippled and I flipped my swords around in the same moment that I lunged, action without thought. I *was* motion and it felt better than anything else could ever hope to.

My left-hand sword swept low, aiming for a point just above the ripples, my right punched forward at chest height. Steel met wood at knee height, jarring to a halt. Clever Devin, advancing a staff instead of his leg. I adjusted my thrusting blade, moving my point left and extending my lunge. Devin had always favored his right slightly. I didn't think he'd give up the advantage of having a drawn sword in that hand, which put his body farther back and more to my left. I was at the very end of my safe extension when I felt my steel touch flesh and sink in—perhaps a half inch.

I wanted to lean forward and press the point, sink it deep, use the anchor of my blade in Devin's chest to catch my balance and finish this quickly. But that was my emotions speaking—anger and the desire for revenge. I needed to listen to my body, my reflexes and training, and my body called a halt, knowing where balance ended. My body was right, as Devin leaped back in the same instant that I struck him, pulling free of my sword with a muffled curse and leaving his staff behind. Had I followed my desire I'd have ended up fully in the water, overextended and off balance.

I was better than Devin, or I had been once, but he was still one of the top thousand or so swordsmen in the world, and he was prepared for my attack, weight back, staff forward, hoping to draw me to him. I could feel it through my sword in our brief connection and see Zass's positioning through Triss's unvision when the two clouds of shadow momentarily intersected each other. Devin landed with a heavy splash, drawing a target in the surface of the water with himself at its center. Somewhere behind me I thought I heard another, fainter splash come in almost the same instant, like an echo. Maylien's boat, I hoped.

"Not bad, Aral," said Devin. "Not bad at all. You plinked me there." He was hiding it, but I could hear pain in his voice. Pain and anger. "Why don't you come see if you can do it again?"

Instead, I withdrew my forward foot from the water and settled back into a waiting stance. This time, with Devin so close, I kept my swords in front of me at high and low guard. Devin would come in fast next time and he would do it soon. He would have no choice. The wound I'd given him wasn't a bad one, and Zass would keep it from bleeding too much at the cost of reducing Devin's shroud. But every second it went untreated was another second the injury ate away a bit of his reserves.

"Come on, Aral, or are you afraid of me now?" The anger came through more strongly this time. He'd expected me to follow him into the water and he didn't like that I hadn't. "I've had time to study what you've been up to the last few years. Drunk. That's what I hear you've become. A fucking sponge for alcohol and not a lot more. What would the priests say to that, do you think? They didn't think much of gutter drunks back in the day."

Don't listen to him.

It's all right, Triss. I know what I am, and I know what the priests would think. I'm not proud of it, but I'm not going to let Devin bait me the way he could when we were ten either. He's desperate, or he wouldn't be trying so transparent a ploy. I wonder why *he's desperate, though. I didn't hurt him that bad. There's an external pressure here that we don't know about.*

"Dammit!" Devin swore. "I told myself I wasn't going to let myself get drawn in like this, but there's something about you that just makes me so mad I can't think. I really do just want to talk. Here." Devin's shroud collapsed, leaving him unmasked in the ford. "Can we please talk?"

He wore watermarked silk, rough and light absorbing, much of a kind with the fabric of my own outfit and cut to the same ancient pattern. But, where the Blade I had seen in the mirror of late held only the straight double-edged dueling swords of Zhan, Devin carried the shorter, heavier swords of Namara, with their slight curve and single edge. The swords of Justice with the unblinking eye on the guards.

I expected rage when I saw that—this traitor to the memory of our goddess still equipped as her champion. What I felt instead was a terrible sense of loss. This was the image of what I was supposed to be, what we were all supposed to be. Zass was with him, a shadow like a giant otter or fisher wrapped around his chest and shoulders—keeping his wound sealed, no doubt.

What's his game? I sent.

I don't know. Maybe he really does want to talk.

Screw that. I don't want to talk to him, and nothing can make me.

We do need to make some noise soon though. That and rough up the water's surface, or he's going to know about Maylien. The ripples from her boat will be coming around the island soon.

Thanks for the reminder. That does change things. Let me think . . . got it. I need control for a moment.

Done.

Triss's conscious presence vanished as he put himself into the sleep state that allowed me to assume control of his actions, a necessary precondition for any more significant work of magic. Reaching out through Triss's connection to shadow, I touched a thousand darker patches on the surface of the water, reflections of the trees in the garden, of the island itself, anything that drank light. Then, I pushed. It was like tossing several buckets of gravel into the lake all at once, creating countless splashes and ripples that met and clashed and combined to churn the surface of the water into a muddled mess.

"Shit!" snapped Devin.

Shadow frothed up around him hiding him from sight.

Clever. He was using my own distraction to cover his movements. I released Triss as I tried to spot any more purposeful set of ripples. But my own trick had worked too well and the surface of the lake told me nothing.

I'm not sure that's the best idea you've ever had, Triss sent as he returned to full awareness.

Point, but it gave Maylien the cover she needed to get clear.

There is that.

Any idea where Devin is now?

Nope, but I'd guess he's here on the island with us.

Yeah, me, too. Dammit. Do you think he's really just here to talk?

I think we're about to find out.

One of the great ironies of Shade unvision is that in the mix of light and dark that is our world at all but its darkest, they find it very hard to pick each other out from among the more mundane sorts of shadows. Whereas in the absolute blackness of the everdark they can easily spy one another. Like me, Triss was reduced to choosing random points of brightness in our surroundings and watching for momentary occlusions as we tried to spy Zass and Devin. That and listening. I tried to cultivate the patience of stone once again. It was harder this time, knowing that Devin had made it onto the island with me. Then I saw it, a pale spot winking out momentarily off to my left, low and fast.

As I twisted that way, Triss shouted into my mind, *Down!*

I threw myself at the ground, hitting the turf with forearm and then elbow as I shaped my right arm into an arc and rolled forward. Through Triss's senses I felt the two Shades overlap above and behind me, as Devin's sword passed through the place where my head and shoulders had been a half beat before. Then the contact was broken as I rolled across a loose pile of silk—Devin's hood thrown to distract. *Nicely done, Devin,* I thought, *nicely done.*

I came to my feet facing back the way I'd come, with both swords extended in front of me. Without really willing it, I found myself taking a series of sliding steps to my right and back.

What are you doing? asked Triss.

Getting out of my own way. When he came onto the island I let the way I feel about Devin and his betrayal push me back into the place where thought interferes with action. I let the vessel of my soul fill with anger and worry when what I needed most was to empty it. Do instead of be. That was a mistake. I won't make it again.

Before Triss could answer me back, I felt the intersection of shadow with shadow—Zass and Devin exactly where my unthinking mind told me they had to be. I pressed in close before they could break contact. With the two Shades overlapping like this, Devin and I were inside the sphere of each other's familiar's senses, as visible as if it were bright day and we were unshrouded. There would be no more playing tag in the dark. In response, both Shades shifted shape, flowing back down into their own chosen forms and leaping at each other. Dragon and tayra faced each other on the ground beneath us, their clawed blows echoing the cut and counter cut of Devin's blades and my own.

At first the contest seemed equal, with Devin giving as good as he got. But things shifted quickly. After the exchange of some dozens of cuts and parries, thrusts and dodges, I found Devin's current measure, and it wasn't up to my standard. Oh, he was better than he had been when we were younger and I was worse, but the gap hadn't narrowed enough to make the contest even.

Beat, parry, lunge, feint. Slice, counter, cartwheel, and cut. Back and forth. I took control of the fight. With it, I forced an opening in his left guard—not a big one, but enough—and drew the point of my blade across the top of his thigh. It was a shallow slice, more an injury of pride than flesh, but it made Devin leap back away from me and swear bitterly.

"Fuck you, Aral, I came to talk not fight! We don't have to do this!"

"Actually, I think we do. If you really wanted to speak with me, you wouldn't have chosen to throw down your hood and try to cut my head off."

"That was wrong. I admit it. But you drive me half out of my damned mind unless I'm actively working to control myself. It started the day you killed Ashvik and it only gets worse as the years go by. Do you know what it was like living in your fucking shadow, yours and, later, Siri's?" He shook his head. "No, of course you don't. You're the great, goddess-blessed Aral Kingslayer, and nothing has ever come hard for you."

He lunged at me then, the best and smoothest attack he'd made since the beginning of the fight—low and fast and totally unexpected. It would have scored on Aral the drunk, back in the days before I'd relearned what it was to be the motion instead of making it. Now, my left-hand blade came down and around, catching the thrust and twisting it aside without my consciously willing it. I *was* my swords again. Bringing my right-side blade across in a backhand response that opened a long shallow cut on Devin's chest was as natural as breathing.

"You can't beat me, Devin, no more than you could when we were boys. If you really want to talk, throw down your swords and we'll see if I let you live."

Something snapped in him then, I could see it in his eyes and the set of his jaw. He didn't say anything else, just started to bore in again. I was still in control, but he pressed me harder now, attacking and attacking and attacking again, forcing me back with hammer blow after hammer blow, though he couldn't penetrate my guard. It was insane and there was no way he could sustain such an attack for long.

At least, that's what I thought right up until he willingly took a nasty cut across the shoulder to get one of my blades in a position where he could catch it between both of his own and shatter it. I had forgotten in my arrogance that where I was fighting with mortal steel, Devin held the swords of the goddess, and suddenly I was fighting one blade against two. Then, a moment later, I had to choose between losing a hand and the shattering of my second sword and I was disarmed.

The reversal of fortune happened so fast that I hadn't any time to prepare for it. One minute I was winning, had won really. The next I was a corpse waiting only for the fatal blow. I threw my hilts down beside my feet then and stood straight to take the coming blow. If I was going to die at Devin's hand, I was going to meet my fate with unblinking eye and back unbowed.

And I *was* going to die. There was no way out for me here, not unarmed against a swordsman of Devin's stature and, we, all four of us, knew it.

Devin paused, too, drawing his swords back into the perfect position for a scissors cut that would leave me in want of my head.

"Go ahead then," I said. "But when you remember this moment, remember that you didn't defeat me. Your Namara-granted steel beat my mortal swords."

Devin's face twisted bitterly. "Gods above, but I'm going to enjoy this."

Good-bye, Triss, we had a good run.

We did. I love you, Aral.

13

———◆———

There is a peace to knowing you're about to die, a peace I never would have expected to find there. It is the peace of surrender, of knowing that you will never again have to fight for anything. No struggle, no pain, no nothing.

I took a deep breath rich with jasmine and osmanthus and surrendered myself to that peace. Peace all too brief. I waited for the blow to come, for Devin to relieve me of the weight of suffering I had borne since the day the temple fell. My only regret was that Triss must die with me.

I waited . . . and waited, and waited some more. The blow didn't come. Devin just stood there, swords in hand, glaring at me, poised to strike, but unstriking.

Until, finally, he threw his swords down at my feet. "I hate you so much, Aral, I can't even express it. Unfortunately, I need you, too. At least for a little while."

Relief mixed with a strange sort of disappointment in my heart. Triss would live, but so must I. "You really did come to talk then? That wasn't another lie."

Devin shook his head. "I know you don't have any reason

to trust what I say, but somehow, even now, I had hoped that you would."

He turned away, leaving his swords at my feet and his back to me. I could have killed him then, easily. He had to know that. I'm not entirely sure why I didn't. Maybe because despite everything that had happened between us, he was still the best friend of my childhood and somewhere in my heart he always would be.

I sighed. "Well then, say what you came to say and get out of my life. Oh, and pick up your damned swords and put them away. I'm not going to put you out of your misery, and you shame the memory of the goddess by leaving them in the dirt like that."

Devin's back tensed like he'd been struck, but then he took a deep breath and visibly relaxed his muscles. "I need your help."

"You *what*? What possible reason could I have for helping you, Devin? You've betrayed everything that ever mattered to me. I wouldn't cross the street to spit on you, if you were on fire and that was the one thing you needed to save your fucking miserable excuse for a life."

Devin turned then and put a toe under his nearest sword, flipping it up into his hand, where he flicked the dirt off before sheathing it over his shoulder. He repeated the performance with the other sword, so that the hilts stuck up on either side of his head. Then he crossed his arms and glared at me. All without saying a word.

Zass slid forward then. "Triss, Aral, I won't make excuses for what happened when the temple fell. All I can say is that you weren't there. Nor will I excuse or defend our behavior the last time we met. Devin has done what he thought was right."

I hissed involuntarily.

"But that doesn't matter," continued Zass. "Not to what we have to say to you now. Please hear this out. That's all I ask."

I wanted to walk away then, but I couldn't help

remembering Zass breaking Devin's bowstring in a moment when I might have otherwise died. I might not owe Devin shit, but Zass was another thing entirely. It was not easy for a familiar to go against their bond-mate's will, but he had done so for me.

I nodded. "All right. Spill. Start with why I should care about helping you."

"It might save the life of your little queen in waiting," said Devin.

That got my attention. "Go on."

"It's the Kitsune. She's quite, quite mad."

"Tell me something I don't know. I had a little encounter with her recently and it ended very disturbingly."

"In Ashvik's tomb," replied Devin. "I know. She told me she'd put you to bed with the last king since you seemed to get such pleasure out of sleeping with the next queen and she'd heard that you go both ways." Devin looked at his feet. "I wanted to go pull you out, but she told me she'd kill me if I did."

"She's good enough to make the threat stick?" asked Triss.

Devin nodded. "More than good enough, and I've no doubt she meant it, either. She hates me. Actually, she hates pretty much everybody but Kelos—damn him for abandoning us—and he's not . . ." Devin trailed off, and suddenly looked very much younger and more vulnerable than he had at any time since our earliest days together. "Look, this is going to be a long story. Can we agree to stop with all the glaring and hating for a little while and just have a cup of efik somewhere like the old days?"

"No. I don't think we can." It hurt me more than I would have expected to say that, and not only because of the thought of efik—so sharp and strong that I had to suppress a shiver from wanting it. I understood and even shared some of what I thought Devin must be feeling right now—the whipsaw of emotions jerking back and forth between love and hate—but I couldn't let him back inside my guard. "You've made choices that closed that door forever. I'll sit with you and listen to what you have to say, but I will not drink or break bread with you. Not now. Not ever again."

He smiled a bitter ironic smile at that. "Allies if I can convince you, but never friends?"

"Pretty much."

"Good to know where we stand," he said.

"Not good," I corrected, "but there's no other way."

Devin took a deep breath and then another, reasserting discipline in the way we had both been taught. Emotion left his face, replaced with the stillness of the professional killer.

"Let's start this again," said Devin. "I came to you because I need help with Nuriko Shadowfox. If you don't help me, she's going to use Thauvik to kill an awful lot of people, and your royal lover is right at the top of the list."

Before I could say something angry, he held up a hand. "I know you have no reason to take me at my word for that, which means I'm going to have to tell you enough of the story to convince you. That's going to take a while and, given the noise of our recent clash, I don't think this is the place for that. Will you take me somewhere of your choice and hear me out? It should probably be someplace close. I've bought myself a fair piece of time, but the Kitsune *will* start to wonder where I've gone at some point."

He was right about the noise we'd made, and already I could hear the approach of people from the great house. Either the earl's guard checking on the noises in his garden, or Maylien's sent against my express request. I nodded. "Follow me."

Triss, shroud me up.

Done.

Do you believe a word he says?

We'll see. Triss gave a mental shrug. *The Kitsune is crazy. Maybe the rest follows from that. If nothing else, I want to hear more about the Kitsune and Kelos. That's information that we may not be able to get anywhere else.*

The Earl of Anaryun's estate stood on the Kanathean Hill, not far from Marchon House, and right off the royal preserve with its hidden Elite chapter house. Not a great neighborhood for any Blade to have a quiet conversation, not with the stone dogs swimming about under the turf. So I laid a shadow trail for Devin to follow that led east into the still-busy construction zone where they were rebuilding the Old Mews neighborhood out of the ashes of the previous one, another legacy of our last encounter. There, I found us a partially completed tenement, and headed up into the skeleton of the upper floors. In a room with a half-laid floor and two walls I dropped my shroud and waited for Devin to catch up. He was less than a minute behind me.

Devin dropped his shroud as well. "Good spot. High up, plenty of room to sail-jump and glide away in any direction if we're surprised. The only real downside is that we run the risk of being silhouetted against the night sky in a couple of places. I approve." He stripped off his sword rig and threw himself flat on his back on the boards to stare up into the stars—a pose I remembered from a thousand nights spent talking the moon down. "Sit," he said, "it's a long story, even if we haven't enough time for me to tell you all of it."

I tucked myself into the corner where the two walls met, while Triss slid over to one of the open sides where he could keep a lookout. Zass joined him there and they began to converse quietly in the way of shadows, a sort of barely audible susurration, like gentle waves hissing across the sand of a distant beach. Again, I was reminded of so many similar moments in my boyhood, though the smells were different here, with fresh cut wood and the sharp notes of drying stucco taking the place of the incense and garden smells of Namara's temple grounds.

"How about you just skip to the point?" I suggested when Devin didn't start right away. I didn't want to spend one instant longer with him than I had to.

"I can't, not without some setup, not if I want you to really believe me."

"Fine. Talk. I'll listen."

"You know the tale of how Nuriko joined our order and became the Shadowfox, so let me skip forward to the night she had her falling out with the goddess, since that's where the story we learned as boys grows sketchy. I don't know all the true details now, but I've heard Kelos and Nuriko talk about it enough to get a feeling for what happened. It seems that after killing her third or fourth in a series of kings and khans in a few short months, Nuriko decided the entire idea of government was corrupt."

"I heard something similar from Kelos not all that long ago," I said.

"Did you?" Devin turned his head my way. "I hadn't heard that he'd talked to you."

"It would have been shortly before he departed Heaven's Reach for points far away. I doubt he told anyone about it."

"So, you had something to do with that, too? Why does that not surprise me?" Devin frowned, then rubbed his forehead as though it pained him. "No. Never mind. It really doesn't matter right now.

"What matters is the Kitsune. She went to Namara and outlined her ideas about the inherent corruption of any kind of government. It sounds like she also demanded that she and her fellow Blades be given orders to kill every official and noble in the eleven kingdoms and beyond from the lowliest village headman right up to the Sylvani empress on her emerald throne. When Namara failed to agree to the Kitsune's scheme, she resigned, rather spectacularly, as you well know. You've heard what happened after that."

I nodded. "She vanished for a while, then took up a career as a paid assassin. Warfare with our order followed, and she won every contest up until the one where Kelos is supposed to have killed her. That's where things get murky."

"Tell me about it," Devin agreed. "I never got a straight answer from either one of them about what happened that night. I do know that Kelos really did bring her sword back to the temple, and that they didn't speak again for more than twenty years afterward. But apparently, something she'd said that night got under his skin and he couldn't shake free of it. Because, every so often, in the last few years he'd go off on the inherent corruption of government thing himself, along with Nuriko, and it was clear they'd been having the argument for a very long time. She insisted that the whole idea of one person being set above their fellows is, in and of itself, immoral, while he argued that it wasn't the idea of government that had to go, but government as we know it."

"Didn't you find it the least bit odd that they were working for the Son of Heaven with that kind of attitude?" I asked. I knew from my own conversations with Kelos what his plans had been on that front, or, at least, what he'd claimed they were, but I wanted to know what Devin thought about it.

"Not really. I figured it was all hot air and rage over being enslaved by the Son, a way to pretend that something could be done about the chains that bind us to him. The only thing they ever agreed on was that the current system needed to burn to the ground. But they weren't the only ones who had plans about what they were going to do once they shook off the Son's control. That whole order of the assassin mage thing I asked you to join the last time we met, is mine. It does exist, but for now it's more idea than action. None of us are planning to serve the Son forever, and we're all working on what to do after he's gone."

Triss raised his head from where he'd been quietly whispering with Zass. "What *does* bind you to the Son?"

Devin grimaced. "The nastiest magical oath you've ever heard."

"There's always a way around those," I said. Witness Devin's betrayal of Namara.

"Not this one, at least not while the current Son is alive. It's much more than your usual magical binding. It draws on the authority of Shan as Emperor of Heaven, and the Son as his mortal representative. It's as much a thing of divine power as it is of magic." He reached over and touched the hilt of one of his swords. "Like these. You can't see the magic, but you can feel it in your bones whenever you even consider breaking it."

I looked at the swords and thought about that. They carried the most powerful enchantments I'd ever known, and yet they were invisible to magesight, showing no hint of spell-light for the simple reason that Namara had willed it so. Divine magic broke all the rules. The gods knew no limits, a fact that I was increasingly coming to believe was a major flaw in the system. Look at the way they had murdered Justice.

"All right," I said, pushing that thought aside. "I guess I can see why a divine oath might play out differently. But how did the Kitsune get drawn in? She wasn't at the temple when the Son's forces attacked. That's for damned sure."

"Oh, but she was, just not on the side of Namara. She was the first Blade to take service with the Son. How he got her to do it, I've no idea. You can't threaten her. She'd have to care about her life a whole lot more than she does to make that work. But I'm getting off course here. You know enough of the backstory now for me to jump forward a bit, to my appointment as Heaven's Shade this winter."

"Son of a bitch!" It was probably a good thing I didn't have any swords just then, or I might have ended up cutting our conversation short, and there were still things to learn, whether I decided to help Devin or not.

Devin winced. "I take it you know what that means, then."

I nodded. "Yeah. You're in charge of all of the Blades who went over to the Son and formed the Shadow of Heaven." I looked to see if Devin was wearing a ring of office as the head of the Hand of Heaven did, but couldn't see one in the dark. "He must have been pretty desperate if he replaced Kelos with you."

Devin laughed at that, a surprisingly genuine sound, if bitter. "You might have a point there, though not the one you think you do. Nuriko joined the Son's forces before the fall of the temple, though not *long* before, if I'm reading my tea leaves right. For a while at least, she *was* the Shadow of Heaven. When the rest of us came on board, she wasn't thrilled that the Son handed the reins over to Kelos, but she seemed willing to let it pass. Mostly, I think, because their agendas were in alignment and she had a lot more than casual influence over Kelos."

"Are you implying what I think you're implying?" I asked.

"Yeah, they were lovers, had been for the better part of a century if I'm not reading the cues all wrong. But it was a weird sort of love, if you could even call it that, more like an extension of their never-ending arguing and dueling displaced into another realm."

"Dueling?" I raised an eyebrow.

"Well, not really, but it was a hell of a lot more serious than any sparring I've ever seen. They drew blood all the time, and I never saw either of them pull a blow. If they hadn't been so evenly matched, I'm pretty sure one of them would have killed the other."

"But, you digress," I said.

"Only because you asked. The point I was aiming for was that when Kelos pulled his rabbit run, Nuriko expected to be named to replace him. She had a good case, too. She was the senior Blade by far, and the best of us in a fight. But after whatever happened with Kelos, the Son really didn't trust her. He wanted someone more . . . biddable."

And Devin didn't like it one bit that the Son felt he fit the bill, if I was any judge of a onetime old friend's tones. Good.

Devin rolled his head to look at me. "You didn't take the opportunity to twist the knife there. Are you going soft on me in your old age or something?"

I couldn't help but grin. "Nope. You seemed to be doing such a good job of cutting yourself up on your own that I didn't want to get in the way. Carry on."

"Thanks. The Kitsune was not happy at being passed over. Especially not for 'Kelos's puppy,' as she called me."

"That had to hurt." Again, good.

Devin shrugged. "Less than you might think. After all, I spent my entire Blade career as the Kingslayer's shadow. I'm used to the shit that comes with being seen as the lesser. Nuriko, however, was not, and she threw a fit about my being named Heaven's Shade. The Son actually seemed a little bit frightened of her. I'm not sure whether that's because she maybe didn't take the same oath the rest of us did, or the fact that she's deeply crazy, or what. Whatever the reason, the Son decided he needed to get her out of Heaven's Reach and far away from him. So he sent her here to play nanny to Thauvik."

I had a sudden realization. "This has something to do with Thauvik being one of the risen, doesn't it? It's the Son that arranged for him to fall to the curse, and Ashvik and Sumey, too, isn't it?"

"Yes. The Son has great power over the risen. Well, some of them anyway. I don't know why or how, maybe it comes from Shan. He can make them do what he wants. If he's close or if they're far gone with the curse, he doesn't even have to speak to them, he can move them around with his mind. Make them stay or go, attack or defend, whatever he wants. But his power fades with distance, and the more of their own mind that they have left the more they can shake off his will. With someone like Thauvik, who's still very nearly human, the Son pretty much has to be in the same room to pull those strings directly."

"So what good does sending Nuriko here do him?"

"Even when he can't control one of the risen by will, he can cause them great pain or kill them outright from a great distance. If he has one of his agents in place, he can send orders through the agent and enforce them with the threat of punishment or death. It only works up to a point though. He can't shut down the blood madness that comes with the curse, or the desire to pass it along to others. He can only limit it. That's why I stabbed Sumey back when I was playing her minder. I thought she was about to bite me and I panicked."

"But the swords of the goddess wouldn't slay her for you."

"No. That magic seems to have left me when I . . . left her service." Devin drew a ragged breath. "I had thought it was the swords that changed, but then it worked for you."

Triss lifted his head from his conversation with Zass again. "Why were you trying to put Sumey on the throne if Thauvik was also under the control of the Son of Heaven?"

"I wasn't. Or, at least not right away, though it turned out she had different plans that she hid from both me and the Son. I was just supposed to keep her busy and ready to take over should something go too wrong with Thauvik. The Son likes to have an heir in place and ready to assume the reins of power. He temporarily loses control over his risen as they transition from something that can pass for human into more obvious members of the restless dead. It's an inevitable decay and he seems to have had some practice at managing it."

"How many thrones does the Son have under his thumb?" I asked.

"I don't know. Even now that I'm the Son of Heaven's personal Shade he doesn't tell me much. Of course, he hasn't had many chances. I've been in the role for less than half a year and I've been here much of that time, thanks to the Kitsune and your would-be queen."

"Are we finally getting to the point then?" I asked.

"Yes. When the Son sent Nuriko to ride herd on Thauvik, he gave her very specific orders for what he wanted. She followed them pretty well, too, at least until the day of the Council of Jade. I don't know exactly what went wrong then, whether it was simply the opportunity the Kitsune had been waiting for, or if Maylien's challenge to Thauvik's authority pushed him into a true blood frenzy, or if the stars lined up wrong. But since then, she's been playing Thauvik for her own goals instead of the Son's. I was sent here to bring things back under control, but neither Thauvik nor Nuriko listens to a word I say. She's had him under her complete control, right down to arranging all the security in the palace for her convenience."

"Don't you have the Son's proxy for punishing Thauvik?" asked Triss.

"I thought I did, but Nuriko's done something that blocks the Son's powers there. I would have expected that to violate her oath to the Son and bring some terrible consequences down on her head, but she seems to have slipped free of her own geas as well."

"So, there *is* a way out of your oath," I said, sitting forward.

"Don't think that hasn't occurred to—" Devin's voice broke off in a whimper and his hand went to his forehead. "Fuckfuckfuckfuck!" For several seconds his breathing came heavy and rough, then it slowed again. "Yeah, no. I don't think the Kitsune operates under the same rules the rest of us do. Maybe it's the structure of her oath. Maybe it's the crazy. Whatever the reason, that particular door doesn't open for me."

"It really seems like the Son doesn't trust you to keep your word to his god. Sensible of him."

"Fuck you, Aral. I knew I was going to regret not chopping your damned head off."

"It's never too late. You're still armed with the weapons of the last master you betrayed, and I've got nothing but a couple of knives to defend myself."

"What did happen to your swords, Aral? Did you pawn them to buy booze?"

I suppressed the flash of rage and the snarling response Devin was so obviously fishing for and smiled sweetly instead. "I returned them to the goddess in her tomb. If I wasn't going to serve Justice any longer, then I had no right to carry her swords." And, that, I could see, drew blood. "But we weren't talking about me. We were talking about you and your problems. Do go on."

"Gods but you're a sanctimonious asshole, and you always have been. Yeah, let's talk about my problems, chief of which is that I really need the help of the fucking king of holier-than-thou. The Kitsune is out of her mind and she's got mad King Thuavik half under her thumb. She's currently trying to get him to declare himself the *Risen King*, and to start slaughtering and converting the masses as the start of some insane crusade of the restless dead. She's promised him that she'll find and murder Maylien for him just as soon as he gets things underway."

"That's completely crazy," said Triss.

"Yes," agreed Zass, "that's what we've been trying to tell you. Nuriko has to be stopped, but we can't do it without you. She's a better swordswoman than Devin and a better

mage, and she's with Thauvik constantly. We can't beat
Nuriko by herself, much less when she's backed up by a risen
who also happens to be one of the best soldiers and duelists
in the kingdom. He rose through the ranks from petty officer
to chief marshal without any help from his brother, and he's
a damned good fighter. We need your help to stop the
Kitsune."

"No," I said.

"No?" asked Devin. "Why the hell not?"

"I don't like you, I don't trust you, and I don't see how
my helping you does a damned bit of good for anything I
care about."

"The Kitsune wants to kill your royal bed warmer. Isn't
that enough?"

"No, as much as I care for Maylien, that's not enough.
I'm pretty sure your plan is for me to bail your ass out with
the Kitsune so you can stab me in the back, kill Maylien,
and put Thauvik back on the throne."

"Yeah, that's pretty much what I was hoping for."

"It's not going to happen. Nothing is, unless I'm calling
the tune." I pushed myself to my feet and walked over to
look down at Devin. "I might, *might* be convinced to help
you out with the Kitsune if it also ends with Thauvik in the
grave, Maylien on the throne, and you headed back to Heav-
en's Reach with your tail between your legs. But nothing
short of that is going to move me."

"I hate you. I really hate you." Devin glared at me for a
long moment and then his face suddenly twisted in intense
pain and he reached for his forehead.

"I think he's actually considering it," said Triss.

"Clearly," said Zass, his voice sad. "Nothing else would
hurt him so."

"Can't say I'm sorry to see him writhe a bit," I replied.
"He deserves a hell of a lot worse."

After a time, the fit passed and Devin rolled over, crawl-
ing to the edge of the finished floor and emptying his stomach into the void below. "I *can't* agree to help you put
Maylien on the throne, or to kill Thauvik," he rasped. "I

can, probably, lend you my swords to fight the Kitsune, and—oh fuck." He threw up over the side again.

Zass went and laid his head on the small of Devin's back. "What you do with Devin's swords before you give them back is up to you, I'm sure. Please, don't make him say what that implies."

"All right," I said. "I won't, and maybe I'll even pull his ass out of the fire, though it sure won't be for old times' sake." I looked down at Devin, who had rolled onto his side so he could watch me. "But before I do any of that, and out of sheer idle curiosity, what happens if I don't help you?"

"I try to take the Kitsune on my own, and she guts me."

"You're sure you can't just pull a rabbit run of your own?" I asked.

Devin nodded. "Quite sure. I don't know how Kelos has slipped the leash so thoroughly, but the oath has certain safeguards built into it. The Son can compel me to return to him, even from a great distance."

"Interesting." I wondered at that. "Why didn't he simply set it up so he could kill you at a distance?"

"It's not personal enough for him, I think. Nor sufficiently frightening."

I raised a questioning eyebrow.

"We're Blades, Aral, even if we have left the service of the goddess. Death at a distance isn't a big enough threat because none of us is all that scared of dying."

"Could have fooled me, or am I hallucinating the part where you switched sides to save your coward's hide?" Devin blanched. "What? Did I hit a sore spot?"

"You did," he said, "though not the one you were aiming at."

"Now I'm confused."

Devin sighed. "You said I turned my coat to save my skin. That isn't quite true, and I don't want to talk about it. But my skin is in serious need of saving now. Do you want to know what the Son of Heaven will do to me if I fail, really?"

"I wouldn't have asked otherwise."

"First, he'll stake Zass out, so that he can't help me and has to watch. I'm sure you can imagine it?"

I nodded, though it didn't need imagination, only memory. I remembered Master Kaman nailed to a cross with his Shade staked out in front of him, the iron spikes that pierced Ssilar burning with a terrible intense light that prevented the shadow from moving. I remembered as well the arrow that I had used to end Kaman's life after I'd offered to try to free him and he begged me to kill him instead.

Devin continued. "Then he'll have me hung up in the center of a room with chains at my wrists and ankles, all spread-eagled for his *artists.*"

"Artists?" I asked, confused.

"Tattooists," said Devin. "Part of the Hand. They do exquisite work, both gently on the willing, and . . . less so, on those who displease the Son. You'd be surprised at how much blunt needles can hurt."

"That sounds like experience talking."

Devin nodded and pulled back his left sleeve. An incredibly detailed and beautiful image of the god Shan adorned the inner side of his forearm. "The Son wasn't happy to lose Sumey, and decided that I should serve as a graphic lesson for my fellows. When he had this done he also had the designs drawn up to expand the piece into a full-body mosaic should the fancy take him. Then he took me into his gallery. Mostly it's filled with bits and pieces, a back panel with a battle scene from church history, a scalp with an earlier Son's death image recreated on it."

"Ugly," I said.

"And beautiful, and terrifying beyond words. He told me that he always has them removed while the subject is alive, and that some of his better healing 'canvases' continue to serve him to this day. He said that the only reason my arm piece wasn't going on display right now was that Kelos had spoken up for me. Then he told me that if I ever disappointed him like that again, I would go into the section of the gallery where the rest of the full-body pieces were displayed. So, you'll understand why I'd rather take a shot at the Kitsune, and force her to kill me, than not, and simply fail."

I found myself feeling a wholly unwanted compassion for Devin. "So what happens if I kill the Kitsune for you, but also Thauvik?"

"I don't know. I'm pretty sure that with both her and Kelos gone, I'll be too valuable for him to end up hanging on the wall anytime soon, though I might get some more decorations. He really doesn't have a better candidate for Heaven's Shade. However, in my perfect world, you and the Kitsune both die of your wounds and I quietly put Thauvik back on his leash until I get his successor lined up."

"Or maybe, I kill the Kitsune and you stab me in the back while I'm doing it?"

"That works for me, too, but I don't expect to get the opportunity."

My compassion was fading fast. "Charming."

"Look, I hate your guts, you hate mine, that's the way it is. Doesn't mean we can't use each other against the Kitsune and sort out the rest of the details once she's dead."

"Sure, it'll be fun."

Devin smiled sarcastically. "Glad you're on board. Now, let's talk plans. There are going to be guards, Elite, soldiers. The palace is filled with Thauvik's loyal subjects. We'll need a major distraction to keep them off our backs while we deal with Nuriko, and any . . ." Devin winced and closed his eyes as the oath squeezed him. "While we deal with whatever needs dealing with."

He was obviously hurting, and after what he'd told me about the Son's artists I wished I had the grace to feel worse about it. "What do you want me to do about that?"

"You have access to Maylien's forces, don't you? I think my oath to the Son will extend to arranging for you to bring some of them along to help me get rid of the problem that Nuriko has become."

"That's got potential." Mostly the potential to get a lot more people killed the way I had so recently on the bridge, but that was all too likely to happen no matter what at this point.

If I could stave off a full-scale war by the advent of leading a smaller assault, I had to at least consider it, no matter how badly things had gone at Sanjin Island. Of course, I would have felt a whole hell of a lot more comfortable with the idea if I'd come up with it instead of Devin. If he was trying to suck me into a trap, the addition of any number of the kinds of seasoned and loyal troops that Maylien would have to send on a mission this important and dangerous would sure sweeten the take.

I thought of Jerik then, as I had not in too long, and of his torments on Darkwater Island, and I wondered how my desire to rescue an old friend had led me from there to here. I suddenly missed the simplicity of having a goddess to tell me exactly what to do and who to kill. Sorting out justice on my own was the hardest thing I'd ever done, and I had no way of knowing if I was getting it right.

14

Sweet and sad the dreams that bring us our dead. Kaman and Loris came to me in mine, master Blades visiting me in the tomb where I lay in place of Ashvik's risen corpse. They brought portents and dire warning, railing against Devin's treachery and speaking darkly of the Kitsune's cruel humor and terrible power.

Master Kaman was a gentle man who had taught me to dance, both court-style and silently among the shadows, the master charged with our instruction in the arts of stealth. Master Loris had taught advanced magery, my worst subject, and not my favorite teacher at the time, but a good man who showed me far more patience than I had deserved on the subject.

Loris had died in the same raid on the abbey that had cost me so much of myself this previous summer. He had given his life to save mine and those of several of his younger students who had been captured by the Hand of Heaven. Kaman had fallen at my own hand when he begged that I give him death to free him from the torture that had broken his soul. That was another crime of pain to be laid at

Thauvik's feet alongside Jerik's more recent suffering, though I did not absolve myself of my teacher's death, only of his reasons for asking that I kill him.

There in my dreams, I got the chance to thank Loris for my life, as I had not when he saved it. Sweet reward, though I knew even then that I thanked the memory of the man, not the man himself. But bitter was the balance, when Kaman thanked me for his death with the very same quiet gratitude that I had showed Loris's Shade. As everything in my life since the fall, light mixed with darkness and no joy came without cost.

In the days when Namara yet lived, I might have taken my dreams for a communication from my goddess. She often spoke to her champions in the quiet darkness of our sleeping minds. But Namara was dead and gone out of the world, and even as I woke, I recognized my dreams for what they were, the voice of my under-mind speaking in the only place where it could be heard.

The first message was clearly born in my heart—my own anger and disappointment with myself crying out to me against this compromise I was considering in pursuit of what seemed increasingly a phantasm of justice. The second spoke more of my fears in facing an enemy who had beaten me so easily in our first encounter—a mad legend out of my order's past.

The transition from dream to waking came with Kaman's quiet thanks and the fresh sprouting of the arrow I'd put in his chest, growing now like a rose. I closed my eyes to a memory I would never erase and opened them to a view of rough carved stone. The light was dim and green and I could hear water gently splashing behind and below me.

Normally, if I haven't been drinking, I wake smoothly and aware of my surroundings, a skill mastered through long practice. Not this time. This time, I had no idea of where I was, and my head was full of cobwebs and creepies carried over from Ashvik's tomb into the waking world.

Triss?

Yes?

Where the hell are we?

Fallback. Used to be a transshipment point for Miriyan Zheng.

Got it.

Zheng was a sellcinders, or fence, who used to deal big money items out of Highside. She'd specialized in artifacts that came out of the nonhuman Other cultures, mostly Durkoth stuff. It made her rich. And then, later, when she got involved with the wrong item, it made her dead. Both the Durkoth and the Elite had come after her, and between the two they'd burned her operation completely to the ground.

I'd built my fallback in what was left of a secret little transshipment point and tuckaside warehouse she'd used for the smuggling side of her operations. Both had been carved into the broken cliffs on the Quarryside face of the harbor where the currents and rocks made the waters far too dangerous for any boat bigger than the tiniest flat bottomed sampans. That was fine by Zheng, who only dealt in small items anyway. The Durkoth had destroyed the tuckaside above me, using their power over earth to collapse the chambers and entry tunnel, but the water cave where the sampans had docked remained because the Durkoth preferred to avoid the interface between elements.

With all the human people who'd known about it dead but me, and the Durkoth avoiding the place, the cave made a perfect fallback. Judging by the light and the level of the water—high tide submerged the cave's mouth—it was midafternoon. I slipped out of my hammock—hung over the water—and swung down to the narrow stone ledge that had served as a dock. It was the only dry ground in the cave, running along the eastern wall. A narrow stair led up into a passageway off the back of the ledge, but ended in a solid rock wall only a few steps up where the Durkoth had closed things off. I'd parked my emergency supplies on the highest of these along with the basket of clothes and other gear I'd stripped off earlier.

As was my wont, I'd put all of my supplies in wide-mouthed

amphorae and sealed them with thick stoppers and preservation spells. That kept things fresh and dry for the months I might go between visits. With a word of opening and a twist of my wrist I popped a seal, set the lid on the step, reached into the jar, and . . . froze. The first thing my hand touched was a twelve-year-old bottle of Kyle's whiskey—I could identify the vintage by the shape even without looking at the label. I'd set up this hidey-hole in the weeks after the affair with the Durkoth, using supplies hauled from another, recently compromised, fallback, and I hadn't cracked into them since I'd mostly stopped drinking.

Finding the bottle just then, so soon after having to deal with Devin and all the bits of my past he brought with him was *not* what I needed right now. With my hand shaking, I pulled the bottle out and held it up in the light. Rich amber heaven stared back at me through the glass. I could already taste the peat and the fine honey notes the twelve always brought with it.

Aral?

I didn't answer Triss. I couldn't. It was taking everything I had not to tear out the cork and drink off half the bottle on the spot. I could feel sweat breaking out on my brows and the palm of the hand holding the bottle as I fought with my own desire. Fuck me but I wanted that drink *bad*. Without seeming to cross the intervening space, I found myself holding the whiskey out over the water, willing my hand to unclench. It wouldn't, and probably better that it didn't. Whoever had built this tiny hidden slip in the long ago had smoothed the bottom when they carved out the rest of the cave to make it into something people could use. Dropping the bottle wouldn't put it out of reach, it would just make it a little bit harder to get at. A little bit harder and a lot more humiliating.

Aral! Triss shifted into dragon form beside me, poking me in the ribs with his nose.

I ignored that and the increased urgency in his voice and used a word of opening to free the cork—a spell where normally I would have simply torn it free with my teeth.

Then, slowly, oh so very damned slowly, I turned the bottle over and poured the contents into the sea. It felt more than half like I'd opened a vein and it was my own blood I was draining away, but I did it. When it was empty, and only when it was empty, did I let the bottle fall into the water and sink to the bottom. I watched it all the way down. Then I sat back against the wall of the cavern and dangled my bare feet in the cool water.

Yes, Triss? I sent back. *What is it?*

Nothing now. Thank you. He slowly slid back around behind me, where the light would have put him naturally—it took effort for him to fight the light.

You're welcome, though I'm pretty sure I couldn't have done the same with a twist of efik powder or a sack of beans right now. I miss her, Triss. I miss Namara like my own soul.

I know you do. I miss her, too. I could hear how much in his mental voice. *She was the foundation atop which we all built the structures of our lives. Now Justice is dead and gone into a cold and watery grave and we who once worshipped her have to stand alone upon the shifting sands of the world.*

Do you know what's hardest for me? The fucking uncertainty. When she lived, I was her instrument, and I always knew exactly what I had to do and who I was. After, when they had slain her and I was a ruin, I knew that she would hate what I had become and what I had to do to live. It was a dark mirror of the way things had been before. Now, now when I am once again trying to follow the path she set me on, I don't know if what I am doing is what I should be doing. I only know that I have to try.

And I know that you will succeed. I can't give you your certainty back, but I can be certain for you. I am so proud of what you just did.

I looked down into the shadowy green depths where I could still see the empty bottle lying on the stone floor. *It's funny. It was hard, it's hard every time, but not because of the booze itself. Hell, I hated the stuff when I started drinking, and just did it to get away from the efik, since I* knew

that would kill me. No, it's hard because it's come to rep-
resent the things I started drinking to replace, if that makes
any sense.

Triss didn't say anything, but I felt shadowy wings settle
around my shoulders briefly. After a few minutes I got up and
went back to the amphora, rummaging around for something
to eat. I found salted pork and rice cakes wrapped in oilcloth,
and a small skin of beer that didn't tempt me at all—stuff
tasted like horse piss at the best of times. I poured that into
the sea and tucked the skin back into the jar, wishing for
perhaps the first time in my life that I had some tea and a pot
to steep it in. Clearly I was going to have to make changes to
the way I stored my emergency supplies, since only a fool or
a suicide would willingly drink the waters of Tien straight.
Even the deepest wells tasted faintly of the sewers.

Once I'd eaten as much of the pork and rice cakes as I
could stand without a drink, I pissed into the sea and
checked the tide level. It was going down. Soon I'd be able
to float the basket that held my clothes out through the gap.
I could have swum out now if I had to, or even at the highest
of tides, but my gear would get soaked in the process, and
it would be nice if I only had to wash the salt out of my hair
and hide. While I waited I dug through my trick bag and
the amphorae to see how much coin I had available. I needed
to shop for new swords since Devin wasn't in a position to
give me his yet. Not without the Kitsune noticing they were
gone, and nothing good could come of that. It was a good
thing that Maylien and several of the others I had worked
for in the last two years were generous, or I'd have had to
play the thief at some poor armorer's shop. It wouldn't be
the first time I was thus reduced, nor probably the last, but
every time I did it, it was another small betrayal of my goddess's memory.

"Perhaps this one?" The smith showed me yet another
Zhani dueling blade, the fifteenth I'd seen over the last hour.
The steel was excellent and the weight and length were

both good. There was another just like it in the rack, and I might even be able to fit them into the sheaths I already owned. Still, I turned it aside with a shake of my head and a feigned yawn, part of the role I'd put on for my shopping. I wanted him to remember me as a pain-in-the-ass of the lesser nobility, not the vaguely foreign-looking fellow who came in knowing exactly what he wanted and bought something quite out of the ordinary.

"No, those won't do at all. I've got dozens like them. Oh, never mind, this is getting me nowhere." I turned toward the door.

"Wait," said the smith, who'd been eyeing my obviously fat purse avariciously for quite some time, "don't go yet. If you're really bored with the usual, I might be able to find something a bit more out of the ordinary."

I'd picked this armorer because I knew him and his stock well. Though that was from back in the days of my old face, so he didn't recognize me. He did good work, he didn't overprice it, and he mucked around with odd foreign designs now and then, both to work on his skills and for the simple joy of it. He took the dueling blade and set it back in the cabinet with the others, carefully locking it as he did so.

"Just stay right there." He ducked through the door into the back of his shop, though he left it open behind so he could hear the bell. A minute or two later he returned wheeling another little cabinet on a handcart, which he brought around the counter. "Don't get much call for this stuff, so there's no point taking up precious space out front. Hang on."

He unlocked the cabinet and opened it. Lined up in hanging slots along the back were a score or so of mixed swords. Hangers on the backs of the doors held more, along with some bigger and stranger knives. I started poking around, first pulling out a forward curving Kadeshi cane knife, then, a hook-ended Sylvani dragon sword. As I worked my way through the offered blades, I kept up a mumbled monologue.

"No. Hmm, nice. Nope. Maybe . . . too heavy. What's this thing? That's a little odd."

Finally, after going through about half the lot I touched

the hilt of a short, single-edged, lightly curved sword in the modern Varyan pattern. This was why I had come here, a sword modeled after those my goddess gave her Blades. Though he obviously hated the idea, Devin had known as well as I did that going up against the Kitsune with mortal steel was suicide and that I would need to use his swords to have any chance at victory. Our own fight had driven the point home hard.

That meant I needed to get back into practice, as it had been seven long years since I last used their like. And since Devin couldn't yet lend me his, I had to find my own swords, and here they were. I lifted the first one free of its hanger and brought it up into a Zhani guard position twisting it this way and that as I did so.

"Hmm, now this is interesting." My words rang strange and tinny in my own ears and the hilt felt like I had caught magelightning in my hand, sending a series of little shocks of memory up my arm and straight into my heart. I *wanted* this sword. "This is Aveni, right?"

The smith managed not to roll his eyes or call me an idiot, but I could see it cost him. "Varyan, actually, but you're very close, my lord. Do you like it?"

I stepped back so I could run it through a couple of Zhani cuts and thrusts. "The weight's a little off." *No, it damned well wasn't, this was what a sword was* supposed *to feel like.* "And I'm not sure about the grip." *Like hell.* "But yes, this might be what I'm looking for." *Wantwantwant!* "Does it come with a sheath?"

The smith nodded. "It does, and a custom belt, since it's actually a double sheath. The Varyans use a two-sword style, so these blades are always sold in pairs."

"Really? How odd." The style had been adapted from half-true reports of the way Namara's Blades fought, just as the swords themselves had been. Even in Varya, the home of the temple, we were not often seen or spoken to by any but our own.

"It sounds like a sneaky way to roll up an extra sale." I started to put the sword back on its hanger, then paused, and took its mate out instead, weighing both in my hands and pretending I had no idea how I ought to hold them. *Need!* "Oh, what the hell, it'd be different at least. How much are they?"

The smith quoted a ridiculous price, and I responded with a scandalous counteroffer, and we went on from there. In the end, I got my swords and the smith got more than they were worth here in Zhan but far less than I'd been willing to pay. Once I'd forked over most of my cash, I put them on. It felt very strange to settle the cross-draw belt around my waist and carry the weight of the sword on my hips. I resolved that the first thing I needed to do was slice away three quarters of the seaming along one side of each sheath so I could rig them for back-draw.

They're good swords, Triss sent as I stepped out into the street. *They cast a shadow very like the swords of the goddess, though they're in the wrong place right now. Add in the proper grays underneath your poncho, and I very nearly feel like I live in a Blade's shadow again.* He'd been strangely silent all during my shopping, and I wondered if this was why.

I very nearly feel like a Blade again, I responded. *Isn't it odd that it took trying to put someone on a throne to get me here?* I turned into a tinker's shop then to pick up a small hammer, a punch, and an awl—the tools I'd need to rebuild my new sheaths. I also bought half a dozen buckles, some metal rings, leather strapping, and a bottle of oris juice to darken everything. *Do you think I should set them up for hip-draw like my old sheaths, or shoulder-draw like a proper blade?*

Hip. Shoulder would feel more natural. But I like the way hip-draw allows you to conceal your weapons with the simple addition of a cape instead of having to rehang them on your rig.

Point. It also felt a bit like the reversal of my own personal flag—a universal sign of something not right, and since I would never be quite right again . . . *Next a visit with Captain Fei so I can bring her up to date. Then I'll need to hang my pack, collect some supplies, and we can head for the country to find Maylien.*

So, we're going to trust Devin then? Triss sounded dubious.

No. I'm never going to trust Devin again, but this might give us a chance to shut Thauvik down short of a full-scale civil war.

Do you think Maylien will agree?

I don't know, Triss, I really don't, but I have to try.

"**There**." I tapped the last rivet into place on the second sheath. "Let's give them a test."

The sheaths weren't originally designed to hang down my back, so I'd added straps to hold the swords in place while upside down. I'd also opened up the seams that ran along the back of the blades for all but the last couple of inches. That allowed me to draw by lowering them so that the tips cleared and then pivoting them free of the sheaths instead of having to draw them full length like a sword hanging on your hip. I'd also added leather loops at the top and bottom so that they could be fastened to the steel rings of my Blade's harness without jingling.

I rigged that now, setting the harness up as though I was about to go on a mission, with knives fastened to the straps on my chest and my trick bag hanging on my right hip. Then, because I couldn't resist, I looked into the nearby stream to see the effect.

A dragon's shadow looked back at me, occluding my reflection. "You look fine, every inch a Blade. What you need is practice."

And he was right. So, I headed back into the middle of the little clearing where we'd set up our camp—a poachers' site Maylien had shown me once upon a time. I took a series of long slow breaths to ground myself. Though I'd done a bit of practice with my new swords already, this was different, more real. I was about to try a proper Blade sword form for the first time in seven years.

Now.

I popped the thumb releases on my swords and pivoted them around with a snap—a slight modification I'd had to add to account for my reversed sheaths. Seven years . . . and not one of them mattered here in the place where my soul would always live—the flow of the swords from instant to instant. Oh, I slipped up and made minor mistakes—I was rusty and my steel was new and unfamiliar—but the heart of the thing felt exactly as it always had.

I was home.

My ghosts were there with me, both the living and the dead. Master Kelos leaned against a tree and I could feel his disapproval with every slipup. Siri stood silently waiting her turn, a pillar of stone, practicing her art even as I practiced mine—as deadly serious on the field as she was wickedly irreverent off. Loris frowned at me from a tower that had long since fallen, and I knew that he wished I would show his lessons the same dedication I gave to sword and shadow. Jax, my onetime fiancée, looked promise from the sidelines. Devin was there, too, laughing with me at the start but closed and withdrawn as I finished my forms.

It hurt me now, as it had not when I was young and oblivious. He was my best friend once, and might have been more had he had the inclination. But he had not, so we had mostly commiserated about our studies and our problems with women, which I preferred, though not exclusively as Devin did. There was Alinthide, a teacher I had loved with a mad schoolboy crush, Jax, whom I nearly married, Siri, who bedded many but favored none of us, and others who left memories less vivid. What had gone wrong between me and Devin? Was it purely the jealousy that Jax had described so starkly when we had met again last summer? Or, was there some inherent flaw in his soul that made him betray me as he had our goddess?

I had a thousand memories of Devin. Hell, if you divided my world into before and after, with the fall of the temple as the inflection point, the Aral who lived in the kingdom of before had very few memories without him. Nowhere in them could I see the flaw, nor more than normal jealousy.

Maybe that was the hardest lesson of them all, that nothing separated us, that the potential to do what Devin had done lived within my own heart as well. Did we all walk the line between man and monster, deciding whether or not to cross it each and every time the opportunity arose? It was simultaneously a profoundly uncomfortable thought and one that freed something deep down in my soul, something I hadn't even known was under lock and key.

I finished my last form then, feeling physically much closer to the old me than I had in years, though it would take many more hours to fully recover my feel for Varyan-style swords. I slipped them back into their sheaths, closed the snaps, and bowed deeply to the memory of my goddess.

That was all that I had left of her, but for the first time in seven long years I was beginning to see that someday, that might be enough.

15

"Absolutely not!" Maylien slammed her fist down on the table. "Are you fucking insane, Aral? Why would you even consider trusting your life to some wild-ass story told by Devin Nightblade!"

Bontrang shrieked a sharp accompaniment to Maylien's anger when she said that name. The little gryphinx might not be as bright as Triss, but he was a hell of a lot smarter than either the eagle or the house cat who supplied his distant antecedents, and he had a powerful hate for Devin. The rogue Blade had once taken him and Maylien prisoner and used a threat to his life to control Maylien—kill the familiar, kill the mage.

Prixia didn't shriek, but she looked even angrier than Maylien and her words came out low and deadly, "After the disaster on Sanjin Bridge, I can't imagine letting you risk more of our troops on another scheme to assassinate Thauvik." She turned to Maylien. "I can't conscience throwing lives away on a mad plan like this one."

I'd expected resistance, but not this much or so angry.

"It's not mad, I was able to slay one of the risen using Devin's swords before, and—"

Maylien cut me off. "And you yourself have said that you don't know why the magic of the swords worked for you where it had not for Devin. Look, I sympathize with the desire to end this short of a war, but there are just too many things that could go wrong. Devin might be lying. If he isn't, he might change his mind and not give you his swords. You told me last time we talked about this that the swords had to come to you freely. If he does hand them over, and they work, you still don't know that you can beat the Kitsune. Your last encounter with her didn't go so well."

"True, but that's no guarantee of how things will go when next we meet. I was surprised before; unprepared, and off balance from the discovery that she was still alive."

Maylien shook her head. "Even if it goes perfectly, you're going to have to pivot straight from a fight with her to taking on Thauvik, and Devin won't have any incentive for you to succeed there. Quite the contrary. What happens if he revokes his permission to use his swords? Will they continue to work for you then? This is crazy, Aral. Don't throw your life away on the word of someone who's already betrayed you more than once."

Triss spoke from the place Maylien had made for him at the council table—a bare patch of white wall with no chair blocking his view. "Maybe they're right, Aral. Maybe this is madness and we just can't see it because we grew up with Devin."

Heyin nodded, but didn't add anything more.

I straightened my back and took a deep breath. "I agree with every word you're saying about the risks. If anyone knows the cost of Devin's betrayals, it's me. But if there's any chance his offer is legitimate, we have to at least think about it. Once the war starts rolling for real, there will be no way to stop it. Thousands will die. Perhaps tens of thousands."

I looked straight at Maylien. "And you're going to have to come out of the shadows to fight it. An army won't rally around a queen they can't see. The second you make yourself visible, you're going to be opening yourself up to assassination by the Kitsune. If I spend every waking second with you, and I see her coming, I might, *might*, be able to stop her. But a betting man wouldn't put any money on it. My fight with Devin has reminded me of the dangers of putting mortal steel up against the blades of the goddess. I can't protect you by fighting defensively."

I turned to Heyin. "You're the commander of Maylien's guard. If the Kitsune comes for her, she is almost certainly going to kill her. The only way to stand any real chance of stopping the Kitsune is to do it before she moves. Tell me that's not worth some risks."

Heyin looked down at the table. "I . . . dammit, Aral, that's not a fair argument."

"No, but that doesn't make it any less true." I flicked my gaze to Prixia. "Look, I fucked up on the bridge about as badly as it's possible to fuck up. I got your brother and half a dozen other good soldiers killed. That's on my soul, and nothing I can do will bring them back or excuse me for their deaths when I face the lords of judgment. I can't begin to express how sorry I am for that. I should have seen the possibility that Thauvik was risen, full stop. I didn't because it's such an insane proposition—that one of the best-guarded men in the whole world could have been given the curse— and I fucked it up completely."

Prixia's eyes flashed and she half rose out of her seat, but I held up a hand. "Wait, let me finish. I owe you a blood price for that. Once this is all over, if we're both still alive, we can settle the debt however you want. Steel against steel, barehanded, poison in one glass, wine the other, and blindfolds for both, whatever you choose. But for right now, you are going to put it aside and you are going to do what needs to be done for Thauvik to go down. Because otherwise, your brother will have died for nothing."

"I . . ." She took a deep breath and sat back down, though her eyes still burned bright and furious. "You're right. I fucked up, too. I trusted you to succeed on the bridge and I ordered my brother to follow you based on that trust."

Ouch! sent Triss.

Yes, but I deserved it. I felt like the world's biggest ass-hole, laying things on Prixia like I had, but it was true. I needed her to put her grief and anger aside and focus on what had to be done. That was one of the harder lessons I had learned at the temple, and there was no gentle way to teach it. *She can hate me all she wants later if we win. Right now I need her help to defeat Thauvik. If we lose, it's not going to matter.*

Oblivious to my exchange with Triss, Prixia kept right on speaking. "If I'm going to pay the debt I owe my brother's memory, I must do as you say for now and focus on defeating Thauvik. But, and I promise you this, I *will* collect what I am owed from you as well when the time comes."

"I would expect no less of you, clan leader." I turned back so that I was squarely facing Maylien. "This has a real chance of working if Devin comes through. If he doesn't, you'll be out one slightly broken-down assassin and a few good soldiers. That's a high price, but not, I think, beyond what a queen must be willing to pay if the need calls for it."

I could see that she wanted to swear at me. If we'd been in private, she probably would have bitten my head clean off. Instead, she gently inclined her own. "Much as I hate to admit it, you might have a point." Before I could say a word, she held up a hand. "Might."

She turned to her field commander. "Prixia, put together a force for a mission that's going to cost a lot of lives even if it goes perfectly to plan. Volunteers only, and make damn sure they know what they're getting into. Tell them about what happened on the bridge. I'm not sure who we can get to command it, since Aral's going to have to focus on the Kitsune and Thauvik once they're inside. That's going to be a problem."

"No," said Heyin, "it won't. I'll lead them, and don't give me that look. If Aral is right and Devin really needs our help to get out from under the Kitsune, and we can use that to kill Thauvik, it's not a suicide mission. If he's wrong . . . well, I'm old and my reflexes are getting slower by the day.

If it comes to war, I'm not likely to see the end of it anyway. This gives me a chance to save a lot of lives at a cost I don't begrudge. And, no, I won't be ordered out of it, or persuaded."

Maylien looked like someone had just stabbed her in the heart, but she didn't argue with Heyin. Instead she turned her gaze my way, and the message was clear. If I got Heyin killed for nothing, I was as dead to her as he would be. I met her eyes and nodded faintly to let her know I understood.

When Maylien spoke next, her voice held not the slightest hint of the pain I knew she was feeling, and I admired her all the more for it. "Aral, talk to Devin again. Work out the details. Make damn sure he's not playing you. If you can convince me that's the case, we'll do this and the credit or blame will fall on your shoulders."

Talking to Devin was proving to be a lot more trouble than I'd hoped. Before we parted, he'd given me the location of a message drop where I could leave him a note asking for a meeting. Since he could only check it as often as he could worm his way free of Nuriko's eye, I was supposed to choose a location and wait for him to signal me back as to when to meet. Of course, I still didn't trust him as far as I could reasonably throw Harad's dragon familiar, so I had picked a location where I could get away easily if he was trying to set me up.

Unfortunately, the signal never came, and every time I checked behind the loose brick Devin had picked for the drop, I found the very first message I'd left for him untouched. And not in a, he'd read it and put it back sort of way—I'd arranged a couple of fragments of mortar so that if the message was moved I'd be able to tell. No, this was a not-checking-the-drop-at-all kind of unmoved. After a week, I did a risky circuit around the outer perimeter of the palace checking for shadow trails, but if either Devin or the Kitsune had come and gone recently, they'd done so without leaving any traces.

As the two-week mark approached, I really started to worry. Two more circuits on consecutive nights produced no evidence that Devin was even alive. By then, Maylien was pushing me hard, saying that if I couldn't get things set up soon, she was going to cancel the preparations. And, she didn't have the resources to let four score of good soldiers sit idle—the number we'd settled on. Tonight would mark the beginning of a third week since I'd left my message. If there was no signal and no sign it had been received . . .

What do you think, Triss? I asked as I watched the drop from a distance—no way I was going to go in to check it without making sure no one else was spying on the spot first.

About what?

Assume for a moment Devin hasn't picked up the message.

Good assumption, Triss mindspoke dryly.

What do we do then? Head up and make another loop around the palace? The drop was in the wall of a tenement in the Little Varya neighborhood, about midway between the palace and the harbor.

That's freaking dangerous and lousy tradecraft. Do you have any reason to suspect we'd find anything different this time? His mind voice sounded deeply skeptical.

No, I replied.

Are you willing to give this up?

You mean step back and let a war start?

That's what I thought. Triss let out a mental sigh. *So, what do you want to do about it? Devin either can't get out of the palace, or he simply won't visit the drop, and we can't make him do either one.*

I think we're going to have to go into the palace and look for him. We have to find out what's keeping him from checking the drop like he said he would.

First, that's insane. Second, "what's keeping him from checking the drop like he said he would"? This is Devin we're talking about. Betrayed you. Betrayed the order. Betrayed Namara. He's not exactly known for keeping his

*word. Third, that's insane. Fourth, did I mention that it's
insane?*

*I'm getting the sense that you think this plan's not the
best one I've ever had, Triss. So, what's your alternative?
Give up and let the war start?*

Sometimes I really hate being your shadow.

Does that mean we're going to the palace?

*Yes, it means we're going to the palace. As much as I
don't trust Devin, he didn't kill us when he had the chance
the other night, though it was damned obvious he wanted
to. That suggests he really is in over his head with the Kitsune. Enough of the rest of his story makes sense on its own,
or checks out—we know Thauvik is one of the restless dead,
and we've heard Kelos spouting that inherent corruption
of governments line—that I tend to believe him when he
says he needs our help. If that means we get one more shot
at ending this short of thousands of gallons of blood spilled
in the streets, we have to try.*

Maybe now you'll admit I'm not so crazy after all.

*No, crazy and right aren't exclusive. I haven't once said
you're wrong about this, just that it's insane. Now shut up
and check the drop so we can justify doing the insane.*

Moving from one shadow to another to maximize the
effect of my shroud, I slipped down to the wall. Devin had
chosen well, picking a spot behind a small tree that kept it
soaked in shadow no matter what time of day or night one
might approach. Now, with that shadow deepened to impenetrable by Triss, I slipped the brick out and looked behind it.

I was so prepared to see what I was expecting that it took
three long beats and a couple of blinks to see what was really
there—a different slip of paper entirely. I plucked it out with
some concern, since it fit neither of the scenarios Devin and
I had set up—my own message untouched, or, a void left
when he finally retrieved the note. The drop was supposed
to be for one-way communication only.

That's odd, sent Triss.

I don't like it. Let's get clear before we give this a read.

I agree.

I finally opened the note some minutes later, sitting atop a water tank on the roof of a private tower on the edge of Highside. It held one sentence, "Scheroc says come find me," a safe enough message given that to the best of my knowledge there were only three people in the entire city who knew both that Fei had a familiar and what its name was. The other two being Harad and Fei herself. Conveniently, Fei's office wasn't all that far from my current location. Fifteen minutes later I was knocking quietly on her back window.

There was a sniff. "Aral."

It wasn't a question, but I answered it like one anyway, "Yes."

The lights went out and the shutters swung wide. "It's about damned time," said a voice from within. "I left that note three hours ago."

"Good to see you, too." I caught the window ledge and pulled myself inside.

Fei latched the shutters behind me, though she left the slats spread despite a slight chill. The familiar shaped the mage, and Fei's sense of smell was about a hundred times better than any normal human's. That was certainly part of why she'd taken a corner office with big windows on both sides. She left the room dark, but enough moonlight filtered in through the shutters for me to see her face.

"I've had Scheroc keeping an eye on things up at the palace and I think everything is about to go straight into the shit."

"What's happened?"

"Well, ever since you told me about the Kitsune, I've tried to keep Scheroc out of the parts of the palace where she seems likely to turn up." Fei shook her head. "That's actually harder than you'd think. Scheroc is a dear little thing, but he doesn't really understand place in the same way that we do. Trying to tell him where he can and can't go gets a bit . . . dicey."

I'd had some experience of that when I'd had to follow the little wind spirit to Fei once upon a time. But that wasn't really to the point at the moment, so I merely cleared my throat questioningly.

"Sorry. The key thing is I've had to keep Scheroc away from the really royal parts of the palace; the grand tower and surrounds, the Elite's master chapter house, the wing where the Lord Justicer stays with the other Crown officers."

"Speaking of which, do you know why Vyan's head isn't hanging over the traitor's gate? I was sure it'd be up by the evening of the day I stabbed Thauvik on the bridge. But nothing was heard from Vyan for a week, and then he was back out in the square making official statements for the Crown as if nothing had happened. Maylien had her initial go-between pull a rabbit run as soon as the assassination went south, and she hasn't been able to get another in close since. She's lost two good people trying."

"Can't you guess?" asked Fei. "You're the one who gave me most of the pieces I needed to figure it out."

"I'm too damned tired for games, Fei. Just tell me."

"How about I give you the one piece I *didn't* get from you, something Scheroc heard while flitting about in one of the servants' quarters."

"Fine."

"Seems one of the footmen ruptured himself when the marble tub they were hauling up to the Lord Justicer's rooms slipped."

"Oh." That was very bad. Especially if it meant the king was starting to warm to Kitsune's idea of an undead crusade.

"Yes, it seems that Vyan has *risen* to the challenge of his king's present needs."

"What about the week he spent out of sight?"

"I have an idea," replied Fei, "but it's more an educated guess than anything solid. I've been trying to learn more about the risen ever since you told me what Devin had to say about Thauvik and the Son of Heaven. With the exception of that silly adventure novel you mentioned, there's balls-all about blood bathing in the Ismere's collection. But when I told Harad what I wanted to know, he dragged out a few stories that aren't in any of his books."

"And?"

"And, some of the most powerful restless dead go into a sort of dormant state while they transition, like a caterpillar turning into a moth. Normally, the risen don't, or don't for long, but Harad thought there might be something special about this version of the curse. Something that makes them smarter and nastier. If so, they might well spend longer in the state between dead and undead, and . . ."

Fei suddenly lifted her head and sniffed the air like a hound catching a scent. "Shit."

"What is it?" I asked.

"The wind's shifting, and not in a natural way."

A moment later, I felt the change as a cold breeze suddenly came in from her palace-side window.

"Scheroc's in trouble." Fei looked stricken.

"The Kitsune," Triss said from the shadows beneath my chair. "It has to be."

"Aral," Fei whispered, "please . . ."

"Just tell me where to go." I was already halfway to the window.

"He was supposed to be checking out the south barracks," Fei said as I opened the shutters.

It was only in that instant that I realized Fei hadn't gotten around to telling me why everything was about to go to shit. Nothing I could do about it now. There was no time.

I hit the ground beyond the window and started running. Fortunately, Fei's offices weren't much more than a couple of stones' throws from the palace complex and I was scaling the outer walls within a few minutes. Given a choice, I wouldn't have come in this way, as it meant I had to take the same path I'd followed on my last foray into the palace. But if Scheroc was really facing the Kitsune, every second counted. And, not only was this the quickest way in from this side, I would be coming in very close to the south barracks where he was supposed to be eavesdropping.

I had to pause at the top of the wall and let a hundred or

so precious heartbeats go by while I waited for one of the
walking patrols to clear the way. I considered killing the
pair of them, but didn't want to leave any bodies behind
where they might draw attention and raise alarms. Not if I
didn't have to. To make up for that slowdown, I sail-jumped
down from the wall, a risk for certain, but nobody started
shouting alarms. I wanted to sprint, but I kept my speed down
to a lope. As much as I wanted to get there fast, I didn't dare
arrive winded. Not if the Kitsune was involved.

You do realize you haven't got Devin's swords, right?
sent Triss.

*That had occurred to me, yes. But I'm not planning on
winning yet, so we should be good.*

*I'm not sure I follow you. Doesn't not winning equal
getting dead?*

I hope not, that would put a real crimp in my plans.

So, you do have a plan then?

*More of an outline really. I don't think we're going to
find Thauvik lounging around the barracks, so I don't want
to beat the Kitsune yet. There's no reason for Devin to give
me the tools I need to kill our risen king if I solve his Kitsune
problem prematurely. My only goals right now are to pry
Scheroc free of whatever's got him, send him on his way,
and then make a daring escape.*

*That was very nearly a joke. Who are you and what have
you done with the real Aral Kingslayer? You know the fellow, serious demeanor, morose, guilt ridden. . . .*

*Don't worry, old friend, if we live through this, I'm sure
he'll be back. It's just nice to have a clear idea of what needs
doing and no moral qualms about it for a little while. I like
Scheroc. I like Fei. Helping them's the right thing to do,
plain and simple.*

*Except that if you get yourself killed here, there'll be no
one left to bust Jerik out of prison and stop Thauvik and
the Kitsune from leading a legion of the undead across the
lands of the East.*

Devin can handle it.

What! Wait. That was an actual joke, wasn't it?

Maybe. I—

I came around a corner and stopped hard. I had found
Scheroc . . . probably. I'd planned on entering the barracks
through one of the windows along the back where it ran
close to the outer wall. In a colder climate the builders would
probably have used the defensive fortification as part of the
structure of the barracks. But here in Tien, where the summer heat could kill, they'd opted to run a breezeway between
the two. The dark slot didn't provide much of a view but it
did funnel the prevailing winds nicely, a good place for an
air spirit like the qamasiin to flit around and listen without
creating the wrong kind of stir.

What I had expected to find there was what I had seen
in the past: a long, narrow, poorly lit alley of the sort that
would attract footpads were it not inside the palace. What
I actually found had two important additions. One was a
floating cage. It was shaped of shadows and magic and gave
off a deep orange spell-light—all invisible to mortal vision.
The second was Nuriko Shadowfox sitting cross-legged atop
a small barrel, her skin glinting gold in the moonlight. Her
eyes were closed and she appeared to be deep in meditation,
but as I came around the corner she raised her head, seeming
to look at me without actually lifting her lids.

"Ah, that was fast," she said, then paused and opened
her eyes. "Is that you, Kingslayer? I'd expected to catch a
very different fish with this particular hook. The sprite is
certainly no familiar of yours. Oh well, you'll make a fine
first course. The only question is whether you'll go down
better sliced thin and raw, or chopped and panfried with
noodles."

Then, she smiled.

16

---◆·◆---

What do you say to a myth? The Kitsune was a tale to frighten young Blades, not a real person. No matter that I had already fought her once. That encounter, with its coda of my living burial, was more the stuff of nightmares than reality. Which was what the Shadowfox was *supposed* to be, a creature of dark dreams and disturbing fictions, not this calm woman sitting on a barrel.

After a few moments, she rolled her shoulders and sighed. "Do drop your shroud, child. Let's exchange a few pleasant words before we get to the part with the swords and the screaming. Thauvik agreed to issue orders that will give us all the privacy we need. So there's no worry about the Elite or the Crown Guard interrupting us. Come, sit, talk."

She snapped her fingers, and the shadow of a nine-tailed fox slid out from beneath the barrel where she sat, growing suddenly long and thin where it stretched out before her. For the briefest of moments it touched its nose to my shroud, then it flickered sideways into one of the nearby windows. In that instant the cloud of shadow that surrounded me dissolved into a puddle at my feet, shapeless and cold.

Triss!

... I'm ... all right. His voice echoed hollowly in my mind as though it were coming back through a door that opened into a place beyond the world. *Give me a moment. There.* The puddle twisted and turned, becoming a small, winged dragon.

"Your Triss is stronger of will than most of his kind," said the Kitsune. "The only other who has ever recovered from Thiussus's kiss so quickly is Kelos's Malthiss, and that one is almost as exceptional as his human pet."

Before I could think of anything to say, the nine-tailed fox reappeared carrying another barrel in jaws grown all out of proportion to the rest of her. She brought it to me like a dog delivering a fallen bird to its master.

But just as she was about to set it down, she grew a second head that said, "Here. Sit. Stay." Then a third, which pitched back in a silent howl of laughter. A fourth bent down to nose Triss, but this time my Shade was ready. He leaped away, coiling himself up and around my back so he could look over my shoulder. The barrel landed neatly on end in front of me. Then, all four heads did the silent-howl bit before looking each at the other, and dissolving back to one.

Mad, and powerful, and more dangerous than I could have imagined, sent Triss.

"Now," said the Kitsune, "are you going to sit? Or am I going to have to kill you without the benefit of getting a shot at converting you to the methods of my madness?"

"I don't think you're likely to convert me to anything, but I'll sit and listen if you feel the need to talk." It would give me time to think, a commodity I badly needed.

"Ah, stalling for time. Good boy." She made a patting gesture. "The smart choice whichever way things go, and the one that leaves you most likely to live. Kelos was right when he called you the best of your generation, or at least that's what I have to conclude from what I've seen of your lot."

"Siri's better," I replied. She was. There was no question.

"A better killer and a better mage. Certainly, that's how

Kelos painted her, though he said you were at least as smart and could be as good at the rest if you had the focus she did. But he still called you the better Blade. He said that you possessed the soul of justice to a degree that none of the others did, and that's what makes a true Blade. It's what made me, it's what made Kelos, and it's what made all of the other legends."

"*You* are calling yourself a true Blade?" I couldn't hide my shock.

"There's none truer, though Kelos comes closest."

"That's completely crazy! It's crazy on the record and it's doubly crazy given the current situation."

The nine-tailed fox laughed beside her. "Little fool, little tool, little child playing by the pool. Thinks he knows the ways and hows, but barely sees the plays and bows."

Did that make any sense to you? I sent Triss.

Not a jot.

Nuriko reached out and scratched the fox behind the ears. In response the fox grew a second pair, and Nuriko scratched behind those as well. Once she was done, she looked up at me and shook her head. "You know nothing, child. Neither about me, nor the true situation, but let's pretend for a moment that you have an opinion worth expressing. Tell me what the situation is here and why it makes me no true Blade."

"You've taken control of Thauvik somehow, wrenched it free of the Son of Heaven. You're trying to push him into a crusade of the undead that will kill tens of thousands or more. Namara created us to protect the weak from the mighty and to see that justice found those that power shielded. You're driving things exactly the opposite way."

"Not an uncommon way of seeing what I'm doing," said Nuriko, "but you miss several points. First, I'm not controlling Thauvik. Not in the least. I have no interest in putting any controls on anyone. Quite the contrary. What I have done is free Thauvik to do whatever he wishes. I have made him a king unchained. No more, no less."

"He's risen and blood mad, and what he wants is death

and destruction without end," said Triss. "He should be destroyed, not freed to wreak havoc on the world!"

Nuriko smiled a sad smile. "Naïve thing. Death and destruction is what they all want . . . ultimately. Oh, they may start out with the best of intentions—many of them do—but the very nature of the power they wield slowly whittles away at their humanity. Thauvik is undead and the worst kind of monster. That's true, but it barely takes him a half step beyond what any king becomes over time. They all want blood, and every last one will take it if they think they can get away with it. Every last one. It is what they are, and why we must destroy them."

"If he's such a monster, why haven't you destroyed Thauvik?" I asked.

"Because he is the perfect example," replied the Kitsune. "If Thauvik embarks on his risen crusade, he will soak this kingdom in blood. Kadesh, too, maybe the northern Magelands. Depends on how far he gets. No one will be able to deny what he did or the evil of it. No one will be able to pretend that the system that enabled him to do it isn't corrupt in its bones. It may not happen right in the instant that he is stopped, but the evidence will be undeniable, the first stone in the avalanche that buries the very idea of monarchy, and of government with it."

"That's mad," I said.

"Is it?" asked Nuriko and she didn't look crazy, she looked unspeakably sad. "Really? Here's the most obvious example. What is the single worst thing for the people? Not the rulers, the people. It's war. Where does war come from? Governments fighting governments. Without government, there is no war. There is no one person wielding power over their fellows and being corrupted by it. Government is the enemy of humanity. Hell, the enemy of all peoples. It's done as much harm to the Other races as it has to ours."

She sighed. "I can see that you don't understand, though I don't know whether that's because you *can't* understand *ever*, or if you're just too shaped by the system to see a world without it. Do you know why I left the service of the goddess I loved more than I love my soul?"

I shook my head, unable to answer the pain that suddenly throbbed in her voice.

"Because despite her love and compassion and divine decency, Namara couldn't be made to see. She was herself a form of authority absolute and had, in that one way, been corrupted by the idea of authority—unable to see its inherent limitations and evils. I tried to show her that what we were doing in her name wasn't justice, not really. It was just another way of propping up the system. For nearly eight hundred years the order provided the people with a false reassurance. We deceived them into believing there was a force in the world that could hold the mighty to account, despite the obvious corruption and inequality of the whole system."

She rose now and took two long steps closer to me. "But there can be no accounting for the great, not as a class, and individuals don't matter. As fast as you can kill an Ashvik, a Thauvik rises up in his place. If I let you kill Thauvik, how long do you think it will be before your pretty princess starts to make the tradeoffs of corruption. A day?" Nuriko came closer to me. "A week? A year? Ten?"

And closer still. "I can't say. Maybe she will play the exception and hold on to her integrity for her entire reign, providing one of those rare shining examples of a just ruler. But even if she does, the ass that follows hers on the throne could be another Ashvik. Or the one after that. As long as thrones exist there is no end to them."

Now she was standing inches away from me. "That's why I've loosed Thauvik, and that's why I'll kill you if you get in the way of what he is about to do. This is the moment when we finally have the chance to lay the whole system bare for all to see. This is when we begin to end monarchy, and theocracy, and all the other forms of enslavement that we have crafted for ourselves. In breaking Thauvik's chains, I have created the tool for breaking all the chains."

"What would you set up in place of what we have now?" Triss asked over my shoulder, his voice small and unsure.

"Nothing at all," she replied. "What possible reason is there for us to set up this man and call him a king? To give him dominion over his fellows while we call that one a serf and treat him as little more than a donkey with wit? Why should we raise up this one and push down that one? Let each rise to what he can achieve without building on the backs of his neighbors. Justice demands it."

The scariest thing about the Kitsune at that moment was that she didn't sound or act crazy. Not in the slightest. She sounded more than anything like one of my better teachers trying to show me something that was quite, quite true but which she knew I wasn't quite ready to understand. It was terrifyingly convincing on some level, especially since some of what she said made sense. Why *should* someone be allowed to rule over those around them just because their parents did before them, or an uncle, or grandmother? Why should the outcome of a duel decide who got to sleep on a bed in a palace and who was stuck on a pallet in the outbuildings?

I shook my head and pushed that aside for now. The system might well be rife with the sorts of injustice I had been shaped to end, but the solution Nuriko was proposing was pure unadulterated horror. I could not let her do what she planned.

"No," I said, "Justice does *not* demand it. At least, not this way. I'm not at all convinced you're right, but even if I were, I would have to oppose you in this. I cannot let you kill tens of thousands in the hopes that it will *somehow* make the world a better place at some later date."

"Hundreds of thousands, actually." She smiled, and once more I saw pain where I expected madness. "And you can't stop me. You can get out of the way, or you can die. I wish I could offer you another choice, but *this* is the moment. I don't have the time to save you from yourself for long enough for you to see that. It took Kelos years to start down the path to pursuing true justice with me, and a hundred years on he's still not all the way there."

She backed up then, giving me room. "This is your last chance, child. Step out of my way or die."

"I'm not going to do either."

"You can't believe how sorry I am to hear that. In deference to the promise I am about to extinguish and the love I know Kelos bears you, I will allow you to draw your swords and meet me above." She leaped to her right, put a foot on the outer wall and bounced herself back left where she did the same off the barracks, quickly mounting to the roof.

Her nine-tailed fox of a shadow remained behind for a long beat, looking at me with a melancholy cant to her head. "Falling down a champion drowns, sinking in darkness and lies, unable to open his eyes to the nighted skies and what the prophet shows him." Again the silent laughing howl, and then she followed her mistress above.

Triss spoke into my mind, *I don't think Thiussus is half as unwound as she's trying to make us believe she is. I feel intention beneath the words and it doesn't match the nonsense phrasings.*

"Come up," the Kitsune said from above, "or I close my fist on your little friend."

The shadow cage holding Fei's familiar contracted briefly, generating an inarticulate shriek of pain from within.

"On my way." If only because I hadn't yet come up with a better option.

I drew my swords, turned and took four running steps up the wall, then kicked off into a twisting backflip. I landed in a crouch on the edge of the barracks roof facing up toward the last place I'd seen the Kitsune. She was waiting for me at the roof's peak and she gently clapped now.

"Nice," she said. "Unnecessarily flashy, and it gave me a clean shot at your back as you kicked free of the wall, but the technique was beautifully executed."

"Somehow I didn't think you were going to take me out with a back strike. Not after all the efforts you've made to give me a fair chance."

"Smart child, and such good form. I'd love to see your Siri sometime if she's really your better in the Blade's arts."

Nuriko waved me forward. "Come at me now, I don't want you to die feeling you've done less than your best." She hadn't bothered to draw her sword yet.

Be very careful, sent Triss. *I don't know how much I can help you, not when Thiussus can put me more than half out of the game with just a touch as she did before. I wish I understood how she does that.*

Is there anything you can do to prevent her from doing whatever it is? I moved my swords into a high and low guard and advanced slowly.

Maybe, given time and practice. I don't think either is likely at this juncture.

Then stick close to me. Don't give her an easy opening to touch you.

I don't think it will help, but I don't have a better idea. Wait . . . maybe I'm looking at this the wrong way. Maybe it's not about her. Maybe it's about me . . . worth a try anyway.

The dim shadow of a dragon that the moon had painted around my feet collapsed inward into a small puddle which flowed up my body, covering me in a cold and silky second skin.

"Oh, is your partner afraid of Thiussus?" asked Nuriko. "That's too bad. Smart. But definitely too bad for you."

What's the plan here, Triss? I sent.

Not a plan so much as an attempt at a sidestep. I want to see what happens when it's you in control when Thiussus makes contact.

Then the nine-tailed fox was sliding across the lead panels of the roof toward me, and Triss vanished from my mind, releasing consciousness as he sank into shadowy dreams. My senses expanded to encompass Triss's and I decided that it would be best to get the experiment over as quickly as possible. I leaped forward, planting one foot firmly in the center of the advancing shadow at the same time I swung a scissoring pair of cuts at Nuriko, one at knee height, the other aimed for her throat.

Without seeming to exert any effort, Nuriko twisted

sideways in the air, turning a cartwheel that lifted her legs above my left-hand sword at the same time that she dropped her head and neck beneath my right hand. I barely registered her dodge because I was too busy trying to deal with the complete overloading of my borrowed suite of shadow senses.

Rapture in black.

A couple of years previously, I had been hit with a deathspark—a very powerful sort of specialized magelightning. It knocked me unconscious and nearly killed me. When I was first awakening from that blow, my senses had been badly scrambled and I had tasted the color blue. The effect of one sense bleeding into another was wild and strange—utterly unlike anything I'd encountered before. This was kind of like that, only more so.

Take the most intensely hot pepper you can possibly imagine and freeze it so thoroughly that you could shatter it with the lightest of blows. Now bite into it. As it fragments into a thousand tiny crystalline shards, each of them melts instantly, releasing an absolute burning explosion of sensation of impossible heat while simultaneously freezing your tongue. Got that? Now imagine that each of those tiny points of contact doesn't hurt you, but instead creates the most intense sort of pleasure. That's what I got secondhand through my link to Triss's senses, a terrible joyous burst of frozen heat all rendered in a palette of shadows.

No wonder Triss was so knocked down by the sensation. I was feeling it at secondhand through senses my mind had never been meant to interpret, and I still had trouble separating myself from the experience. It wanted all of my attention and all of my focus. All of me. The man I was even a few months previously would have fallen then, dropping everything to become one with his enraptured senses—easy meat for the Kitsune. But I had left that man behind at Darkwater Island, and where thought failed me, the flow of body and sword did not, continuing my motions in the absence of conscious will.

I pivoted on the point of rapture that was my right foot,

bringing my left leg up and around in a fan kick that followed the original path of my higher sword. In turn, I dropped that sword to follow the still-rotating Kitsune as I brought the other up, forcing her into a second, slightly less graceful, cartwheel. I ended my motion sideways to the Kitsune in a stance like a horseman in his saddle, my left blade held vertically between us. I shifted my right into a high diagonal then, slanting it down over my head to point at her heart.

"Better and better," Nuriko said with a laugh. "Now, try again." She still hadn't drawn her sword or even a knife—that slighting of my skills was beginning to grate on me.

I took a deep breath and recentered myself. Both feet were squarely on the Kitsune's shadow now, and I had to keep about half of my attention focused through Triss's senses on Thiussus. So far, she hadn't decided to do anything more than laugh silently and send wild shocks of sensation rolling up my body from the place where my feet met her substance. Coping with that flow *was* growing easier with each breath as I learned to accept it and let it pass through me, but that could change in an instant if Thiussus switched tactics.

I snapped my left wrist forward, flicking my sword at Nuriko's shoulder like a whip. She didn't seem to move, but when my point passed through the place her shoulder should have been, it touched nothing but air. I continued the motion of my sword as I rotated forward around the ball of my forward foot. Twisting down and to the side I brought my left sword into a cross guard while I swung the other in a whistling cut at her face.

She bent backward like a dancer sliding under a pole, moving impossibly fast. An instant later, she took a short, shuffling step that put her between my right-hand sword and my shoulder and stood up, gently touching a finger to my neck as though she were checking my pulse.

"Point?" she asked as though we were practicing on the field.

I growled, but nodded as she leaped back and away from me.

"That was an excellent combination," she said. "Master Eskilon created the form it's based on, and he was the best of my teachers at the temple. Once more."

I could feel anger boiling away under my heart at being treated so lightly, but I knew I mustn't let emotion rule me. Instead, I tried to do almost what Triss had done, letting go of the consciousness of the mind in favor of a sort of bodythought.

Shift the swords. Reflect and distract. Lean back. Stomp a kick at the Kitsune's ankle. Miss. Deepen the knee. Turn a front flip, lashing blades at chest and thighs. Kick. Thrust. Twist. Slice. Spin. Stab. Slice again.

Each time I attacked, the Kitsune shifted out of the way, never avoiding any attack by more than the smallest fraction of an inch, but never seeming to be in any real danger either. Twice more she pressed a finger to my body, once over the heart, once sliding across the inside of my thigh over the big artery there. Both times she asked, "Point?" Both times I nodded.

I was sure she could have scored more often if she'd wanted to, but she didn't seem interested in anything but the most perfect and deadly of mock attacks. I backed her most of the length of the barracks but couldn't lay steel on her. It was maddening. When we had almost reached the edge of the building, she held up a hand and I stopped for a moment.

"You are a credit to your teachers, Aral. Every motion is perfect, every thrust and kick and spin the purest expression of the forms upon which they were built. Your mastery of the arts of the Blade is a great strength, but also a great weakness. For generations your predecessors tried to kill me, but each time they met with failure. Let me show you why."

She produced a pair of long, lightly curved knives from the sheaths at her waist, like miniature versions of my own swords. "Oh, and don't worry, no poison this time."

She came at me and I lost all sense of the moment or anything but avoiding the steel that sought my blood. I

parried and dodged and spun, and never once had a chance
to strike back. Twice she cut me lightly, a shallow slice on
my chest over the heart, and a crease along the back of my
neck that sent a trickle of blood running down my spine.
Add the three times I only barely dodged or parried a blow
that would have ended me, and that was five times I would
have died in half as many minutes had she been using full-
length swords. Then, as abruptly as it had begun, the stun-
ning series of attacks ended. She had backed me almost to
the place where we started.

"Do you know what you're doing wrong?" she asked,
returning her knives to their sheaths.

I shook my head mutely, too winded for words.

"Would you like me to tell you?"

"Yes," I managed to gasp.

"Nothing."

"Huh?"

"You're doing nothing wrong. As with your attacks, every
block and parry and spin is perfect . . . and predictable. At
least for me. You have learned to fight in the best tradition
of the Blade. But you have never learned how to fight against
that tradition. Your submission to the authority of your
teachers will destroy you, just as authority is destroying this
world. A master of another school would find you a very
hard nut to crack, but for one who helped design and refine
those forms, you are an open book. Do you understand?"

"I do." Both what she had said, and what it meant.

"You can't hope to beat me, child, and I am loath to kill
you. Won't you step aside and let me do what I must without
destroying you?"

"No. I can't, and I won't."

"I'm sorry it had to end this way, Aral. You were the best
to come against me in all the long years, save only Kelos."

17

The most finely crafted tool is nothing more than a dead weight if you can't let it go when it becomes a burden, and even a master has things to learn. Kelos had told me that many years ago, and I had pretended to understand what he meant. Only, I hadn't. Not until now, when I faced the Kitsune and, very probably, my death.

"I'm sorry, too, Nuriko," I said, "but I thank you for the lesson."

Then I lunged, delivering a demonstration-perfect thrust of the burning water form, which I subverted at the last possible instant by throwing in a twist I'd perfected with the Zhani dueling swords that had been my primary weapons for seven years. It was ugly and a bit clumsy, as my Varyan-style blade with its curve and single edge had never been designed for such a maneuver, but it did something I had not managed to do previously that night. It connected. The blunt back of the blade caught the Kitsune high on the cheekbone. Not hard enough to split that metallic golden skin, but hard enough that I felt the shock in my wrist. It also forced her to make an ungainly leap to get back out of range before I could follow up—the first ungraceful move she'd made.

A mocking voice spoke from the shadow beneath my feet, "The kitten that fights and bites may scratch and claw, but there's very little blood he'll draw."

I ignored Thiussus's words, listening only for action, straining for any hint of threat with my borrowed senses.

Meanwhile, Nuriko reached up and touched her cheekbone. "I do believe you've bruised me, child. That's very well done, indeed. Your death will be the most honorable I can deliver."

Nuriko's left hand went to the hilt sticking up over her left shoulder. With a lift and flick she drew her greatsword, bringing it down and around into a guard position in front of her while placing her right hand on the hilt below her left. Like the Varyan-style swords I carried, it had a single edge. But it was straight as a Zhani dueling sword, and well over a yard in length—a warrior's weapon, a good foot and a half longer than my own shorter assassin's blades.

Without Triss's senses augmenting my own, the blade would have been all but invisible to me. The smoky blue gray tint of the goddess-forged steel drank the light with a special kind of magic. The oris juice I'd used to treat my own swords was a sad echo of the effect inherent to Namara's. The guard, like my own, was a simple oval. But where mine were of bronze, worked with bas-relief dragons chasing their tails eternally around the base of the blade, Nuriko's was set with a simple piece of lapis as magically unbreakable as the rest of the sword.

The misty blue stone looked down the length of the sword at me as it was supposed to—the Unblinking Eye of Justice. Only, the true eye of Justice had closed forever. Having the order's greatest renegade pointing it at me now felt like blasphemy. Anger surged through me in a great wave. Were it not for a lifetime of training, it might have sucked me under completely, dragging me down into the madness of the berserker. Instead, I took my rage and rode it—setting the whole of my being to the task of destroying the Kitsune.

I leaped forward before Nuriko could act, and once again I lost track of the details of the thing. Giving myself over wholly to the play of steel against steel, I focused only as much attention on any given move as I needed to keep myself from falling into the patterns of my temple training. I drove her back and back again, though she gave ground more slowly than she had before and not every blow was simply avoided. Three times she had to interpose her own sword between one of mine and a vital point. But I still couldn't touch her, and she had yet to strike back.

When she finally made a move, she nearly ended me. It was a simple double-handed cut swung down and around from a high guard and aimed at cutting me in half. From the expression on her face to the loose relaxed set of her arms and shoulders the blow looked slow, almost lazy. It was anything but, coming in harder and faster than anyone but Kelos had ever struck at me.

Instinct told me to set my feet and take the blow with a hard block. Instinct would have killed me. Instinct wanted my swords to be those Namara had made for me. They were not and they would have shattered had I followed my instincts. Instead, I interposed my left sword at an angle to deflect the blow up and out while simultaneously jumping backward.

Sparks danced in my vision as my parrying sword was driven into my forehead, side on, and my wrist burned where it had been wrenched out of line. If Nuriko had followed up then, she could easily have killed me, but she didn't, waiting for me to reset myself.

"I really am sorry that this has to end with your life," she said, and there was genuine pain in her voice. "Kelos was better when I first faced him, but you adapt faster. Given time I think you might surpass your teacher. Killing you is going to be as much a tragedy as the destruction of a Chang Un master sculpture."

"It's not over yet," I replied, though that was pure bravado.

In addition to the minor injuries she'd inflicted on my

wrist and forehead, Nuriko's blow had shaved a hair-thin strip of steel off the side of my left sword. The peeled away piece was a foot long and half an inch across. I revised my earlier thought about her shattering my swords. A direct hit wouldn't break them, it would cut them in half.

"Keep telling yourself you have a chance, child, right up until the end," said Nuriko. "Maybe it will allow you to die happy. Now, come at me again. You're getting better with every exchange, and I want you to end on the highest note you can reach in the time that you have."

Her words should have sounded condescending. They didn't. They sounded true.

I lunged for her heart, then spiraled my point off to the side to aim for a wrist while dropping my second sword into a cut at her forward foot. She moved. I missed. She drove a skull splitting slice down toward my head. I got out of the way somehow, but now my sword had matching stripes of raw steel on both sides.

The part of me that was coming to really fear the Kitsune made the stripes symmetric and intentional—markers set down by a master. The remaining rational bits recognized that was bullshit and me mind-gaming myself, but that helped less than I would have liked.

She attacked again as soon as I'd set myself, following up immediately with a cut that sliced off the top of my cowl and some of my hair. And once more—driving me back to our starting point with her third blow. There, she put up her sword to let me breathe. I took her charity, realizing suddenly and against all odds that I *wanted* to live in a way that I had not in many years.

I was just resetting myself for what I knew would be our final pass when a voice whispered in my ear. "She honors you, and that is the only reason I haven't closed my jaws around your spine." It was the nine-tailed fox speaking in something other than riddles for a change.

It was only in the instant that he spoke that I realized I had lost track of Triss's senses and Thiussus both in my focus on Nuriko. The fox had put herself behind me without my even noticing her movement, though, of course, a tail of shadow still connected her to Nuriko. The line of it passed directly between my legs, and I had no doubt of the message. Thiussus wanted me to know that even if I somehow managed to defeat Nuriko, I still couldn't win because she outmatched Triss in a way that left me fighting all but alone.

That's when a mad idea occurred to me, an insane little plan dropping into my mind all in one piece, though I don't know where it came from. Perhaps the ghost of the goddess had whispered inspiration in my ear. Perhaps my newfound desire to live was pushing me into new ways of thinking. Or, perhaps it was simply the glimmer of reflected moonlight dancing along the raw steel where Nuriko had shaved the oris-treated darker layer off my sword. Whatever, it was mad and simple, possible only because Triss was already playing the second skin for me as he would for any finicky bit of magic.

Even as I thought about how to implement it, I had already begun. Reaching deep into the well of my soul I drew up more of my life force than I had ever expended on a single spell before. Holding the image of what I wanted in my mind, I cried out an ancient word of power; one I normally avoided at all costs. As I spoke the word I channeled all of the nima I had drawn from my soul's well and sent it roaring down the lengths of my swords. They exploded in light. Pure, brilliant, white light, like the sun.

It tore at the shadow stuff coating my palms, and deep stabbing pain spilled through my link to Triss as every shred of him that faced the light burned with agony. Thiussus, who had been gloating over my shoulder, screamed and collapsed down into Nuriko's shadow. She grunted in turn as his pain washed back through her. But I wasn't done yet. Thrusting one of my bright blades straight through Thiussus, I drove it deep into the roof and one of the underlying beams beneath with all the strength in my body.

"Kill you!" Nuriko shouted, leaping toward me. And, I had no doubt that she still could.

Which was why I had already jumped to the side myself,

dropping back down into the space between the barracks and the outer wall. I had judged my positioning properly and, as I fell past the cage of shadows that held Fei's familiar, I sliced it in half. Neither light nor steel could harm the little air spirit, but shadow bars shattered when they encountered their opposite element, freeing Scheroc. Even as my feet touched the ground, I pivoted and began to run, knowing that Nuriko must first free Thiussus from my spike of light before she could follow. As I ran I sheathed my remaining sword and released Triss.

I didn't know how long it would take Nuriko to come after me, having only seen the technique I'd just attempted once before, and that, in very different circumstances. The stakes that had pinned Kaman's shadow to the ground in front of the cross they'd hung him on had likewise been charged with pure light—both a gall and a trap for his Shade. I had no idea what it might have taken to loose those stakes, for I had given Kaman a different sort of freedom in the shape of the death he craved.

I had taken perhaps ten steps when I heard Devin's voice call out from behind me, "Which way did he go?"

"He's mine," snarled Nuriko. "Just as soon as Thiussus can move."

"I've got this," Devin yelled back and I could hear that he was running my way. I didn't know what he was up to, but I didn't dare hang around to find out.

Bring me up to date, Triss sent groggily, distracting me from Nuriko's angry response to Devin. *That* was *Devin, right?* he asked, reminding me that his sleeping state meant he'd missed out on the entire fight. *Also, why do I feel like somebody dipped me in pitch and tried to use me for a torch?*

Sorry, the torch thing was me. And, yes, Devin. No time for more. Right now we need to run and I need a shroud.

All rig—Fire and sun! What the fuck is that on your back!

My remaining sword, and you're going to have to cover it if we're to have any chance of living out the night.

Fire and sun. Fireandsun. Fireandsun! Ow! And then I was shrouded again.

Which was good, as I had apparently reached the edge of whatever cordon the Kitsune had established with Thauvik. There were Crown Guards everywhere, as well as the Elite with their stone dogs scattered amongst them. I aimed for a gap where there were no Elite, but otherwise didn't slow down. This was a race, and it was win or die. Somehow I managed not to collide with anyone in that angry ring, and passed out the other side still running.

Did I mention the part about this hurting? Triss demanded.

Yes. I'm aware and very sorry, but you need to hang on at least till we're past the gate.

The gate? The main gate?

Shortest line from here to the river, and if we don't make the river, we die.

Good thing you're back in top form again then. One more question?

Make it quick.

Why is your sword burning a hole in my hide?

Later, but the other guy looks worse.

Oh, good. He let out a sort of mental whimper. *I hope this isn't going to become a habit.*

I doubt it. I got burned, too, and I hate hurting you. For what it's worth, the light should probably start fading soon. Which was a damned good reason to run faster.

But I didn't actually increase my pace, I was already going as fast as I dared if I wanted to have anything left for swimming. When we got to the gate, I grabbed the portcullis chain and blasted the brake loose. As the great spiked portcullis dropped across the passage, I rode the chain to the top of the wall above. From there, two steps and a hop put me on the outer wall.

Wings! I sent as I leaped into space.

Crazy man, replied Triss, but he shifted shape and density, spinning panels of shadow out from my arms like great sails. He let out a sighing *better* as he moved away from the agony of light leaking out along the seams of my right sheath.

I felt his move away from that source of pain as a sort of deep release, though the underlying aches of his injuries continued to echo along the link that bound us. I had hurt him, badly, and I hated myself for it.

Together, we wafted down toward the river. It was lovely and would have been lovelier if I'd dared let us sail-jump the whole way. But the combination of a sword-shaped magic lantern on my back and no shroud made us all too visible. The first arrow had already zinged harmlessly through my right shadow sail by the time I felt we'd gotten low enough.

Drop me.

You're the boss. Insane, but still the boss.

My wings vanished and we dropped, though not before a second arrow dug a burning crease along my left side just below the armpit. We landed with a splash in the topmost tier of a huge fountain that Thauvik's great-great-grandmother had built to commemorate some victory over Kadesh. I had a grumpy, swearing skin of darkness in place by the time I dropped to the next tier, and a full shroud for my third splashdown.

That was good, because Crown Guards were converging from fucking everywhere by then. I'd just slipped past the first couple when I heard Devin's voice cry out from behind me, "Aral!"

"Fuck you!" I yelled over my shoulder.

Then I hopped over the spear of a smarter than average guard who was searching for me like a blind man with his cane, and started running. Again, I could feel Triss's pain at covering my lighted blade pouring through the bond between our souls. It galled me like an iron spike driven into my shoulder. I was slower, too, much slower, and had begun to develop a stitch in my side. It was only then, after that first wild burst of energy that always came with a chase had faded, that I realized my mistake.

I'd been pacing myself like a runner in his second mile,

not a sorcerer whose injured familiar was actively fighting against his opposite element. Triss's draw on the well of my soul was as much of a drain as a freely bleeding wound would have been. My knees started to go spongy about then, and I had to slow even more or risk a fall. That's when Devin caught up to me, though I didn't know he was there until he'd put one arm around my waist, taking some of my weight.

He whispered harshly as he dragged my left arm over his shoulder, "Keep moving, you fool. She could be on her way already and the river's our only chance of giving her the slip."

I wanted to argue, but didn't dare. I just let Devin take more of my weight and kept on going in what had become a half run. If Triss had any thoughts on the arrangement, he kept them to himself in favor of the mental equivalent of continuous sub-verbal swearing. At the end of another two blocks, we all more or less fell off the bridge together, landing with a huge and inelegant splash.

Before I could figure out how you went about swimming when you felt like I did then, Devin had hooked his arm across my throat and started quietly dragging me backward through the water. He kicked more than he stroked, minimizing both sound and ripples. Triss shifted up away from my now submerged sword to form something of a half shroud over the bits of me that remained above water. I could feel his relief at leaving the light behind again.

"You have a plan?" I asked Devin after a couple of seconds. Or, I intended to anyway. It came out more like, "Youvaplun?"

"Hush," Devin said very quietly. "Boat, just ahead."

A narrow sampan, painted a dull black, was whispering along the water toward us—obviously a smuggling boat. Devin rocked back in the water and flicked his free hand, dropping the knife from his wrist sheath into his palm. As the boat came closer, Devin snapped his arm, sending the knife into the left eye of the smuggler at the back. He slumped forward over the vessel's skulling oar, lifting it out of the water.

When the smuggler's companion turned to see what had become of his rower, Devin pointed his palm at the man's back and spoke a word of opening. It was answered with a brief flare of purple spell-light as the smuggler's back opened like a door. He fell into the water about a half a beat behind most of his organs. Nasty, but effective, like all of Devin's best work. He dragged me over to the boat, which had already started to turn in the current. I caught hold of the low gunwale and hung there, trying to work up the strength to pull myself into the boat.

"Gods but I wish I could just let you drown," Devin said as he slipped aboard.

Then he reached down and caught my arm to help me in. I rolled onto my back in the bow while Devin went aft, where he recovered his knife and pushed the second smuggler into the river. Then he took up the scull, finished the turn the sampan had begun on its own, and began to stroke us rapidly downriver.

We had to dodge two customs boats along the way, but the combination of the light-drinking paint of the smuggling boat and our shrouds got us through all right. Devin didn't say another word until after we'd passed under the final bridge, and the river started widening out into the mouth of the bay. Triss was equally silent, though I could feel that was from exhaustion as opposed to the seething anger that was practically pouring off Devin.

"Okay," Devin finally said, "if the bitch can hear us out here we're both dead anyway, so we might as well talk."

"Where the fuck have you been?" I husked in not at all the demanding tone I'd intended.

"Hang on a beat," Triss said, sounding very nearly as wrung out as I felt. "Let's see." He slipped out from beneath me, where the moon had put him, and slid under the low curved roof that provided the sampan with a tiny cabin at its midsection. "Thought so."

He returned with a dark bottle that gurgled invitingly as he handed it to me. " 'Spirits for the drained spirit.' " He quoted the old saying about magic and booze.

I tilted the bottle this way and that, listening to the alcohol move back and forth. "I . . ." Fuck but I *needed* a drink, and this one would be medicinal, not a drunk getting his drink on. Who could argue with that?

I dropped the bottle into the bottom of the boat and said quietly, "No, Triss, I really can't."

The light shifted and I realized Devin was standing above me, though I hadn't heard him move. He was looking past me to the dragon perched on the gunwale beside me. "Does that rot really work, Triss? I've heard the saying a few times since the fall of the temple, but it seemed ridiculous in the face of our priests' teachings."

"It works," said Triss.

"Good enough for me." Devin knelt to pick up the bottle, and pulled the cork.

Before I had a chance to figure out what he intended, Devin pressed the bottle to my lips and tilted it high. I got a huge mouthful of some incredibly strong anise flavored liquor, and swallowed it down—I couldn't help myself. Sweet liquid fire poured down my throat and into my belly where it vaporized as my nima-starved soul sucked away the vital essence of the liquor. Seemingly of its own accord, my hand reached up and caught the neck of the bottle. I drank off maybe a third of it in huge gasping gulps before I needed to pull it away from my lips to breathe.

I took another long pull, hating myself for needing it. Then, with an effort of will that I could only compare to the effort of building a greatspell, I sat up and threw the bottle out into the bay. I hadn't done anything that felt quite so hard since the day I'd dropped my last few efik beans into the river. The exertion left me shaking and sweating as I fell back against the bow of the boat.

"Is that enough?" Devin asked. "Or will you need more? It's a smuggling boat, I'm sure there's lots."

"Fuck. You."

"Is that a yes? Or a no? I don't speak drunk. I'd better just get you another bottle." He ducked into the cabin in the waist of the boat.

Triss.

Yes? I could feel his pain and anger and worry burning down the link between us.

Break them all, I sent. Devin reappeared with another bottle, pulling the cork as he turned toward me. *Start with that one.*

Done.

I felt a light drain on my nima, and the bottle exploded in Devin's hand. He yelped and swore and I could see blood on his palm where shards of glass had cut him. Good. Triss snapped his wings and slipped past Devin into the cabin. I heard more bottles shattering.

"Not strong enough to just turn me down?" Devin's voice dripped poison as he pulled shards of glass from his hand. "Had to get Triss to bail you out?"

"Again, fuck you, Devin. Sideways. With an iron-bound battering ram."

I hated him more in that moment than I had ever hated anyone but the Son of Heaven. If I'd had the strength for it, I might have killed him, but I didn't. Despite the temporary boost from the booze, it felt like someone had wrapped me in a hundred pounds of thick lead foil.

Devin glared at me. "Even now, when you're nothing but a dried-up husk of what you once were, you still think you're better than me. Don't you?"

"Simple reason for that. I am."

"I want to kill you so bad."

I suddenly realized what would hurt him the most. "You're a coward, Devin. I don't know if you always were, or if it was the fall of the temple that broke you. I don't actually care either, because it's not really important to me. *You're* not really important to me. And yes, I am better than you. Now. I don't know about the old days. I was better at many things than you back then, but as a person . . ."

I shrugged. "You'd be a better judge of that than me. But now, when I'm a half-broken thing always a half step away from a slide back into the gutter? Oh yes, I'm the better man now. My soul may be stained and ragged around the edges,

but it's still *my* soul. You sold yours to the enemy for cowardice's sake, and there's nothing you can do to win it back.
It's *easy* to be the better man now. You're not even human
anymore, Devin. You're a bitter thing in a man's shape."

Devin's unbloodied hand reached back toward his sword
and I could see that it was shaking with rage, but he stopped
short of drawing. Instead, he spat out, "When this is over,
you and I are going to settle this thing once and for all."

"Anyplace, anytime."

18

---◆·◆·◆---

Moonlight on the bay beneath a sea of stars. Salt breeze and gently lapping waves. Shadows speak in whispers, dragon and tayra. Old friends in the dark. Two men who desperately wanted to kill each other.

It was like something out of a pastoral poem, except for that last part. While Devin and I spat hate at each, our familiars had once again slipped aside, quietly conversing in their alien tongue.

I glared back at Devin. "In the interests of getting this whole business over with so we can get down to killing each other, why don't you tell me whatever you dragged me out here to tell me. You could start with why the hell you haven't been by the drop to pick up my message. Last time we talked, you told me you needed my help to take down the Kitsune and you promised that you would be there when I was ready. Mind, I'm not even a little bit surprised at the lack of reliability from you, but what happened?"

"I would have thought it obvious," replied Devin. "The Kitsune happened. Every time I've gotten within fifty feet of the outer walls of the palace, there she's been, just happening by to see how I'm doing. I figured there wasn't much point in trying to pick up messages if I got dead in the process. Nuriko hasn't threatened me outright, but she doesn't need to. She's killed more Blades than any other individual in our history."

"Excepting your boss, the Son of Heaven."

Devin clenched his fists and blood dripped from his injured hand. "Fine. She has personally, with her own two hands, killed more Blades than anyone else, ever. Does that make you happier?"

I nodded, but couldn't resist adding, "Except for the implication that you're still a Blade of any kind, but let's move past that for now."

"Let's," Devin snapped.

"You've been too scared of Nuriko to come out and check your mail. Got it. But here we are, so let's talk about the details for me saving your ass from the Kitsune, and by extension the Son of Heaven. When do we hit the palace?"

Devin looked very uncomfortable. "You don't."

"What do you mean by that?" I asked.

"Thauvik's decided he likes this whole risen crusade thing, but he's paranoid and, I think, a little scared of the Kitsune."

"Meaning?"

"He's planning on shifting his operations to the fortress at Kao-li. He was going to do it later this week, but after what happened between you and Nuriko tonight, I imagine he'll move faster."

I was stunned. Kao-li changed everything. "So, what? The deal's off, Thauvik spills blood over half the world, and the Son of Heaven makes you into a wall hanging?"

"No. I am not going to end up hanging on the Son's wall. I'll hand you my swords and bare my neck for the chopping first." He grimaced as he said that and closed his eyes for a second in obvious pain—that oath again.

After a moment, he went on, "We're going to have to make some changes to the plan is all. I don't know the fortress, so it's going to take me a few days of looking around to figure how to set things up for your assault force. I don't think I'll be able to get loose again after today, so I'll have to send you a message somehow and you can take it from there. Maybe we can use that wind spirit you rescued tonight."

"No."

"What do you mean 'no'?" demanded Devin, with more than a little panic in his voice.

"I mean no. I didn't trust you beforehand, and that's doubly true now. I won't do this. It smells too much like a setup. Even if I was willing, Maylien hates your guts. I had to push really hard to get her to agree to risking her people on an attack at the palace, and Kao-li's a hundred times nastier. There's no way she'll agree to this, and you said yourself that without an assault force there's no way this can work. It's over. Do you want to settle what's between you and me now? Or would you rather let someone else kill you? I'll make it clean, at least."

Devin reached for his swords. I went for my remaining blade as well, but my position hampered me badly and Devin's points were hovering an inch away from my face before I could more than half sit up.

"I didn't want to do this," said Devin.

"Kill me? I thought you'd been dreaming about this for years."

Killing you is not his intent, sent Triss—which explained why my familiar hadn't tried to intervene.

"No," said Devin. "That, I want. This, on the other hand . . ." With a flourish he spun his swords into an underhand grip and extended the hilts to me. "This is the last fucking thing in the world I wanted to do, but I don't see any other way."

"I don't understand," I said.

"We both know there's nothing I can promise or say that will get you to trust me. I more than half expected that, so Zass and I have been discussing how to salvage things. He pointed out there was one thing I could *do* that might suffice.

This is it." He twitched his hands and the swords slid a bit closer to me as his grip shifted from hilts to the backs of the blades.

"You're offering me your swords?"

"No, I'm fucking proposing we do a betrothal dance with them!" He rolled his eyes, visible even in the dark by the flashing whites. "Yes, I'm offering you my swords, though I damned well intend to get them back. It struck me as the one thing I could do that you would have to take seriously. And, since you brought it up, I figured it also might serve to convince your royal bedmate."

I nodded, though I didn't yet touch the hilts—this worked for me and it might do it for Maylien, too. "What are your conditions?"

Last time I had borrowed a sword from Devin we'd done a deal with very specific parameters. I didn't know if that had anything to do with my ability to kill risen with his swords where he could not, but I didn't want to screw this up over a missed detail.

"I hand over the swords, you rid me of the Kitsune."

"That's it?"

"No. If you decide you can't do it, you give me my swords back as soon as possible thereafter. If you do manage to eliminate the Kitsune, you have to give them back afterward."

"How soon afterward?" I needed them to kill Thauvik, and somehow I didn't get the feeling I'd have the chance while Nuriko was still in a position to protect him.

Devin took a deep breath and gritted his teeth, a man bracing for pain. "As soon as you deem that you have achieved your purpose or—ow! Fuck!" He went to his knees, but kept his grip on the swords, still holding them out for me to take. Gasping, he continued. "Or one week after you've dealt with the Kitsune. Whichever comes first."

"Done." I took the swords.

I took the swords.

For the first time in the seven years since I had returned my own temple blades to the hand of my dead goddess, I held a pair of her swords. The exhaustion and pain that had weighed heavier and heavier on me since our encounter with the Kitsune vanished. I felt light and fit and strong, almost seventeen again—the year I had first taken up my own swords and gone out to kill Ashvik. Though Namara was dead, I felt a sort of echo of the purpose that had once filled me, like an ideal's ghost blowing her champion one last kiss.

I had no memory of rising, but I found myself standing on the gunwales with Devin still kneeling before me. He seemed diminished somehow, no longer an object worthy of my hate, if not quite deserving of my pity either. I held the swords high over my head, making a triangle with the moon at its apex, and I knew that though my goddess was gone, this was what I was born to be.

The moment passed, and I fell back down into myself, a broken man reassembled from pieces, holding another's swords and wishing I could be what I once was. It was a very long fall. But I couldn't find it in me to regret the heights or be downcast about their loss, and my fatigue had not returned. With a movement as natural as breathing, I slung the right-hand sword in my sheath, a too-loose fit that I would have to adjust with a few carefully placed rivets as soon as I had the chance.

Then I flipped the left-hand sword to my right, and drew my own left-hand sword—still dimly shining, especially along the scars Nuriko had carved in its sides. I touched it briefly to my forehead in salute to the service it had given me—service that had all but destroyed it—and consigned it to the deeps of the bay, which seemed a fitting enough burial. Before its light had entirely vanished into the darkness, I had flipped the sword of the goddess from hand to hand again and sheathed it as well.

"Aral?" It was Devin, who hadn't moved so much as a hair through the whole maneuver.

"Yes?"

"If you flip my swords around over water like that ever again, I will kill you on the spot, deal or no deal. I think my heart stopped."

For some reason that struck me as one of the funniest things anyone had ever said to me, and I threw my head back and laughed long and hard. Devin shook his head like I was mad and backed away to sit atop the low cabin. When I was done, I smiled at him.

"And that's your tragedy," I said. "Because you never will understand. I couldn't drop one of Namara's swords into the sea if I wanted to, but you could, couldn't you?"

"Did I mention how much I hate you?" asked Devin.

"Once or twice."

"Well, add another one, because I'm really going to hate what I have to ask you next."

"What's that?"

"To beat the living shit out of me."

I didn't ask why. It was obvious. He couldn't return to the Kitsune without his swords, not unless he had the injuries to show he'd lost a fight badly.

I hopped down into the boat. "Where do you want the apparent knockout blow?"

"Just in front of the temple, I think," he replied. "And it's going to have to bleed."

"Broken nose?"

"You'd probably better. If nothing's broken, she'll be suspicious, and that's the quickest to heal. You're going to need to cut me up some, too, probably at least one solid stab wound." He pressed a thumb into his thigh. "Here, maybe two or three inches deep and along the grain of the muscle so it's not too serious."

"You want me to do it on the boat, or ashore?"

"I'd love to have some witnesses to the end of the fight and you stripping the swords from my fallen body, but I'm going to have enough trouble holding still and letting you do this without trying to play pretend at the same time. Better do it out here and dump me ashore."

"Unconscious?"

He nodded. "The sleeping guard spell?"

"I was never any good at it." It was one of Loris's favorites. It worked a bit like a carefully applied sap, but whenever

I tried it the magical flare was always far bigger than I wanted—too likely to draw the attention of anyone magesighted.

"I'll have to do it myself then, because there's no way I'm letting you do that neck squeezing thing Kaman taught you as a substitute."

"I've never killed anyone with that yet." I replied. "Not accidentally anyway."

"No."

"Fine, but I'm not going to mourn if you fry your brains by casting something like that on yourself."

"Tell me something I don't know," said Devin. "Can you make sure the city guard finds me before I wake up? That'll make things a lot more convincing."

"Shouldn't be a problem. Anything else?"

"No. But we'd better nail down the details of how we're going to communicate once I'm inside Kao-li."

So we did that to the extent we could, given the uncertainties. When we were done, I flicked a wrist to put a knife in my hand. It was time.

"I'll start with the head." That would give him more time to recover his faculties before trying a spell.

I threw the first punch with my knife hand, hitting him above the point of his right eyebrow with the pommel and skidding the steel knob from there up and back toward his hairline. It opened a long ragged tear over his temple that immediately started bleeding. Devin clenched his teeth and grunted but didn't cry out. Next, I reversed the knife and put a shallow cut in his left cheek, nicking his ear. Devin hissed and glared hate at me. I punched him in the nose, though I found that every blow made me feel sicker. He touched the right side of his mouth and nodded, so I hit him there as well, though not so hard this time—I wanted to split his lip, not knock out any teeth.

After that, I alternated knife and fist work on his body, aiming for lots of light bleeding and superficial bruises. There's a skill to doing that well. To my shame, I'd learned it back at the Gryphon's Head while playing the shadow jack—freelancing on the wrong side of the law. I'd tried to mostly stick to bodyguarding and courier work, the kind of stuff I could do and still look at myself in the mirror, but I'd taken less savory jobs when I got desperate enough for whiskey money.

That included collecting on loans for the nastier sort of moneylenders, which involved very precise beatings. You wanted the slip scared and hurting, but not injured so bad they couldn't earn. That meant lots of mess and pain, but nothing broken, at least not right out of the gate. I refused to get involved with what they did to people they'd written off completely.

I had enough stains on my soul without that, and even the first-pass work made me drink myself into a stupor after. Not that I didn't drink myself flat most nights in those days, but after working for the moneylenders, I drank with intent. Triss hid himself in my shadow while I worked on Devin, just as he had in the bad old days. I did as thorough a job on Devin as I'd ever done on any debt slip, and when I was finished, I turned and vomited over the side of the boat.

Devin laughed through bleeding lips. "You always were too sentimental, Aral. I don't know why Namara favored you so."

"Fuck you, Devin."

"Truth hurts, huh?"

"Perhaps she favored him *because* he was sentimental," said Zass, completely surprising me and causing Devin to turn and glare at his shadow.

"You still want me to stab you in the thigh?" I asked after a long uncomfortable silence.

"You'd better," Devin said quietly.

So, I did. Then Devin knocked himself out and I sculled us back to the docks, where I dumped him and made a ruckus. I shrouded up and hung around long enough to make sure he didn't get rolled and dumped back into the bay, then headed for Fei's office. We needed a talk.

Aral? Triss sent as soon as we had left Devin behind.

Yes?

I spoke with Zass about Thiussus and the Kitsune while you and Devin were chewing on each other. In fact, we talked of little else, since Zass is even more frightened of her than I am. We compared our encounters with her.

And?

I think it might be possible to lessen the effect she has on me, though I won't know for certain until we meet again.

How? I remembered how raw and powerful Thiussus had felt through Triss's senses and wondered what you could do to fight that.

It's hard to express in human speech. Thiussus is—Triss hissed something in Shade—*of the everdark. Touching her is like touching the heart of shadow. What I feel is powerful by itself, but it's not the strength of her that's so overwhelming, it's the everdarkness of it . . . the sense of being home rather than here in the sunlands. That . . . nostalgia? Homecoming? I don't know the right term, but it is very hard to be here-now, at the same time I feel so there-then.*

All right, I think I can see that, but how do you fight it?

By anchoring myself to this world and to you. Maybe. I must think on it, and then we will have to see if my thinking is right.

He kind of slipped away at that point and I took over maintenance of the shroud while he did his thinking. As we had been talking, I could feel the swords of my goddess slopping around in the too-loose sheaths on my back and I resolved to ask Fei if she had any rivets.

But once we got closer to Fei's office, I realized I had to change my plans. Crown Guard had put a cordon around the area, locking out everyone, *including* the city watch, a fact that had the latter visibly enraged. They were buzzing around the edges of the cordon in angry little groups of yellow and black. Never had the Stingers' nickname seemed more apt.

What's happening? asked Triss.

I haven't the slightest . . . oh. A nasty thought had occurred to me.

What?

We cut our outgoing shadow trail when we went into the river with Devin. . . .

Triss let out a little mental hiss. *But if the Kitsune followed our backtrail, it would have led her straight to Fei's office. We need to find the captain, fast!*

Fei was nowhere in evidence, so I looked around for any of her personal command. I was hoping for Sergeant Zishin, but couldn't find him. Nor any of Fei's other senior people either—a very bad sign. I did finally spot a familiar face standing at the mouth of a small alley: Corporal Anjir. He was with a couple of other low-ranking Mufflers and looked very nervous. They all did, passing a little flask around to bolster their courage. As always, the regular members of the watch were giving them a wide berth. I went up over the rooftops and down into the alley so that I could come up behind them unseen.

"Anjir," I said quietly, though I maintained my shroud.

He and his fellows started, but none of them bolted. Anjir tucked the flask into his shirt, then turned and leaned against the wall. Moving slowly and casually, he glanced sidelong into the alley. "Who's there?"

"I won't say my name here, but we met once before, nearly a year ago in Captain Fei's office. You were delivering a poster and—don't run!" I hissed the last when I saw the memory hit him—he paled visibly. "You won't like the results."

"Are you threatening our corporal?" one of the privates asked angrily, stepping closer to the alley mouth.

"Don't," said Anjir, touching the woman on the shoulder. "It wouldn't go well. I need a moment to talk with an old . . . acquaintance. Keep an eye out for the Crownies and give a whisper if any of 'em start coming this way. We don't want to get scooped up like Zishin did."

"All right, Corp, it's your call, but I don't like it."

"Neither do I, Private, neither do I." Then he stepped into the deeper dark of the alley and I backed up to give him room.

"What happened?" I asked.

"Don't know, something up at the main office." He jerked his head back toward the others. "We were doing a little job for the captain, and when we came back things was all stirred up."

"Dammit! I need to know where Fei is."

"Couldn't say, though Sergeant Zishin told us she rabbited when things went bollocks."

"You talked to Zishin?"

Anjir nodded. "But only for a minute or two. He told us to rabbit, too, when a bunch of Crownies came our way. We went, but not too far, and we saw them scoop him up. That almost started a riot out there." He jerked a thumb over his shoulder. "Most Stingers hate our guts, but when it comes to the yellow and black against the Crownies, we're all on the same side. Especially these days."

"Did Zishin tell you anything else I might want to know?" I asked.

"'Fraid not. He just told us the captain had pulled a fade and warned us to do the same. Said we should go deep and dark and wait for the war to sort itself out and see who ended up in Fei's office after."

"That's good advice, especially now." I tried not to blame myself for leading the Kitsune straight to Fei's office. Cutting Scheroc loose probably balanced the scales there for the captain, but it did nothing for the rest of the Mufflers. "If you've got a retirement plan, you might want to be thinking about it." I pictured the risen crusade that might be brewing and shuddered. "Hell, if I were you, I'd be thinking about relocating to Radewald for the duration. Things could go very wrong very fast."

"We was just discussing that when you arrived. Captain made sure every one of us had backup plans in case someone up the line decided Silent Branch was a liability. Made us think both in-country and out. Paid for a fair bit of it out of her own purse even. Good thing there's not that many of us. You think this could really go bad enough that we need to get out of Tien? I've got a little place I bought outside of Ar. . . ."

"That's a good start, but if this goes wrong, the Mage-lands might not be far enough to run."

Nor anyplace else this side of the mountains, Triss added mentally.

"Oh. The Crownies closed the palace up tight after that thing on the bridge, but—" Anjir tilted his head to one side. "That was you, wasn't it, trying to mark another crown on your sword hilt?"

"Something like that."

"Wish you'd gotten steel into him, then."

"I did."

"Funny, I wouldn't expect a guy like you to only do half the job when you got that close." He paused, and I could practically see him thinking. "Or did you? I was about to tell you the Crownies had shut all the doors in the palace and threw away the bells, but that we were still hearing some really crazy rumors out of there. Now I'm thinking they might not be so crazy. And that's all I've got. Guess I'll be taking the next boat to the Magelands and waiting to hear how it all settles. Give me a tick to get the kids a running?"

"All right."

Anjir turned and walked back to the little knot of Muf-flers. I didn't listen to what he told them, but the discussion was short and they all faded immediately after. While he was doing that, I took a moment just to breathe. It felt good.

"So why are you still here?" he asked when he came back. "I mean, if what I'm hearing in between what you're actually saying is true, Zhan's about to go in the shitter and ain't nobody gonna be able to stop it."

"Without getting into the sort of specifics that someone might wring out of you later, I'm not quite convinced that I can't put another crown on my hilt."

If there's a way, we'll find it, Triss agreed silently.

Anjir paused and I could see him thinking again. Finally, he said, "I don't know if it's my place to tell you this, you being what you are and me being what I am, but I'm gonna say it anyway. Let it go. I was a kid when you done for

Ashvik, and like most kids back then I resented the idea of someone killing our king. I even rooted for the Son when his people put down yours."

I hissed angrily, and Anjir held up a hand. "Please, let me finish, because I was wrong. I joined the Mufflers because I cared about what happened to this city and I was from the wrong kind of family for the regular Stingers—my people mostly ply the cinders trade, selling hot goods. Back when you ghosted Ashvik, I didn't understand what a monster on the throne really meant. This last year, as Thauvik's gotten worse and worse, I started seeing how much the world needed something like your order. If he's what they say he is, you don't have much of a shot."

"No, I don't."

"Then walk away. I don't know much about mages, not the nitty-gritty anyway, but instead of throwing your life away on this, wouldn't it be better for you to start a new order, carry on the mission, that kind of thing? You did us a hell of a good turn once. I'd hate to see you die trying to do us another one."

His words hurt . . . in a good way. "I have to try."

You mean, we *have to try,* Triss corrected mentally.

The corporal nodded. "Well then, good luck to you, and if I don't see you again . . ." Anjir drew himself up, straightened his shoulders, and gave me a parade ground salute. Then he turned and walked away.

19

Sunrise, the devourer of shadows. Even before first light, I could feel it prickling at the edges of my shroud like the sharp feet of a thousand hungry locusts slowly shifting in their hungry sleep. By the time the sun blossomed above the waters of the bay, the locusts had long since begun to nibble and chew, fraying the darkness around me. I was in Spicemarket and miles from the palace by the time the sun had risen to a half disk, so I let Triss collapse down into my shadow rather than feeding him the nima he would need to fight it.

Thanks, he said sleepily. *It's going to be a bright day, and I'm exhausted. Wake me if you need me.* Then he dropped away into a sort of semi-dozing state where he was vaguely aware of what was going on, but not really all there—his normal response to my spending time out in direct sunlight.

I found Fei at her fallback soon after. Or, rather, she found me. Like every smart operator with a foot shadowside, Fei had multiple hideaways. Mine were in places like that old smuggler's cave and abandoned breweries with structural problems. That was because I was broke. Fei was rich, which meant she didn't need to share her digs with rats and slinks. Her Spicemarket place was a very nice little house. It was also compromised, and not just because I knew about it. Kodamia's spy services had put an eye on it, too—a side effect of the same mess that had seen the place revealed to me.

I knew that if Fei really wanted to vanish completely, she would never come by the place again. But it was the only fallback address I had for her, so I started there. Of course, she wasn't home. There was no evidence of her having been there anytime recently, either. But just as I was leaving by the back door, a spritely little breeze came up from nowhere. I followed and it led me straight to Fei. She was sitting at a table in the nearly empty patio of a small cafe.

The interior tables were packed with spice merchants having breakfast on their way to their stalls, with more waiting for an open seat. But, with the sun less than a finger's breadth above the waters of the bay, it was still a touch chilly for any but the hardiest or most impatient to eat out of doors. That gave Fei an excellent excuse to keep her cowl up as she sipped her steaming tea and ate fried bread with a breakfast soup of boiled rice and fish. I followed her hooded example as I slipped into the seat across from her.

"I'm sorry," I said in the same breath that Fei said, "Thank you."

"I didn't mean to bring the Kitsune down on you," I continued, "but I didn't have a lot of choice."

She waved it aside. "You have nothing to apologize for, my friend. Not now. Not ever." She twisted a hand and a little swirl of air plucked at the edges of my cowl. "For this one, I owe you everything. Besides, you didn't bring anyone down on me. Scheroc came straight back to let me know what had happened. I added that to what you've told me in the past about your kind being able to track each other and figured I'd better give the order for all of Silent Branch to rabbit."

"So, you weren't the only one who ran?" I asked. "I was

worried. I talked to Anjir and he said the Crown Guard nabbed Zishin."

Fei's jaw tensed and she looked down. "I was afraid that might happen, but he insisted we needed someone to stay behind and warn the rest of our people off as they came back from patrols and the like. He also insisted that it be him. Damned fool. I don't know how many times I've told him never to volunteer for anything."

"They'll send him to Darkwater," I said, though I knew that they might as easily kill him. "We'll get him out along with Jerik after we've put Maylien on the throne."

"Aren't you just little Lord Sunshine this morning?" she said. "I suppose it's possible, but the smart money's on them torturing him half to death and then feeding him to the risen."

"Is that the bet you want to make?"

"No, nor will I, but it's the smart one, and it means I'll owe Thauvik and the shadow bitch a personal blood debt come the day."

"I can help you collect on that," I said. "Let me tell you where things stand. Then you can tell me what you meant when you said everything was about to go to shit."

Before I could start, a waiter came by and asked what I wanted. I was cold and tired and half starved, so I ordered a huge bowl of the same conjee Fei was eating and brought her up to date while I ate it. When I'd first moved to Tien it had taken me a few years to warm to the idea of rice and fish for breakfast, despite temple training that included learning to eat pretty much anything with a smile—part of teaching us how to hide in plain sight.

In Varya, I'd grown up on breakfast that mostly involved sausages, slabs of bacon, and porridge with bits of toasted bread to dip in it. These days that sounded positively alien by comparison to the spicy soup the waiter had fetched me along with a pot of dark and smoky tea. Though I normally disliked the more strongly flavored teas even more than the regular kind, tired and cold worked wonders on the taste this time around. To my surprise I found myself half enjoying its bitterness. Before I'd finished telling my tale, I actually flagged the waiter to bring me another pot.

"That clarifies things," said Fei, as I poured myself a fresh cup. "Scheroc's view of events can be a might eccentric, and more so when something's agitated him. Kao-li is going to complicate things mightily, but there's no way around it, and the move fits well with what I was going to tell you earlier, which was that the Crown Guard was packing up. That, and that several of Thauvik's more prominent commanders and Crown officers have vanished recently. Each one reappeared about a week later."

"You think they're undergoing the transformation to risen," I said.

"I do. It fits with what Harad had to say about this version of the curse, and the whole undead crusade thing. If we don't shut the king down soon, Zhan is going to end up looking like a prime slice of hell."

"I guess I need to talk with Maylien about organizing our assault. Do you know a good place we can meet near Kao-li?"

"I do, there's a fishing village just downstream with a tavern under the sign of the rooster and the monkey. . . ."

"**There's** the tavern." I nodded toward the Rooster and Monkey, its sign just visible in the fading light.

"Why don't Prixia and I wait over there," Heyin pointed toward a gap between the tavern and its nearest neighbor. "There are enough wanted posters with my face on them to make me nervous this close to a royal fortress."

Prixia's face hadn't turned up on any posters yet, but she followed Heyin into the dark passage without a word—no doubt happy to get farther away from me. Since that made two of us, I couldn't object.

I wish we didn't have her along, sent Triss.

Me, too, but both she and Maylien insisted, and honestly, her plan is better than the one Devin and I put together. She understands war a hell of a lot better than I do. If she didn't hate my guts, I'd be delighted to have her here.

What happened on the bridge wasn't your fault, Aral.

Actually, it was, and I have eight more unnecessary deaths on my tab because of it, but that's neither here nor there. What matters is whether this works.

There had been some deviations from Devin's original proposition—most notably a second, much larger group of raiders who would spread fire and chaos through the surrounding countryside. That would help draw the attention of the royal army away from Kao-li at the same time the assault group led by Heyin drew the Crown Guard away from whatever part of the fortress housed the king and the Kitsune.

The sequence now ran: One, Triss and I would enter the fortress and meet up with Devin and Zass so they could show us the layout. Two, while we were doing that, Prixia would start fires and make a lot of noise on the riverbank on the opposite side of Kao-li Island. Three, Devin would open the doors for Heyin and his volunteers to do an inside the walls version of whooping and burning. Four, I would take out the Kitsune—I'd been practicing alternate sword styles, but this was still where things were most likely to go wrong. Hopefully, I would have Devin's help for that—dealing with the Kitsune, not making things going wrong, which would almost certainly take care of itself.

Assuming I was still alive to make it worth his while we would move on to five, where Devin would attempt to stab me in the back. It wasn't on the official schedule, but I had no doubt it was coming. Six, I would kill Thauvik. Seven, if I hadn't had to kill Devin in the process, he got his swords back. Eight, extract Heyin's people from the fight they would by now be losing. I figured Thauvik's head on a spike would go a long way toward convincing the Crown Guard that killing their new queen's favorite guard captain was a bad plan. Nine, collapse in a heap. There were more steps after that, culminating in putting Maylien on the throne and getting

Jerik out of prison—which is where I had come in originally—but mostly those didn't need me in the picture.

But then I was stepping through the door of the tavern, and I found that I had more immediate concerns. Like the fact that the place was packed with Crown Guards—most of them looking idly at the newcomer. Or, that there were three Elite sitting at the best table. I sent Triss an urgent *stay hidden* and suppressed the impulse to turn right around and march out the way I'd come in. There was no better way to arouse suspicion. Instead, I stepped to the side of the door and looked around the room as though I were planning to meet someone. I had been, of course, but I no longer expected Fei to be there, not given the makeup of the crowd.

I was doing my second pretend scan of the tables and making damned sure I looked disappointed, when I felt a brief little chill breeze along the back of my neck. Really? On my third pass I actually looked at each table, but I still didn't see Fei. I had just decided that I'd imagined the breeze, and I was about to go over and lean on the bar for a bit—pretending to wait—when it came again. This time, when I looked around for the captain, I noticed a barrel-chested bald man lifting a finger as my eyes skipped across his table. I stopped and took a closer look then. The skin was darker than it ought to be, but there were scars on both of the man's cheeks.

Fuck me, I thought as I stepped out in the swirl of the taproom.

What is it? sent Triss.

Lady doesn't go in for half measures. Unless I'm going crazy, Fei's over there with a shaved head and bound-up breasts. She'd picked a tiny table hanging off of one of the posts that supported the roof, and the closer I got the more sure I was of my sanity.

Sounds imminently sensible on her part. Why the swearing?

It's pretty drastic. Only a few yards separated us now, and from this close there was no doubt it was Fei. She just looked so . . . different.

Really? It sounds mostly cosmetic.

Well, yeah, but . . . How do you explain to an inhuman shapechanger the meaning a woman like Fei might attach to her hair?

The thick brown braid had always been perfectly groomed and cared for—the captain's one vanity of appearance. Seeing her without it felt almost like seeing her naked. The impression was deepened by the worry I saw looking back at me out of her eyes.

But she didn't wave me off, so I touched the back of the chair across from her. "Kind of crowded in here, mind if I join you while I wait for a friend?"

She shrugged and drawled huskily, "If'n you don't mind knocking knees a might. There's not much room under this 'un."

"Fair enough." I sat, even more exquisitely careful than usual to make sure my swords didn't clunk against the back of my chair.

After all these years, such caution was mostly a matter of reflex, but I couldn't help remembering that the swords in my sheaths now were of no ordinary steel. Though they didn't shine with spell-light, no one, mage or otherwise, would ever mistake them for anything ordinary if they saw them unsheathed.

"It's a bit busier than the last time I passed through town," I said.

"It is that," agreed Fei in that same husky voice that disguised her normal almost sweet tones. "I'm just passin' through my own self, an' I asked about that. It's cause t' king is up at Kao-li. Barkeep says every tavern and inn within walking distance of t' fort look t' same."

That was when a harried-looking waitress appeared at my elbow. "Could you get me a bowl of the Anyang chicken with fried noodles," I said—the house specialty according to the board behind the bar. "Oh, and a pot of tea."

"Of course." Then she plunked a cheap sake cup down in front of me. It was empty but still confusing.

"Excuse me?" I said, really looking at her for the first

time. In addition to the cup she'd brought me, she had a dark
bottle and a ceramic bowl on her tray.

"First drink is on the king." She nodded toward the table
with the Elite who were all looking my way now. "They say
it's to make up for the crowds."

I smiled and nodded, first at the Elite, and then at the
waitress, even as my stomach filled with acid. She lifted the
bottle off the tray and I recognized a traditional Varyan
liquor—thick, black, and laced with efik. Niala. I needed
every ounce of control I'd learned in my years at the temple
and since to keep my face blank. Even so, I couldn't do
anything about the sweat I felt starting to break out all over
my body.

She poured a good inch into the cup and it might as well
have been blood for the way it made me feel. Then she
reached into the bowl and pulled out a perfectly roasted efik
bean to drop into the cup. Seven years since I'd last touched
the stuff, all of them gone in an instant.

Oh, Aral, Triss whispered into my mind.

"That's an interesting drink," I said, forcing myself to a
cool detachment I didn't feel. "What is it?"

The girl shrugged. "Some weird Varyan thing the Elite
brought. Don't know why they didn't just go for sake, but
they're paying the fare, so no one's arguing."

"How do you drink it?"

She shrugged again. "Don't know how it's supposed to
go. Mostly folks around here have just been tossing it back."

"Fair enough." I lifted the glass and swirled the black
liquor under my nose—buying time, though I didn't know
what to do with it.

The scent of efik filled my nostrils and I wanted to cry
for the needing of it. I knew in that instant that this wasn't
a ploy of the Elite. This was pure Kitsune. The lady had
done her homework since our last encounter, and I had no
doubt that every bar in walking distance had its own little
clump of Elite and its own bowl and bottle.

It was the cruelest of tricks and not designed to catch
me—she had to know I could drink it down without ever

giving a hint to the Elite of how much it hurt me. No, she wanted to destroy me no matter how our next meeting ended. Then, I was all out of time to think. The moment had come to find out whether she had succeeded. I turned to the Elite, smiled, raised my drink, and knocked it down.

Heaven and hell in a single glass.

"What d' you think?" asked Fei, her voice coming from impossibly far away.

"Not bad," I lied, and my own words didn't sound any closer. "But not great either." A far bigger lie. "Don't think I'd pay for another glass." The biggest lie of all. It was taking everything I had not to offer up my soul for a few magic beans and a bottle of booze.

The waitress had vanished, off to scare up my noodles and tea probably—ashes and bitter water—and the Elite were already back to doing whatever inane thing they had been doing when I came in. And it was all too late. I could feel the burn of the alcohol settling in my belly, not that big a drink for a man with my tolerances, and far too big for a man with my weaknesses. But that didn't begin to touch the icy joy of the efik. I couldn't feel its effects yet, but I could anticipate them with a combination of loving promise and pure horror.

Aral?

Wait.

I smiled at Fei and we carried on the sort of conversation that two strangers in a bar carry on when they don't really want to get to know each other better. But I wasn't present in any real sense of the word. My tea came and my noodles, and I ate and drank as though I cared. They could have been dirt and piss, or ambrosia and nectar for that matter. I didn't taste anything. All I could focus on was the efik slowly working its way through my system.

First came the cold rush of calm. All of my problems seemed to fade into secondary importance, even the problem of the efik itself. With the efik in my system I *knew* I could beat it. Ironic that. Then my heart slowed and everything felt better. My aches and pains winked out one by one,

giving me extra room to focus on my expanded senses.
Finally, my mind cleared.

I thought about killing the Elite who had bought my drink.
There were three of them, and I was certain their stone dogs
lurked just below the flags, ready to rush to their masters'
aid. A good two score Crown Guards surrounded them as
well. But I knew I could do it. Nothing was impossible right
now, and the perfect plan laid itself out in my mind, step by
step. I was an avatar of death herself, and nothing could stop
me from my purpose if only I chose to implement it.

I had missed this and I didn't want to let it go ever
again—wasn't at all certain that I even could.

Aral, is there anything at all?

*No. I've got to do this alone. That's the only way it
happens.*

I let the efik fill me and take me completely. I didn't fight
it. I couldn't. That wasn't the way. I don't know how I knew
that, but know it I did.

The swords of the goddess? sent Triss.

I thought of the relief their touch had brought me when
Devin first gave them to me, and my hands twitched, but I
stopped them. This couldn't come from outside me either.

Triss.

Yes?

Shut up. Please. I love you, but you have to shut up.

He did, and I could feel him withdrawing into the farthest
depths of my shadow. The efik made it ten times as easy to
track his position and emotion. I'd hurt him with that, and I
would have to apologize for it later . . . if I had a later. That
was an open question, no matter how much the efik told me
I *had* this. It wouldn't kill my body, or even hurt it, but it
might well slay the part of me that mattered. The fight here
was for my soul, and it was me against the efik and the
Kitsune.

When I'd finished my food, I waved the waitress over
and paid her. I made some polite noises at Fei. That included
a hidden message about where to find me when she got the
chance to follow me out—down by the river among the

cherry blossoms. Then I got up and walked out the front
door. The efik continued to put a fine edge on everything I
did, and a flick of my attention told me Heyin and Prixia
were still waiting for me. From the jerky sounds of their
movements, patience had long since left them. I wandered
past the gap, made noises about a walk by the river, and then
I went on.

As soon as I was certain I had gotten clear of any watch-
ers, I let Triss know that I wanted a shroud and control. He
passed the reins over silently—desperately worried. I
walked down to the river and into the orchard. Heyin and
Prixia followed soon after, and Fei a bit farther behind.

I didn't speak to them. Not yet. I couldn't. My soul was
still in doubt. Once the battle was won or lost, I would join
them, and together we would kill the Kitsune and Thauvik.
Afterward? Well, that would depend on whether there was
any point in my continuing on from there.

The three consulted, worriedly on Heyin and Fei's part,
angrily on Prixia's. Only Fei knew me well enough to have
any tiniest notion of what I might be going through, and I
wasn't about to explain. I moved silently away from the
others, heading into the darkest part of the orchard, where
I settled down into a meditating pose to wait for the efik to
clear my system. Again, I didn't know how I knew, but it
was absolutely imperative that I not *do* anything. I couldn't
let the efik help me accomplish anything, or I would be lost.

The efik told me that wasn't true, that now was the perfect
time for me to make my way across the river to fight the
Kitsune and Thauvik. The efik told me a lot of things. It told
me about how much more I could accomplish with it than
on my own. It pointed out that I was a better man with efik
in me. It told me how to conquer the Son of Heaven, slay
the Emperor of the Gods, and revive Namara. I listened and
I waited and I did nothing, until, finally, it shut up. That's
when the silence began to devour me, and I waited some
more, until the silence had finished chewing on me, and it
spat me out, too.

Then I made a decision, and it was the hardest decision

I'd ever made. I decided not to go back to the Monkey and Rooster, and not to sneak into the backroom, and not to steal me a bottle of Niala and a bowl of roasted beans. I wanted to. I wanted it so very much. But I chose not to. I had beaten my demon.

For today.

Tomorrow I would fight it again. And the next day. And the next after that. If I held out, the fight might get easier over time, as my struggles with alcohol seemed to. At least, I hoped it would. But there was no guarantee of that. There was no guarantee of anything but the fight itself, because this wasn't a foe you could slay. You could only push it aside. If I was lucky and I was strong, I would keep it at bay till death took me, winning finally in the silence of the grave.

20

———◆———

"**W**here the fuck have you been?" Prixia demanded in a hiss—I had only just dropped my shroud and joined the others in the orchard.

"Hell, but I'm back for now."

"I suppose you expect me to think that's funny," she said.

"Not really. It wasn't for your benefit."

"I've just about had it with you, Assassin. If you think you can fucking well—"

I burned a bridge then—knowing I would regret it later. I did it because I was all out of patience. Drawing my right-hand sword, I put the point just under the tip of her jaw. "Are we done? I promised you a shot at me when this is all over. If you want to live to take it, you'll let this one go."

"I . . . yes." I sheathed my blade and she backed away, visibly shaken.

That was not well done, Triss sent.

I know, but I don't have it in me to do better right now. I feel like one giant bleeding wound.

"How did you do that?" asked Prixia. "I'm a damned fast

hand with a sword and I didn't even see you move. Not when you drew, and only barely when you put it away."

Fei rolled her eyes at Prixia. "Girl, you're good, one of the best young fighters and duelists I've seen in a lot of years of dealing with violence. Don't make the mistake of thinking that puts you in a league with the legends. This is the Kingslayer, much as it pains me to swell his head by pointing it out. If you do choose to go against him when this is done, pick a duel where luck wins, because anything else is simple suicide. Now, if you're done trying to pretend you've got the biggest dick, we have a war to win."

Prixia glared at Fei but didn't argue with her. She understood when to cut her losses and move on, which is part of what made her such a brilliant tactician. I wished once more that my failure at Sanjin Island had not put us on opposite sides of an unbridgeable divide.

You have made an enemy, sent Triss.

Yes, the afternoon I got her brother killed and then ran away.

That was not your fault, it didn't have to lead to this.

Even if I agreed with you about that, I don't think she would. Either way, there's very little to be done about it now. Also, I'm sorry for snarling at you earlier. I was not myself.

It's all right.

"Now that Aral has finally decided to grace us with his presence, we can move on to the next step," said Prixia. "You've been able to get in contact with the other assassin?"

"Devin," said Fei. "Yes, I have. If we want to withdraw to someplace a bit closer to the fortress, I can send Scheroc to flag him and see about setting up a discussion. If we're lucky, he'll be able to talk with us tonight. If not, we'll have to wait."

I nodded. "Do it."

A few hours later, we had settled ourselves in a briar patch a half mile upshore from the fortress. It was cold and damp and uncomfortable, but it was as close as we could get without running into heavy shoreside patrols, and distance mattered. Scheroc wasn't equipped to haul physical messages back and forth, but he could relay short verbal communications, mimicking people's voices. With a minute or more of travel time for the wind spirit each way, it was like having a very slow conversation, with really long pauses between phrases.

I verified when and where I was supposed to meet Devin, then settled down into a half nap while Prixia and Heyin talked back and forth with him to nail down details and timing. It was nearly dawn by the time they'd hammered everything out and were ready to return to their respective commands.

Prixia left first. She had the longest way to go since her people were across the river on the north bank. We would not see her again until after everything was over, which was probably for the best on my part. If we didn't send her a message changing the plan, she was supposed to start burning her way across the countryside about an hour before midnight. Heyin went next, pausing only to confirm our meeting here at that same hour. That left Fei and me, and Scheroc and Triss.

"How are you doing?" Fei asked me. When I didn't answer right away, she continued. "Scheroc found you for me in the orchard. He's not good at things that aren't moving generally, but breathing registers for him much the way a light flashing on and off might for you and me. He recognizes people by the patterns. He wasn't sure it was you at first, because your breathing wasn't right, but I had no doubts. Then, later, he knew you. Are you all right?"

"No, not really." I felt a wave of wordless comfort from Triss, a sort of mental squeeze.

Fei frowned. "I don't know what that drink meant to you, though I could tell it was nothing good. I recognized the efik, of course, when I had one a couple of days ago—they're making everyone who wanders into any of the local bars have a glass the first time they arrive. I wasn't thrilled by the idea, but it didn't seem all that strong once I'd swallowed it."

"The dose wasn't a big one, and efik's a mild sort of drug, especially if you don't chew the beans."

"Unless you've got a problem with it," said Fei, and it wasn't a question.

"Unless you've got a problem with it," I agreed.

"I'm sorry, Aral. I didn't realize it was a trap set for you until I saw the hell in your eyes when she poured you that drink. If I'd had any idea how bad it was going to be, I'd have sat out in the street day and night rather than let you walk into that. But in the five years I've known you, you've never touched the stuff. I know. I ask around about the people I hire shadowside, and all anyone ever said was that you liked your whiskey a little too much."

"There's no way you could have known," I said. "It's a Blade thing and not one we've ever let get bruited about on the street. For that matter, it wasn't a problem while the goddess was still alive; it was a tool. For some of us it still is. Devin seems to use it just fine."

"But not you."

"No."

"Is there anything I can do?"

"No." She opened her mouth again, but I held up a hand. "Let's talk about something else."

"Like what?"

"Like your hair. That's pretty drastic."

"It'll grow back."

"But that braid was such a part of you. Even looking you in the face right now, I find it hard to imagine you without it."

"That's the point. If you can't let something go when you need to, you're its prisoner."

"It was hard, then," I said.

"Very." She got up. "I need sleep and so do you. See you back here tomorrow night."

"See you then." She left.

Aral?

Yes, Triss?

I'm proud of you. You fought it off.

For now. Tomorrow's another day. Fuck but I missed certainty.

You'll do it again.

I hope so, Triss, I hope so.

That's *the damnedest thing,* I sent as I tugged on the rope that Devin had let down for me. *I'm not comfortable with things being simple.*

The fortress of Kao-li was a huge pile of masonry completely covering a stony island in the middle of the Zien River about fifty miles upstream from Tien. It was connected to a second, much smaller island by a drawbridge. The little downstream island, known only as the tollbooth, sat at the midpoint of a big stone-piered bridge between the north and south banks.

The Zien was very wide at that point and all traffic into Kao-li had to travel across a hundred feet or more of thick wooden planks to the center of the river and the tollbooth. From there it crossed a short drawbridge to the smaller island, passed through a barrel-vaulted passage in the base of the tollbooth tower, and then on to the second drawbridge. In addition to the gates and drawbridges, the wardens of the tollbooth had the means to cast down the main bridge spans on either side.

An army couldn't hope to get in. An unaided assassin would have had plenty of trouble, too. As I prepared to shift my weight to the rope, I drew a knife and sliced a long gash in the tiny hide coracle I'd paddled across to the upstream wall of the fortress. It sank quickly, weighted down by several large stones.

Easy makes me nervous. I started up the rope.

This isn't the part you should be nervous about.

I have plenty of room to be nervous about the Kitsune and *the rope.*

Without the latter, the climb would have been all but impossible. After they set the stones of Kao-li's walls, powerful magic had been used to fuse them all together, creating a single seamless whole with a finish as slick as any volcanic glass. The lowest wall, on the downriver side was fifty feet of backward-angled glass coming straight up out of the water. On my side, the height was sixty-five feet, and for all but the last ten I wasn't hanging close enough to the wall to so much as brace my feet on it.

I was sweating by the time I reached the top, though more from nerves than exertion. For perhaps the dozenth time that night I thought about how much better I'd have felt with a couple of efik beans calming my nerves and sharpening up my focus. Every time I pushed the thought aside, the effort cost me a tiny bit of what felt like a very finite will, like I'd started the day with a block of the stuff and I kept chipping away at it. I shuddered to think about what would happen if I ran out.

As soon as I pulled myself up onto the lip of the parapet, Devin let the rope fall away into the water below. "Come on, I've cleared a path to the north tower where the king has his nightly bath."

"Nightly?" I asked, appalled.

"Since he got here, yes. I don't know whether he's reached a new stage where he needs them more frequently, or if he's simply indulging himself because he feels more secure at Kao-li." Devin started walking. "The Kitsune's there with him right now, discussing what comes next. Once I've got you in place, I'll go open the front door for your little queen's soldiers."

There was a guard's body slumped at the first stairhead we passed. I nodded toward it. "When will his relief be along?"

"Never. I poisoned the whole of the next shift and killed the cooks before I started in on the guards up here."

Nasty, sent Triss. *I don't like it.*

I agree with you, but there's nothing to be done about it now.

We passed a dozen more corpses as we worked our way around the perimeter wall. We were in less danger of discovery than we would have been walking down one of the main streets of Tien in broad daylight. It was disturbing in a very different way from the holes that the Kitsune had built into security at the palace. Here, there was no mystery. You could see exactly what had happened. Devin.

"How many?" I asked.

"Counting the next shift?" He shrugged. "I didn't bother to keep track. Don't tell me you've gotten even *more* sentimental in your old age." I didn't answer, and Devin continued. "It's better this way, we won't have any immediate interruptions. Once I've let your slinks in amongst the mice at the main gate, it should preclude any latecomers joining the party."

"You sure you don't want help with the gate?" I asked. The less I had to do with Devin, the happier I'd be, but I didn't want a failure on his part to waste all the blood he'd already spilled.

"Quite sure. I wouldn't want the great and mighty Kingslayer to have to dirty his hands unnecessarily. Though, I must admit, *that* made me wonder if you hadn't finally wised up." We'd just come around a corner then and he pointed across the river to what looked like a hundred fires burning away madly. Farms, mostly, but also at least two entire villages. "I didn't think you had it in you to be quite so ruthless on the diversions front, but this is inspired."

Triss swore bitterly in Shade, and I thought, *Oh, Prixia, what have you done?*

"It looks like a good portion of your little queen's army is out there burning and looting," continued Devin. "The garrison commander wanted to ignore it at first, since no one is supposed to bother the king when he's a-bathing. But then the first village went up, and she decided she really ought to lead a major force out to deal with it rather than try to explain it all to the king later."

"That's mad," I said. "The toolbooth will be locked down tight now, and very hard to crack. Are you sure you can handle it alone?"

"Oh yes, I've got it well under control. I had *lots* of poison and plenty of time to figure when and how to deliver it.

Speaking of which, we really should stop sightseeing now. I need to get you to the tower and point you in the right direction before my little added something extra starts hitting."

I took one last sick look at the fires on the north bank—burning on a scale vastly beyond anything Prixia had implied might happen—and then I followed Devin. What other choice did I have? Walk away and let it all have been for nothing?

"Up that way." Devin pointed to a high tower window a few minutes later. "There's an identical window around the other side that opens on the king's bath. Just let me . . ."

He snapped his fingers and a tiny dot of magefire like a dim candle's flame shot up to a place just below the crown of the tower. I couldn't make out what it did there. Neither with my eyes nor Triss's senses. But Devin reached a hand outward a moment later, sending a thin thread of spell-light from his fingertips to the nearest wall.

"Don't worry, there's not a mage alive anywhere close enough to see." Then he made a fist and pulled. An almost invisible line of blackness detached itself from the wall and swung our way as the spell-light winked out. "There we go."

He caught the silk rope and handed it to me. "The tower walls are even slicker than the outer defenses—there's no way up the outside without using serious magic or a rope. I set this up last night as soon as we were done talking. Let it fall back when you're done, I'll need it to rejoin you and I don't want to fight my way past the Elite in the lower levels."

"I can't wait."

"Don't start without me if you can avoid it," said Devin. "I want to see the look on Nuriko's face when you kill her. Or, failing that, the look on yours when she does for you. Either way I'll have one more happy memory to carry me along to whatever comes next."

Before I could respond, Devin assumed his shroud fully and vanished into the night.

*What do you think, Triss? Should I cut the line when
we're done with it?*

*Tempting, very tempting, but no. We're probably going
to need him to back us up.*

I was afraid you'd say that. Shroud me up. With a sigh,
I swung across the fifteen-foot gap to the tower and started
hand-over-handing my way up the rope.

A few minutes later, I stepped down beside the body of
the guard atop the tower. She had taken a crossbow bolt in
the base of her skull—a very clean shot an inch below the
rim of her helm. It would have severed her spine in the
instant before it drove up into her brain.

On the far side of the tower I released Triss to slip down
over the edge. As expected, he found a second rope there.
It was bound up in a black silk bag with a wax seal holding
it shut. When Triss released the seal, the rope fell silently
to hang a few inches to the side of the window that was my
target, just as I would have set it. Pulling the rope up a few
feet, I looped it several times around my calf and knee to
act as a rough brake. Then, headfirst and shroud in place, I
slipped over the edge.

The scene I witnessed when I slowly poked my head
down over the edge of the window could have come straight
out of one of the more lurid descriptions of the thousand
hells. The room took up half the top floor of the circular
tower. In the center, a few feet out from the only flat wall,
Thauvik lay at his ease in a red marble tub filled with what
looked like a mix of blood and water.

An iron pipe circled the base of the tub in a loop that was
anchored in a small fireplace, presumably to keep everything, well, blood warm. Near the door a half dozen pale
corpses were partially covered by a huge waxed silk sheet.
Gilded fetters hung from a crane-like apparatus above the
tub to make the bloodletting easier.

The Kitsune sat on a chaise lounge somewhat in front of
the king and to his right, her sword lying across her thighs
and the nine-tailed fox curled up beside her. She and the

king were speaking quietly but amiably about how best to arrange for him to keep up with his soaks while on campaign. It took another big chunk off the block of my will not to swing in and attack them the instant I realized what I was witnessing.

The only reason I was able to hold off was knowing that if I failed and died, there was no one to follow me. Namara was gone. There would be no second assassin if I fell, and no third to follow them if they went down in turn. When I'd killed Ashvik, I was the fourth Blade my goddess had sent to make the attempt. And, though I had been aware in the abstract that I might well fail and fall as my predecessors had, I had also known deep down in my bones that another would follow me, and another. I had known that justice would be done no matter what happened to me.

Until this very moment, with the prevention of a slaughter almost beyond imagination hanging in the balance, I hadn't realized how reassuring that knowledge had been for the younger me. But I was older now. I knew that I could fail and I knew anyone could die. The fall of the temple had brought both those lessons home in a way nothing else could.

So, I used the time while I waited for Devin to plot out my every move and contingency instead of simply rushing to attack. Originally, I'd figured on fighting the Kitsune before dealing with the king, but now I decided that I had to kill Thauvik first if at all possible and even at the cost of my life. Without him, there would be no risen crusade, no matter how dangerous and powerful Nuriko might be. I was mentally rehearsing my slide in through the window for perhaps the dozent time when a loud clanging alarm sounded from off toward the front of the castle.

"What's that?" demanded Thauvik.

"I'm not sure." Nuriko slid off the chaise, reattaching her sword to her rig as she rose. "Bide a moment." She crossed to another, smaller window. Pulling an eyespy from her trick bag as she went, she set it on the ledge. "There's heavy fighting on the south end of the bridge, but no one's cast the bridge into the waters. That means the tollbooth's fallen. Yes, and the inner gate with it.''

She twisted the eyespy and made a gesture that would allow it to see around corners. "There's a much larger enemy force on the north bank—an army really—and fires in the lands beyond. They're trying to throw down the bridge to keep what looks like your garrison force from returning to relieve the fortress." She turned away from the window and put her back against the wall to one side. "But then, there's no way they could get back here in time to make a difference anyway, is there, Kingslayer?"

"Kingslayer!" Thauvik sat up, sloshing bloody water over the edge of the tub. "Where?"

Nuriko didn't answer the king, choosing instead to make a slow scan of the room while Thiussus darted this way and that sniffing at every shadow.

"I know you're here, Aral, and that you've subverted Devin. That's the only way this makes any sense. He's let the raiders in at the gates to draw attention away from this tower and the king. *That's* why you didn't kill Devin when you took his swords. It wasn't sentimentality on your part, he gave them to you. I should have seen it before."

She drew her greatsword. "Come on then. You wouldn't have set this up if you didn't think you'd learned enough from our last fight to take me. Let's see if you're right." She turned her gaze to the window where I was hiding at the same time the nine-tailed fox indicated the spot by pointing his nose like a hound. "Ah, there you are. Whenever you're ready, we can begin."

Thauvik rose to stand naked in the tub. He had a double-bladed axe in one hand dripping with red, and I wondered rather macabrely what else might be hiding under all the bloody water.

The Kitsune turned her gaze on him. "Don't. Aral made this personal at our last encounter and he's mine alone. Touch him before we're finished and I will end you."

"I'm immortal," replied the king.

"Not when you're chopped into tiny bits and stuffed into that fireplace over there, you're not. Stay out of my way."

I thought they might come to blows for a moment, but then the king settled back down into the tub like a man getting ready to watch a show.

Devin was still nowhere to be found, and I knew I might not get this clean a shot at the Kitsune ever again. So, I dropped my shroud and slid headfirst into the room, using the window ledge as a springboard to flip myself onto my feet. I was already drawing the swords of my goddess as I landed, but the Kitsune hadn't yet moved.

She nodded now. "We're not playing this time, child. Say good-bye to your Shade and let's get this over with."

Thiussus struck then, bounding forward and opening her jaws as she went for my leg. She was pulled aside by a shadow dragon darting in from the side and biting her shoulder at the last possible moment. I felt the shock of that contact through my link to Triss. Hot-cold ecstasy echoed in my own jaws, but only for an instant—Thiussus doing whatever the hell it was that she did to other Shades again. Triss released her as soon as he'd diverted her attack.

You all right? I sent.

No, but I think I can handle this if you don't take too long about killi—His mental voice went silent as the nine-tailed fox swiped wicked claws across one of his wings.

He leaped back, and she pounced, trying to pin him to the floor. As soon as she landed, he darted around and nipped at one of her tails. She spun and he jumped away, like a small dog worrying a bear. With each contact I felt the shock again, but weaker now, as whatever Triss had chosen to do about Thiussus seemed to be working.

That was the last I saw or thought of the battling Shades for some time. Nuriko had slid silently forward in the brief moment while I was distracted by the clashing shadows and swung a blow that very nearly beheaded me.

Reflex saved me, with a simultaneous parry and backward crowhop that I had no memory of attempting. A moment later, reflex nearly killed me when I executed a form-perfect riposte that went exactly where Nuriko expected it to. That allowed her to hammer my right-hand sword aside and go for my shoulder when I tried to recover. I couldn't afford to operate on pure bodythought against the Kitsune. I had to both become my swords *and* plan ahead.

For the next several seconds I had no idea what was happening around me as I desperately tried to bounce back from my initial mistake. By the time I was actually thinking again instead of just reacting, she'd backed me around and past the tub. If Thauvik had been in the game with us, I'd have died as he split my skull from behind. Fortunately for me, he continued to follow Nuriko's orders, playing the spectator with a happy smirk on his undead face.

Back in control of myself now, if nowhere near in control of the fight, I parried and parried again, as Nuriko pushed me back around to my starting point. I did manage to get off one or two cuts of my own, forcing myself to stay within the weird hybrid style I'd developed for the fight, but I didn't come close to scoring on her. The main reason I was still alive at that point was the slender advantage my second sword gave me over her single blade, that and the fact that this time my steel was every bit as unbreakable as the Kitsune's.

"You've improved." She spoke easily, a sharp contrast to my own heavy breathing. But she didn't let up for a moment, coming at me again and again with shockingly powerful blows of her longer, heavier blade. "You're more unpredictable."

"Thanks." I would have liked to respond with a bit of banter or a clever insult that might put her off her game, but I had neither the wind nor the wit to spare. I needed everything I had simply to keep from dying.

"Namara's swords have saved you four times by my count. I'll have to make Devin pay for that."

I didn't answer, just parried and parried again . . . and spun, and jumped and generally danced to the tune she was calling as she backed me toward Thauvik again. I resolved to take a shot at the king this time if I got the chance. I also spared a glance for the shadows that danced alongside us. They had shed their assumed shapes for something more fluid and elemental, a pair of flickering patches of darkness that I couldn't have identified, one from the other, were it not for my soul-deep ties to Triss.

"Thinking about trying the trick with the light again?" Nuriko asked, driving a thrust at my left eye.

I limboed under it, flicking a backhanded cut at her forward knee with one sword while I brought the other into position to deflect the drawing slice she made as she brought her sword back into position for a more devastating attack. Again, I didn't answer her. I simply didn't have the spare attention.

It would have been nice if I *could* have managed that ploy again, but it wasn't going to happen. Not with Devin's blades. I'd tried a less drastic version in practice, but the same light-drinking enchantments that made Namara's swords so hard to see in the dark simply devoured any mage-light thrown at them. They belonged to the element of shadow as surely as any Shade.

Nuriko pressed in harder then, and I had no attention for anything else. Before I knew it she'd pushed me past Thauvik's bath again. He clapped lightly when she opened a long shallow cut across my ribs.

"I'm happy that I chose not to interfere earlier," he said into a lull. "I would have missed a gladiatorial contest the likes of which no lesser king has ever staged."

Nuriko was starting to breathe a touch harder now—little enough comfort when I was practically gasping—and she eased off a tiny bit as the fight slid back around to the window where I'd come in. As we approached Thauvik a third time, she picked up again, and I realized that she was intentionally keeping me too busy to shift my attack to the more vulnerable primary target. So, of course, I had to try. Leaping up and back to go over the tub instead of going around this time, I spun a downward cut at the king's exposed throat.

It should have worked. Instead, it nearly killed me.

Nuriko moved forward impossibly fast, catching my sword with hers and twisting it down and around to strike the heavy marble wall of the tub instead of Thauvik. The impact felt like a hammer striking the palm of my hand and the stone chipped and flew. I very nearly lost my suddenly numbed grip. The shifting of my sword had turned me in the air as well, and I landed badly, stumbling into a backward roll as the Kitsune vaulted the tub behind me.

I came to my feet with both swords low and parallel, and couldn't get either up in time to block the cut that burned a bloody line across my chest, nicking a collarbone in the process. The pain was breathtaking, like someone had branded me. The traitor that lived forever in the back of my mind cried out for efik. I managed not to die for the next several beats by shifting to a wholly defensive strategy and backing even faster than I had before.

In no time at all, Nuriko had driven me most of the way back to the king. Thauvik had climbed out his bathtub and was now swinging his axe back and forth menacingly. It looked like my luck was about to run out. But when Thauvik leaped forward with an inarticulate yell and chopped at my neck, the Kitsune's sword interposed itself, spearing the haft of the axe and ripping it from the king's grasp.

"I *said*, stay out of it," she growled as she snapped her sword and sent the axe flying across the room. "I meant it. That was your one warning. Interfere again and you won't have anyplace to wear a crown."

I tried to take advantage of her momentary distraction and the weight of the axe on her sword, flowing in to make a double attack. But even as she cast the axe aside, she caught one of my swords on the hilt of her own, blocking my edge with the bare half inch of grip between her hands, while skip-hopping over the other. I sliced open the leg of her pants and left a bleeding nick along the outside of her calf, but that was all.

"You're a treasure," Nuriko said as she gave me a third nasty cut, this one above my right ear. "It really is going to be a shame when I kill you."

That moment wasn't far off now, and we both knew it. She was my better and by a longer margin than either Siri or Kelos. I was only delaying the inevitable.

Then Devin finally arrived, though I didn't know it at first. Slipping in through the window directly behind Nuriko, he drove his knife straight for her left side. I discovered his presence only after Nuriko dropped into a low, spinning, back kick aimed somewhere behind her. In that same moment, she caught my left sword in a drawing bind and yanked it out of my hand, catching it in the air.

Several things happened all at the same time then. A knife suddenly sprouted high in Nuriko's shoulder. Devin's shroud fell away and he grunted as she swept his feet out from under him, then shrieked as she used the sword she'd taken from me to pin his right forearm to the floor, driving it between the bones and deep into the planks. And, I slashed at the back of her neck with my remaining sword, slicing away her ponytail and putting a deep cut in the scalp beneath it.

I grazed her skull, but missed the killing blow that would have severed Nuriko's spine by a couple of hairs. In response, she threw herself forward and away from me into a diving roll. Shifting to a two-handed grip, I followed. But I was too tired and slow now, and she was back on her feet and mostly facing me in time to take the huge double-handed chop I aimed at her neck with the flat of her sword. Still, I knocked her back into another roll, and for the next few beats, as I backed her up again and again, I thought I might win.

I was wrong.

As I hammered my sword down at the top of her skull in what I was sure must be the killing stroke, she simply slipped aside. It was only as my sword, driven with all of my remaining strength, struck the rim of Thauvik's bath for the second time that I realized she'd played me. Shards of marble flew and both of my arms went momentarily numb as my goddess-crafted steel shocked deep into the stone.

Before I could move or think, Nuriko brought her own blade around and down in a smashing blow aimed at the back of my trapped sword. I could see what was to come and I knew there was no way I could hope to keep my grip, but I had to try if I wanted to live. So I called up what will I had left in me, and braced for the impact. But nothing could have prepared me for what happened next.

My sword broke. My blade of Namara, the unbreakable signature of my order and the steel of my soul, snapped. Watching it break hurt me more than all of my wounds combined.

This could not be.

But it was.

I seemed to have all the time in the world to watch a dream shatter. The Kitsune's sword continued onward, sinking deep into the planks and giving me the opening that I could have used to finish things if I'd had a sword in my hand or the wit to think of my knives.

But all I could see was the breaking blade. The useless hilt fell from my nerveless grasp in the same moment that the broken shaft of the blade rebounded from the marble, spinning end over end. It was with a sort of mystical detachment that I watched the point of my own sword sink deep into the meat of my left thigh.

Broken.

Jagged steel like a crooked lightning bolt tipped the dark blade where it stood out from my thigh, but I couldn't bear to believe it. Horrified, I reached down and caught the blade where it pierced my leg, gripping the steel so tightly that the edge opened deep gashes in my fingers. Despite the blood and the pain, I couldn't bring myself to let go. I was finished and I knew it.

I reached out for Triss to say good-bye, but there was only silence at the other end of our link. Thiussus had beaten him as thoroughly as Nuriko had beaten me. All was lost.

"You are the greatest champion to stand against me since I faced Kelos."

At first the words registered as little more than a mad buzzing—a bee trapped in a bottle. But on the second or third repetition they started to make sense. The Kitsune was talking to me, telling me something. Not that it mattered. Not like the broken sword in my leg. My own death would be nothing beside that. I could see Nuriko's feet and shins from my hunched position. Hers and Thauvik's, both on my right. She was within easy striking distance and he was standing only a few feet beyond.

"What?" I finally managed, though the word sounded dragged out and dull in my own ears.

"You deserve the best death I can give you," said Nuriko. "Do you want to face the sword? Or would you rather meet it as you are, bowed and on your knees."

How could that possibly make any difference? I wondered as I looked again at the jagged point standing out from my thigh. *The blade of the goddess is broken, and it's all been a pointless . . . wait . . .*

"Well?" she asked. "What is your choice?"

Madness, I thought. But isn't inspiration a sort of madness? "Face," I husked, forcing myself not to think about what I had to do next, lest I give something away by action or omission.

Focus on the steps, I told myself, *not the plan.* And . . . begin. I dragged myself to my feet, using the side of the bath and my free hand. Razor-edged steel did further irreparable harm to my thigh. The pain . . . didn't matter. I remained bent over, thinking, judging, still trying to win. I turned slowly, facing my fate one way or the other. Nuriko shifted her stance slightly, waiting for me.

I began to unbend, my eyes slowly rising till they were level with Nuriko's chest. Pause. Breathe. Everything came down to this point. I jerked myself upright with one great convulsive effort. With the same impulse, I clenched my hand even tighter around the sword in my leg and yanked. I felt it cutting my thigh and my fingers, slicing deep into already torn flesh as I wrenched it free of my leg. Then I drove the broken end of the sword into the soft spot under Nuriko's ribs, angling that jagged second point up into her heart and twisting it sharply.

For one brief moment, Nuriko's face and mine were only

inches apart, her eyes looking straight into mine. She smiled at me. She smiled at me and she died. I wanted to do the same, but I couldn't. Not quite yet. The real job was still undone, and there was no one to do it but me.

Before I could begin to think about what to do next or how, Nuriko's shadow boiled up from the floor. Sliding in under her clothes and covering her in a second skin of liquid night, Thiussus took Nuriko within herself. I'd never seen anything like it. But then, the only Blade I'd ever seen die had been Kaman, and Ssilar had been staked to the ground in front of him when I killed him. Maybe we normally went like Nuriko when the time came, ending our lives in one final embrace of shadow. It was a comforting thought.

For one more beat of my heart I looked into Nuriko's dead eyes, darkened by lenses of shadow. Thiussus started to change then, becoming darker, and darker still. Finally Nuriko's eyes were gone and I could see only the impossible blackness of the everdark. With a pop like a bubble sighing its last, she was gone, leaving behind an empty suit of clothes, and two falling swords. I caught Nuriko's out of the air with my good hand. Then, pivoting on my one working leg, I swung it around in a whistling arc that severed Thauvik's head.

I got one good look at the shocked expression on the undead king's face before it landed in the tub with a red splash, and I had a moment to hope that Nuriko's sword of the goddess retained enough of its holy enchantments to slay him. Then, the world went away for a time. When it came back I was leaning against the tub and Devin was standing over me holding his remaining unbroken blade like he wanted to split my skull. I didn't . . . couldn't, blame him for that.

"I should kill you now," said Devin. "I really should. But I can't decide if that would hurt you more than letting you live knowing you're responsible for that." He kicked the hilt of his broken sword into my lap. "What do you think? Is that suffering enough, when you add in the fact that you'll never walk without a limp again? Or hold a sword with that hand?" He pointed a finger at the ruin I'd made of my right hand.

But I wasn't really paying attention to him anymore. I was looking at the hilt on my lap and the broken blade on the floor beside me. How could I go on living knowing what I did now? How could I move past the breaking of the unbreakable? With my good hand I reached down and picked up the fallen shard, cutting that hand, as well, as I did so.

"Are you even listening to me?" I recognized Devin's words. Understood them even, but they didn't matter.

Nothing mattered but the broken blade. Somehow, despite fingers that could no longer close properly, I picked up the hilt with my ruined hand. How could I have done something that led to *this*? Helplessly and hopelessly I fitted the broken ends together, both now smeared with my blood. The match was perfect—a perfect break for a perfect blade—but there was nothing more I could do.

It burned my soul to see this last symbol of my goddess broken, just as she herself was broken. Broken and dead, a stone corpse lying on the floor of the sacred lake.

"I would give my life to fix this," I whispered. "Without thought or hesitation."

Then, from an impossible distance, a voice spoke into my mind. *I know that you would.* For a long lingering moment I felt a cool touch on my brow, a touch that held something of healing and something of benediction. *I know that you would.*

Triss? Is that you?

There was a long silence, and then I felt a stirring. *Whazza? Do we yet live?* The voice sounded so very like the one I'd heard a moment earlier, but somehow I knew that it was not the same.

I started to reach out with my mind again, sending Triss reassurance, but not yet finding any words that were adequate to the moment. Before I could complete the impulse, I was interrupted by Devin, speaking my name in a frightened hiss, "Aral!"

"What?" I asked.

"Give me my sword," Devin said in that same fearful tone.

It was only as I reversed the hilt and offered it to him that I realized the sword was whole once again. Covered in my blood, but a single unbroken piece of steel. Devin gave the sword a flick that cleared the mess from the steel—another magical gift of the goddess—and held it up in the light. There was no evidence that it had ever been broken.

I reached for the sword, wanting to take it back and look at it more closely. "That's not"—I stopped as I realized that it was my right hand that I'd used and that it no longer hurt—"possible."

I turned my hand around and looked at the palm. It too looked as though it had never taken any injury. My thigh was the same, though the long cut over my ribs where the Kitsune had nearly speared me remained. So did the bloody gash on my head and every other wound that I'd taken from her. I braced myself on the bath and pulled myself to my feet.

Devin hadn't spoken since he cleared the blood from his blade. Now he held it up between us, looking at me over its edge with something of awe and something of terror in his eyes. "How did . . . what *are* you?"

I didn't know what I had done or how, or how to answer him. But the shadow of a dragon appeared between us then and spoke. "The better man," said Triss.

Devin looked down and away. "Maybe you really are." He sheathed his swords and walked to the window, shrouding up as he went. An instant later he vanished into the greater darkness of the night beyond.

Epilogue

---◆---

Dim green light filtered down from the surface far above, painting the broken stone form of a goddess in stripes of sunlight and shadow. Namara was still dead.

The sight tore at my heart every bit as painfully as it had the last time I was here, seven long years before. But after the events at Kao-li I knew I had to come back, and Triss had agreed.

Not to check. Never that. The dead do not return to us, no matter how much we might wish that they did. No, I had returned for a different reason, the narrow wool-wrapped bundle that lay in the fallen hand of my goddess. As I set Nuriko's sword in that open hand and reached for the bundle I could feel Triss's approving presence in my mind, though he said nothing.

My lungs were practically bursting as I attached it to my belt and turned to stroke for the surface. I could have used a spell to allow me to breathe underwater for a time, but that seemed somehow wrong given what I had come to do and prove. Stars danced in the darkness around the edges of my vision by the time I finally broke the surface of the sacred lake. I had to tread water and rest for a time before swimming back to the island and diving under the arch that led to the pool of Namara.

There, in the same place that I had first accepted my Namara-made swords, I laid the woolen bundle on the stone. It was soggy and cold, but no weeds grew in the folds of the fabric, nor barnacles clung to the weave. A high contrast to the state of the goddess herself—covered in lumpy green and gray as time slowly blurred away her form. The sheaths and hilts within were equally pristine, with the lapis eye of the goddess staring at me from each of the paired guards.

Unsheathed, they were virtually identical to the blades I'd borrowed from Devin, dark, sharp, perfectly balanced, and yet I could feel the difference. These were the swords of the Kingslayer. The old Kingslayer, the one who'd drawn his name with Ashvik's blood. I smiled and reached into the bag I'd left behind on the grass while I made my dive.

Are you sure about this? Triss asked.

Absolutely. I lifted out a small brush and went to work.

I'd borrowed it and the black paint from Harad after telling him what had happened at Kao-li and promising him that I would fetch Faran back for his ministrations as quickly as I could manage. I'd also asked him about what might have happened with Devin's sword, but he'd had no better ideas than mine. He did promise to look through the library catalogs and see if he couldn't find a volume or two that might help me understand the matter. It was an interesting conversation, one of many I'd had in the previous weeks and perhaps the most rewarding.

The one time I'd spoken with Maylien had probably counted more as an argument. It had come shortly after she rode in through the gates of Kao-li with Prixia at her right hand and an army behind her. I was mad that she'd tricked me into believing she was only sending a raiding force when she had actually intended to make a real battle of it. She was mad because my plan had ended with Heyin losing a leg. Our meeting hadn't gone well, though she had promised to lift the Crown's price on my head and restore Jerik to his bar.

Jerik was another of the good talks. To my surprise he hadn't held his imprisonment against me, though he *was* a bit grumpy about my swearing off whiskey. Said he was losing one of his best customers. Then he gave me a completely unexpected hug and told me to get out and come back when I could make him some profits.

I finished my first careful bit of brushwork then and laid my sword aside to let the paint dry.

Fei was another talk that went well. She'd promised me that if I ever needed anything at all, including Prixia boxed up and shipped off to Kanjuri as fish cakes, I need only ask.

It was a favor I hadn't needed to call in. Prixia and I had settled things . . . for now. When I offered to meet her so we could finish what lay between us, she'd declined. That had surprised me. So, I asked her why she was willing to let it go. I expected her to tell me to go to hell, of course. Instead, she told me exactly why she had made the choice she did. Mostly, I think, it was because she thought knowing would bother me more than not knowing. She might even have been right. It seemed that when Heyin was first wounded and everyone thought he was done for, he'd asked Prixia to promise not to complete her duel with me.

"You'll lose," he'd told her. "You'll lose, and I'll be gone and there won't be anyone standing between that bastard and Maylien, and there needs to be someone. There needs to be a wall between them. You be that wall."

And she had promised him that she would, and now I would always have a nemesis in Tien's royal house. Which was probably for the best, though I didn't tell *her* that.

I finished the second sword and set it to drying beside the other. Once it was done, I would mount up and head for Dalridia. I had business there with Jax and her school as well as with Faran. One more of the many unfinished things I had to do.

Like making sense of Triss's explanation of why Thiussus had been so overwhelming and how he'd come to fight it off. It had involved a lot of untranslatable Shade words and how touching Thiussus felt like an *actual* return to the everdark whereas other Shades simply felt like Shades. Thiussus made him homesick, because Thiussus *was* home in some incomprehensible Shade way, and knowing that had allowed Triss to do something . . . I still didn't understand that part beyond the fact that the words involved a lot of esses and long vowels.

After a time, my swords were ready. I picked them up and went quickly through a couple of my modified forms. They felt exactly as they always had—the missing limbs I'd sacrificed to the memory of my goddess were restored at last.

I'm not sure I like it, Triss sent as he nosed at the freshly blackened guards of my swords.

I am. The Unblinking Eye of Justice has closed forever.

But the world needs *justice.*

Yes, it does. That's part of why I painted them over. It will serve as a constant reminder. The goddess may have closed her eyes, but that doesn't mean I have to.

Terms and Characters

———•———

Alinthide Poisonhand—A master Blade, the third to die making an attempt on Ashvik VI.

Alley-Knocker—An illegal bar or cafe.

Anaryan, Earl of—A Zhani noble.

Anyang—Zhani city on the southern coast. Home of the winter palace.

Aral Kingslayer—Ex-Blade turned jack of the shadow trades.

Ashelia—A smuggler.

Ashvik VI, or Ashvik Dan Pridu—Late King of Zhan, executed by Aral. Also known as the Butcher of Kadesh.

Athera Trinity—The three-faced goddess of fate.

Balor Lifending—God of the dead and the next Emperor of Heaven.

Black Jack—A professional killer or assassin.

Blade—Temple assassin of the goddess Namara.

Blinds—Charms of confusion and befuddlement, mostly used by thieves in the Magelands.

Bontrang—A miniature gryphon.

Calren the Taleteller—God of beginnings and first Emperor of Heaven.

Caras Dust—Powerful magically bred stimulant.

Caras Seed-Grinder—Producer of caras dust.

Caras Snuffler—A caras addict.

Channary Canal—Canal running from the base of the Channary Hill to the Zien River in Tien.

Channary Hill—One of the four great hills of Tien.

Chenjou Peninsula—The peninsula to the north of Tien.

Chief Marshal—Head of the Zhani military.

Chimney Forest—The city above, rooftops, etc.

Chimney Road—A path across the rooftops of a city. "Running the chimney road."

Coals—Particularly hot stolen goods.

Code Martial—Ancient system of Zhani law.

Cornerbright—Magical device for seeing around corners.

Crownies—A derogatory term for the Crown Guard in Zhan, used by the watch.

Crown Law—Zhan's modern legal system.

Dalridia—Kingdom in the southern Hurnic Mountains.

Devin (Nightblade) Urslan—A former Blade.

Dian—A black jack in training in Tien.

Downunders—A bad neighborhood in Tien.

Dracodon—A large magical beast, renowned for the ivory in its tusks.

Dragon Crown—The royal crown of Zhan, often replicated in insignia of Zhani Crown agents.

Drum-Ringer—A bell enchanted to prevent eavesdropping.

Durkoth—Others that live under the Hurnic Mountains.

Dustmen—Dealers in caras dust.

Eavesman—A spy or eavesdropper.

Elite, the—Zhani mages. They fulfill the roles of secret police and spy corps among other functions.

Emberman—A professional arsonist.

Emerald Throne—The throne of the Sylvani Empire.

Erk Endfast—Owner of the Spinnerfish, ex–black jack, ex–shadow captain.

Everdark, the—The home dimension of the Shades.

Eyespy—A type of eavesdropping spell.

Face, Facing—Identity. "I'd faced myself as an Aveni bravo."

Fallback—A safe house.

Familiar Gift—The ability to soul-bond with another being, providing the focus half of the power/focus dichotomy necessary to become a mage.

Faran—A onetime apprentice Blade.

Fire and Sun!—A Shade curse.

Ghost, Ghosting—To kill.

Govana—Goddess of the herds.

Gram—The name of the world.

Greatspell—A major permanent work of magic, usually tied to a physical item.

Gryphon's Head—A tavern in Tien, the capital city of Zhan. Informal office for Aral.

Guttersiders—Slang for the professional beggars and their allies.

Hand of Heaven—The Son of Heaven's office of the inquisition.

Harad—Head librarian at the Ismere Library.

Hearsay—A type of eavesdropping spell.

Heyin—Lieutenant of the exiled Baroness Marchon.

Highside—Neighborhood on the bay side of Tien.

Howler—Slang name for the Elite.

Inverted Crown—A Zhani brand applied to the cheeks or foreheads of traitors.

Ismere Club—A private club for merchants.

Ismere Library—A private lending library in Tien, founded by a wealthy merchant from Kadesh.

Issa Fivegoats—A sellcinders or fence.

Jack—A slang term for an unofficial or extragovernmental problem solver, see also, shadow jack, black jack, sunside jack.

Jax Seldansbane—A former Blade and onetime fiancée of Aral's.

Jenua, Duchy of—A duchy in Zhan.

Jerik—The bartender/owner of the Gryphon's Head tavern.

Jindu—Tienese martial art heavily weighted toward punches and kicks.

Jinn's—A small cafe near the Ismere Library.

Kadeshar—Chief city of Kadesh.

Kaelin Fei, Captain—Watch officer in charge of Tien's Silent Branch. Also known as the Mufflers.

Kaman—A former Blade, crucified by the Elite, then killed by Aral at his own request.

Kanathean Hill—One of the four great hills of Tien.

Kao-Li—Fortress retreat of the Zhani royal family, upriver from Tien.

Kayarin Melkar—A master Blade who joined the Son of Heaven after the fall of the temple.

Kelos Deathwalker—A master Blade who taught Aral.

Keytrue—A charm to prevent lock picking.

Khanates, the Four—A group of interrelated kingdoms just north of Varya. Also known as the Kvanas.

Kijang, Duchy of—A duchy in Zhan.

Kila—The spirit dagger of the Blade, symbolizing his bond to Namara.

Kip-Claim—Pawn shop.

Kodamia—City-state to the west of Tien, controlling the only good pass through the Hurnic Mountains.

Kuan-Lun—A water elemental, one of the great dragons.

Kvanas, the Four—Group of interrelated kingdoms just north of Varya. Sometimes referred to as the Khanates.

Kyle's—An expensive Aveni whiskey.

Last Walk—The road leading from the Smokeyard to the traitor's gate in Tien.

Leyan—A onetime journeyman Blade.

Little Varya—An immigrant neighborhood in Tien.

Loris—A former Blade.

Magearch—Title for the mage governor of the cities in the Magelands.

Mageblind—Mage term for those without magesight.

Mage Gift—The ability to perform magic, providing the power half of the power/focus dichotomy necessary to become a mage.

Magelands—A loose confederation of city-states governed by the faculty of the mage colleges that center them.

Magelights—Relatively expensive permanent light globes made with magic.

Magesight—The ability to see magic, part of the mage gift.

Mage Wastes—Huge area of magically created wasteland on the western edge of the civilized lands.

Malthiss—A Shade, familiar of Kelos Deathwalker.

Manny Three Fingers—The cook at the Spinnerfish.

Marchon—A barony in the kingdom of Zhan. The house emblem is a seated jade fox on a gold background.

Maylien Dan Marchon Tal Pridu—A former client of Aral's.

Mufflers—Captain Fei's organization, so known because they keep things quiet. Officially known as Silent Branch.

Nail-Puller—Tienese street slang for a freelance torturer.

Namara—The now-deceased goddess of justice and the downtrodden, patroness of the Blades. Her symbol is an unblinking eye.

Nest-Not—A ward to prevent vermin infestations.

Niala—A Varyan liquor flavored with efik.

Nightcutter—Assassin.

Nightghast—One of the restless dead, known to eat humans.

Night Market—The black market.

Nima—Mana, the stuff of magic.

Nipperkins—Magical vermin.

Noble Dragons—Elemental beings that usually take the form of giant lizardlike creatures.

Nuriko Shadowfox—A legendary renegade Blade killed by Kelos Deathwalker. Also known as the Kitsune.

Oil-Smear—A charm to ward against eyespys.

Old Mews—An upscale neighborhood in Tien that burned to the ground.

Orisa—God of sailors.

Oris Plant—A common weed that can be used to produce a cheap gray dye or an expensive black one.

Others—The various nonhuman races.

Palace Hill—One of the four great hills of Tien.

Petty Dragons—Giant acid-spitting lizards, not to be confused with noble dragons.

Poison—Gutter slang meaning toxic or too hot to deal with.

Precasts—Active spells kept precast and at the ready.

Pridu Dynasty—Hereditary rulers of Zhan from around 2700 to the present day.

Prixia Dan Xaia—Clan chief of Xankou.

Qamasiin—A spirit of air.

Quink—Slang word meaning, roughly, freak.

Rabbit Run—An emergency escape route.

Rehira—A high-end black jack in Tien, one of the few who's not a mage.

Render's Way—A street in Tien.

Reshi—A clanate in northern Zhan.

Resshath—Shade term of respect meaning, roughly, teacher or sensei.

Restless Dead—Catchall term for the undead.

Riel—Currency of Zhan, issued in both silver and gold.

Right of Challenge—Part of Zhan's old Code Martial.

Risen, the—A type of restless dead, similar to a zombie.

Royal Monetist—Chief financial official of Zhan.

Sailmaker's Street—A street in Tien.

Sanjin Island—Large island in the river below the palace in Tien.

Scheroc—A qamasiin, or air spirit.

Sellcinders—A fence or dealer in hot merchandise.

Serass—A Shade, familiar of Alinthide.

Shade—Familiar of the Blades, a living shadow.

Shadow Captain—A mob boss.

Shadow Jack—A jack who earns his living as a problem solver in the shadow trades.

Shadowside—The underworld or demimonde.

Shadow-Slipping—The collective name for the various stealth techniques of Namara's Blades.

Shadow Trades—The various flavors of illegal activity.

Shadow World—The demimonde or underworld.

Shaisin—Small town in Zhan, baronial seat of Marchon.

Shanglun—A river dragon.

Shan Starshoulders—The god who holds up the sky, current Emperor of Heaven, lord of stability.

Shatternot—A charm to keep windows from breaking.

Shinsan—A water elemental, one of the great dragons.

Shrouding—When a Shade encloses his Blade in shadow.

Silent Branch—The official name of the Mufflers.

Siri Mythkiller—A former Blade.

Skaate's—A premium Aveni whiskey.

Skip—A con game or other illegal job, also a "play."

Sleepwalker—An efik addict.

Slink—Magical vermin.

Slip—A person who tries to get out of paying back a money-lender. Also known as a debt slip.

Smokeyard—The prison in Zhan where traitors are held on their way to execution.

Smuggler's Rest—The unofficial name of the docks near the Spinnerfish.

Snicket—Alley.

Snug—A resting place or residence.

Son or Daughter of Heaven—The title of the chief priest or priestess who leads the combined religions of the eleven kingdoms.

Sovann Hill—One of the four great hills of Tien.

Spinnerfish, the—A shadowside tavern by the docks.

Sshayar—A Shade, familiar of Jax.

Ssithra—A Shade, familiar of Faran.

Starshine—Elemental being of light.

Stingers—Slang term for Tienese city watch.

Stone Dog—A living statue, roughly the size of a small horse. The familiar of the Elite.

Straight-Back Jack—A shadow jack who gets the job done and keeps his promises.

Stumbles, the—Neighborhood of Tien that houses the Gryphon's Head tavern.

Sumey Dan Marchon Tal Pridu—Baroness Marchon and sister of Maylien.

Sunside—The shadowside term for more legitimate operations.

Sunside Jack—A jack who works aboveboard, similar to a modern detective.

Sylvani Empire—Sometimes called the Sylvain, a huge empire covering much of the southern half of the continent. Ruled by a nonhuman race, it is ancient, and hostile to the human lands of the north.

Tailor's Wynd—An upscale neighborhood in Tien.

Tangara—God of glyphs and runes and other magical writing.

Tangle—Charms of confusion and befuddlement, mostly used by thieves in the Magelands.

Tavan—One of the five great university cities of the Magelands.

Tavan North—The Magelanders' quarter of Tien.

Thalis Nut—A nut that produces a poisonous oil.

Thalis Oil—A toxic oil used by the Blades both as a poison and for the oiling of hinges and other hardware.

Thauvik IV, or Thauvik Tal Pridu, the Bastard King—King of Zhan and bastard half brother of the late Ashvik.

Thieveslamp/Thieveslight—A dim red magelight in a tiny bull's-eye lantern.

Thiussus—A Shade, familiar of Nuriko Shadowfox.

Tien—A coastal city, the thousand-year-old capital of Zhan.

Tien, Duchess of—Jiahui Dan Tien, cousin of the king.

Timesman—The keeper of the hours at the temple of Shan, Emperor of Heaven.

Travelers—A seminomadic order of mages dedicated to making the roads safe for all.

Triss—Aral's familiar. A Shade that inhabits Aral's shadow.

Tuckaside—A place to stash goods, usually stolen.

Tucker—Tucker bottle, a quarter-sized liquor bottle, suitable for two or for one heavy drinker.

Underhills—An upscale neighborhood in Tien.

Vangzien—Zhani city at the confluence where the Vang River flows into the Zien River in the foothills of the Hurnic Mountains. Home of the summer palace.

Vesh'An—Shapechanging Others. Originally a part of the same breed that split into the Sylvani and Durkoth, the Vesh'An have adopted a nomadic life in the sea.

Warboard—Chesslike game.

Wardblack—A custom-built magical rug that blocks the function of a specific ward.

Westbridge—A bridge over the Zien, upriver from the palace and the neighborhood around it.

Worrymoth—An herb believed to drive away moths.

Wound-Tailor—Shadowside slang for a healer for hire.

Xankou—A clanate on the Chenjou Peninsula, near Kadesh.

Xaran Tal Xaia—Bastard half brother of Prixia Dan Xaia.

Zass—A Shade, familiar of Devin.

Zhan—One of the eleven human kingdoms of the East. Home to the city of Tien.

Zishin—A sergeant of the watch answering to Captain Fei.

Currency

————◆•◆————

Bronze Sixth Kip (sixer)
Bronze Kip
Bronze Shen
Silver Half Riel
Silver Riel
Gold Half Riel
Gold Riel
Gold Oriel

Value in Bronze Kips

~0.15 = Bronze Sixth Kip
1 = Bronze Kip
10 = Bronze Shen
60 = Silver Half Riel
120 = Silver Riel

Value in Silver Riels

0.5 = Silver Half Riel
1 = Silver Riel
5 = Gold Half Riel
10 = Gold Riel
50 = Gold Oriel

Calendar

(370 days in 11 months of 32 days each, plus two extra 9-day holiday weeks: Summer-Round in the middle of Midsummer, and Winter-Round between Darktide and Coldfast)

1 *Coldfast*
2 *Meltentide*
3 *Greening*
4 *Seedsdown*
5 *Opening*
6 *Midsummer*
7 *Sunshammer*
8 *Firstgrain*
9 *Harvestide*
10 *Talewynd*
11 *Darktide*

Days of the Week

———◆———

1 *Calrensday*—In the beginning.
2 *Atherasday*—Hearth and home.
3 *Durkothsday*—Holdover from the prehuman tale of days.
4 *Shansday*—The middle time.
5 *Namarsday*—Traditional day for nobles to sit in judgment.
6 *Sylvasday*—Holdover from the prehuman tale of days.
7 *Balorsday*—Day of the dead.
8 *Madensday*—The day of madness when no work is done.

No one can escape his past.

FROM

KELLY McCULLOUGH

CROSSED BLADES

a FALLEN BLADE NOVEL

For six years, former temple assassin Aral Kingslayer has been living as a jack of the shadow trades, picking up odd jobs on the wrong side of the law. But the past is never dead, and Aral's has finally caught up to him in the beautiful, dangerous form of Jax Seldansbane—a fellow Blade and Aral's onetime fiancée.

Jax claims that the forces that destroyed everything Aral once held dear are on the move again, and she needs his help to stop them. But Aral has a different life now, with a fresh identity and new responsibilities. And while he isn't keen on letting the past back in, the former assassin soon finds himself involved in a war that will leave him with no way out and no idea who to trust...

"McCullough evokes a rich and textured setting of back alleys, rooftop hideouts, dank dungeons, and urban magical grime. Call it fantanoir." —SF Reviews.net

kellymccullough.com
facebook.com/Kelly.McCullough
facebook.com/ProjectParanormalBooks
penguin.com

M1257T0213

FROM AUTHOR

KELLY McCULLOUGH

the faLLeN BLAδe series

BROKEN BLADE

BARED BLADE

CROSSED BLADES

BLADE REFORGED

---

praise for the faLLeN BLAδe NoveLs

"Stories by Kelly McCullough are one of a kind."
—*Huntress Book Reviews*

"A fascinating world."
—*Fresh Fiction*

kellymccullough.com
facebook.com/Kelly.McCullough
facebook.com/ProjectParanormalBooks
penguin.com

M1258AS0213

THE ULTIMATE
WRITERS OF
SCIENCE FICTION

John Barnes	Jack McDevitt
William C. Dietz	Alastair Reynolds
Simon R. Green	Allen Steele
Joe Haldeman	S. M. Stirling
Robert Heinlein	Charles Stross
Frank Herbert	Harry Turtledove
E. E. Knight	John Varley

penguin.com/scififantasy

ACE   RoC